THE SPRING OF MALICE

"A blessed companion is a book"— JERROLD

THE SPRING OF MALICE

*

JOHN HARRIS

THE COMPANION BOOK CLUB
LONDON

Pride is the spring of malice and desire for revenge, and of rash anger and contention.

Archbishop Leighton.

A man that studieth revenge keeps his own wounds green, which otherwise would heal and do well.

Bacon. Essay IV: Of Revenge.

Made and printed in Great Britain
for The Companion Book Club (Odhams Press Ltd.)
by Odhams (Watford) Limited
Watford, Herts
S.463.V.

PART ONE

★ I ★

THE sudden sound of the telephone in the top apartment of the Maison Rollin jarred the stillness with the urgency of a bomb.

The Maison Rollin had been erected in the Rue Sainte Foy, just north of the river, long before Napoleon III had opened the streets of Paris against insurrectionists, and the sudden shriek of the bell seemed to stir up the ancient spectres of all its past occupants and brought the building to a quivering alertness that rippled through every one of its seven storeys.

Sam Hardy stirred in his sleep. Out of the suffocating folds of darkness the clamour of the telephone came, insistent and emphatic, frightening him with its demand for attention, and his unwilling hand reached out to shut off the irritating and unwanted sound.

As he surged upwards towards reality, the sound stopped and he became aware of the girl alongside him, one hand clutching the sheet to her throat, the other pushing the telephone at him. He took it from her slowly, his eyes questioning, and she shook her head, and swept back the thick lock of hair that fell over her eyes. Wide-awake at last, Hardy stared at her—his thin face dubious, wary and uncertain.

"Who is it?" he asked.

"I don't know. It's for you."

"Me? Who the hell knows I'm here?"

Hardy lifted the telephone. "Hello," he said, his voice low and cautious, ready for an immediate change of step if necessity demanded it. "Hello, who's that?"

"This is Cellini," the voice said in his ear, and Hardy glanced at the girl alongside him and smiled reassuringly. "It's all right, Ernestine," he whispered. "It's nothing."

He turned his attention again to the instrument and shouted into it, his voice cheerful now and riotously confident.

7

"What in the name of the Great Lord God of Stresses and Strains do you want at this time of the bloody night?" he demanded.

The voice at the other end had a faint note of annoyance. "Never mind that now. Are you alone?"

Hardy glanced at the girl alongside him, still clutching the sheet to her throat. "Er—not exactly," he said.

The annoyance became more marked. "I didn't think you would be. Look, I want to see you. I've got something I've got to talk to you about."

Hardy shrugged. "O.K." he said. "Are you coming up?"

There was a faint feminine cry alongside him and he turned sharply, putting one hand over the mouthpiece. "Better get some clothes on, for God's sake," he said quickly. "We've got company."

He spoke into the telephone again. "A slight impasse," he pointed out easily. "We weren't expecting visitors. What's the trouble?"

"I had a hell of a job finding you." Cellini sounded frustrated and weary. "I've been jazzing up and down Bonne Nouvelle and Sébasto for twenty minutes. Look, there's a bar open here. Right opposite the Porte St Denis. The Méphisto. I'll wait for you there."

"Christ, you do pick a time," Hardy complained. "I hope it's going to be worth while, that's all."

As he put the telephone down, he saw the girl staring at him angrily. "I've got to go," he pointed out quickly.

Her face darkened at once and he hurried to explain.

"It's business," he said. "I'll be back."

His words triggered off an explosion of anger in his face and for a while he listened to the tirade, gesturing one-handed from time to time as he attempted to object, then he swung his feet to the floor in disgust and went into the next room, his shoulders hunched, ignoring the protests. The girl followed him, and stood in the doorway, demanding angrily to know where he was going, her voice shrill with temper. She was small with the red-brown hair and high white forehead of Normandy and her anger had raised two bright spots of colour on her cheeks.

"Why are you leaving me?" she kept demanding. "Who wants you at this hour? Where are you going?"

For a long time, he didn't bother to answer her questions and went on dressing doggedly, closing his ears to the shrill enquiries, until, after a while, infuriated by his silence, she began to push at his shoulder with her hand in short angry jabs, trying to force him to reply.

"There's another woman somewhere! She's waiting for you! Isn't she?"

Hardy looked shocked and disbelieving and quite unconvincing. "There's no other woman," he said firmly. "It's business, I tell you. Cellini's on to something and he wants help. I can't afford to say no. I'm broke and Jimmy Cellini usually means cash. The great American public needs news and the Inter-Continental News Agency's prepared to pay well for assistance. They always have been. I wait for their telephone calls like a dog with its tongue hanging out. They pay my debts."

She followed him about the room as he reached for his clothes, complaining all the time, and he listened stoically as he slipped on his jacket and pulled his tie straight.

"It's only for a while," he said.

The explanation only produced another tirade which grew shriller and angrier as he moved towards the door, and as she reached for the metal bread-basket which stood empty on the sideboard, he began to run.

"For God's sake," he shouted back, angry at last. "Put *something* on! A girl should never stand swearing at a chap looking like that!"

Leaping outside on to the landing, he heard the bread-basket clatter against the door panel and fall to the floor, and he stood, listening intently for a moment until the sound of anger died away. His mouth widened into a grin and he stared at the closed door with the crafty unruffled look of a fox interrupted in its maraudings.

As he straightened up, he heard a car shoot out of the Place St Denis nearby and into the Rue Sainte Foy below. The sound of its engine seemed to burst through the door and hurl itself like a misdirected rocket up the spiral staircase to where he was

ocp/7018—A*

9

standing, and he heard a disturbed baby wail from a room on one of the lower landings.

The stairs were illuminated by a solitary bulb, far too small to offer much comfort or light, that was repeated staircase by staircase all the way down to the street, and Hardy lit a cigarette and set off slowly towards the floor below, which was merely a repetition of the top floor, except that the scents of the Rue Sainte Foy hadn't collected so firmly on the landing there as they had under the roof and the grubby skylight of the top floor.

All the way down the stairs he passed dog-eared cards drawing-pinned to doors. *Alphonse Daudi, Plombier; Theodore de Ring, Insurance de la Cité; Odette Bronsky.* They went past him like a procession of failures as he descended. The Maison Rollin was the sort of place where failures inevitably found themselves. It went with the husband who had walked out on Ernestine two years before and the job he just managed to hold down by the skin of his teeth at the Institut des Langues Européennes, and all the charming inefficiency, the misdirected industry and the stubborn arrogance of the Alphonse Daudis, Theodore de Rings and Odette Bronskys who lived there. That was perhaps why Cellini hadn't wished to explore it, he decided. To Cellini, only recently transported across the Atlantic from New York where success was still a measure of happiness, the place had a depressing appearance of neglect.

On the street door, he noticed with interest a shining red Communist poster. *Homage to the heroes of the Commune of 1871*, it said. *Service at the Wall of Père Lachaise. Sunday, 11.30.* That was a new one, he thought cheerfully. It hadn't been there when he'd arrived. The Rue Sainte Foy, with its battered walls and narrow corners and odd unused doors, was a bill-stickers' paradise, and the Parisians loved groping back to past glories and martyrdoms—even the Reds, with their sanctifying of the mobs of the Commune.

Outside in the street, he stopped and raised his head, feeling the cobwebby touch of drizzle on his face. The rain fell gently, silently. It always seemed to fall lovingly on Paris, he thought with a warm flooding affection for his surroundings, caressing the boulevards and the unhurrying passers-by, and the last late bars and the dark shops with their cavernous interiors redolent of stored fruit and vegetables and wine.

Behind him, the Maison Rollin was already vague in the anonymity of night time, peering after him with the blind-eyed stare of darkness. On the nearby wall, someone, smarting under the indignity of governments that changed every few weeks, had scrawled the words, *"A bas les politiciens. 1957, and still we wait. Bring back de Gaulle and stability,"* and the chalk strokes stood out boldly in the dusk like the plea of the French nation to the monolithic figure of the General who had withdrawn, brooding and incorruptible and secure in the knowledge that some day he would be wanted again, to his country home at Colombey-des-Duez-Eglises.

The Méphisto Bar, opposite the brown bulk of the St Denis Gate, was open, but only just, in spite of the juke-box moaning a down-beat jazz tune in the shadows. The waiter, his black apron discarded already, had piled up the bright red and yellow chairs outside on the tables and was occupied in pulling the grills down over the glass front with a clamour of rattling metal.

There was an Algerian in a skin-tight suit with a high white collar and yards of white linen cuff playing a pin-ball machine under a flickering neon tube with a red pom-pommed sailor, both of them reflected a dozen times in the mirrors that lined every inch of wall space. It was a dim barren little place with a few late drinkers, attended by the bored proprietor.

Cellini was deep inside the bar, almost as though he didn't wish to be seen, tall as a steeple and gangling in a wiry American way, immaculate in spite of the late hour in a dark blue suit and a broad-ribboned hat. He smiled as he saw Hardy but managed at the same time to look faintly uncomfortable, his handsome brown face heavy, as though he were disapproving.

He raised his eyebrows questioningly and Hardy nodded.

"Beer," he said shortly. He lit a cigarette and drew a deep breath. "It's amazing," he observed cheerfully, "how that sort of thing works up a thirst. How the hell did you find where I was?"

Cellini gestured deprecatingly, as though ill at ease away from his office in the Place Vendôme and the bright lights of the First Arrondissement.

"They told me at the Snick Snack bar," he said.

II

Hardy frowned. "They would," he commented. "I can see I shall have to be more discreet." He reached for his beer and drained the glass at a gulp. "Well, how's the American and Inter-Continental News Agency?" he asked.

"O.K.," Cellini said. "Look, I'm sorry to chase you, Sam. I'm not poking my nose into your affairs."

Hardy gestured airily. "Doesn't matter," he pointed out. "They're as wide open as the window of Pan-American in the Champs Elysées. They always have been."

Cellini's smile faded and his voice grew hard. "Look Sam," he said, "I've been looking all over the damn' place for you. I want some help?"

"What's the trouble?"

Cellini rubbed his nose. "You've heard of Murphy?" he asked.

"Which Murphy? I know bags of Murphys. You can scrape them off the bars in hundreds in Dublin."

"No, dammit——" Hardy could see Cellini was growing faintly irritated with him as he always did in the end. He always started by being friendly and ended up looking as though he'd be glad to get away—"I mean *General* Murphy."

"Which General Murphy?"

"Hell, there's only *one* General Murphy. General John Forrest Murphy."

Hardy looked up, his interest caught. "The chap who liberated Percéval and the Bligues?" he asked.

"That's him. Washington's sending him to Paris. Didn't you know?"

"Well, they didn't write to *me*."

Cellini breathed deeply. It seemed to him just then that he'd spent half his life breathing deeply to avoid losing his temper with Hardy. He'd started in London not long after the war and he'd been doing it on and off ever since. Now he let out his breath in a vast explosive sigh.

"Look," he said patiently. "He's arriving in ten days' time——"

Hardy's eyebrows rose. "Well, for Christ's sake," he said loudly, "what do you want me to do? Go and meet him at the airport and sing *The Star-Spangled Banner*?"

"If it weren't for the fact that I'm needing assistance," Cellini said with difficulty, "I'd walk out of this damned place right now.

Look, I want your help. I'm on to something. They tell me there are rumours flying about of an attempt to demonstrate against him when he arrives."

"That's the worst of the French," Hardy said, unmoved. "They're what you might call a prey to historical and social crises. They used to boast that they once made even Eisenhower slink in like a thief."

Cellini contemplated French arrogance and ingratitude with a frown. "Murphy's a national hero," he said. "To Americans he's Montgomery and Mountbatten rolled into one. If somebody threw stinkbombs at Monty or Mountbatten in Singapore, it'd be news in England, wouldn't it? It's the same with Murphy. It always hits 'em hard back home to find American heroes aren't quite so popular in other countries as they are in the States, and when someone takes a poke at them it always hits the front page. I looked you up," he explained, "because I thought you might know something about it."

"Me? I've had nothing to do with it."

"I wouldn't be surprised," Cellini said bitterly. "It's just the sort of thing you would do."

For a moment they stared at each other, then Hardy grinned suddenly, an unexpected melting grin that completely disarmed the angry American.

Cellini could never understand Hardy, much as he liked him. To Cellini, with his aptitude for success, Hardy seemed a saddening figure, tragic beyond redemption, and he could never conceive how he managed to remain cheerful under the disasters that persisted in assailing him.

"O.K.," Hardy said. "Let's have it." He pulled a stool forward with his foot. "Better get the weight off your feet."

Cellini sat down. "There's a lot of wild talk of posters and placards, and things being thrown," he said. "For all I know, it might end up in quite a houpla, though so far it's only talk, and rumours floating round the cafés in the Boul' Mich' and the Place St Germain and the Sorbonne."

Hardy shrugged. "That's where *all* the rumours start in Paris. Students with nothing better to do. They always keep a few cops handy, just in case. No one enjoys an upheaval like the students. They're always ready to man the barricades."

13

"Barricades are out of date!" Cellini snapped.

"Not in Paris. They flung up the barricades when they threw the Germans out in 1944——"

"A fat lot of use they'd have been against an 88-millimetre gun!"

"It's part of the Paris scene to have students demonstrating about something," Hardy pointed out blandly. "Just to prove they know how. Barricades are a gesture. This district's famous for 'em. They do no harm. They don't dig up the cobblestones any more and the police play according to the rules."

"Well, this time it might be different. And they've picked an American and a national hero at that."

"What the hell has the poor bastard done to them?"

Cellini sighed. "You've heard of General Boderin, haven't you?" he asked. "You know the one. The guy had a name as long as the Boulevard Haussmann. De Lespinasse-Boderin du Crest. Remember?"

Hardy nodded sombrely. "I was here at the time," he said. "It split France wide open. It once even damn' near stopped the war. Was Murphy Boderin's commanding officer?"

Cellini nodded and Hardy whistled. "And was it Murphy who gave him the old heave-ho at Percéval?"

"Yes."

Hardy nodded slowly. "O.K.," he said. "You've got me on the edge of my chair. My British instincts for minding someone else's business are aroused. What's the rumour?"

Cellini rose, ordered another drink and stood fiddling with the saucer of change. "You know what these French students are like where their damned honour's concerned," he said. "Boderin was a French officer. He was leading French troops. He was liberating France. He was in the spearhead of the Bligues advance. When Murphy removed him, it was a personal insult."

"As I remember it, it didn't seem to be much of an insult to his men. Plenty of 'em testified against him at the court-martial anyway. I heard they got on well with Murphy."

"The complaints didn't come from the men who were doing the fighting," Cellini said. "They never do. They came from all the long-winded French politicians who were more concerned with winning the peace for their party than with winning the war for their country. They took the line that it was a studied attempt to belittle France, to prevent the French from taking any part in the liberation of their own country. You know what a damned fuss there was about letting the French be the first into Paris."

"It always seemed to me difficult enough just to stay alive in wartime without worrying about things like honour," Hardy observed.

"Well, that's the way the French tick over," Cellini said. "There's talk now of the Communists muscling in again. After the war there was an outfit called the Partie des Abandonnés. They were Boderinists or Boderinards or whatever they called themselves. They managed to stir up a lot of trouble for the Americans in 1945. Maybe they're going to try again. There's talk of trying to create some rift they can blame on the Government. So they can throw it out."

"Oh, God, not again! It's the only stable one we've had. It's been in at least two months now."

The waiter approached them, his shopworn face disgusted, and ostentatiously began to wipe the counter in front of them and stack chairs around them. Hardy ignored the hint and looked curiously at the American.

"What's Murphy coming here for, anyway?" he asked. "Surely not for fun?"

Cellini shook his head. "Missile development," he said. "Murphy's an expert on guided weapons. There's a new NATO committee being formed and he's coming over to organize the programme. The French aren't keen on rockets and atom bombs on their soil and it's part of his job to see that they change their minds. He's got to go down well."

"And how come you know all about the demonstration?" Hardy asked.

Cellini shrugged. "I don't know all about it," he said. "I wish I did. Fred Groszwicki, my leg man, got wind of it. His *femme de ménage*'s got a son who's one of the students. Mind you, the police know about it but they regard it as just another day of the week. Why not? Someone's always demonstrating in Paris. You said so yourself. It's just that I'd like to do a special on it, that's all. My boss has a theory that Americans shouldn't take it for granted that everyone loves us just because we won the war and saved civilization with Lend-Lease and Marshall Aid and tins of Spam. He thinks we ought to work harder for friendship and he likes this kind of story because it jerks the politicians back home out of their self-satisfaction. You know the mood. *We can lick the Japs in Six Weeks*. It was all over the country in 1942."

"How much did Fred Whatever-his-name-is get to know?"

"Not much. The son suddenly decided he might have said too much and clammed up. I want to know who's behind it. And why, and where? That's why I came to you. You know all these damned students, Sam. You teach 'em. They come for extra tuition down at the Institute. Can't you pump a few of 'em?"

He fished in his wallet and passed across three or four large notes. "That ought to help you along for a bit," he said. "Give me a ring if it runs out."

Hardy grinned. "God, what it must be to have an expense account! I always swear to myself I'll not sell my soul to you for money any more; but you've always got so much of the damn' stuff it seems easier just to let things slide. I might say, you arrived just in time. I was just thinking of packing up and leaving."

"Leaving what? Paris?" Cellini looked concerned. "St. Germain'd never be the same without you propping up the bars."

"It might have to struggle along one of these days. I owe too much money, and the Institute was never noted for over-paying."

Cellini stared at Hardy. "Where were you going?"

"London. I'd been offered a job. Teaching 'the pen of my aunt' to snotty-nosed schoolboys. Some grimy dump in a street a thousand miles long, with a million gaslamps and a couple of million houses. I was expecting to moulder rapidly and go to seed in an atmosphere of duty and 'play the game, you chaps'. But not now. No, by God, not now! You've saved my life, old boy, if you only knew it. Where do I start?"

Cellini paused, faintly embarrassed by his own success in front of Hardy's failure. "I'll leave it to you," he said slowly.

"O.K." Hardy flipped the money with his thumb. "I'll start tomorrow. There's enough here to buy drinks for the whole of the damned Sorbonne, and most of 'em would give anything for the price of a pernod. I'll give you a ring in a day or two."

He walked to the door with Cellini. The bar was empty now. The waiter had gone home in disgust and the proprietor was waiting to lock up behind them.

The rain seemed to have stopped and the night air was refreshing after the stuffy atmosphere of the bar. Hardy stopped, listening to the roar of a heavy lorry heading towards the markets at the Halles, and stared thoughtfully up at the houses beyond the Porte St Denis.

The last restaurants had long since darkened their *terrasses,* and the waiters outside the last bars were sweeping up the cigarette ends. It was only at Pigalle and along the Champs Elysées, where the brilliant neons marched in rows up to the Etoile, that the glare reached up to thin the darkness of the sky.

The streets were empty now except for the last few strollers and the home-going policemen from the late Métro trains. The last lunatic taxi-drivers were screeching out of the boulevards, leaving the lights behind them as they plunged into the canyon-like backstreets towards their garages.

The rolled corrugated metal blind of the Méphisto Bar roared briefly and the striped awning disappeared abruptly. As the lights went out, the mansard roofs of the high apartment blocks faded, and the yellow patch on the wet pavement vanished. To the north the spires of St Laurent, St Leu and St Eustache had long since merged into the darkness.

Cellini had begun to walk along the Boulevard Bonne Nouvelle, on the look-out for a prowling taxi to take him home, and Hardy stood on the corner, flipping the bundle of notes in his hand. Then Cellini, realizing he was alone, stopped and waited for him, half-expectant.

"Coming?" he asked.

Hardy grinned. "I was thinking," he said, "that I ought to go back to my place at St Germain."

Cellini gestured vaguely. "It'd be a help if you had a stabilized address for a bit," he agreed.

Hardy laughed. "Ernestine and I were like an old married couple," he said. "It's funny how these lonely women have a habit of finding their way into a bloke's bed. The least he can do is make 'em feel at home."

Cellini turned his attention again to finding a taxi. As he swung away once more Hardy's eyes strayed round in the direction of the Rue Sainte Foy, and he hesitated a moment longer; then he shrugged the thought aside and set off after Cellini.

"There'll be hell to pay when she finds out," he said.

★ 2 ★

IN New York, the taxicabs and cars were bumper to bumper in the wet streets, their horns roaring a chorus. From above, they looked like some curious species of ant, threading and pouring through the concrete and glass canyons of the city. On the sidewalks, thousands of people, caught in the glare of the neon signs, moved purposefully towards the entrances to the subway, their faces pale and tired as they made their way home from the wearisome city centre of the offices to some other weary centre where they lived.

High up in a room of the Woodrow Wilson Hotel which pushed its neon and glass and chrome-steel portico over the sidewalk, the newspapermen were beginning to think of getting back to their offices, of deadlines, of cups of coffee and cold beers and hamburgers. The press conference was almost over.

The room was crowded with people, and the pale yellow carpet that covered the floor was marked here and there with little dark marks where the dirt their shoes had picked up from the rain-wet streets outside, had rubbed off. The hotel management had provided the room for the press conference because they'd decided General Murphy's apartment would not be big enough, but even this room, with its mustard-coloured carpet and grey leather chairs—looking more like a board room than a hotel lounge—was already far too full. General John Forrest Murphy had been a national figure so long now that every move he ever made got into the papers.

General Murphy had been far under age when his country had declared war on Germany in 1917, but in spite of his youth, he had managed to make sergeant by the time the United States landed him in the Argonne in 1918. He was already a big nutty youth from near Nashville, named after Tennessee's favourite Civil War general, and living there in the Tennessee hills, he knew how to handle weapons and how to stalk wild animals. In spite of his youth, he was twice decorated for bravery and finally commissioned on the field just before the end of the war.

In December 1918, just when the country was basking in the newspaper stories of his fame and prophesying a great military future for him, his mother, whom he had taken the precaution of keeping in the dark about his exact whereabouts, angrily reclaimed her erring son from the War Department and it was discovered that in spite of his commission and his decorations, he was still legally under age. There was a tremendous and delighted uproar in the press that spread throughout the country, and the Army had no alternative but hastily to discharge its youthful hero.

However, having decided that he had found his true metier as a soldier, Murphy quietly bided his time until he was of the right age, avoiding all the time all the publicity they tried to shower on him. He spent the intervening months reading every military history he could lay his hands on, and as soon as he was old enough he promptly rejoined the army as a Regular soldier, dodging his mother and the town band which turned out to see him off. Within a week he was a sergeant again and within two months he had his commission back. By the time World War II came round he was a lieutenant-colonel.

He fought in Bataan and somehow contrived to escape to fight again in Tunisia, Italy and the South of France. He found himself conducting rearguards during the Ardennes breakthrough and distinguished himself in one of the few successful actions at the beginning of the Korean War. By the time he was posted to SHAPE in Paris, he was one of his country's most decorated soldiers and a three-star general. Having clearsightedly spent all the postwar years studying nuclear weapons, he'd become an expert on atomic and guided missile warfare and, inevitably, when the new three-dimensional warfare agency was set up by NATO in Paris, he was ordered to go to Europe to make it work.

He sat at the table—there was a picture of him that week on the front of *Life,* looking just as he did now—calm and smiling with an easiness of manner that had always been his even as an overgrown schoolboy when he had distinguished himself in World War I; his uniform neat but not precise, casual yet not sloppy, that mass of ribbon vivid on his left breast. His rocky brown face was full of humour and immense American commonsense, quite different from the Hollywood conception of a soldier's face that Ridgway had—and his dignity was extraordinary in a man not born to it.

Watching him, Colonel Walter Edsell Franks, his personal assistant, was impressed not only by his bearing but by his patience and forbearing in what, to any man, was a formidable operation. Some of these journalists were no respecters of persons and some of the more spiteful actually took a malicious delight in tripping a man up—particularly a top-brass name.

Franks was always impressed by Murphy. He openly and frankly admired the general, not merely because he was a brave man—braver than Franks knew he could ever be—but because, with all the disadvantages of so inconspicuous a background, he had made so much of himself. Franks knew all of Murphy's faults and he was still impressed by him. He was one of the easiest men to work with that Franks had ever met, and, because he was so honest, Franks always felt faintly protective towards him when he was faced with men who weren't quite on the same level of integrity.

Because no man who had succeeded quite so successfully as Murphy had, could have been normal without enemies as well as friends, there were many who were jealous of him and claimed he had reached his present rank simply because he had decorations. A few of his detractors round the Army clubs and bars still called him "The Sergeant", but there was never anything stiff and military about him. He had an incredible easiness about him, that curious civilian quality that seemed often to adhere to successful American soldiers, sailors and airmen, and roused a startling sense of loyalty in Colonel Franks.

Franks had sat beside him, the light glinting on his spectacles, watching him as he'd skirted pleasantly round all the secret stuff they kept plugging at, smiling yet giving nothing away, not even hints that would lead to further questions which would be difficult to dodge. He felt Murphy was now on the last lap, and he still had hopes that he'd get through the session without someone raising the one awkward question he knew Murphy wished to avoid. He'd expected it long before now, but had begun at last to think they might make it without it cropping up.

"General," the *New York Times* man said from the front row. "What's *your* view on this trip to Paris—your *personal* view?"

"Well"—Murphy grinned, sidestepping neatly—"you know what they say about Paris in the spring. It'll be May when I get there."

"What's going to be your first job, General?"

"My first job?" Murphy smiled again. "To get myself a quiet house somewhere—probably out St Cloud way—for when Mrs Murphy joins me in two months' time, and put a double lock on the door so we won't be bothered by you guys."

There was a ripple of laughter, then a young man representing the magazine *Now* stood up and jabbed a pencil at Murphy. "What's the programme, General?" he demanded.

Franks frowned, not only because of the insolently jabbing pencil but also because he didn't like the magazine *Now*. *Now* had put out a paragraph on Murphy only that morning, he remembered, and he riffled through the few papers and magazines on the table in front of him and opened *Now* at its snippets of news. *"Plump balding Lt. General John S. Murphy,"* he read, *"leaves New York next week for Paris. At 58, bulky John S. is one of the fit men of the top brass in the Pentagon. In spite of weighing 250 lbs. he has always breathed down the neck of the avoirdupois brigades."*

Franks could see Murphy pausing before he replied. He was fifty-six and his weight was under two hundred pounds. That hearty back-slapping columnist's style that said he was plump always annoyed him, Franks knew, and he eyed the young man in front of him with a hostility that he knew Murphy would never allow himself to show.

He wasn't so damn' thin himself, come to think of it, Franks decided, eyeing the young man's well-fed frame. And no one had done more than Murphy had to discourage, not only by decision but also by example, the tendency of United States military men to allow themselves to become over-corpulent.

"The programme," Murphy was saying, staring at the young man with a bland undisturbed air. "The programme. Well, now, I'm flying out——"

"Army plane, General?"

"No," Murphy said shortly. "Pan Am."

A few pencils flickered over notebooks.

"What's the idea, General? What's wrong with the Army?"

"I've got a few things to do in London, that's all. You might recall I was over there in the last shindig. I made a few friends there."

"How?" someone asked from the back in a bored voice. "Come to that, why?"

Murphy smiled, though he tried hard to hide it. "I'm just going back to look up a few of them," he said.

"And then?"

"And then? Then I guess the Allied Missiles Research Agency starts to claim me. I'll have to get down to work. I'll fly to Paris from London——"

"Civil again, General?"

"Why not? I'll still officially be on holiday. I can please myself."

"What about national prestige, General?"

Franks sighed. Why couldn't a man do as he wished once in a while without having to tell the nation why? The Army didn't mind what Murphy did. He'd had his plans O.K.'d and the airline people didn't mind him flying in their planes. Besides, once in a while, he knew, Murphy enjoyed travelling by ordinary plane, or ship, or train. He supposed that when a man had been forty years in the Army it was pleasant occasionally to get away from it.

"I don't think we need worry about national prestige," Murphy was saying calmly. "Nobody else's worrying. When I arrive in Paris I guess I'll have a day or two squaring up and then I'll get down to work. That's all."

He looked at the *Now* representative as he spoke and Franks found himself thinking how nice it would be to get a simple straightforward paragraph in the magazine, written in intelligible English instead of that slot-machine slogan style that somehow managed to make a man look a clown or some sort of national hero, when he wasn't either—just a hard-working soldier, beginning to look forward to retirement.

Someone looked at his watch and got to his feet and Franks thought they'd finished with Murphy. But a tall thin smooth-faced man from one of the tabloids stood up and, knowing him, having had dealings with him, knowing his paper, Franks knew what was coming. All the others had been discreet enough to leave it alone. But not this merchant. He'd never been known to leave anything alone in all the time he'd been visiting Murphy's conferences. He'd even waited until everyone was finished so they'd all be quiet and would hear exactly what he had to say and know it hadn't been forgotten. Franks knew all the tricks.

Murphy glanced at Franks and seemed to brace himself. The sixty-four-dollar question was coming somewhere in this lot, they both knew.

"General," the smooth-faced man said. "Aside from AMRA—how do you think you're going to get along with the French?"

"Fine! Why not?" Murphy answered lightly, but Franks knew that wasn't the end of it. That was only the first of the sparring blows before the heavy punching. There was more to come.

The smooth-faced journalist was pausing now, as though seeking a way to frame his questions. "Wasn't there a time, though, General," he said, "when you and the French didn't quite see eye to eye?"

Murphy nodded briskly, not dodging the question. "There was," he agreed. "I hope it's finished now, though. It was a long time ago. Twelve years ought to be enough for anyone."

"Some people have long memories, General."

One of the other reporters tried to pull the man down into his seat, but he shook off the hands, and Franks saw Murphy tense. This was it. The thin-faced man had "bird-dog" written all over his features.

"What about this guy"—the reporter glanced at his notebook as though to confirm the name—"this guy, General de Lespinasse-Boderin du Crest, General? I hope I pronounced that right." He beamed at Murphy, as though he were only trying to get the matter straight.

"You did," Murphy didn't return the smile. "What about him?"

"How do you think *he's* going to regard you being in Paris?"

Murphy drew a deep breath. "I don't know," he said frankly. "As far as I'm concerned, that affair's over and done with. I hope *he* thinks the same way."

"Suppose he doesn't?"

"That's something I'll have to face when—and if—it arises."

"Isn't it a fact that this General Boderin had quite a few followers? Isn't it a fact that the *Affaire Boderin* became a national issue in 1945?"

Franks knew Murphy was beginning to get angry now, though he still didn't permit himself the pleasure of showing it.

"I believe he did have a few followers," he said. "And if it did become a national issue, it was a French national issue and didn't concern me."

"Suppose they try and bring it up again, General?"

"Shall we wait and see if they do?" Murphy suggested quietly.

The newspaperman wasn't finished yet though. "I understand," he went on, "that General de Gaulle—whom we all know is still regarded as a man worth listening to, though he has no political power in France at this moment—I understand he took General Boderin's side against you at the time, and even tried to get President Truman to intervene. I just wanted to know how you feel about it. That's all. Just for the record." He sat down, his face a mask of patience and sweet reason that made Franks boil.

"I don't feel about it," Murphy said evenly. "I stopped feeling about it when it finished ten to twelve years ago. That's over and done with. This is 1957 and General de Gaulle's no longer the leader of the French nation. However, it's my guess he would still very probably be consulted before the appointment was made and I take it he must have offered no objection. He strikes me as a man big enough to think in a big way. This way—this way of harking back to something that's been dead for twelve years— isn't a very big way. In fact, it seems to me to be mighty small."

Franks saw the newspaperman frown and knew Murphy would have to pay for the satisfaction of letting himself go. All the same, he noticed, there was a ripple of applause from the back that indicated that the smooth-faced young man and his paper weren't any too popular even with the press and that if they picked on Murphy he might expect support from the rest of them.

Franks was glad. This job of Murphy's—probably his last before retiring—was the biggest he'd ever tackled and Franks had heard whispers that his background was too homely for the rarified atmosphere of Paris where he'd be in daily contact not with

24

fighting men but with politicians and polished diplomats from all over Europe, all trying, with their shrewd Continental experience, to get the best bargain they could for their countries. It was a job which demanded size and, above all, dignity; and it had been said that Murphy, lacking an Academy background, would be at an immediate disadvantage against the crafty brains of the Old World. Colonel Franks, however, suspected that Murphy was sharper than most people—even the people who'd chosen him—believed. He felt Murphy could do the job and he hoped he'd succeed in spite of malicious journalism and the whispers of the envious.

Murphy seemed in no way perturbed by what lay ahead of him, Franks had to admit, and he was answering smoothly with an urbanity that was completely unruffled. "I'm going to do a job with NATO for the United States in Paris, France," he was saying. "And if you guys'll let me, I'd like to start giving a little thought to my packing."

"But, General——"

There were shouts of "Sit down" and Franks sighed, feeling somehow that the questions had left a nasty taste in his mouth. For a Middle Westerner and a man with no intellectual background Murphy had, through two world wars, developed an affection for France, he knew, that was somewhat out of character. He had talked often to Franks about the size of the place and its grandeur, about the curious nihilist atmosphere of Paris, the wry self-pity of the French, and the immense intelligence that seemed always to lead nowhere.

The conference hadn't gone as well as they'd hoped. There was at least one paper that was hostile to Murphy, Franks decided. But then, he reflected, it was hostile not only to Murphy but to everyone else also. It lived only to feed on its own spite.

He knew how it would go: *"Lieutenant-General ('The Sergeant', they still call him in some circles)—"* Franks knew they'd bring that one up, *"—Lieutenant-General John F. Murphy leaves New York next week for Paris, France."* After years of reading the reports of Murphy's conferences he knew exactly just how each man would write his paragraph.

"Flying by Pan-Am instead of by Army plane—what's his quarrel with Army planes?—the general intends to visit old

buddies from the war in London before going on to Paris to take up his appointment at NATO Headquarters.

" 'Murph,' it will be recalled, served in France 1944–1946, when he tangled with the French Government over a matter of prestige and honour." Franks sighed. That's what they'd say, he decided.

He was right—they did.

The Paris newspapers put it differently. That day, there'd been a shooting in the Avenue Hoche where FLN, the Algérist terrorist party, had rubbed out the nephew of an Anti-Algérist Senator, and the murder story, complete with grisly pictures of the dead man sprawled on the pavement in his own blood, had grabbed all the headline space. Nevertheless, Murphy's appointment had not gone unnoticed and they'd all got a paragraph about it on the main news page.

Figaro announced simply *"General Murphy for Paris."* The Leftist *Paris Soir* stated. *"Yet another American General for Paris,"* while the Communist-controlled *Emancipation* tried hard to reopen old wounds by announcing *"General Murphy for Paris. Affaire Boderin recalled"* and made a point of referring in its leader to what it called *"the twelve-year-old stain on the honour of the French Army."* There were other versions, too, but those were the ones that caught the eye.

In the Place des Epars at Chartres, sixty miles south-west of Paris, the warm spring sunshine was bringing out the coffee and apéritif-drinkers. From the Bar Normand, it was possible to see the green tiles and flying buttresses of the cathedral over the crooked roofs of the town. General Marceau, cast in bronze, and surrounded by shrubs and flowers, leaned against a group of Revolutionary War armaments and stared down his long nose into the Rue Delacroix.

The business men sitting by the Bar Normand shook out their newspapers and settled back in their minute chairs to blink at the glare of the midday sunshine, and watch the children with their blue smocks and brief cases coming from school.

It was said of Chartres that you could say "Good morning, General" in the main street at any time of the day and at least half a dozen men would stop and raise their hats, and the soldierly-looking man in the grey suit sitting in the shade of a blue-and-red-striped parasol sipping a coffee didn't look much out of place as he put down his cup and opened his *Le Monde*. Slowly he read the streamers without taking the trouble to explore the mass of type for the greater details of the stories, then his eye fell on a double-column headline half-way down the page— *"General Murphy to Return to Paris"*. It was insignificant and *Le Monde* had refrained from comment, stating nothing but the bare details, but giving the paragraph a bigger headline than the announcement normally would have warranted.

For a moment he stared at it, and at the smaller type just beneath, *"Liberator of the Bligues will take up NATO Post"*, then he laid down his newspaper on the unoccupied chair alongside him and took another sip of coffee. He sat silently, motionless almost, staring ahead of him while the Orléans and Paris traffic roared past in its circle round the statue of Marceau. He was an old man, but not as old as he looked. The white hair round his ears was tufty and frail-looking and his face was pink and bright, but thin with the delicate bones beneath showing through. He was a tall man and very straight, with a narrow sensitive, yet somehow stubborn face.

For a long time he sat staring in front of him, indifferent to the noisy squabble of the sparrows on the pavement, then he took up the newspaper again and, folding it carefully into a neat square, settled back to read the article once more, his washed-out blue eyes distant, browsing over it for some time, reading it again and again, dwelling particularly on the concluding few lines: *"In the Assembly yesterday, Monsieur Romane (MRP) asked what steps had been taken to protest against the appointment of General Murphy. It was a disgrace, he said, that one of the principal participants of the Affaire Boderin was to be allowed back in Paris, especially at a time when the country was looking forward once more to a measure of calmness and settled government."*

It was some time before the old man put down the paper again. He sat, slim and erect and frail in his chair, staring at the traffic moving noisily in front of him, then he slowly lit a cigarette, drew a deep puff at it and swallowed the rest of his coffee. Finally he

27

began meticulously to fold the paper again and picked up his hat, gloves and stick, then he rose abruptly, tucked a hundred-franc piece under the saucer and walked briskly away.

The man at the next table who had been watching him keenly ever since he had sat down, looked across at his companion.

"He saw it," he said.

"Saw what?" His friend had been busy with the sports news in *L'Equipe* and hadn't noticed anything. "What did he see?"

"The bit about Murphy."

The other lowered his paper and began to look around him with interest.

"You should have seen his face. It was a picture." The first man gestured with his cigarette. "There, by the gunsmiths. He looks as though he's seen a ghost."

The second man shrugged. "Well, he has, hasn't he?" he said.

The old man in the grey suit was standing still and erect outside a shop at the other side of the Place des Epars. The gold letters over the doorway, *Arquébusier, Pêche, Armes, Coutellerie,* caught the sunshine. He was staring through the window at the miscellany of fishing rods, knives, pistols, rifles and shotguns.

For a long time he stood gazing thoughtfully at the assorted weapons and sporting equipment in the window, then he continued slowly past the prosperous houses of the doctors in the Boulevard Chasles to the Place Pasteur where the bust of the scientist stared glumly down the Rue St Brice. On his left the narrow streets of the city fell away steeply to the river with its huddle of crooked houses.

Turning into the Rue St Brice, the old man walked briskly for a while, then he swung in at the door of a shabby block of apartments. The concierge put his head out of his cubicle, nodded and withdrew to his newspaper, watching cautiously over the top of the sheets. The old man in the grey suit waited impatiently for the lift to descend, then with a clashing of grilles he climbed inside and ascended to the fourth floor.

Taking a key from his pocket, he opened the door of his apartment and went inside. The apartment was a dark place and his face was in shadow. On the walls were crossed sabres and over the door a long lance, its yellow pennant gathering the dust.

28

The wallpaper was studded with portraits, all of them grouped about one large painting of a soldier in the uniform of the First Empire which seemed to hold pride of place. There were daguerrotypes of men in shakos and dolmans, and water-colour sketches made in battle. There were several of the attack on the Malakoff at Sebastopol in the Crimean War signed *Boderin du Crest*, and more of troops moving up for the Battle of the Marne signed *de Lespinasse-Boderin du Crest*, which were neither as colourful nor anything like as good. Here and there were framed newspaper cuttings dating back to 1870 and 1914, and written despatches and letters signed by people as eminent as Marshals MacMahon and Joffre, and General de Gaulle.

The old man's eyes wandered over them slowly, and he seemed to stand before them almost as though in front of a shrine, absorbed in worship, then he appeared to shrug off the thoughts that were filling his mind and strode into the bedroom.

For a long time he was occupied in rummaging through a desk, throwing papers and documents out on to the bed, then he stopped dead, staring into the drawer. Slowly he reached down and lifted a small automatic pistol from among the disturbed papers . . .

The shadows in the room had grown longer when he returned to the lounge. He glanced briefly at his watch, clicked his tongue irritably, and deposited an armful of documents in a chair. Again, he glanced at his watch then, picking up the newspaper again, stood staring at it, not reading it, his expression unchanged since he had first seen the paragraph that interested him outside the café in the Place des Epars. It still had about it the same mask-like quality of tension—pale, taut and trembling, a small muscle flickering at the angle of his jaw, his eyes with a blank unseeing look about them. He was still standing there with the paper in his hand, still not reading it, when the door opened.

He started to life abruptly and turned to meet the newcomer, a thickset middle-aged man with a curiously hard moustached face that stamped him distinctly as an ex-N.C.O. The little eyes in the square leathery face moved from the old man to the chair loaded with papers, and the eyebrows rose slowly.

"You're late, Blot," the old man snapped irritably.

"I've been shopping." The newcomer's face was blank and faintly defiant.

"Well, get a move on. We're going to Paris." The old man laid down the newspaper and began to pick up the files of documents he had unearthed. "You'd better pack your things, Sergeant."

"Very good, Monseiur. When are we leaving?"

"In an hour."

The sergeant's face registered a faint imperceptible sadness. "I see, Monsieur," he said.

The old man suddenly became more animated and began, in his frail uncertain way, to fiddle with the documents in his hands, his washed-out eyes alight.

"And Blot," he said. "We'll want all the maps from my study and the typescript of the court martial proceedings. It's in the cupboard there. You'd better take these with you."

He handed over the papers, and Sergeant Blot nodded—in a way that seemed to suggest he was coming to attention.

"The American, General Murphy, is coming back to France," the old man went on gaily. "I think we should be in Paris to meet him. Perhaps we can change his mind about the affair at Percéval."

The sergeant sighed again, with the air of a man who has heard the whole story before. "Perhaps so, Monsieur," he said in a flat voice.

"We shall need two suitcases, Blot. One for clothing. One for all my papers and books, and the brief case for the dossier I prepared on the court martial with Monsieur Robert."

Sergeant Blot nodded again, then he turned away with a stiff gait that spoke of an artificial leg. When he returned, he was wearing a harsh black suit which looked as though it were his best, a starched collar and black tie, and a grey felt hat that seemed almost to be made of wood. He carried two suitcases and a brief case.

The old man had been stuffing papers into a second brief case and, as Blot appeared, he straightened up, eager now in a childish excited way.

"We're ready, Monsieur," Blot announced.

The concierge had come out of his cubicle by the time they reached the bottom floor. As the lift gates clashed, he looked round from where he was talking to the postman by his door.

"Going away, Monsieur?" he asked.

The old man turned his face towards the concierge. Only the brightness of his pale eyes revealed his excitement.

"For a while," he said. "For a while."

"What about the mail, Monsieur?" the postman asked. "Will you be away long?"

"I don't expect so."

The concierge and the postman exchanged glances as the two men headed for the door, and moved farther into the hall for a better view.

The old man waited at the edge of the pavement, tapping impatiently with his stick, while Sergeant Blot vanished in search of a taxi. Almost immediately, however, he returned and the concierge moved slowly into the sunshine as the vehicle disappeared.

"That was sudden," he said.

The postman, his *képi* pushed back on his head, was still staring after the taxi, his face interested, his mouth widening into a grin.

"Did you see his face?" he asked.

The taxi drew up near the cathedral. The two men climbed out and, while Blot paid the driver, the older man walked slowly past the nun sitting by the west door with her offertory box. Inside, the stone walls were violet from the sun on the stained glass of the circular window overhead, and flecks of red, blue and yellow touched the worn paving and the dark wood of the confessional boxes. Cascades of notes were flooding from the organ and echoing round the high vaulting.

For a long time, the old man stared towards the altar, then he crossed himself and sat for a moment in the rearmost of the rows of rush-seated chairs, his head bowed in prayer, then abruptly, as though he had put behind him all thoughts of emotion, he rose and walked to the door, pushing through the groups of tourists gathered in the gateway.

At the station at the bottom of the hill, a low huddle of ugly grey concrete buildings, the old man paid for two tickets and, crossing under the track, pushed among the crowds waiting for the train towards Le Mans. A little boy making water on to the track moved over to let him pass and a porter wheeling a couple of bicycles along the low platform stopped in front of him.

"Good morning, General," he said. "Going far?"

The old man shook his head. "Only to Paris," he said.

The porter indicated the metallic silver train waiting at the rear of the platform. "That's your train, General."

The old man nodded and walked towards the train. Blot followed, his face expressionless, studiously ignoring the porter who stood holding the two bicycles, still staring after them. As another of the station staff approached, the porter stopped him.

"He's seen it," he said.

"Who's seen what?"

"Boderin. He's seen the bit about Murphy. He's off to Paris."

On the north-east fringe of Paris the cemetery of Père Lachaise stretched its hundred and nine melancholy acres along the slopes above the Boulevard de Ménilmontant. It was a hot sultry day and the dark trees overlooking the massed tombs—the horse chestnuts, the cypresses and the acacias—threw the crowded avenues into deep and sombre shadows. Even the birds seemed to be oppressed into silence by the low clouds.

A small shabby man picked his way carefully between the serried rows of tasteless monuments towards the Porte Principale. There was a smell of decay in the air as he hurried into the Rue du Repos and past the funeral parlours that surrounded the cemetery.

The café he chose was a dingy place of brown woodwork and fly-specked smoke-pickled paint where even the glasses had the same worn look as the walls—as though they'd been handled so often the shine had worn off them. Ordering a beer, the little man moved along the counter to the telephone and dialled a number. The voice that answered him was soft and wary.

"He's still in Père Lachaise," the little man said. "I've been following him most of the morning."

"What do you think?" the wary voice asked.

"Early to say yet," the man in the café replied. "Give me a chance to make contact. He's lonely and he's easily influenced and, like most of 'em, he can't recognize politics when he sees 'em."

"Where is he now?"

"He's up in the old part. By the family tomb. That damned place gives me the creeps, especially on a day like this."

The voice at the other end of the telephone broke in irritably, as though its owner were unconcerned with the moods of Père Lachaise. "What's he doing?"

The little man shrugged. "Just standing there," he said. "Staring. He's been at it an hour now."

"What's he contemplating?"

"God knows."

"Very well," came the wary voice. "Keep an eye on him. Don't let him out of your sight. We might be glad to use him."

"I'll watch him," the man in the café said. "I wish he'd get a move on, though. There's too much death and glory in that place for me, and he's been there over an hour now. It's just as though he's trying to draw courage from all the other Boderins in there. I think it's crossed *his* mind too."

Master-Sergeant Eddy Sligo of the U.S. Army's Weapon Training Park at Achensee in Bavaria put down his beer and stared at the paragraph in *Stars and Stripes* which was resting on the table in front of him. The bar of the club behind him was filled with sergeants and their wives, but Sligo, a bachelor, was quietly absorbed with his lunchtime beer and with what he was reading in the paper.

He was a heavily-built man, past his prime, too old now for active work but comfortably ensconced in an office which he ran with complete efficiency. For a moment longer he stared at the paper, then he finished his beer and pushing away the glass, walked briskly out of the club and across to the headquarters block.

Passing under the brilliant red, white and blue of the flag which hung outside, he made his way to his own office. There he threw down the paper and taking a leave form from a drawer, hurriedly filled it in. Then he slammed the drawer shut and walked along the corridor to the adjutant's office.

The adjutant looked up as he arrived, and smiled.

"Hi, Eddy," he said. "Thought you'd be in the club now with your beer."

Sligo grinned and saluted. "I was, sir," he said. "Only I saw this." He flicked his copy of *Stars and Stripes* across the desk to the adjutant and indicated a paragraph set in a box. The adjutant looked up.

"Yeah," he said, "I've read that. It's Murphy. He's coming back to Europe."

Sligo nodded. "That's it, sir," he said. He pushed across the completed leave form. "I'd like you to sign this, sir."

The adjutant glanced at the leave form, then up again at Sligo. "You haven't filled the dates in," he pointed out. "When do you want it for?"

Sligo gave him a sheepish grin. "I'd like you to sign it, sir, leaving the dates open. I'll fill 'em in. You can trust me."

The adjutant looked puzzled. "What's the idea, Eddy?" he said.

In spite of the rows of ribbons on his chest and the grizzled hair at his temples, Sligo managed to look remarkably like a small boy asking a favour.

"Sir," he said, "it's like this: You know how I feel about the general."

The adjutant chuckled. "Well, you've told me often enough," he commented.

"Sure, sure," Sligo agreed. "Only you know how it is, sir. He was my company commander on his first stretch. I was only a kid then. He wasn't much more himself but he'd already gotten enough medals on his chest to make a cub scout go green with envy. We thought he was a pretty hot shot even then. Every one of us. He fetched me out of that goddamned river, sir—I've told you about that. That gook of a driver tossed us all in. If it hadn't been for the General I'd have been hearing taps through six feet of soil. I'd got one leg broken and the other all goofed up with my rifle sling. I'd got a full pack on pulling me down, too. He got himself another medal for that. He came to see me once in hospital and brought me some cigarettes and books. Me. Just a kid, and him on the way already to being the most decorated man in the States. I always swore I'd try and do something to repay—

34

at least to stand up in front of him and throw him up the best god-damned salute there ever was in the history of the United States Army. But, you know, sir, I've never once saluted that man. The only time I ever saw him I was lying on my back with a broken leg."

"You certainly make a lot out of it, Eddy," the adjutant said with a grin. "Hell, he only saved your life. *You've* saved a few lives in your time, I've heard, but I've never noticed you beefing because they didn't all come and pay their respects."

"This is different, sir."

"Why? Because he's General Murphy?"

Sligo grinned sheepishly. "I guess so," he said. "It isn't every guy gets the privilege of being hauled out of the river by the most famous man in the army. I've followed his career all through the years. It sort of grows on you, sir. It becomes a—hell, an obsession, if you like! I just want once before I retire and lose the opportunity for good, to throw him one up and probably shake his hand."

The adjutant grinned and stared up at the old sergeant, standing in front of him, straight-backed and unashamed of his emotions.

"But I've never caught up with him since, sir," Sligo was saying, his voice brittle with his earnestness. "When I came out of hospital, he'd left the post. I had several tries to get sent after him but the rank I had in those days didn't carry much weight, and nobody took any notice. When he was in the Philippines I managed to be in the States. When I went to the Philippines, he'd gone to Pearl. When I went to Pearl he was back in the Philippines. After Bataan he went to North Africa."

The adjutant opened his mouth to speak but Sligo, carried away by his emotion, interrupted. "Sure, sir. I know. I went to North Africa too, but by that time they'd dropped Murphy into Sicily. When I went to Italy they'd pulled him out and put him in charge of a new division and sent him to the South of France. I just never caught up with him. For thirty years I've been promising to shake his hand and I haven't got much time left now. Like always, just when they send him here to take over, I'm due for home and finish for good and all. I've not done badly," he said humbly. "I reckon I've got most of what I want—*but one*

35

thing. Sign that pass, sir, though, and I'll be in Paris when he arrives. I won't miss him this time."

The adjutant reached for his pen. "You goddamn old soldiers," he said good-humouredly, "you're all the same. You're more sentimental than an old schoolmarm. O.K. Eddy"—his pen scratched across the paper—"there's your leave pass. All you've got to do now is go when you want."

Sligo gave the adjutant the smartest salute he could manage. "Thanks, sir," he said earnestly. "This sure means a lot to me."

★ 3 ★

THE rain on the circular iron grilles at the base of the mutilated trees of the Boulevard du Palais, close to the Cathedral of Notre Dame, made the ironwork shine in the yellow light that was streaming eerily through a split in the heavy clouds. Across the Quai des Orfèvres that overlooked the crowding Seine barges, the dark trees and flat-fronted houses of the Left Bank peered northward in a blank futile stare.

The tall military man, curiously English with his walking stick and pipe and smooth tweed suit, who appeared from the West Door of the Préfecture, strode quickly across the boulevard between the hurrying traffic and passed through the tall iron gates touched with gold at the east end of the Palais de Justice. Turning right, he slipped through a shabby side entrance, noticing with an experienced eye the words, *Vive de Gaulle*, scratched on the stonework with swastika decorations. "*A bas les politiciens*" was scrawled with heavy French disgust underneath in chalk, and he wondered casually when the country would decide it had had enough of the petty manoeuvrings of the coalitions that had followed one upon another with dreary monotony since De Gaulle's departure from the political scene and would have the sense to recall that sombre figure, stiff with integrity and the honour of France, to lead them back to dignity.

Stepping gingerly through the crowd of bicycles parked among the dusty legal notices at the bottom of the stone stairs, he clattered upwards to the vast domed marble hall that led to the law courts. His heels clicked across the black and white floor in the tremendous silence inside, where a uniformed man sat opposite the vast war memorial to the Paris advocates, heavy with the names of the Marne, Ypres, Verdun and the Argonne, and passing through to the other end, he marched briskly along the corridor until he came to a door marked "*Service de Sûreté de la présidence de la République et de protection des members de gouvernment et hautes personalités.*"

Pushing it open, he went inside and spoke to the clerk. "Inspector Souprosse, please."

"The name, sir?"

"Major Schneider."

"Of course, sir. I should have known."

The clerk stood up respectfully and as he opened the door, Schneider followed him, a tall slender man with a clipped greying moustache and sharp alert eyes, one hand twisted like a claw by an old wartime injury. He had an aristocratic face, but it had the brisk awareness of healthy intelligence and he smiled distantly as he shook hands with Souprosse, a small plump man with a curious toughness about his round frame.

"Schneider," Souprosse said gaily, his eyes alight with pleasure as Schneider sat down: "I know what you've come about: Murphy."

Schneider nodded and leaned back.

"When does he arrive?" Souprosse demanded.

"The 21st."

"Orly?"

Schneider nodded again, his eyes on the window where he could see the flat roof of the Théatre des Nations with its *Sarah Bernhardt* sign.

"Expecting trouble?"

"No," Schneider's manner was brusque. "There may be something, of course, but we're watching. The Communists or FLN may try to start something."

Souprosse smiled. "Well, we've had others," he said placidly. "Eisenhower. Ridgway. Montgomery. Mountbatten. Speidel." He looked up again. "De Gaulle," he finished with a wry smile.

Schneider nodded again. "Murphy's different," he said. "For a time he was part of French politics."

He lit a cigarette, then started to polish the edge of the desk

37

with one finger of his maimed hand. "I'm not worried about the Communists, though," he said. "Or the Boderinists. They're defunct. As defunct as the Dreyfusists and the Pétainists and the Boulangists and the Bonapartists. I'm afraid of the Extremists who might use Boderin to upset the government. That organization that supported him in 1946. The Society for the Friends of Truth. They're allied now with FLN and the Sidis. I kept track of them. They'll join anyone who works against security and common sense."

Souprosse watched him for a while, rubbing away in his curious detached way, as though he were occupied with the patina of the desk rather than the problem of the arrival of General Murphy.

"Think someone might have a go at him?" he asked.

"It's always possible. Anything's possible in France. We're incurably political."

Souprosse grinned at Schneider's flat cynicism.

"I've heard that the students are contemplating something," he said.

Schneider nodded. "Probably no more than a demonstration. A few crackpots from St Germain and the Sorbonne. We'll learn more about that later. At the moment we've nothing to go on. But I don't want anything to develop. I want nothing that the press can get hold of. We don't want that damned *Affaire Boderin* bringing up again if we can help it."

Colonel Franks was driven out quietly with General Murphy to the great Pan-American Boeing standing at the far end of the tarmac. The grey-green staff car, its lights blazing, followed the airport jeep, heading quickly away from the neons of the airport buildings where the buses were picking up travellers. A wireless was playing music softly in the darkness but, even as the car came to a halt, it ceased abruptly, and the announcer's voice began to summon the passengers for the London flight.

The distant lights played on Frank's lean, unsoldierlike face as he stared out of the window, making his spectacles and smooth cheeks gleam. It was a warm night and he could see Murphy dabbing at his moist face with a handkerchief. As they descended in front of the great machine, the crew appeared at the top of the steps, waiting for them, and Murphy and Franks paused while the chauffeur unloaded their brief cases.

"It's going to be a good trip," Murphy observed, glancing at the sky.

As they walked towards the plane, a mechanic who was standing by a trolley-load of batteries smiled and gave Murphy a salute. "Pleased to see you again, General," he said. "I was with you on the run up into Alsace in the Fall of '44."

Murphy gave him a grave salute in return, then his mouth widened with a responsive smile.

"What outfit?" he said.

"General Wilchau's, sir. I didn't do so well as you, though. I only made corporal."

"We can't all be generals," Murphy said.

"I got a Purple Heart though."

"All right now?"

"Yeah, fine, General. No harm done."

"Glad to hear it. I see you've deserted to the Air Force now, though."

"Got to earn a living, General."

Murphy laughed. "Haven't we all?" he said.

"Hope you have a good flight, General."

"Thanks. I hope you fixed those engines O.K."

There were smiles all round as Murphy began to climb the steps into the plane. He was greeted at the top by the captain and the crew, then he moved forward and took his place, Colonel Franks following close behind, marvelling as he always did at Murphy's gift for putting everyone at their ease.

Franks was a man of good family. His father, who was a wealthy man, had been a soldier too, but illness and bad eyesight had prevented Franks from being accepted for the peacetime army before the war and he had gone into publishing. Already on his way to the top of his profession when the war had broken out, he had gladly thrown it all up and joyfully offered himself to the Army which had been delighted to have a man not only of proved skill in his own field but also of a strict military background. Franks had done well as a desk soldier and, in the vast expansion of the army after the war and the threat from the East, he had elected to remain where he was and had been allowed to.

He was used to high-ranking officers and he recognized Murphy clearly as a man who had dragged himself up by his bootstraps, but it was still a matter of wonder to him that he was so capable at making people confide in him—that curiously intimate manner that was never flattering, never searching for cheap popularity, but always managed to make the people with whom he came into contact feel important. He hoped like hell that Murphy would confound all his critics and make them realize that, in giving him the Paris job, the Pentagon had judged more wisely than they knew.

Murphy had stuffed his brief case on to the rack by this time and was stretching his legs in his seat.

"Anything from France, Frankie?" he asked, busy with the magazine and papers they'd bought for the journey.

Franks nodded. "A nice note from SACEUR saying they'll be glad to have you over there," he said with a grin. "A lot of stuff from AGARD. It's all new and we'll have to go through it, but it's not urgent. A request from CINCENT and CINCHAN for your views on their position with regard to the Agency. I think they're after anything new that's available. They want to be there when the curtain goes up."

He continued to read through a list in a notebook he held in his hand, looking vaguely like a professor giving a lecture, an appearance that always tickled Murphy when he thought about it and led him to call Franks "Prof." from time to time when he was in a good mood.

"There's also something here that'll please Mrs Murphy," Franks said. "A list of addresses. Houses vacant for letting furnished."

Murphy looked up from his magazine and took the list that Franks held out to him. "I hope they're what we want," he said. "Where are they?"

"Mostly south and south-west of Paris. St. Germain-en-Laye. Meudon. Versailles. Le Vésinet. St Cloud."

"Sounds all right. They're good residential districts. What have we got temporarily?"

40

"They've fixed you up with an apartment in the Avenue Foch until you make your mind up which you want."

"What about you?"

"I'll find somewhere."

Murphy looked up, his eyes smiling.

"How big's the apartment in the Avenue Foch?" he asked.

Franks grinned. "Pretty big," he said. "You know what it's like in the Avenue Foch. Film stars. Diplomats."

"Americans," Murphy added.

"And Americans." Franks laughed. "You can use part of it as an office."

"Why not shack up with me till we both find something. It'll be useful having you handy. We can work longer hours. Save trouble."

"That's what I thought," Franks admitted, "but I didn't fancy saying so."

"Well, I've said it for you," Murphy retorted. "If there's as much room as you say there is, I'll rattle round inside the joint like a pea in an empty pod. I'll be glad of company, Frankie, and there'll be all those damned people to look after me. They'd only be wasted. And, for God's sake, when you get yourself a house out there, don't get it too far away from mine. Lilian gets along fine with Sue. They'll be glad to swop hairdressers and dressmakers. No reason why they shouldn't travel over together, in fact. Company's good on a trip that long."

Franks nodded gratefully and took back the papers Murphy passed over.

"Anything else?"

Franks nodded. "They've got it," he said.

Murphy's face clouded.

"Got what?" he asked cautiously. "The Boderin Affair?"

"Scraped up from the very bottom of the barrel!" Franks passed over a folded slip of paper to Murphy, who took it and stared at it.

"That's a summary," Franks pointed out. "Lancy prepared it. Headlines and salient points. Lancy's part French and was once an assistant editor. It helps."

"Sure does." Murphy tapped the paper with his finger, pointing to one of the paragraphs. "That's a lulu," he said. "Still, I

41

suppose we ought to expect it from that lot. Communist, aren't they? They'll try to drive in all the wedges they can. What about the others?"

"They've all of them got you, but most of them haven't mentioned Boderin yet."

"They *will*, when they get around to it."

"Those who have, are being pretty vague about it still," Franks went on encouragingly. "Lancy's sent a full re-write of them all. In English. Here it is." He fished in his brief case and produced a wad of paper. "The Leftist papers are complaining again about the number of American generals in Paris. That crack of the *New York Times* about them being the worst straggler of the lot still hurts, it seems, and they're having a crack back. The Communists, of course, have brought out Boderin himself, all dusted and clean and ready for use."

"Pity," Murphy said. "I just hoped they might not. I like the French, as it happens. I had a lot of 'em with me during the war. I got on all right with 'em. Not so starchy as the English, bless 'em—though they had a sticky pride in those days."

"One of them calls it the 'Dreyfus Case of the Fourth Republic'."

"Kind of strong, that, isn't it? Hell, you couldn't call it a miscarriage of justice. I had good reason to pull Boderin out. None of his officers ever complained. Some of them even agreed with me. Anything else?"

"A letter. In French."

"A fan?"

"I guess not."

"Who's it from?"

"You'll never guess."

"I'll buy it."

"I don't suppose I'll pronounce it properly."

Murphy looked at Franks with a faint trace of humour in his eyes.

"Have a go," he said.

"Nicholas Jean St Omer de Lespinasse-Boderin du Crest. Companion of the Liberation Legion of Honour. General de Brigade."

"The old boy himself?"

"The old boy himself!"

"Wow! What's he want?"

"He presents his compliments and expects to meet you as soon as you arrive in Paris. He trusts that he'll then be able to put right the great wrong you did to him."

"Is that all?"

"That's all."

"Doesn't say much, does it?"

"That's what I thought."

Murphy scratched his nose. "That's a hell of a beginning," he said. "What's he mean, I wonder. What's he after?"

Franks shrugged. "Could mean anything," he said. "Could be he just wants a chat. Could be he wants to present you with a treatise on the case, setting out his side of the picture. You know these old birds when they get a bee in their bonnet. Could be he wants to stick a bullet in you."

"That's what occurred to me too." Murphy grinned ruefully. "He didn't take it very well, I guess. Wonder if the papers have got this."

"Apparently not."

"Maybe it's as well. If they could get him to talk they'd tear me apart." Murphy thought it over for a moment. "Any address on that letter?" he asked.

"Nope. Postmarked Paris. That's all."

"It might be the work of a phony, though I guess it's like his writing, as I remember it. Let's leave it to the boys in Paris. They'll know of it, if Lancy does. They'll know what to do about it. Let's just enjoy the trip. What's the forecast?"

"Pretty calm this side. A few electrical storms over the other side. Nothing to worry about."

The sudden roll of thunder sounded over the single bell of St Germain-des-Prés and the rising wind flapped the café awning and sent the cigarette ends and monkeynut shells and coffee tickets swirling into the gutter like confetti. The vestments of a passing priest flapped against his legs, and the people waiting for buses crowded forward urgently to climb aboard before the rain came. A grubby tricolour on a stand advertising an exhibition began to flutter, and the windows and blinds of the apartments

43

across the street, drawn against the thundery heat, began to move and rattle. The geraniums in their pots outside the upper-storey windows began to wave agitatedly, and a couple walking arm-in-arm in spite of the crowd began to move more quickly. The pigeons round the short spire of St Germain burst abruptly into the air at the sound and whirled round the whipped acacias at the top of the Rue Bonaparte, white against the dark cavern of the church door with its carved lettering, *Venite Adoremus*, then came to rest on the ivy-covered walls of the little garden alongside.

As the rain came down, Hardy edged his chair farther back against the wall to make room for sheltering pedestrians. The thunder rolled again and a small boy in tight shorts, his legs like sticks, who was carrying two tins of tomatoes home for the family supper clapped them against his ears to keep out the noise. There was a sudden flurry among the waiters as they dragged chairs and tables under cover, then the water began to drip from awnings and coloured umbrellas and bounce off the surface of the road.

Hardy sipped quietly at his brandy, his eyes on the students from the Sorbonne as they passed, the men in soaked shirts, the girls in wet blouses which clung flatly to their bodies showing the white outlines of their brassières. A woman carrying a saturated paper bag began to gesticulate as it burst and scattered apples on the pavement, then philosophically, she picked up the apples and put the remainder of the bag over her head to protect her hairstyle. Hardy grinned. Whatever else was lost, *le chic* must not disappear. All around him, women were dumping brief cases on café chairs and putting plastic bags and newspapers over their heads, ignoring their clothes completely.

A girl with ash blonde hair and a meridional skin pushed through the crowds and sat down at the next table, shaking the rain off her coat, and Hardy stared at her for a moment with interest. After a while he turned to the student sitting across the table from him, and raised his eyebrows.

"That her?" he asked.

The student, a young boy in jeans, who wore an immature beard as though it were a badge of freedom, shook his head and went on smoking.

Hardy sighed regretfully. "Pity," he said.

44

The boy stared at him, puzzled.

"Why do you want to see Nicole Lacquart, Monsieur Hardy?" he asked. "She's not one of the inner circle. She's not really had much to do with the demonstration. She's not even on the committee."

"Just a hunch," Hardy said. "I don't think her name's Nicole Lacquart for one thing."

The boy looked startled. "Oh? What is it then?" he asked. "That's what she's registered as. I've seen it written down."

"Doesn't mean a thing."

"She'd get into trouble if she gave a wrong name."

"She might get into worse trouble if she gave the right one."

"I don't understand, Monsieur Hardy."

Hardy shrugged. "I don't suppose you do," he said. "I don't much myself. I just want to know what's behind this demonstration of yours. That's all."

The boy gestured irritably and hitched his jacket over his shoulders like a cloak. "She can't tell you any more than I've told you already," he said patiently, as though he were dealing with someone elderly and stupid. "We object to the United States sending their soldiers over here. That's all. When we sought Marshall Aid after the war, instead of getting tins of beans and spam, we got Air Force installations and rocket sites."

"They've got 'em in England too," Hardy pointed out blandly.

The boy shrugged, magnificently indifferent. "Nobody in France worries about England," he said calmly. "Even the most eminent Englishmen can hardly be taken seriously as intellectuals."

Hardy laughed. "All right, then," he said. "They've got 'em in Germany. *And* Spain. *And* Africa. What's so odd about that?"

"French situations can't be explained away in a few words," the boy said, prickly with the honour of his country. "France is composed of a tangle of many incoherent things. She's been rotting away for too long. It started in 1940 and it's gone on ever since. Indo-China. North Africa. Here in Paris. We have a new government every few weeks and none of them last. There's no honesty anywhere. There's distrust in the very air we breathe."

"One more American general won't make all that difference. Why pick on this one?"

"Because the appointment's just an indication of the *manque de psychologie*—the lack of psychology—of the Americans. They shouldn't have sent this man Murphy. They're still in the nursery stage in international politics. Because *they* like it, they think everyone else will like it. They let us down again and again."

Hardy gestured with his cigarette. "You wouldn't have said that if the Russians had tried to walk across Europe in 1947," he said calmly. "Only the Americans being here stopped them. They didn't let you down then."

The boy shrugged off the difficult question with the ease of a man with an *idée fixe*.

"It's easy for American generals to be brave," he pointed out, "with their homes across the Atlantic in safety."

Hardy sighed. Sometimes, the ardour of young Frenchmen wearied him.

"You've heard of the *Affaire Boderin*?" the boy asked.

"Too often," Hardy said.

"How could they send the one man who was the cause of it?"

"The President doesn't seem to mind."

"The President isn't all of France. His hands are tied. He has to tread warily. But what he can't say, *we* can. We intend to let this Murphy know he's not welcome."

Hardy said nothing. With Cellini's money, he bought the boy another coffee and himself another brandy, and sat back waiting.

It had started with a few questions at the Institut des Langues Européennes and had progressed to the Amphithéâtre Richelieu at the Sorbonne where all the students gathered. It had continued in the bookshops near the Ecole de Médecin, and among the boys selling virulent pamphlets in the square off the Boul' Mich'. His inquiries had led to the Alliance Française and the Cité Universitaire and even the Berlitz School. All the students seemed to be concerned in it.

Nobody seemed to know much, however, beyond that in their concern for the honour of France, they were anxious to make a demonstration of some sort. Any sort. To their logical French minds, it didn't seem to matter, so long as it was a demonstration. Just to show they cared. Just to show that they were the same students who had raised the barricades in 1789 and 1830 and

46

1848 and 1871. Just to show that the spirit of France wasn't dead.

He'd tried all the little student bars with their sawdust and predatory pimps, in the twisting alleys round the Panthéon and the Odéon, and on all the long straight roads of the St Germain area where the drunks slept off their wine on the benches outside the Ecole de Médicin. He had pushed among the everlasting market stalls that jammed the gutters of the Rue de Seine and crowded at the long oilcloth-covered tables of the shabby restaurants under the flat-fronted leprous houses in the Rue de Buci; searching dark little eating places with interiors of mahogany and mirrors and built-in hatstands, full of gilt and glass and the tarnished pomp of the Nineteen Hundreds, their banquettes jammed with fat businessmen in high built-up belly-holding pants who were absorbed with their eternal stomach pills.

During the course of his inquiries, one name had cropped up repeatedly and, acting on a hunch, he had gone to the American library at the top of the Champs Elysées. It had been a profitable morning because, not only had he found there the name he'd been seeking, but he'd also met an English girl who wore a two-inch ring and a sack dress left over from last year and not much else. The glow the episode had left in him had been dimmed only by the sight of Ernestine waiting in his room for him when he'd got home the next morning. The ensuing uproar had brought all the occupants of all the rooms on all the floors of the building out into the corridors and had continued even into the street as he had fled.

The rain had stopped now and he leaned back and watched the smoke from his cigarette whipped away by the gusty wind. The air had cooled considerably and the passing boys had taken off their jackets and put them over the shoulders of the girls. A few Americans came past, looking surprisingly tall, as they always did against the French students and the slender North Africans. The advertisement on the awning, *Pils-Schutz, Bière de Strasbourg*, flapped sharply. A boy in Roy Rogers pants with wet hair came among the tables carrying a basket of nuts. He shoved it in front of Hardy and said *"P'stache, Monsieur?"* but, seeing Hardy was lost in thought, he left a single nut as a sample and wandered away again.

Then, as Hardy came back to earth, he saw Cellini standing in front of him.

"You said you wanted to see me," the American said. "You left a message."

Hardy sat up and called the waiter. "That's right," he said, indicating the boy by his side. "Meet Yves Hall. Demonstrator. Leader of the Band. The Daring Young Man on the Flying Trapeze. I've persuaded him publicity's a good thing to have. He'll tell you the time and the place, and you can have your photographers ready to send pictures back to a shocked America of their national hero being actively disliked in France."

Cellini gave Hardy a sharp look and, while Hardy sat back to admire the blonde girl, he began talking to the boy. They began arguing immediately but after a while the boy stopped his jeremiad abruptly and touched Hardy's arm, nodding his head at a girl who was approaching.

"This her?"

"This is her, Monsieur Hardy."

The girl who had pushed between the tables and now stood looking uncertainly around her, was dark but had dyed her hair blonde and wore it long and brushed diagonally and flatly across her forehead and one eye. She was small and slight, with firm young breasts and slender hips and legs. Hardy eyed her with approval.

"She shouldn't be blonde," Cellini said at once. "She's not got the right complexion."

"You must tell her."

"And those clothes!" Cellini waved a hand vaguely at the olive-green jersey and black leather coat she wore. "Man, I thought these French girls knew their stuff."

"She's just feeling her feet," Hardy said gently. "You should have seen me at the same age. Horses reared and old ladies passed out."

Cellini grinned. "Who is she?" he asked. In spite of his disapproval, there was a look of interest in his eyes.

"She calls herself Nicole Lacquart."

Cellini glanced again at the girl. She had delicate features which hinted at Indo-Chinese blood, with a small nose that flared at the nostrils. She was too heavily made up, however, particularly round the eyes, and the make-up and the pouting mouth made her seem as though she were trying to look like Brigitte Bardot and not quite succeeding.

Then she saw the boy alongside Hardy, smiled quickly, and came towards them.

"You wished to see me," she said.

The boy introduced them then began to back away. "Perhaps I might leave now," he said. "I've got a date. Nicole will be able to help you. She'll tell you everything."

As he hurried off between the traffic, glad to get away, the girl sat down and when Hardy asked what she wanted to drink, she ordered a Pernod. Cellini's eyebrows rose in disapproval.

She was obviously ill-at-ease and for a while they talked politely about the rain, then she seemed to make an effort to come to the point. "What do you want to know?" she asked. "I've brought a list of names with me if you want it. We're meeting at Corvisart. It's on the way to Orly. There'll be a lot of cars and we have to give them time to get there. Her voice was loud and important with nerves. "They're not all fast," she went on, "and some of them are very old. I've been in charge of getting everyone together. I have about a hundred names. I ought to have more but it's surprising how indifferent politically most people are. They're more concerned with eating and drinking and film stars. France has lost its sense of leadership and they'll have to be re-educated if they want to live."

She spoke quickly, her words youthful and shallow and defiant, and full of catch-phrases picked up from political pamphlets and the arguments that took place nightly round the St Germain bars. Hardy and Cellini listened politely for a while, then she stopped, aware that they weren't taking a great deal of notice.

"Are you sure you're interested?" she asked suddenly.

"Oh, we're interested," Hardy said.

"Then I've told you all I can," she pointed out, standing up.

"Not quite all." Hardy gestured. "For instance, you're not going out to Orly to demonstrate against Murphy because you're convinced politics is a racket, and that all political ideals and isms are a matter of salesmanship."

She looked down at him, puzzled and faintly disturbed.

"What do you mean?" she asked harshly.

"Your name's not even Lacquart, is it?" Hardy said.

She sat down suddenly, her expression altering subtly. With her petulant young mouth and drab clothes, she looked just like all the other students who hung about the St Germain bars and round the narrow streets that led up to the Butte de Montmartre: Unsettled by a childhood spent in Occupied France; watching their elders corrupted by the necessity to keep alive; Chauvinistic, uncertain about the future; trusting no one and ready to flare into anger when their pride was touched. Her face stiff with the perpetual arrogance of the French, she stared at Hardy with cold disinterested eyes.

"Your name isn't Lacquart really, is it?" he repeated.

"No," she agreed after a long pause. "It's not."

"Would it be de Lespinasse-Boderin du Crest?"

Cellini sat up so quickly he knocked his drink over and the liquid ran off the table and spilled to the floor alongside his feet. A waiter came up immediately and mopped the table.

The girl had not moved but under the dead-pan pale-lipped make-up her hard little face had gone white and she suddenly looked vulnerable. After a while she nodded.

"Yes," she said. "That's my name. I'm not ashamed of it."

"Why did you change it?" Hardy asked.

She paused before she replied. "Because things have often been difficult for my family. We *all* changed our names at times."

"All of you?"

"My mother. My brothers. Myself."

"Not your father?"

"No."

"Why not?"

"He said his name was too old and too honourable to put aside. It dates back to the Army of the Revolution and beyond. There's a Lespinasse on the Arc de Triomphe."

"There's a Hardy too." Hardy spoke flatly. "I've seen it. I expect he was some turncoat Napoleon got hold of."

The girl's eyes flashed indignantly. "De Lespinasse was a great soldier," she said. "Napoleon honoured him."

Hardy nodded. "But there's really very little of the Comte de Lespinasse in your family, is there?" he asked.

50

She looked at him expressionlessly, and Hardy found it hard to tell whether she were angry or merely indifferent.

"You know a great deal about my family," she said.

He nodded. "It was all public property once," he reminded her. "I looked it up. Your father married a Thérèse Lacquart. Daughter of another soldier. She came from Amiens. That's what made me wonder—the name. I put two and two together."

"You're good at sums, Monsieur. Are you a policeman?"

Hardy shook his head. "No, I'm not. I'm a teacher. Not a very good one either." He paused, then went on. "You have a brother, Robert," he said. "He's a lawyer. He works for a firm on the Boulevard Haussmann. He has an apartment near Père Lachaise."

She looked angry and full of pride. "Let me put you right," she interrupted. "I had four brothers. Jean-Michel died in 1940 with the cadets of Saumur. Raoul was shot by the Nazis in 1943. There's a tablet on the wall at the top of the Avenue Hoche where he fell. You can see it for yourself if you take the trouble to look. Etienne was killed in Indo-China. Now there's only Robert left. He's a cripple. The war broke up my family. The Germans started it. The *Affaire Boderin* finished it for them. Why shouldn't I have an interest in General Murphy?"

Cellini leaned forward, speaking as though to alleviate the hurt she was obviously feeling. "Does your brother Robert take an interest in General Murphy too?" he asked.

"My brother keeps himself to himself," she said quickly. "I very rarely see him. He's not easy to get on with. He worked for years on my father's case."

"I see. What about your father? Will he be meeting General Murphy?"

"I don't know. My father lives out of Paris and I don't go home much. He could answer your questions better than I could."

It was an unsatisfactory interview. The girl was not very willing to answer questions. She was resentful and full of bitter words, and it was chiefly Cellini's charm that pulled them

51

through. It was Cellini who finally got her promise of help and an unwilling offer to meet them again.

After she'd gone, Cellini sat for some time staring after her as she crossed the Place St Germain towards the church, where the canvas-covered stall on the corner sent strong wafts of caramel across to them. It was growing darker now and the street lamps had come on, and the yellow and red of the traffic lights were tinting the leaves of the acacias. At the next table a man and a girl who had sat down to shelter from the rain were kissing. He had his hand on her thigh and she was stroking his cheek. On the table in front of them they'd spread their wet cigarettes and money to dry.

Cellini stared for a long time after Nicole Boderin then he sat back and lit a cigarette.

"You were a bit rough on her," he commented.

"You more than made up for me," Hardy said. "Anyway, why not? This family of hers collects glory like a film star collects fans. This de Lespinasse they claim is actually no relation of Napoleon's de Lespinasse. They like to say he was and so did he, but he wasn't really. He was a brewer of lager beer in Alsace who'd bought an estate in the Bligues district so that people would think he was landed gentry. Du Crest was a minor nobleman from Chartres who married one of the Boderins, probably because the Boderins had money and he didn't. Then a Boderin-du Crest married a de Lespinasse and they grabbed at the name with both hands because it added another measure of glory to their already over-full escutcheon."

"They're entitled to think whichever way they like," Cellini said.

"Oh, sure. Why not?" Hardy gestured. "The French have been making a business of La Gloire for a hundred and fifty years. For a nation as sophisticated as they are, it amazes me that they're taken in by a thing that's so damn' naïve. These Boderins, for example. Their courage often seems a bit fly-blown if you look at it closely. Gravet quoted them in an appendix to his book on the French Army. It produced a libel action but Gravet managed to win it and one of the counsel at the court-martial of this girl's father in 1947 brought it all out again—made the poor bastard admit it all in public. What Gravet didn't mention I found out from the people who'd known him. And what they didn't know, I got from the transcripts of the court-martial. It's all there."

Cellini sat still, and Hardy could see he was suffering a little from second thoughts at having set it all in motion.

"One of them who'd been decorated for bravery in Mexico in the 1860s," he went on remorselessly, "was broken in 1870 for doing a bunk at Sedan. And one who was decorated for bravery in Indo-China got himself mixed up in some service scandal in Algeria. There was another in the First World War who was unofficially accused of encouraging his regiment to join the mutinies of 1917. This girl's father—he declared for Free France at a time when it required a certain amount of guts to do it, yet he managed to make a hash of his career tangling with Murphy. There's a funny strain running through them all, a curious thing that taints the glory."

"It doesn't sound a pretty history," Cellini said uncomfortably.

"It's not. Though they distinguished themselves in their own way, I suppose, most of them were military madmen who preferred to die magnificently even when there was sense in surrendering. While one of them was doing a bunk at Sedan, another was getting shot full of holes at Floing. While Great-Uncle Alphonse was popping into bed with the Colonel's wife in Algeria, his nephew was hacking out history in Mexico. While this girl's great-uncle was being cut in the messes for his regiment's defection at Chemin-des-Dames, they were still busy framing the decorations her grandfather won on the Marne. While her brothers were getting themselves shot by the Germans for their courage, her father was working himself up to this damned stupid affair with Murphy that finished his career."

"You've certainly got it all," Cellini said with a faint trace of bitterness.

"I spent a whole day in the library," Hardy pointed out. "If you want the details I have 'em down on paper. They collected glory and disgrace together in equal proportions. They'd just got themselves nicely allied in 1870 to what they liked to suggest was the De Lespinasse family and worked up this resounding bloody name that takes half the day to say, when one of them mucked up the whole thing by fathering a child in Tonkin—you can still

53

see the Tonkinese blood in her. But he must have had more of Lager Lespinasse than Boderin or du Crest in him because he insisted on marrying her and, as the child was a boy and heir to the name, they had to make the best of it. The present Boderin's the grandson of that child. This girl's the great grand-daughter. After the *Affaire* had quietened down, they returned to Paris. Then the wife died and they all moved about a bit. Rheims. Rennes. Chartres. They seem to be breaking up a bit now."

"If you ask me," Cellini said, "she needs someone to straighten her out and get rid of all this family nonsense."

"You're the very person," Hardy said slyly. "I can think of no one better."

"It'd be an interesting experiment."

"It always is. These Continentals are smaller than your stag-like American women. Much more cosy."

"I didn't mean that," Cellini said, quickly.

Hardy laughed. "They're harder to throw off, of course," he persisted. "Ernestine's been phoning twice a day." He sat back and spread his hands. "Well," he said. "You're got your story. You know there's a demonstration on. You know the time and the place and the ringleaders. You've even got a de Lespinasse-Etcetera. Now you can have a wonderful time raking over all the muck once more."

"We don't work like that," Cellini said. He sipped his drink and sat frowning. "I wonder how General Murphy's going to feel about all this," he mused.

A thin island rain was falling in wavy showers across London as General Murphy stared through the window of his apartment. The park opposite looked curiously drab in the damp. The roar of the traffic came up to him, muted and muffled, and the occasional blare of horns. The trees were rich in their late spring foliage but the greenery had a curious dead look about it, as though the weight of the rain took all the life from the foliage.

"I'm glad I'm not English," Murphy said feelingly, jiggling the ice round in his glass.

Franks, at the other side of the room, looked up.

"*American troops abroad,*" he said gravely, "*are advised not to make unfavourable comparisons between modes of life in Britain and America. They are urged not to criticize Royalty or speak in a familiar way about the Royal Family.*"

"It's nothing to do with the modes of life or the Royal Family," Murphy said. "Or even the cold houses or the warm beer. It's just the weather, that's all. Look at it now! May, too! Yet the English seem to *like* it."

"'*Of all the extraordinary things about England,*'" Franks quoted, "'*the most curious are the English.*'" He started to riffle through the pile of newspapers on the table by the door, then he stopped, read for a while, and finally crossed over to the General, carrying a bundle of them with him.

"I see some guy called Cellini's dragged up one of the family," he said. "There's an interview here with her."

"What's she say?" Murphy turned from the window to face him.

"Not much. Still, she's only nineteen. I suppose we can't expect her to. There's some talk of a student demonstration when we arrive."

"That'll be nice. Anything on that letter from old Boderin?"

"They've not been able to contact him."

Murphy shrugged. "I guess it was a phony," he said.

"I don't know so much." Franks looked worried suddenly. "He's disappeared."

"Disappeared?" Murphy's eyes opened wide.

"The police tried to look him up but he'd gone. Now they're scared. So's Lancy, by the tone of his letter."

"Don't they know where he's gone?"

"Not according to Lancy. Think we ought to lay on some sort of security guard?"

"No." Murphy looked up quickly and spoke sharply.

"It might be a good idea," Franks urged.

"I don't want guards," Murphy said firmly. "If I can't walk among the French people without a god-damned guard, I'll throw up the job. There are other people can do the job. Tom Hertzer, for instance."

"He couldn't do it as well as you."

"He wouldn't be plagued by people dragging up his past." There was a trace of bitterness in Murphy's voice.

"Begging his pardon," Franks said, "but General Hertzer's got no past. He's a desk general."

"All the same, if I can't work freely, I'll go home."

"Could be that's what the Commies are hoping." Franks pointed out. "To scare you off."

Murphy nodded. "Could be," he agreed. "Well, they aren't going to. I'm going, and I'll take a chance. Remember when De Gaulle went into Paris in 1944? Bullets were flying all round him and everybody else was lying flat on their faces. But not De Gaulle. He just went on walking. And you know what a target that guy is. It made a hell of an impression. Maybe I'll make an impression."

"It was only a gesture, General."

"The French likes gestures. Maybe I'll make a gesture or two. It might do a hell of a lot of good."

"Not if there's some guy with a gun."

Murphy shrugged and grinned. "They won't shoot," he said. "A dead American general doesn't help anybody. A live general they can throw rotten eggs at's much more use. Besides"—he paused thoughtfully—"Boderin would never countenance shooting. More likely a challenge to a duel in the Bois de Boulogne at dawn."

Franks' eyebrows raised. "Do they still fight duels?" he asked.

"Sure they do. He wanted to fight a duel then. I told him to go suck eggs."

Franks didn't smile. "Maybe he wants to fight another duel now," he said, "and it wouldn't do Franco-American relations a hell of a lot of good if he tried."

Murphy rubbed his nose. "That was twelve years ago almost. He'll be well over seventy now. He wasn't young then and, hell, he never seemed any too robust—even in those days. Tall and skinny. I guess as a young man he must have looked like every boy's idea of a hero. Only he was all nerves."

"What *did* happen, General?" Franks looked at Murphy expectantly. "Even *I* don't know the whole of it."

Murphy thought for a while. "No, I guess not," he agreed, "and under the circumstances, perhaps it's as well you should. I think he was always a bit hard to get on with. You know what these old families are like. He did all right in the First World

56

War but then he became a Carmelite monk or something queer. You know—the pacifist period, the revulsion against war. It hit 'em over here as it never hit the States. They lost so many men in the trenches. We were always digging them up." Murphy paused and Franks found himself staring back over the years to a tragedy his generation had not experienced.

Murphy was silent for a moment, lost in thought, then he went on in matter-of-fact tones. "He went to work in French Equatorial," he said, "and he was there when it started again in 1939. After the Occupation, he offered his services. His family were in France, I think. One or two of them had got themselves bumped off. One of them was with the Saumur cadets. Maybe you heard about them. What they did stands out like a beacon among all that rottenness in 1940. Another one was shot in Paris by the Nazis. He was a student at the time. You can't say they hadn't got guts."

Murphy paused again. "But it was the sort of guts that doesn't help much," he said, shrugging. "Desperate charges and last stands. You know the stuff. He made a lot of noise with a lot of other students, and the Germans turned a burp gun on them."

He turned away from the window and began to walk up and down, holding his glass, his eyes on the floor. "He had three other youngsters who were only kids then," he went on. "There are only two now, I think. He was always a bit unbalanced. He wasn't ever sure whether to be a saint or a soldier. However, because of his record, he pretty soon found himself a colonel. When Leclerc made his march from Chad, Boderin decided to make a march too. He called himself Colonel Domrémy or some such name. It was the fashion for Free French leaders to change their names in those days and it was just like Boderin to pick something that suggested Joan of Arc and a crusade."

Franks lit a cigarette. "He sounds as though he might have been quite a soldier, all the same," he observed.

Murphy shrugged. "That's just it," he said. "He *might* have been. Only he never was. There was always something missing. Maybe it was that his office work was never very hot. Slapdash. He picked a bad route to the north for example, and he lost a lot of men and a lot of health. He could have done it an easier way, but it was gallant to do it the way he did it and to some of these French guys gallantry's the whole art of war. But this *Mort pour la France* stuff isn't much good these days. We try to keep 'em alive now. They're more useful that way."

"Go on," Franks said.

"He got himself pretty severely mauled by Rommel at Sidi Ifna, but the English refitted him, and he got a medal from De Gaulle and was made brigadier. Then we went into the South of France and got up to the Bligues. Mostly it was easy, but there were tough spots. As Georgie Patton used to say, it was like a kid playing Mendelssohn—mostly straightforward, but full of little hard bits. And Boderin always seemed to find 'em.

"At first I thought he was just unlucky, then I began to realize that it was because he goofed up his staff work, and you couldn't afford to goof up your staff work with the Germans, Frankie. They were so damned hot at it themselves. I guess it was his own fault he got knocked about. He was too much in favour of *La Gloire*. Wave the flag and charge. To his way of thinking, it was still the way to win battles."

"What happened?"

Murphy thought a moment and held out his glass. Franks refilled it. "Sorry there's no ice," he said.

Murphy didn't seem to hear. "He sure knew how to pick the wrong time to get into trouble," he said. "Hell, I'd got plenty to do without him just then. I'd got a pretty mixed bag of troops at Percéval. The Poles wanted to fight everybody—us included— and the British I'd got were commanded by a one-eyed old bastard who spent all his time being resentful because we were winning the war and they weren't getting enough credit for standing up to Hitler on their own. There never seemed to be any answer to him but, dammit, it didn't always seem to me to be anything to be proud of. They asked for it, didn't they? That gang of Ivy Leaguers they had for politicians before Churchill took over had let Hitler get away with Austria and the Rhine and Czechoslovakia and Sudetenland. What did they expect but trouble and standing alone? The way he complained, though, you'd have thought he wanted to *go on* standing alone."

He paused and even Franks felt the strains of nationality that had set them all—in spite of their avowed common enemy—at other's throats.

Murphy sighed, as though he seemed still weary of the arguing he'd heard. "Just when I was trying to calm him down," he said, "offering him Hemingway and Ernie Pyle to write 'em up for the States—that sort of thing—in walked Boderin.

"He'd been twice wounded," he went on slowly, "and he'd twice collapsed through ill-health and exhaustion. He wanted to be the spearhead, he said—because his family had some connection with the Bligues or something. Either they'd lived at Percéval or one of his ancestors had fought a victory there. I don't know the story. He felt he had to lead the way. Besides, De Gaulle was beginning to cut up rough by this time. He felt it was due to the honour of France that French soldiers should be in the vanguard. You remember, they insisted on Leclerc going first into Paris. Our people didn't fancy the idea. The Fighting French were becoming a sight too important for us by then. Anyway, I said no."

"Why? Instructions from Washington?"

Murphy shook his head. "Not this time. His boys were just exhausted. They needed pulling back for a bit and refitting. That's what I did with 'em. Pulled 'em back. Next night, he appeared at headquarters in the biggest god-damned rage you ever saw, talking about the honour of France. It was one of those beat-up towns we were going through in those days and nobody felt full of the joy of life. He walked straight into headquarters, dizzy with weariness, a dose of malaria and a new head wound he'd picked up. That guy was never very lucky. I took one look at him and decided he was more in need of a rest than his men were."

"What happened?"

"I asked him to go into hospital for a while but he started raving, and I had no choice but to tell him his outfit was being pulled back and that was that. Then the balloon went up. He had the gall to go out there and send his boys in near St Roth. Got himself in a fine old mess. Sent his lorries straight up the main drag without looking."

Murphy took a turn up and down the room, puffing at his cigarette before continuing, his eyes on the carpet, and Franks waited, patient, until Murphy was ready to give him the rest of it.

After a while, Murphy stopped and looked up.

"The Germans were waiting for him," he said briefly, gesturing with his cigarette. "They'd been sitting there on their butts, waiting for days with everything they'd got. I'd told him so, but he didn't take the trouble to listen. They pinned him down near St Roth and he had to send for help. I told him to hang on and sent the tank boys up from Percéval. Hell, we could still have saved the day! But he'd lost a lot of his men and he seemed to go to pieces. His Chief of Staff—guy called Gallifet—got himself killed and everything began to fall apart. It was just as I'd always suspected. It was Gallifet who'd done all the thinking. Boderin supplied the heroics and Gallifet the brains and the energy. When Gallifet went—a mortar bomb got him—Boderin seemed to stop bothering about his troops. He'd got 'em into a mess because of his god-damned honour and now he couldn't get 'em out. The whole line crumbled and he just let it. He never could take casualties. By the time I got the tanks and the reserves up from Percéval, there was nothing in front of us. It took me three days to sort out that damned mess. We nearly lost Percéval. Fortunately, there was nothing that one-eyed Britisher liked better than a fight, and I found a guy called Devéria—an ex-Legionnaire Colonel on Boderin's staff—so I pulled Boderin out and pushed Devéria in his place. He did all right."

"What happened afterwards?"

"Hell, I did it as nicely as possible. We all knew the French were a bit prickly about their honour. But I was the boss and I had to do something. He'd got me into a battle I didn't want and wasn't ready for and then, having started the affair, he just let the whole thing come to pieces in his hands. He'd lost a hell of a lot of his men and he lost me a hell of a lot of my men too, to say nothing of tanks and vehicles. We had to back right up against Percéval again. I had to scrape up cooks, clerks, the lot, to stop the Germans. I told him he was going to hospital whether he liked it or not. I wrote to Ike, who was sitting on my neck wanting to know what had gone wrong at Percéval, and told him, and he was all in favour. But, of course, Mr God-damn' Boderin had to take it as a personal insult. It was the old story. Inexperienced America trying to order experienced France about. You know how they feel about their Army. It had become an obsession with him. In the end, I had to tell him to get the hell into hospital before I put him in arrest."

Franks said nothing and Murphy paused for a while before going on, his face troubled.

"I guess it wasn't his fault," he said finally, with compassion. "He'd got too much to live up to and he just couldn't do it. He just hadn't got what it takes, and like most people of that kind, he made more of loss of face than anybody else would. I was quite prepared to forget what had happened and find him a job behind the lines somewhere when he'd recovered but he made a mess of the whole thing by not keeping his appointment at the hospital. He simply disappeared. I took no action since by this time the Bligues had fallen and, in fact, most of France was liberated and he was free to go anywhere he wanted. Only it appeared when he didn't get another command that he'd been removed for cowardice. As a matter-of-fact"—Murphy's face grew angry—"that's damn' near what it was. But I wasn't going to say so."

He puffed his cigarette again and waved the smoke away impatiently. "The Communists—they were just starting the papers again in Paris—they went for it like hell. *Emancipation* got out the brass band. They said I'd used Boderin's men until they were all gone—the old song about us fighting to the last Frenchman. They said that when Boderin had refused to sacrifice any more of his men, I'd had him removed for cowardice. They started called me *General Méfait*——"

"*Méfait?*"

"Play on my name. It means *Misdeed*. Favourite trick of the Paris journalists." Murphy chuckled. "Hell, that's nothing," he said. "They started calling Matthew Ridgway *General Plague* when he arrived, and put on anti-American plays for his benefit. He'd once made the mistake of talking about germ warfare, I think. They tried to make me out to be a hell of a rat. Georgie Patton hadn't helped much. He wasn't any more popular with the French than he was with the British.

"I was back in the States by then—they even tried to say I'd been recalled in disgrace—and Boderin had it firmly in his head by this time that he'd done no wrong. Some guys can convince themselves of anything if they try hard enough, I've found. I suppose it's some form of mental cushion against the knowledge that they're duds. He demanded a court martial. He got one all right. It upheld what I'd done. I think it broke him. They said he looked an old man when it was over."

Murphy put down his glass, frowning deeply.

"But he didn't give up," he said. "I think his family was pushing him a bit. He started asking for a re-trial. By this time things had quietened down a lot and De Gaulle had resigned in a huff. That guy always seems to be in a huff. Of course, he still had a hell of a lot of power in France and they asked him to support Boderin's application for a re-trial. But, although he'd met Boderin at St Cyr or somewhere and knew him well, he wasn't playing. He knew what had happened, of course. He'd got it from Devéria, who'd become a Deputy by that time. But, in addition, of course, just then the French didn't like the Americans much. They were conducting a private war with us and no one even bothered to announce *why* Boderin didn't get his redress. They let it look as though we were putting pressure on them to keep it dark. There were some god-damn' silly things going on then." Murphy looked puzzled. "Considering we'd just won the war, we were all making a hell of a poor job of the peace."

He strugged. "Later the Communists said we were putting the pressure on in case it upset the NATO project, but it wasn't *us* who put him off. Finally even the Communists dropped him."

Franks drew a deep breath. "That's one hell of a story," he said.

Murphy shrugged. "Yep, I suppose it is," he smiled. "I expect I'll carry it round with me for the rest of my life. When I die they'll remember it again. It wouldn't have mattered if I hadn't been sent over here, I suppose. Now it's all going to be dragged up again."

Franks looked worried. "General," he said. "You sure we oughtn't to do something about a guard?"

"Negative. Not necessary."

"Resentment makes assassins."

"Hell, I'm not scared of that kind of assassin. The FLN are twice as dangerous. I see in today's paper they've bumped off a Deputy now. Walked up to him in the Champs Elysées. They

62

weren't caught. They never are. They're threatening to start on foreigners now, I notice. Part of a new policy of terrorism. They're tired of keeping it domesticated and French."

Franks looked sober. "That's something else for me to worry about," he said. "Maybe *you're* not worried, but I am. I've got used to you, General. I like working with you. I wouldn't like to change now. Besides, think what a mess it would make of Franco-American relations if somebody *did* decide to poop off at you."

Murphy stared out of the window again. "We'll chance it," he said. He stared for a moment longer through the streaming glass. "Hell," he said. "This weather! No wonder the English are so frigid."

<h1 style="text-align:center">★ 4 ★</h1>

MAJOR SCHNEIDER's office was a small place—private-looking to Inspector Souprosse, and faintly too homely for a work-place. It had curtains and a carpet—things which Souprosse preferred to do without, but which somehow seemed to go with Schneider's background.

Souprosse knew he came from an ancient Alsatian family with a name almost as long as the one the Boderins claimed, but he never thrust his heritage at Souprosse, preferring in that arrogant manner of his, to let it flow quietly over the lesser men with whom he came in contact.

The walls were yellow instead of the utilitarian green of Souprosse's office and there were small photographs about the place—Schneider as a young officer, Schneider's father in full uniform. And a discreet case of medals which Souprosse had long since discovered contained several for bravery. But somehow, even these didn't intrude—almost as though Schneider liked to have them around to remind him of the past, but was afraid that they might give offence to others by their suggestion of pride.

He was sitting back in his chair now, that maimed hand of his touching the desk top, his greying hair brushed flatly across his large skull so that it concealed the scar just below the scalp line that he'd picked up in 1940. He stared across at Souprosse, looking down his nose at him in a way Souprosse delighted to mimic for his family, and made a portentous gesture with his pipe.

"It's building up," he said solemnly.

Souprosse gave him one of his fat smiles. "*Emancipation*'s working hard at it," he agreed.

Schneider reached across the desk and picked up a slip of paper which he threw towards Souprosse.

"He wrote to Murphy in London to say he was waiting for him," he said. Souprosse picked up the paper and stared at it for a moment.

"That's a copy," Schneider pointed out. "The Americans sent it on to us for action. They thought we ought to know about it." He paused. "No address, you see." He pushed across a newspaper. "There's an interview there with his daughter."

Souprosse stared at the headline and the name beneath. "Cellini." He made a moué with his mouth as he read. "I know Cellini." He read the report. "Doesn't say much, does it?" he commented. "Nothing that we don't know already."

"Where's General Boderin staying?" Schneider asked quickly.

"We haven't been able to trace him yet," Souprosse admitted. "Paris is a big city and there are a lot of people in it. So long as he lies low, we're going to have a job finding him."

"What have you arranged, for when Murphy arrives?"

"Plenty of police at Orly and an escort into the city. What are you expecting?"

Schneider's cold intelligent face lifted from his papers. "Nothing, I suppose," he said. "A little noise from the students. Probably a very embarrassing interview with General Boderin and an escort laid on by you to see that he goes safely home. What about the other Boderins—his children."

Souprosse tapped the newspaper. "I don't think we need worry," he said. "The girl's too young, and the son's part crippled. Works with a law firm in the Boulevard Haussmann. Mistress with a flat in the Vincennes district. She comes from the South. Fréjus or somewhere. Chief interest seems to be a re-trial for his father."

"Not another one? You'd think they'd begin to understand after a while."

Souprosse grinned and Schneider stared at him disapprovingly.

He never quite managed to understand the policeman. He was something quite alien to Schneider's background, something that had been thrown up by the war—efficient, effective, but somehow faintly vulgar. With his old army outlook and his ancient family manner, Schneider sometimes found it hard to see things the same way as Souprosse, though he had an immense respect for his skill. There was never any affection visible between the two of them but they worked well together and even on occasions, invited each other out to dinner; chilly little meals that they both curiously enjoyed, Schneider sitting coolly and stiffly, appraising the wine, Souprosse bent over the table more concerned with the food, neither of them speaking much except to discuss work.

They never visited each other because Schneider was a bachelor, while Souprosse had an adoring and nagging wife whom Schneider couldn't stand; but between them there was an odd understanding that overlapped their minds and allowed them to think as one.

"Any documents?" Souprosse asked, ticking off the last of the notes on a little list by his elbow.

Schneider gave another shrug.

"Just the letter he sent to America," he said. "It's hard to understand what he's getting at. But from what I can make out, the Boderins were never very clear about anything they *ever* did."

Souprosse grinned and nodded. He always enjoyed listening to Schneider's coldly aristocratic sarcasm. He regarded Schneider as a bit of a joke with his spartan monasticism, an old joke, perhaps, but a good one, that you could regard with affection. There weren't many like him any more.

"Anybody tried to contact any of the Boderins?" Schneider went on.

"Just the ones we know about?"

Schneider nodded. "We'll have to keep a look-out for him, of course. We've got photographs. Fortunately, there were hundreds taken of him between 1944 and 1946. There'll be plenty of prints for everybody and he shouldn't be hard to pick out. After all, there can't be so many tall thin military-looking men of seventy-odd at Orly at any one time."

Master-Sergeant Sligo sat at a little table under a jazzy

umbrella on the right-hand side of the Champs Elysées, somewhere near the Pan-American Airways Offices, staring up the
slope towards the Arc de Triomphe. The mellowed stone of the
arch with its gigantic bas-reliefs caught the yellowing sunshine of
the afternoon, standing out starkly against the sky over the
fringe of acacias and limes. Twenty yards away from Sligo, a
photographer and another man were trying to photograph a
girl smoking a cigarette.

Obviously some sort of publicity stunt, Sligo decided, because
they seemed to be having a little difficulty getting her to smoke it
gracefully. The photographer was leaning on his camera, bored,
while the other man kept sweeping a lock of black hair from his
forehead and pushing the girl's arms into a more elegant posture.

Sligo watched with a faintly amused contempt for a while, then
started to read the Paris edition of the *New York Times*. There
was a picture of General Murphy on the front page and Sligo
stared at it for a while affectionately. The old guy hadn't altered
much, he thought. He could still remember him vividly. Bit
thicker round the gills, he thought. That was all. Like Sligo
himself. Neither of them had much longer to go before the axe
fell. For Murphy it would probably be a farm down in Tennessee
where he came from. For Sligo it would be New York. Some sort
of apartment. Something small and neat he could look after on
his own. A few beers at midday. A few more at night. God only
knew what else. Sligo didn't. He wasn't looking forward to retirement. The prospect of being alone in New York, with nothing to
do, with all the things he was used to taken away from him, made
him want to shudder at the bleakness of it.

It wasn't shortage of money that was worrying Sligo. He'd
got plenty of that put away. It was shortage of work, something to
keep him busy. That was something you couldn't bank and draw
on when you wanted it. He wasn't a technician and a proficiency
with weapons or at running an orderly room wouldn't find him
many jobs in civilian life.

Sligo pulled himself up sharp, as he realized he was becoming
sorry for himself. He'd never been sorry for himself in his life—
not even in the Philippines or Tunisia or in the Ardennes—but
this problem of what he was going to do with himself in his retirement kept cropping up these days with a disturbing regularity.

He wasn't a young man any more but, by God, he wasn't an old one either and he could look forward to a lot more years of life.

The photographer seemed to have finished his work at last and he was loading his equipment into a small red Rénault that was pulled up off the road. The girl followed the man with the sweeping lock of hair, wiggling her fanny like all the French dames did.

Sligo watched her with interest. He liked Paris. He was a strictly moral man who'd never made a habit of running after women—he'd been hurt often by the things he'd heard said about American troops—but he enjoyed Paris because he felt Parisians knew how to enjoy life. They were the most companionable of people, Sligo had found, and there was something about the city that had got hold of him long ago. Not just the monuments he could see and the galleries he could visit. He'd made the rounds on his first visit years before, not long after the war. Nowadays he found he preferred to spend his time sitting on the sidewalk just watching. There was always such a hell of a lot to watch in Paris.

He studied the passing crowds a little longer, the neat little Indo-Chinese girls, and the lanky black students from Senegal and Chad with their faces scarred by tribal markings, the languid rich and the hurrying poor. Then he ordered another beer and sat back to read the paper again.

Murphy, it seemed, was spot ball at the moment. The papers seemed to be gunning for him. Some business during the war. He remembered reading about it at the time. It had come as a shock to him to find that anyone could criticize Murphy. To Sligo, a hero was a hero. There were no half measures.

He began to wonder just how he'd go about meeting Murphy. He'd been to the Allied Armed Forces Information Centre across the road from where he was sitting—which was why he was in the Champs Elysées instead of one of the less glossy cafés along the Boulevard Montparnasse that he preferred. They'd told him the time of the arrival of the General's plane but they hadn't been able to guarantee any meeting with him. They'd taken him into an army major who'd listened to him carefully but without a great deal of sympathy. The major was fat and comfortable-looking and didn't seem to have much faith in the sort of sentiment that motivated Sligo. He'd promised—rather cursorily, it seemed to Sligo—to contact the General when he arrived. But

67

obviously, he'd said, he could promise nothing before the General had even set foot in the country. In fact, he seemed to regard Sligo as vaguely demented. Doubtless, he'd said, Sligo might be able to contact the General through his staff.

All of which might sound all right to the Major but to Sligo, knowing the ways of the army, it sounded highly doubtful. Besides, he had no wish to stand in line with a lot of other people to have his hand shaken. He wanted ten minutes' chat with the General.

In the end, he decided to go out to Orly and to try to tackle him there. There would surely be a V.I.P. lounge where the General would wait while they were going through the formalities of arrival. After that point, it might be difficult. Inevitably there'd be a round of official meetings with the top brass of Europe, where a master-sergeant's stripes wouldn't carry much weight, and after that apparently, General Murphy was to make a tour of Army and Air Force installations. By the time that was finished, Sligo would be back in Achensee waiting for a plane to the States.

It looked like being Orly or nothing.

The high-shuttered houses that crowded round the Church of St Séverin looked faintly disapproving with their flat grey façades—like the faces of a lot of elderly spinsters pressed against a window—their plaster crumbling and faded paint peeling from the shutters.

A pair of grey underpants was hanging out of one of the windows and there were a couple of young self-set acacias growing in a vacant lot which looked as though it had been scooped out by a bomb. A linnet in a cage was filling the air with liquid notes just above a shop that specialized in skeletons for students of the Ecole de Médecin in the Boulevard St Germain not far away.

Hardy glanced out of his window quickly, staring up and down the street, then went back to his shaving, moving about his small rooms, half-dressed, one eye on the street, absorbed more in what went on around him than in what he was doing.

Two old ladies in a doorway were examining each other's teeth in the sunshine and, somewhere to their right, he could hear the chip-chip of a mason's hammer as repair work was carried out behind a length of suspended cane matting that dripped little driblets of grey dust to the pavement. Below it, politically-minded Frenchmen had scribbled their slogans—*"Paix en Algérie"*, *"Non à De Gaulle"*. *"Pas de bases militaires Allemandes en France"*.

Above him he could hear the thin nasal strains of a piano accordion, and it seemed to him that wherever he heard a piano accordion, wherever he heard it during the whole of the rest of his life, he'd think of Paris. Not loud, it never seemed to be loud, and you never seemed to see the player, except occasionally when it was some beggar in the long arches of Montparnasse-Bienvenue or Chatelet in the Métro. It was always hidden, always playing something unbearably nostalgic and French, and he was seized with an unutterable affection for his surroundings.

" *'Paris has my heart*——' " he quoted softly—" *'I love her tenderly, even her moles and blemishes.'* Christ," he said aloud, turning away, "I couldn't leave this damned place!"

He had thought often and unwillingly of leaving Paris as his debts crowded in on him but he knew he'd never be able to take the final step. He envied the Parisians the way they managed to mind their own business, and liked the little rooms they lived in, rooms like this one; the rickety chimneys and the myriad roofs of the frenzied horizon that stretched all the way from Issy to the north; the courtyards with their uneven stones and the puddles of dishwater that always seemed to be lurking in the hollows; the way the night porter let you in in his pyjamas without turning a hair, rigid with the unshakable barriers of French officialdom; the café that was always next door, shut in by apartment houses that rented hot lopsided rooms under the eaves to impecunious tenants; the abundance of joy and the absence of comfort, and the amount of sorrow. To Hardy, because he was a drifter, even the absence of the deeper joys of home-making seemed to make the place easier to live in.

He moved towards the kitchen, still shaving, staring down with affection at the blue-overalled concierge in the courtyard, sitting by the inevitable group of geraniums, his head against the peeling sign of the plumber who carried on his noisy affairs in a cavernous stable at the back—stretching his neck a little to catch the sunshine that threaded its way through the houses down

69

to his little domain. About his head were two lines crowded with washing that would reflect the sun for an hour or two and then be in shadow, and just above him, there was a window that showed lace curtains, old overcrowded furniture and a wide bed with a patchwork quilt on it, and a pair of stockinged feet— one with a white toe showing—sticking out from somewhere out of sight. As long as Hardy had been in that room, those feet seemed always to have been there, just opposite, their owner always out of sight and always, it seemed, asleep.

He finished shaving and crossed to the front window once more, just as Cellini manoeuvred his car into a position where it didn't quite succeed in jamming all the traffic passing up and down the Rue des Prêtres de St Séverin. Cellini was just climbing out, his eyes on a crimson placard on the wall that announced, with typical aplomb, that the Federation of Anarchists were holding a meeting the following week. Cellini's face seemed a little startled, as though he still felt a faint surprise that any city could permit such an organization to exist with impunity in its midst, almost though he expected a sub-heading below, *Bring your own bombs*.

All about him, the walls were plastered with columns of abuse from *Humanité* and *Emancipation*, stuck on the plaster with the adverts for holidays in Corsica, cinema daubs for Fernandel and Fernand Reynaud and the *affiches* for the Opera and the nude shows.

A workman pushing through the passing crowds with a long roll of bread and an equally long sausage stepped to one side as Cellini opened the car door for Nicole Boderin to climb out. The petulant mask she wore seemed to be having difficulty struggling for survival, Hardy saw. Beneath it there was a lost air, an uncertainty that submerged the arrogance. She seemed a little scared and unsure of herself, though she still wore with an air of defiance the black leather coat she affected over the olive green jumper.

As they passed out of sight beneath him towards the door, Hardy began to hurry. Cellini's telephone call dragging him out of bed to the ancient instrument situated at the bottom of the stairs had been urgent. Cellini had rung Souprosse that morning, it seemed, in the hope of information, only to be confronted with the news that General Boderin, contrary to all expectations, had not yet been traced.

Cellini's alert mind had translated the information into a story at once and he had gone immediately to search out Nicole in her rooms among the seedy old landings above the Rue Jacob. Cellini had been a little startled by the bearded young men in beatnik shirts and the long-haired girls in leather belts and shield-sized metal brooches, who'd turned out to watch him arrive. As he had spoken to Hardy, his voice had still been trembling with indignation at the number of American accents he'd heard.

At the knock on the door, Hardy crossed over and opened it, still fastening his trousers. Cellini looked faintly annoyed that he wasn't dressed.

"I thought you said you'd be ready," he said bitterly.

"I did. But I never am. I've discovered the reward for vice is exactly the same in the long run as the reward for virtue? Have a drink?"

Cellini accepted unwillingly the glass that Hardy put into his hand and stared round the shabby room. Then through the window his eyes fell on the pair of feet in the room opposite. Hardy saw his eyes on them and grinned.

"One of these days I'm going down to investigate," he said. "I've an idea he's been dead for six months."

While they were talking, Nicole had drifted across to the window where the light was better and was riffling through the pages of *Match*. There wasn't much to choose between her and the picture of Brigitte Bardot on the front. She still looked hard, under that over-applied make-up on her face, though Hardy suspected her dislike of people was only a façade that hid the fear of insecurity. Outwardly she looked like the rest of the noisy youngsters who absorbed the pseudo-intellectual atmosphere of St Germain-des-Prés, but he was certain she was really just another doubtful little creature trying hard to make herself worldly with her over-applied mascara and fin-de-siècle hair style and her boy friends, who tried for the same reasons to look like nothing on God's earth.

She had registered no surprise at seeing Cellini, it seemed, and there and then, on the old-fashioned telephone that hung behind a curtain in her room, they had tried to ring her father's apartment at Chartres. But there had been no reply, just that empty hollow ringing that indicated the owner was out, the emptiest, loneliest sound in the world.

"So I thought we'd better get out there," Cellini concluded, "And quick, too. Besides"—he indicated Nicole—"I guess she's already had enough to worry about in her life, with this damned Boderin Affair hanging over her head."

"There are fifty million Frenchmen," Hardy said with flat cynicism, "and most of them have a secret tragedy. What do you think he's up to?"

"I don't know." Cellini shrugged. "Nicole thinks he might be going to hand over some dossier of his grievances to Murphy. She says he's been working on the thing ever since 1946. Over a matter of twelve years, you can imagine it's reached quite considerable proportions, especially since his son qualified as a lawyer and took a hand at setting it in order."

"Is that why we're going to Chartres?"

"We might find someone there who knows where he is. We might find the dossier. We might get a better story than anyone else. Hell, it is a story, isn't it?" Cellini ended. "A man being confronted with a grievance twelve years old."

There were cars outside the grey block of apartments in the Rue St Brice at Chartres when Cellini pulled the big Chevrolet into the side of the road under the trees, and a policeman was talking by the door to a couple of men who were waving newspapers under his nose.

"Press," Cellini said flatly, disappointed that he wasn't first on the scene. "That's Félibien, of *Figaro*."

As they approached, the two men turned away, and one of them nodded as he saw Cellini.

"You're too late. The bird has flown," he called out in a stilted English that sounded curiously old-fashioned.

They moved to the cars, still shouting over their shoulders at the policeman, then with a great slamming of doors they roared off in the direction of the Place des Epars and the Versailles road to Paris.

Cellini got out of the Chevrolet and opened the door for

72

Nicole. The policeman, his thumbs hooked in his belt, was standing inside the entrance to the block of apartments now, talking to the concierge, and as they approached, he broke off the conversation and stepped in front of them.

"You can't go in there, monsieur," he said.

Cellini introduced himself and the girl. The policeman stared at her curiously and they could see the dark inquisitive eyes of the concierge over his shoulder.

"Boderin?" the policeman said. "The daughter of General Boderin?"

She nodded, and the policeman stared at her doubtfully, then he shrugged.

"*Vos papiers, Mademoiselle,*" he said.

The girl offered her identity card and the policeman stared at it for a second, reading it out loud, "—*Nicole Christiane Françoise Lacquart de Lespinasse-Boderin du Crest—*" He looked at her quickly, his eyes a little startled, before handing it back, then he nodded to the concierge and stepped out of their way.

"I'll come with you," the concierge offered quickly. "I'll bring the key to the apartment."

"Just give it to me," Nicole said. "There's no need for you to come up."

"It's my job, Mademoiselle. I'm responsible for everything in there."

"I'm his daughter," Nicole said imperiously, and the concierge gave up the key with a sullen face.

Inside the apartment, Cellini walked straight across to the window and stared out. The policeman was just strolling into the entrance of the building opposite.

"I'll bet you an even dollar," he said bitterly, "that he's gone to phone Félibien."

"Why doesn't he use the phone downstairs?" Hardy asked.

"I expect the concierge wants to use that one." Cellini's voice was heavy with the suggestion of treachery. "He'll have been slipped a *mille* or two to ring up if anything like this happens. They'll be back from Paris this afternoon like a lot of vultures."

Hardy didn't answer. He was standing in the middle of the room now, staring round him almost as though he were trying

73

to make up his mind what sort of human being would choose to live in this dark mausoleum of an apartment. The place was gloomy, with the heavy curtains of an earlier period at the windows, and the walls were covered with a crimson paper that seemed to be the colour of blood. There was a picture of the Christ child that proclaimed the Boderin religion and a harrowing crucifix, and paintings, trophies and weapons that jammed every inch of space.

He stared for a while at the loaded walls, then he indicated a large portrait opposite the window, where it caught what light there was.

"Who's that?" he asked. "Somebody we ought to know?"

"That's the Comte de Lespinasse," Nicole said quietly.

"Ah!" Hardy nodded. "*La Gloire*. Of course. I ought to have guessed. And these others? Odd Boderins and Du Crests, eh?"

He walked slowly round the room. The whole history of France seemed to be spread out in front of him, the whole closed caste of senior officers, the aristocracy of their profession; men of influence and education who'd retained their hold over their troops, whatever the political disasters of their country. Even through the victories the framed chromos depicted—*Colonel Alphonse Boderin du Crest at Beni-Abbès, The defence of the wall of the Legation at Peking by Lieutenant de Lespinasse-Boderin du Crest*—an atmosphere of calamity hung like a miasma in the room. Almost as though to heighten it, someone had hung small prints by Détaille and De Neuville's *Dernieres Cartouches,* among the photographs, almost as though they were France's crown of thorns. There were last stands and desperate charges, and squares breaking under the weight of squadrons of horse-men. There were links with Ney and Lannes and Lyautey; with Wagram and Borodino and the Marne. There were pictures of groups of cadets taken at the Saumur cavalry school and a few names like Faidherbe, Chanzy and Denfert-Rochereau, that had blazed out in brief moments of splendour in the long line of defeat in 1870. But, somehow, through it all, the room was a sepulchre rather than a tribute, a monument to an atrophied stiff-necked military background that had smelt the stench of defeat half a dozen times and still remained arrogant. Somehow, Hardy seemed to hear the derisive words of the Great Duke on

74

French leaders as he surveyed the unedifying prospect of French Marshals changing sides before Waterloo. Two busts, one of the Comte de Lespinasse, and one of the Boderin who had been sieved by German machine-gun bullets on the Marne, were the most living things in the apartment.

He stared at the portraits, his eyes wandering back again and again to that of the man in the Napoleonic uniform in the big portrait opposite the window.

"You know," he said. "Damned if I don't think they're graded in size according to importance! What are we looking for?"

"Anything," Cellini said. "Anything that might indicate where he's gone to."

Hardy joined in half-heartedly, disinterestedly following Cellini and the girl as they moved about the apartment.

They began to go through drawers, but there was only the usual conglomeration of rubbish from a long and valueless life—pipes, meaningless photographs that had faded to yellow, clothes that were out of date, ancient golf balls, trout flies that hadn't been used for thirty years, and boxes of cigars that had been forgotten and gone dry.

Hardy stood sniffing one of them. "Twenty years too late," he mourned.

Cellini and the girl were in front of a large desk now.

"It's locked," Cellini pointed out.

"It doesn't matter," Nicole said. "I know how to open it."

She pressed down on the handle of the drawer and as the lock slipped she pulled it open. "It's always been like that," she said. "We used to help ourselves to cigarettes when we were children."

They were carelessly dragging out papers now and scattering them on the desk top. There was a publisher's letter, dated 1953, which said that, while the firm could not make an offer immediately for Monsieur the General's account of the battles for the Bligues, they would always be delighted to read such an account, written from the General's own standpoint, with a view to publication. Everyone, they said, was anxious to know the truth of the *Affaire Boderin*, but owing to the time that had elapsed since the affair had become public property, they could not be more definite until they had seen the completed manuscript.

"Poor old bastard," Hardy said under his breath, staring at

75

the letter. He turned over the attached bundle of notes to which were clipped sketch maps that General Boderin had clearly drawn himself. They were headed *The Bligues* and signed *Nicolas Jean St Omer de Lespinasse-Boderin du Crest, ancien général de brigade,* followed by a list of his decorations—tacked on at the end like a funeral oration.

"Did he ever actually write this up?" he asked.

"No." Nicole shook her head. "He was never much good at writing. My brother later worked out the story for him and had it printed as a pamphlet. Nobody ever wanted to read it," she ended flatly.

There were several books—Gravet's *Explanation for 1870 and 1940,* the book which had provoked the libel action, with a sheet of paper placed in the appendix dealing with the Boderins; *The Enigma of Percéval,* by Jean-André Devéria, a tough-looking customer whose face was on the book jacket; and a copy in French of *Bataan to Berlin,* by Lieutenant-General John Forrest Murphy, which flipped open in Hardy's hand at a chapter marked *The Bligues.* Obviously the old man had browsed often through this chapter, looking for things that might help him. But there was nothing useful. Murphy had wisely kept the controversy out of his book. He was careful to pay a compliment to the Fighting Frenchmen and even to General De Gaulle who had led them, but there was no reference to the Boderin Affair at all.

There were a few yellowing newspaper cuttings, *"Where is General Domrémy?"* one of them said. *"Has he been cashiered?"* And another, *"Why did General Méfait sack Domrémy? De Gaulle Should Act."*

He flipped through the bundle which started with deep thirty-two point headlines that gradually dwindled down to nine point. The size of the cuttings dropped, too, from column lengths with double—and treble—column heads to mere paragraphs—while the columnists' comments disappeared altogether. He could imagine with what despair the old man had filed away the last of them, aware that his case was not only closed in the official files but in the memories of the public too.

"When did it all die out?" he asked.

"It was all over and done with by 1948," Nicole said. "By that time we'd exhausted everyone who might help, everyone my father knew at the Ministry, every lawyer my brother could lay his hands on, every soldier, every friend. No one would touch it any longer. Some could see no money in it. Some could see no success. Some thought it was tainted by Communist fingers. The Communists were the only ones who were ever interested," she ended bitterly.

"Naturally," Hardy said. "What a knife to stick in the Right Wing's august back."

He wandered round the room, still, to Cellini's disgust, showing more interest in the pictures and the trophies than in searching. Then suddenly he became aware that Nicole was opening and shutting drawers at speed and that Cellini had crossed over to the desk too.

"My father had a pistol," she was saying with a quick intake of breath. "It was a little Belgian automatic. He bought it years ago. I remember it well. Lots of people had them after the war. It was at the time when he felt he had many enemies. It didn't look big enough to do anyone any harm, but there was a box of ammunition that went with it. He had another gun, too—a big one, an English one he got during the war."

"Perhaps he's got rid of them since," Cellini said.

"I asked him to," she agreed. "I was afraid that he might try to commit suicide. But he never did. They were always in there."

They began to search through the drawers more eagerly, then Cellini straightened up. He held in his hand a small square brown cardboard box that rattled as he showed it to them.

"That's the box," Nicole said quickly. "That's the box the ammunition was in."

Cellini opened the box slowly and held it out for them to see. There was one bullet inside.

"It looks to me as though he was in a hurry," Cellini said. "As though he just scooped the lot into his pocket—and he didn't notice he was one bullet short."

"And it looks to me, Jimmy old boy," Hardy said, "as though your demonstration at Orly's going to be a great deal rougher than you thought."

77

★ 5 ★

THEY had to wait in the corridor outside Schneider's office for some time, sitting on a leather-covered bench below the black and white sheets of official announcements. Clerks and uniformed men stared curiously at them as they passed in and out, and someone offered them cigarettes and eventually coffee. After a while Hardy sent Cellini to ring the Institut des Langues Européennes to say that he was ill and wouldn't be in that day, but the official at the other end of the line sounded angry and dubious—as though Hardy had had too many days off for them to believe his excuses—and Cellini came back looking annoyed, as if he'd been asked to do something against the dictates of his conscience.

The evening sun had been falling across the black and white Gothic face of Notre Dame as they had parked the car in the square and walked across to the Préfecture, between the Police sentries in sunglasses lovingly cradling their tommy-guns by the great East Gate with its rows of bullet marks—honourable scars from the Liberation and the entry of De Gaulle.

As Hardy stared moodily through the window at the tricolour and the words *Mort Pour La France* on the War Memorial, he caught the faint whiff of salt from the Seine by the Pont St Michel and the throb of a barge's engine pushing its way through the dusty stone silence of the ancient building. Inside the courtyard, by the entrance to the Salle Louis Lépine, there were black camions and cars and a group of red-booted motor-cyclists, looking like men from outer space.

When they finally began to think they'd been forgotten, they were ushered in and Schneider rose to greet them. Souprosse stood in the background, plump and sly-looking with his flabby cheeks and his shock of cropped fair hair. About Schneider there was the same arrogance that Hardy had seen in the photographs and paintings out at Chartres, and he felt that Schneider would have understood the Boderins without difficulty. But about his face there was something else, a hard look, an inner toughness that the Boderins didn't seem to possess.

Cellini introduced Hardy and Nicole and set out quickly what they had discovered at Chartres. For a moment no one said anything. Schneider was rubbing the edge of his desk with his

78

maimed hand as though he were trying to keep up the polish on it.

"Do you think your father would use this gun you mention?" he asked at last, facing Nicole.

"I don't know," she said quietly. "I would have thought so once, but now I'm not so sure. He used often to suggest that only something dramatic could draw attention to his cause but he never did anything and I stopped thinking much about it."

"What about the other gun? The British gun? Are you sure he had one?"

She nodded, "I saw it," she said, "many times."

Schneider made a quick note on a piece of paper. "Have you any idea where your father is?" he asked, and she shook her head.

All the high-handed arrogance had gone from her now, as though she doubted even her own background, as though for years she'd believed in the sanity and the sense of her family and was now suddenly faced with indisputable proof that they were less stable than she'd always imagined. It seemed to have frightened her, as though suddenly everything she'd clung to had been proved to be unsound.

"Perhaps my brother knows where he is," she said in a low voice.

"We've just taken the precaution of telephoning him," Schneider said. "Inspector Souprosse also went to see him some time ago. He knows nothing of your father's movements. He was unable to help us at all."

"We'd not kept in touch with each other much," Nicole admitted quietly, almost shamefacedly, as though she felt her family were lacking in the qualities of ordinary contact with each other.

"You never visited your father?" Schneider asked.

She shook her head. "I didn't like the apartment. I still don't. I——" she paused and Schneider looked closely at her.

"Yes——?" he prompted.

"I don't think I liked living with this obsession of my father's."

Schneider's pen skated swiftly over his sheet of paper, then he looked up. "It hasn't stopped you taking his side, I notice," he said. "You're one of the organizers of this demonstration at Orly. Why?"

She paused for a moment. "It seemed the thing to do," she said

79

wearily. "It's not really anything to do with General Murphy. Not as far as I'm concerned, anyway. It's just that my family seems to have suffered from what happened at Percéval and St Roth and it seemed people ought to know that an injustice's been done."

"Are you *certain* an injustice was done at Percéval?" Schneider asked quietly.

She looked up quickly, her eyes angry. "Aren't you?"

Schneider shrugged and she burst out bitterly.

"I can't really see why we came here then," she said.

"Perhaps not," Schneider admitted. "But whatever we may think of the Americans privately, our country's agreed to them being here, and we must try to avoid trouble with them. We must certainly not go in for violence."

"The demonstration isn't going to be violent."

"I wasn't thinking of the demonstration, mademoiselle. I was thinking of your father."

The girl looked at the two of them sharply, a trace of anxiety on her face.

"You won't hurt him?" she asked.

Souprosse shrugged. "It depends chiefly on him," he said. "If we pick him up in time, we'll try to escort him quietly out of the way. If he doesn't object, no harm'll be done. But if we don't find him and he tries anything, then that's a different matter. Anything might happen."

"Could I see him if you find him?" Nicole spoke in a very low voice.

"Most certainly, mademoiselle," Schneider said. "In the meantime, I suggest you visit your brother and talk to him about it, too. Together, you may be able to recall something that might indicate where your father is. If you do, telephone us at once. We'd like to talk to him. *Before* General Murphy arrives at Orly. *Not afterwards.*"

The sky had clouded over when Hardy and Nicole came up from the Métro station at Père Lachaise. Hardy stared round him gloomily. Why the hell is it, he thought, that whenever I'm near this damn' place, the sky always seems to be dark?

There must be a private and special set of clouds, he decided sourly, that hung over Père Lachaise, something that didn't affect the rest of the city, but just added a little more gloom to the cemetery. Something that went with the prison-like walls, the cypresses, the decaying vaults and the rusting iron-work, and the smell of death that seemed to permeate the whole grotesque district, dedicated as only the French knew how, *à la douleur*.

It always amazed him that the cafés were as lively here as they were anywhere else in Paris, that people even made fun of it—*You're better off in here,* the notices in the bars announced, *than in the cemetery opposite*—and that people ate and lived and slept and made love and had children all under the influence of these massed monuments to the dignity of death and the glory of France, with their attendant cohorts of stonemasons' workshops and undertakers' rooms, and the florists with their vast piles of waxen lilies.

They crossed the wide double track of the Boulevard de Ménilmontant and one of the *gardiens* of the cemetery came forward with his little map to direct them. Hardy waved him aside. He had a feeling that Nicole—like all the Boderins—would know this vast necropolis like the back of her hand.

They began to walk up the wide Avenue Principale, beneath the heavy horse chestnuts and the acacias and the dark assembly of crowding monuments like sentry boxes. The willow growing from the tomb of Alfred de Musset seemed strangely ostentatious and in as bad taste as the bronze supine statue of Felix Fauré who had terminated his office as President by dying of an embarrassing heart attack in the arms of his mistress. A few women shoppers moved about, traversing the cemetery on their way to the main street, and he could hear the sound of scuffling cats among the tombstones.

For a moment, he wished he were back in the apartment in the Rue Sainte Foy. He'd once tried to ring Ernestine to make his peace with her but there'd been no reply and he'd guessed she was sulking. He'd been more disappointed than he'd expcted and had begun to wish he'd never got himself involved in this half-baked masquerade round the history of France. Before he'd been able to protest, Cellini had left them outside the Préfecture, anxious to get back to his office in the Place Vendôme to write up his story.

"See if the brother has anything to say," he'd told Hardy softly.

"Give me a ring if he has. Then get her home, for God's sake, before Félibien and the others find out about her." He had pushed money into Hardy's hand. "Use taxis," he said gently. "Don't drag her through that damned Métro. Look after her. She looks all in."

They hadn't taken a taxi, though. She'd seemed to prefer the company of crowds, and Hardy had stuffed the money back into his pocket, wondering whether he could use it to buy something to placate Ernestine.

"Do you come here often?" he asked. "To visit the family tomb, I mean."

"No," she said in a flat voice. "I never do. Never since I was old enough to say no. They used to bring me as a child. And once every year there was a priest and a ceremony. Only my brother ever comes now."

"Why does your brother live here?" Hardy asked. "There must be better places to live than overlooking Père Lachaise."

"The apartment's been in the family a long time," she said. "It's old now and I don't like it. My grandmother bought it in 1914 when my grandfather was killed. He was buried here and she wanted to be near him."

They moved towards the South Gate between age-bulging walls that were mouldering into grey leprous patches under the overhanging trees and the cloaks of dripping ivy. As she passed, Nicole seemed to make a shy obeisance before the memorial columns of Masséna and Suchet, and at the flat wall-surrounded tomb of Marshal Ney—as though their glory were linked some-how with her own family's fame. It was something you grew up with, Hardy supposed, this obsequiousness to everything military, this bobbing to flags and respect for medals. It couldn't possibly be of interest to her, but she'd been so aware all her life of her menfolk dropping on one knee in front of glory that it had become a habit with her too.

The red marble sepulchre of the Boderin family under the shadowing cypresses stood curiously alone, its colouring separa-ting it from the crowding grey tombs. Cut in the stone, Hardy caught a glimpse of names and date and battles, ranging it seemed from Waterloo through the Crimea and the disasters of 1870 to the Great War and the Nazi War. The newest of all, he saw, were

82

the names of Jean-Michel de Lespinasse-Boderin du Crest, *cadet de Saumur, mort sur le champ d'honneur*, 1940; Raoul, aged 19, *fusilé par les Nazis*, 1943; and Etienne, *mort pour la France en Indo-Chine*. In the centre of the tomb were three deep red roses, quite fresh and unwithered, like a splash of blood on the stone.

"Someone's been here," she said. "It must have been my father."

For a while she stood in front of the red marble, apparently oppressed yet at the same time awed by it, while Hardy waited impatiently, anxious to get away from the obsessive atmosphere of gloom.

In the Rue du Douleur, they crossed to a tall old house, and on the first floor she stopped opposite a huge oak door with its brass knob set between heavy ornate panels. It seemed to open immediately, as though the occupant had been expecting them, and the young man standing in the entrance stared at Hardy without any sign of friendliness.

He was tall with the same small nose and flaring nostrils that Hardy had seen in all those pictures out at Chartres. He had a small body and long legs, shapely in tight trousers. His suit was grey, and his narrow black tie was strikingly severe on his white shirt. He wore a small beard—*tres chic, tres snob*, Hardy thought sourly, *tres Left Bank*—and his soft black hair was cut in a thick mop that allowed it to fall over one eye in a way that seemed to Hardy not quite natural. It was too tidy, too careful, too effeminate to be unconsidered and he suspected that this boy with the same striking features as Nicole was more than a little conscious of his own good looks and the dramatic effect he produced —faintly like the pictures that existed of Byron, startlingly handsome and faintly unreal. These damned Boderins were all too good-looking to be true, he reflected.

"My brother, Robert," Nicole introduced him. "Robert, this is Monsieur Hardy. He's a friend. He's English."

Robert Boderin stared at Hardy arrogantly. "The English still think they are the greatest nation on earth," he said, "though they never tell you so because they're convinced you know it already. Your fleet shelled our fleet at Mers-el-Kebir in 1940."

Hardy blinked at the insults, and saw Nicole's eye flicker

83

miserably, but he recovered quickly. "It shelled it at Trafalgar too," he responded cheerfully. "In 1805. Remember?"

There was another young man in the background, lounging on a chair, who was smoking and slow to get to his feet. He was younger than Robert Boderin, and squarer, with a peasant's frame that was squat compared with the aristocratic leanness of the Boderins. His clothes were not so well cut and he seemed to have yards of white collar and cuffs. He wore high-heeled elastic-sided boots such as they'd taken to wearing a lot round St Germain and a small moustache that had the effect of making him seem cheap and nasty. His lips were red and wet and his eyes had the sly uneasy look of a man caught in the middle of a doubtful story.

Robert Boderin was staring with disapproval at Hardy's shabby jacket and untidy collar, and it seemed an age before he stepped back and held the door open for them, walking behind them with a stiff puppet-like walk that was a picture of pride, arrogance and narcissism.

Nicole nodded to the other young man—with a marked absence of enthusiasm, Hardy noticed—but he held her fingers tightly and the nervous look changed quickly to the practised beam of a lady-killer.

"Pierre-Auguste Blot," Boderin introduced him to Hardy. "We're almost related, you might say. He was brought up with us. His father's always been with our father. Pierrot works in a house agent's office.

There was a faint trace of condescension in his manner as he spoke, as though in spite of himself, he regarded young Blot vaguely as belonging more properly to the servants' quarters.

As he glanced around, Hardy was struck at once by the similarity between this apartment and the one at Chartres. There were the same portraits, he saw, a couple of crossed sabres and a yellow pennant that seemed to be the partner of the one at Chartres. Even the silvered horsewhip that lay on the table seemed to be part of the scene. Hardy half-expected to see it labelled, *Whip used to flog the troops into action. General de Lespinasse, 1871.*

The walls were covered with photographs, and studying them more closely while Boderin fished in a sideboard for a Martini bottle and glasses, he noticed that most of them were pictures of the other Boderin, the General Boderin of the Bligues. There were one or two old ones, faded and brown, of a youthful-looking officer in the chalky trenches of the First World War, and several newer pictures, better pictures, taken by press photographers, showing General Boderin with Leclerc and Koenig and De Gaulle, pictures taken in the desert and in France, pictures of reviews and inspections, and a framed newspaper cutting in English—*Magnificent Stand of Fighting French at Sidi Ifna. General Domrémy Wounded.* There was nothing else, though, no photographs taken since the days of glory, no cuttings of what had happened afterwards. The searchlight rested squarely on General Boderin's days of victory. Discreetly, nothing was said about what came later.

Nicole and her brother had been talking in undertones as he prepared the drinks and he was speaking to her now in low insistent tones, as he handed Hardy his glass.

"He's not been here," he was saying almost irritably. "I've not seen him for months."

"They say he's somewhere in Paris," she told him. "They say he's got a gun. You remember those two he had in his drawer? They've vanished."

He shrugged, his eyes strangely blank suddenly. "So they told me," he said. "They came to see me with their damned officiousness. They telephoned again today about the guns. But he'd not contacted me."

As he moved. Hardy noticed that he limped heavily as though some old injury had shortened his right leg a little.

"Why did he leave?" Nicole asked, her voice unsteady.

"*Un peu gaga,*" Robert Boderin said sullenly. "Why else?"

She stared at him angrily. "Don't you care?" she demanded in a high unnatural voice.

"Care!" Boderin swung round on her. "Of course I care. It means as much to me as it does to you and to him. Haven't the Americans interfered enough in our affairs? Didn't they fire me from Gillet Frères because I was who I was? Didn't they prevent me from joining the army? Haven't we been accused of cowardice?" He had been calm, even cynical, until this moment; but now the flood gates of his bitterness were flung open and the

85

passionate hatred for everything that wasn't French poured freely over them, sharp, acid, full of venom. He seemed to regard his father's humiliation as his own, Nicole's, the whole family's a cross that they all bore with mutual grief.

They were all looking faintly embarrassed when he stopped suddenly, his tirade quietened. "Of course I care," he said more steadily. "But what can I do? I have no influence with the people who matter. The damned politicians are all the same—concerned only with hanging on to the ship, swopping places all the time as though they're playing musical chairs. Schumann. Queuille. Mendès-France. Mollet. Pflimlin. One after the other and back again. Let's have De Gaulle again—or Poujade or even Thorez for a change. Let *them* join the dance too. They've let France slip to a state of a third-rate relic. She breathes still but the vultures are already in the sky."

"Robert——" Nicole tried to interrupt, but he didn't seem to hear her.

"No matter how many of us vote or how we vote," he went on, "it's always the same predatory combination in that House of Imbeciles across the Pont de la Concorde that run the country. We can depose politicians but we can't produce honest statesmen. And because the Communists once saw a chance of political gain in my father's misfortune nobody else is interested in case they're stamped as fellow-travellers. Only the Communist deputies bother with us now—and who wants *them*?"

His tirade ran down suddenly and he swallowed his drink quickly, staring at them with his fine crazy eyes. Blot sat back, staring appreciatively at Nicole, and anxiously at her brother, his expression changing curiously as his eyes went from one to the other, as though they were the lens of a camera and reflected what they saw. Nicole stood before her brother, hurt and puzzled and not understanding.

"I've looked for him," Robert Boderin ended lamely, almost gently, as though suddenly aware of his rudeness. "I couldn't find him."

"He's been to the tomb," Nicole said. "There are fresh roses on it."

Boderin turned. "No," he said. "I put those there."

"Why?"

86

He shrugged. "It was a gesture," he said despairingly. "That's all. Just a gesture. Why did you come here?"

Nicole hesitated a moment. "The police said I ought to talk to you. They thought we might be able to recall something that might indicate where he's gone. They're going to be at Orly. They hope to pick him up there."

"And you helped them?"

"Yes. Why not?"

"That was a stupid thing to do!"

"Robert!"

Boderin turned away and seemed to calm down again. "Perhaps it wasn't, though," he said thoughtfully. "If nothing else, it'll keep them occupied." He saw his sister staring at him and managed a twisted smile. "It'll draw attention to our cause, of course," he said.

"Robert"—Nicole's voice was pleading and to Hardy she seemed suddenly to be begging for mercy—"I don't think anybody's bothered about our cause any more."

Robert stared at her, his eyes startled and not understanding. "What do you mean?" he demanded.

"Robert, the war's been over twelve years now. All the people who were important then are beginning to disappear now. A lot of them have gone already. Many people who're adult now don't even remember it. Aren't we counting on too many people being interested? They weren't interested in 1946. Why should they be interested in 1957?"

"France remembers," Boderin snapped, his voice harsh. "France remembers everything—France remembers the *Horst Wessel* sung in the Place de la Concorde, and the Elysée Palace a prisoners' camp, and the whole of the Avenue Kléber reserved for the German staff, and that old stuffed uniform, Pétain, appealing to French women to produce more babies to enlarge the German armies. We've never recovered from the moral shock. We're a nation of failures. When we managed in the end to beat the Germans, we promptly surrendered to the Americans. They've taken possession of the Champs Elysées and Montmartre, and we've become one of their Coca-Colanized buffer states. Churchill kicked us out of Syria and the Americans swept us aside at the Oradour trial to get the Germans into their

87

European Army. They want to make France like America—a paradise with klaxons replacing harps, and cherubs six feet tall, all playing American football. What is there left for us—a rotted country run by political children."

Blot was trying hard to avoid his eyes, Hardy saw. Robert Boderin's working mouth was foam-flecked and furious and there was a curious quality of unreality about the whole scene.

"Robert——!"

Nicole tried to interrupt the storm but Boderin had worked himself up into a rage now. "The Americans are big talkers, and Dulles is the biggest of the lot," he said, and there was something of the actor that gave body to the well-worn phrases from the pamphlets of defeated politicians.

"They don't remember as we do," he said, "when the lights of Paris were tinged with the blood of the dead, when the place was grey with humiliation, and all the skies were dusty and drained of hope."

"Robert——!"

"They don't remember the graft and the corruption, the strikes, the sell-outs, the hypocrisy of politicians, the wantonness of girls and the disillusioned boys. We're the generation of the sacrificed, with nothing left but barbiturate pills for suicide——"

"Robert!" Nicole's scream startled Hardy. He got the impression of someone who had tried for years to believe in something, secretly hating it all the time, and finally reaching breaking point.

Robert Boderin had stopped dead, in the middle of a gesture. Blot had got to his feet, scared-looking and unhappy. Hardy laid a hand on the girl's arm.

"I think we'd better go," he said.

She nodded her head miserably and Boderin stared at Hardy before turning to his sister.

"Who did you say this is?" he asked coldly.

The girl looked round at Hardy, as though begging him not to provoke her brother.

"Hardy's the name," Hardy said. "Edward Sampson Hardy."

"You're English, you said?"

"Yes."

Boderin nodded, his face composed again but still bitter, his voice chilly and distant. "Then what can *you* know of how we think here in France?"

"I've a pretty good idea. I've been here twelve years—from choice. I like it."

Boderin seemed a little startled by the information and tried a new tack.

"Why?" he said bitterly. "Don't you have pride in your own country?"

"Yes, I do."

"You're lucky. You have *something to be proud of*. In England you have forty makes of cars but only two political parties. Here we have two makes of cars and forty political parties. Our Parliament's full of *arrivistes*, band-waggoners, collabos and careerists, and France's a voice crying in the wilderness."

"Maybe you're just going through the mumps and measles of the Fourth Republic," Hardy suggested cheerfully.

"What we need is the spirit of the Republic in danger again. We should throw out the Americans and stand on our own. Go down, if necessary, but at least go down *alone*—in a *folie glorieuse*."

"One seems to hear the muffled roll of Bonapartist drums," Hardy commented dryly.

Boderin stopped dead, his eyes cold.

"It's not an occasion for jesting!" He was stiff and unfriendly again, and Hardy began to grow tired of the humourless political diatribe.

"That's where you Frenchmen always go wrong," he smiled. "It's one of your greatest failings. Let's go, Nicole."

He took Nicole by the arm and led her from the room. The two young men, one slender, over-intelligent and angry, the other square and dull-looking and nervous in the commotion, stared after them.

They travelled back to St Germain by Métro, sitting silently in the old-fashioned coaches crowded with home-going workers, all of them looking a little stupefied in the heat. A man with a beret and the red ribbon of the Legion of Honour in his lapel was reading *France-Soir*. There was a picture on the back of a girl, and the heading, *Ex-Reine de beauté, trouvée morte, nue dans sa*

89

chambre. Across the other side of the aisle there was an American tourist with the *New York Herald Tribune.* The headline there was *Body found jammed in Garbage Can.*

Somehow, he thought, there you had the essential difference between the two nations. One corpse was a beauty queen, naked on her bed. The other was a man, probably ugly and ridiculous in his underpants, jammed with as little dignity as possible into a dustbin. The difference between legend and realism.

They got off at St Germain-des-Prés. A porter with a whisk broom was sweeping the platform and there was a stale smell of wet sawdust in the air. The adverts for tombola and the National Lottery, even the appeals for sobriety, seemed curiously stark, and the glaring St Raphael adverts that plastered the seats *ad nauseam* and the metallic clash of the wicket gates seemed the gibberings of a neurotic.

The Café des Deux Magots opposite the entrance was jammed with tourists, but with the occasional student smoking yellow cigarettes and trying to look intense and *fine de siècle,* and the odd elderly tight-panted fringe-whiskered pansy; all of them busy believing in disbelieving.

Hardy and Nicole sat with their backs to the building, facing the seedy streets that led down to the Rue Jacob, silent and preoccupied with their own thoughts.

Hardy ordered a Pernod for Nicole and a brandy for himself, feeling he needed a stimulant after the run-down atmosphere of the Boderin apartment. For a long time, she seemed unaware of his presence, then finally he offered her a cigarette, and she took it, lit it and, laying it down on the ashtray, sat with her glass in both her hands, staring over the cross-roads at the teeming traffic and the numberless people gasping in the still hot air through the heavy-hanging petrol fumes and the smell of hot oil.

"It's Blot," she said angrily at last, as though she'd been debating her brother's behaviour with herself all the time. "He's got too much influence on Robert."

She seemed to be hinting at all sorts of dark connections that she didn't want bringing out into the light.

Hardy shrugged. "I'd say it was the other way round," he commented dryly. "I think Robert's got too much influence on Blot."

She didn't disagree. "Robert's strange," she said, nodding. "He always used to be kind and generous and affectionate. But he was always moody. One minute he'd be sad and the next full of happiness. He was pampered a bit, I suppose, because he was the last of the boys, and he was always vain and a bit disobedient."

She put her glass down and sat holding her elbows, lost in thought for a moment. "He becomes so obsessed, he frightens me," she said at last. "I sometimes think he's never grown out of his schoolboy ideas. Once he twisted my arm. He said I ought to know what pain was. He said all the Boderins knew what pain was, because they'd suffered for France, and he thought *I* ought to know about it too." She spoke quietly, staring straight at Hardy as though she were ready to take offence at the slightest sign of irony.

But Hardy's face was sober. "Has *he* suffered pain for France?" he asked.

"No." She looked embarrassed. "Not really. Not for France."

"Why does he limp? The war?"

"He was knocked down by an American lorry during the Liberation. The driver was drunk. It broke his leg. After the war, when he wanted to go into the army, he couldn't because his leg had been badly set. He was very embittered about it."

"Naturally."

She stared at him, bewildered and unhappy, and Hardy felt faintly as though he'd struck her.

"Go on," he said quickly, and then as though the urging were all she needed, she continued in a hurried breathless voice.

"He'd hoped to go into my father's old regiment," she said. "He was the last of the family. Since the Germans killed Jean-Michel and Raoul, and Etienne was killed in Indo-China, he felt it was his duty. I think he feels now that somewhere, somehow, he failed the family. "

"It doesn't seem to have been *his* fault."

She gave him a wry smile. "That isn't the point," she said. "He just *felt* that way. Perhaps that's why he worked so hard on the documents of the case with my father. Perhaps he felt he could make up for it. Perhaps that's why he feels so strongly about France."

"France doesn't need help all that much," Hardy said with firm cheerfulness. "She may be a trollop but she has a curious habit, when the buffoons and charlatans are stealing all the limelight, of throwing up something good and solid and bourgeois who sees that power gets into the hands of the right men in the end. The Deputies aren't France any more than the whacky lot who hang round here. Let's have another drink and forget it for a minute."

She nodded and tried to smile but she seemed to find it harder to put everything behind her than she'd thought, and she remained preoccupied and detached.

"I suppose my family had got too fixed in their ways," she admitted at last.

"That might seem to be the explanation."

"The Boderins served the same regiment for generations. They always served in the same one."

"Of course," Hardy observed dryly. He paused. "Tell me," he went on, "what did he mean when he said the Americans got him fired from Gillet Frères?"

She sighed. "After he found he couldn't go into the army, he tried various things. For a while he tried the stage——"

Hardy wasn't surprised to hear the source of all those dramatic gestures Boderin had used.

"——only it wasn't very rewarding. They told him he always overacted."

"I imagine he might."

"Besides, because of his leg, he was a little limited in the parts he could play. You can't have a Cyrano or a Romeo with a limp."

"So——?"

"He tried politics for a while, but I think it was only really to help my father. He wanted a Deputy to take up the case and couldn't find one. So he decided to be one himself. Unfortunately, he couldn't make up his mind which side to work for. Only the Communists would have anything to do with us and that was only because they wanted to stir up trouble. He never joined anything in the end, except an anti-bomb movement and a few things like that which all seemed to fizzle out. He finally went in for law, but even that didn't turn out as he expected. He handles property transactions. That's all. Nothing's happened as he expected. He's frustrated and bitter."

"And Gillet Frères? You haven't told me about them yet."

"It was a law firm. They dealt a great deal with Americans, and Robert was naturally rude to them because of my father and because of his leg. In the end he was asked to leave."

"Not because the Americans fixed it, but because he was rude?"

Her eyes flashed angrily. "Yes," she said. "But you see, the Americans had disgraced my father. And they'd broken his leg."

Hardy sighed. "The way I have it," he said, "your father brought it on his own head. And as for your brother's leg, there were plenty of people injured accidentally by the Americans in some way or other, who don't carry it round like a cross. There was a war on, after all, and the Americans had their hands rather full with the Germans. Some people were hit by lorries, some were hit by bullets, some by shells, and some by bombs. Some of them were girls who were unlucky enough to find themselves with GIs who hadn't seen a girl for a long time and they got hit emotionally. I suppose they were war victims, too. It happened in England as well. Didn't your brother dislike the Germans for the way they treated your country?"

"Of course." She sounded indignant. "We all did. But this was more personal."

"I'd have thought that having Nazis swaggering round the streets, filling the cafés and eating all the food, getting rid of the Jews and sending Frenchmen off to forced labour camps was pretty personal too."

She seemed puzzled and he could see that the *Affaire Boderin* had been so close to her for so many years she'd never thought to consider the other things, the bigger things that had happened to her unhappy country.

"I'm sorry," he said. "I'm sorry if I appear to be rude and unsympathetic. But you see, I lost *all* my family in the blitzes. Not just my honour. Not just my leg. All my family. There was only me left. I got over it, though. Time healed it all. It heals everything, Nicole, even wounds, unless you keep them open yourself."

"Yes, I suppose so. He felt so strongly about things, that was

93

the trouble. Perhaps I didn't. We used to quarrel. You've seen us together. We don't get on. He didn't approve of my friends."

"Why not?"

"I was friendly with an American student. He was at the Sorbonne on a scholarship. He was kind and made me laugh. My brother came to my room once when he was there."

"So?"

She stared at him, her eyes unashamed. "Do I have to tell you *exactly* what he saw?" she asked. "Robert went away. He came back with a horsewhip."

"A what?"

"A horsewhip."

"The one I saw on the table?"

"I suppose so."

"Good God!"

She seemed indifferent to his amazement. "There was a scuffle," she said in a flat voice.

"And the American got horsewhipped?"

She shook her head. "No, he didn't. Robert wasn't strong enough. All he got out of it was a split lip and an assault charge from the police."

Hardy sat in silence for a moment or two and she went on with a trace of bitterness. "You don't admire my family, do you?"

"Shall we say I think your menfolk are a little obsessed by glory? The blood they shed seems a little bloodier than anyone else's. I think it's unhealthy. Your brother's rooms looked exactly like your father's rooms. Are *your* rooms the same?"

She shook her head.

"Thank God for that! There are too many people already with a taste for thinking backwards in terms of glory instead of forward in terms of hope."

"It was the war," she said. "We all look back now, because there's nothing to see if you look forward. When De Gaulle came back to France there seemed to be so much hope, but the politicians forced him out and now I think there's not much security left anywhere in France and less in Paris than anywhere else. I think often I'd like to go away. Even leave France."

She seemed young and serious and lost. Hardy leaned forward and she made a movement to rise.

94

"I'd better go," she said. "You've too much to think about without the troubles of my family."

He put his hand on hers. "Forget it," he said. "I'm being paid for it. I just think you take much too gloomy a view of things. The art of living's to survive, not to wither like a rotten fruit on a dead branch. If life gets a bit cock-eyed occasionally, you've got to wrench it back into shape. That's all. Maybe St. Germain and the Left Bank aren't Paris, any more than the Champs Elysées. Try the northern suburbs where the café lights don't come on so early and the taxis are little Rénaults instead of big Citroëns, and they don't expect first-class tickets in the Métro because no one ever travels first class. The air's not so rarified out there, and they still manage to laugh now and again."

She stared at him, uncertain whether he was pulling her leg or not, and he went on with a grin.

"It just happens," he said "that I like France. Even if her deputies can't discuss the weather or sing 'Auprès de ma Blonde' without bringing down the Government. If I didn't love France I'd have given her up long ago."

She stared at him curiously, warming to the cheerfulness, the good humour in his face, the wry self-denigration that was so unfamiliar to her in her family of stiff-necked humourless males.

"Why are you here?" she asked.

Hardy grinned. "Because I can't afford the fare home," he said. "I came here after the war for a few months' study. Unfortunately, I fell for an English girl who was studying French at the Sorbonne. I thought she was like all the rest but I discovered too late that she wasn't. *She really was studying French.* But by then, we were married, and I discovered she was all set to go back to Bradford and live in a suburb and spend the same number of hours every day at a school cuffing kids' heads." He shuddered. "That's not a life," he said gravely. "It's a habit. In the end, she decided she couldn't live with me after all and went off on her own."

"Was she awful?"

She seemed very young as she spoke and Hardy gave a wry grin. "No," he said. "As a matter of fact, she wasn't. She was just honest and normal and decent and dignified, and very moral."

"And now——?"

"I've been waiting ever since for her to agree to divorce me. But she won't. She believes it's better to live in misery than face facts. She ought to have been a Boderin, Nicole."

She managed a smile and he went on.

"So I stay here. I've no future and no money, but I wouldn't have it different—well, only the money! I live in a room where the bedspread's too small and the water heater was bought secondhand in the Flea Market. After three months you're entitled to a reduction, so long as you abide by the rules, but you mustn't use drawing pins to hang pictures or bring in a girl without paying extra, and if you pinch the maid's bottom you're out on your ear because maids are hard to get. There's an old soldier in the room above who uses his wooden leg to pound the ceiling if I come home bottled and a chap below as big as the Zouave on the Pont de l'Alma who once went three rounds with Primo Carnera."

She was laughing at last, really laughing.

"It's not really as grim as it sounds," Hardy said. "It's just that I'm not much good at my job. That's the trouble. I'm not much interested, I suppose, so I can't be bothered. The students call me *Mister Trop Tard*. You must have heard the name. Because I always miss the boat. *Les catastrophes Hardy* are well known at the Institute. One of these days they'll give me the push and then I'll *have* to leave if I don't want to end up making a living writing pornographic literature for tourists to buy."

"I'm sorry." She looked up at him, her eyes full of sympathy.

"So am I." Hardy grinned cheerfully, clearly unperturbed by the disaster that was hanging over him. "So, for what it's worth, I'll do anything I can to help you. I've been known to act out of character once in a while. But, in the name of Heaven, don't chuck all this business about the Bligues in my face, Nicole. You're too young and far too pretty for that."

She glanced at him under the corner of her eyelashes and for the first time managed a real smile.

"So, do me a favour," he said. "Back out of this half-baked demonstration at Orly. It can't do any good. Don't go."

"But I must!"

"In the name of God, why?"

"My father will be there," she said, her voice sharp again. "If something were to happen, I ought to be on hand to help him."

"Your brother's going to be there. Isn't that enough?"

"What could *he* do in an emergency?"

Hardy finished his drink. "O.K.," he said at last. "I'll go along with you. I have an idea. It's been with me for some time, as a matter of fact, but I kept hoping I shouldn't have to dig it out. Now it seems I'll have to. Suppose this student demonstration did take place after all? Would it get rough?"

"That's not the way it's planned."

"Perhaps we might let it go on then, after all. If your father's proposing to use one of those guns that are missing, ten thousand students getting in his way won't help him, will they? They could well mask Murphy from anything he might be intending. Let's see if we can't make some arrangements to lay on enough transport to get the whole of the Sorbonne and the Alliance Française there—even the Berlitz and the Institut des Langues Européennes and anybody else who wants to go."

★ 6 ★

THERE were already crowds on the visitors' balcony at Orly when Robert Boderin and Blot arrived. They were outlined against the brilliant blueness of the sky, men and women and a great number of children. It was Saturday, and Orly was one of the sights, like Fontainebleau and Versailles and Robinson and the chateau at St Germain-en-Laye.

Boderin parked his car, and Blot watched him nervously as he stood looking up at the crowds and the silent aircraft—BEA and blue-and-white Air France Viscounts, and the huge Pan-American Boeings, great silver machines with their coloured company crests and square identification letters, and the rows of small round windows picking up the sun in bright golden lights. From the hangars, they could hear the roar of an engine being tested, a rippling metallic roar that momentarily drowned all the rest of the noise round the aerodrome, then died away to a murmur and finally stopped, so that the sounds of motor cars came through again, and the whirring of the little electric luggage trucks, the low tones of mechanics and officials, and the high voices of children.

Boderin watched for a little while longer, then he limped slowly towards the exit hall. Blot hesitated for a second before following him, then he moved unwillingly after him out of the sunshine.

They stood for a moment watching the hurrying hostesses, the lounging police and customs men, and the passport officials sitting in their little booths. Boderin glanced round nervously, searching for his father, then he stood waiting in a corner, silently, almost as though Blot weren't with him, erect, one hand held inside the heavy mackintosh he wore in spite of the warmth; his face pale, his breath coming quickly.

Blot watched him silently. After twelve years of knowing him, he knew just when to speak and when not to. He had grown up almost as one of the Boderin children, first in Amiens, then in Rennes, and finally in Chartres and Paris. He had shared in the sorrow of Etienne Boderin's death in Indo-China, had felt as keenly as the family the humiliation of the court-martial at Rennes, and had taken part even in the endless whispered talk about the chance of a re-trial.

He had been one of them for twelve years, yet never quite one of them. Because of his peasant background, there had never been any envy. He had accepted his place as natural. He was one of them to the point of sharing their hurt pride, their humiliation, their anger and scorn, but never sufficiently to be unable to view their activities without a certain amount of detachment.

As a child he had suffered Robert Boderin's tantrums and quick temper with the placid nature of a country boy, and he didn't worry a great deal that Robert regarded him with contempt because he was only a clerk and frowned on his alliance with a woman near the Place des Vosges who had a husband serving with the artillery in Algeria, a nagging, sharp-featured woman who nevertheless gave him far more happiness than he had ever felt with the uncertain Boderins.

He had entered into business agreements with Robert Boderin, knowing they would be scrupulously honoured even while they were regarded as faintly demeaning. He had made money for him, offered comfort in his darkest days, entering ever since childhood into the spirit of all his crack-brained escapades merely because it seemed to be his duty to dance attendance on him as it was his father's duty to look after General Boderin—always smiling except when he was afraid, wanting only to succeed at his job and conduct his little affair in peace with the woman in the Rue St Antoine—stupid, shiftless, always bullied, often complaining and whining, without the strength of character that his father's army service had given him.

He was analytical of Robert Boderin through long acquaintance, but afraid of his anger. So he held his tongue now, knowing the present mood would soon pass and was best unreferred to.

The gesture of approval he'd been waiting for came at last. Robert Boderin nodded to him and moved to a fresh position close to the passport booths where chattering women were waiting for their documents to be stamped. They could see well and Boderin was in a position to move forward quickly.

"The students should be coming soon," Blot said, but Boderin brushed the idea aside irritably.

"The students don't mean a thing," he said. "I've seen them before. A few hotheads shouting under the Arc de Triomphe. It always stops as soon as they feel the lead weights in a policeman's cloak."

Blot nodded. "I wish it were over," he said nervously. "I shouldn't be here. I should be at work. Martine would play the devil if she knew."

Boderin looked down his nose at him. "Martine! Martine! Martine! That's all you ever talk about. That damned woman of yours. Why don't you marry her and have done with it?"

Blot managed a smile. "It's easier not to," he said.

"You ought to be ashamed of yourself."

"Who're you to talk? What about that girl of yours out at Vincennes?"

Boderin calmed down and drew himself up with a stiff dignity. "That's finished," he said. "It's all over and done with."

Blot turned, interested, on more familiar ground.

"What on earth for?" he asked, puzzled, "I thought it was all so easy. Her own apartment. No parents around to be difficult."

Boderin shrugged. "Sentimentality's a failure of feeling," he said. "It's a pity, of course. I thought at one time we might eventually marry, except that her family's so ordinary. It would be a good thing for me to marry. I ought to have a son. There should be another generation to follow on. But now's not the time to have my life cluttered up with extraneous affairs. I have things to do."

The airport authorities had put a small room aside for Schneider and Souprosse and it was occupied now by police officials, officers with silver braid on their *képis*, red-booted motor cyclists, one or two men wearing riot helmets, double strap firm under their chins, plain-clothes men and one or two worried American officers.

"God knows what they're making all this goddamned fuss for," one of the Americans was saying nervously. "Surely nobody's going to take a pot at John F.—Hell, Lancy, with Patton and Bradley and a few more, he did more to give their damned country back to 'em after the war than anybody else!"

"Exactly!" Lancy—a small dark man with French features, spoke calmly. "Perhaps that's what gripes 'em so. They'd have preferred to have won it all back themselves—with Leclerc and Koenig and this guy Domrémy. You got his name right——?"

"De Lespinasse-Boderin du Crest. That's one thing I have got straight."

Lancy chuckled. "How much nicer it would have been for 'em to see *that* plastered all over the battle honours instead of *Eisenhower* and *Patton* and *Bradley* and *Murphy*. The French like their heroes to *sound* like heroes. They like 'em to have trumpet calls as handles, not names that sound like the horn of a Model-T Ford."

The first officer lit a cigarette. "O.K.," he said. "You know all about 'em. You had a French grand-daddy. All the same," he ended stubbornly, "I can't see that anyone's going to take it so seriously they'll want to shoot old Murph'."

Lancy shrugged. "The guy who assassinated President Garfield did it because he thought he ought to have been given a job in the administration," he pointed out. "The guy who killed President MacKinley did it because he'd got a grudge against presidents having so much attention. The guy who shot Lincoln did it because he thought it would make him immortal."

"You've sure been reading it up."

Lancy grinned. "I thought I ought," he said. "I came to the

100

conclusion they were all a bit nuts. Maybe this guy's nuts, too, and you can never tell what a nut's going to do."

As they finished speaking, Schneider came into the room, followed by Souprosse. They crossed over and shook hands with the formal solemnity of the French that faintly embarrassed the two Americans.

"I believe everything's in order." Schneider gestured with his maimed hand. "We have men stationed at intervals in every room or corridor overlooking the area where the General will appear. I've suggested that all the formalities should be undertaken before he leaves the plane. We can run a car—with outriders and escorting cars—right up to the aircraft. I gather there's to be no inspection of a guard of honour."

"That was the general's express wish, Major," Lancy said. "I think he'd like to arrive here with as little fuss as possible. He said no guard of honour and no inspections. Just the necessary introductions. He goes straight on from here to the Embassy. There's a formal reception there."

"I see," Schneider gave his chilly smile. "Very good. Well, everything's ready. Every one of my men has General Boderin's picture." He offered two or three pasteboard slips to the two Americans. "Perhaps you'd like to see them, too. They're wartime pictures blown up, but they're very good. It shouldn't be hard to spot him. I've arranged for General Murphy to be allowed through as quickly as possible, of course. There'll be special arrangements to get him away through a side gate."

Lancy nodded. "That sounds fine, Major," he said. "That's exactly as we got it from the Embassy." He glanced round him through the door into the entrance hall which was rapidly filling up with people. "By the way, Major," he said anxiously. "What about these students? There are getting to be a hell of a lot of them."

The odd procession of cars had drawn up just short of the aerodrome. There were old Citroëns and Rénaults, a Volkswagen, an ancient bull-nosed English Morris with a growling klaxon and *Rosalie* painted on the stern and on the side *Why is petrol so expensive? A nous la liberté.* An elderly *deux chevaux*, inevitably tipped forward, inevitably noisy, inevitably grey, with an advertisement for a jazz trio painted on the stern, shuddered to a halt with a rolling and twanging of springs and the tinny slamming of doors.

The youngsters who climbed out of the odd selection of vehicles looked as though they'd been scraped from all the cafés along the Boul' Mich' and the Boulevard St Germain and the dusty grassless walks of the Luxembourg gardens. There were Texas cowboys, Yul Brynners and Toulouse-Lautrecs, in rabbit-skin coats and shiny black mackintoshes; Brigitte Bardots, Van Goghs and Gauguins; high-shouldered negroes with heavy swinging hands and Senegalese girls with the kinks combed out of their hair; tight-trousered boys and girls with too-short ballet skirts and dimpled knees. From one of the cars there was the sound of a gramophone playing one of Shirley Bassey's records, and on a Lambretta that whirred past, a student sitting sideways on the rear seat was pumping at an accordion.

They drifted into a group, shaking hands solemnly with each other, then sat down at the side of the road, their feet in the gutter, smoking and chattering and talking in groups. Several of the youths were dragging placards from their cars—*Non à Murphy*, and *Pourquoi Percéval?* and *Boderin, Martyr aux U.S.A.* There were the usual *A Bas Les Américains* and *Go Home, Yanks*, but most of them were thinking more of the *Affaire Boderin* than they were of any enmity to the Americans. The rest were there merely for a joke because it was Saturday and there were no lectures to attend and not much to do.

They were all still swarming round the entrance to the airport, when Hardy and Nicole Boderin arrived in Cellini's car, and Nicole smiled quickly at Hardy as she saw them. She suddenly seemed to have found some truth somewhere among the confused explanations she had given to herself, and clung close to him as though his very lack of seriousness appealed to her, as though his indifference to conventions acted as an antidote to the humourless formality of her own family.

"Well, they're all here," Cellini said. "And there sure are plenty of them."

"There should be enough, if they're manoeuvred properly," Hardy grinned, "to make the finest screen John F. Murphy ever had in his life. He might not like it but at least no one's going to

102

be able to take a pot shot at him if we can once get that lot in between."

He put his arm round Nicole's waist and pulled her with him through the crowd, holding off the swaying weight of people. She gave him a quick grateful glance and seemed to lean even closer. When a police official stepped forward to speak to them, Cellini showed his card and the cards he'd obtained for Hardy and Nicole, and the policeman nodded and let them through.

Almost immediately, the students tried to follow, swarming round the entrance in a colourful noisy crowd, waving their placards, shoving, and shouting cheerful insults. Immediately half a dozen more policemen came from nowhere and stood in a tight line, arguing with the ringleaders.

By the time Master-Sergeant Sligo arrived at Orly, in hired taxi, the crowd had become enormous. There were people who were there merely to watch the aircraft taking off and landing—there was always the chance one would crash. There were those who'd come specially to see Murphy, both Americans and French, their interest tickled by all the press activity in recent days. There were the police and the officials, and there were the students.

This was one hell of a disappointment, Sligo thought bitterly. He'd put on his best uniform and all his decorations just for the pleasure of being able to throw up a salute to the general, but by the look of it, he was going to be damned lucky even to *see* the general.

The crowds seemed to be increasing rather than decreasing by the time Murphy's plane circled the airport. Murphy was deep in conversation with Franks, his hand running over a map, not interested in the vast plan of Paris spread beneath the wing of the turning machine.

"I want a garden," he was saying firmly. "I want a house where I can breathe. I'm not going to stay in that damned flat in the Avenue Foch all my days here. My boy wants to bring the kids out and I want a bit of grass where they can enjoy themselves. Besides"—he grinned—"what would Lilian do without a bit of garden to weed?"

He paused, staring through the window for the first time. "In five minutes, Frankie," he said, "we'll be down."

Franks nodded, watching his face. "What's it feel like to be back?" he asked.

Murphy shrugged. "It's like coming back to a football ground where you once made an end run," he said. "Where you were hero of the game." He paused, then went on thoughtfully. "You know the first thing I'd like to do, Frankie?" he said.

"What's that?"

"I'd like to visit another football ground. I'd like to visit the Bligues. I'd like to go back to Percéval. Can you fix it? The first thing. The very first."

Franks nodded.

"I suppose I can," he said. "It doesn't sound difficult. What's on your mind?"

Murphy grinned with a faint trace of shyness. "I've done all right, Frankie," he said, "For a farm boy." He sounded humble and grateful. "I was doing all right even before the war, I suppose, considering where I came from, but it was at Percéval that I got my chance. That clinched it. Percéval and the Bligues made General John Forrest Murphy, and General John Forrest Murphy's duly grateful. In fact, he's got a sneaking feeling he ought to go back to Percéval, on a sort of sentimental journey— a sort of homage job. See what I mean?"

For the thousandth time since he'd known Murphy, Franks realized afresh how much he liked him. There was nothing about him of arrogance. Outside of his job he was still the farm boy from Tennessee who'd surprised himself and everyone else by becoming a national hero.

"There were some great guys there in the Bligues," Murphy went on reflectively. "They'd been resisting for years—ever since the Occupation started. There'd been no collaboration in the Bligues and there weren't many Communists either. They were good joes. Old Chatelin de Bruneval, for one. Do you know, that guy had had a cork leg since 1918 but it didn't stop him riding on a tank. And Marchand. Poor bastard, he got blinded. I'd like to see them again if they're still around. Fix it, Frankie, will you?"

"I'll enjoy fixing it," Franks said sincerely, and Murphy looked through the window again, his eyes sharp and interested but suddenly doubtful as he gazed at Paris.

"Well, there it is, General," Franks said, trying to gauge his mood.

"Yep." Murphy nodded. "There it is. All of it. I guess it'll be my last battleground, Frankie, before I retire. I sure hope I'm up to it."

Franks turned. It was the first time Murphy had expressed any doubts about his ability.

"Sure you're up to it," Franks said firmly.

"Yes, I guess so. They seemed to think so when they picked me. I hope they were right. It's a big step though for a country boy like me." Murphy smiled at Franks but Franks saw a little of the anxiety behind his eyes.

"Wonder what the reaction'll be?" he said thoughtfully. "Wonder what they'll think when you actually put your feet on the ground?"

"Well," Murphy said flatly, turning away from the window. "We'll soon see."

Inside and outside the reception lounge, the crowds had increased immensely. The students milled around in large groups, streaming in and out of the other crowds like a multi-coloured snake, clinging close to each other, all a little nervous and anxious for the near support of their friends, all a little noisy, and in spite of their noise faintly embarrassed by the banners they carried.

A large number of people had made their way downstairs from the balcony when they had heard that Murphy was due. They all knew who Murphy was and they were all anxious to see what he looked like. In addition, there was a junior minister and an official or two, one or two soldiers, a few American top brass, a few British. It promised to be quite a spectacle in the end.

As the big silver machine landed, someone started a chant, *"Non à Murphy"* which was taken up by the students. After a while, though, as the big machine waited at the other end of the runway before taxiing up to the airport buildings, the chant died away. Once or twice there were cries of *"Justice à Géneral Boderin"* and *"Pourquoi pas un autre jugement?"* but the plane was late and they'd been there a long time and they were all beginning to grow bored.

As the plane finally stopped in front of the airport buildings there was a surge forward, but only a few priority passengers descended. As they passed through the booths and the police barriers, the crowd of students edged forward once more for a sign of General Murphy and his aide.

Cellini began to curse under his breath, irritated by the numbers which, while they aided Schneider, impeded Cellini in his search for General Boderin. He had a pretty shrewd idea that the old man was there somewhere among the crowd, and he decided gloomily that in his search for the bigger story of an attempted assassination, he was going to miss seeing Murphy arrive. However, he decided confidently, Fred Groszwicki, his assistant, could look after that. He was out there now with the other journalists, waiting in a huddle on the apron for Murphy to appear. There'd be nothing but formalities, and from what they could gather not even many of those. It was chiefly a photographer's assignment out there anyway, and Cellini felt certain that General Boderin was inside somewhere and that in General Boderin lay the better story.

Hardy stayed close to Nicole during the shouting, trying to hold off some of the weight of the surging crowds. "See your father?" he asked.

"No." Standing on tiptoe, she tried to peer over the jostling heads. "But my brother's over there," she said. "It's Robert."

She tried to wave, but the intense young man with the dark hair and pale set face didn't see her. He was standing in a corner by the exit, wearing a mackintosh in spite of the warm weather, one hand inside it in a Napoleonic stance, watching the barriers with a taut expression on his features. In spite of the crowds, he was lost in a bottomless isolation, his cheeks drawn in and his mouth tight; and there was something about his feverish eyes that was a mixture of pride and anguish and determination.

Master-Sergeant Sligo, standing on the edge of the crowd, could see at once that the chances of coming face to face with General Murphy were going to be even more slender than he had at first thought. It hurt him to see the placards *Non à Murphy* and he took it as a personal affront. For a while, he tried to push forward, startled by the noise, but after a while he gave up trying and allowed himself to be swept about by the surge of the crowd.

More people were leaving the plane now, in ones and twos, carrying small cases and mackintoshes, but there was still no sign of Murphy and the students were beginning to shout.

"He's afraid," they yelled. "Murphy's afraid!"

Hardy could see Cellini pushing among them, his eyes darting here and there in search of General Boderin. He'd carefully studied all the available photographs so that he'd recognize him at once.

Suddenly there was a shout. *"C'est Murphy,"* he heard, and he knew that the general had appeared. A few students in front of him began to jump up and down and he began to wonder if they were going to be more of a hindrance than a help. He hadn't dreamed they could raise such a crowd as this.

Someone shouted *"Le voilà"* and he guessed they'd seen Murphy at last, and almost in the same instant he saw the man they were looking for. He was standing on the fringe of the crowd, tall, handsome in a frail brittle way, white fluffs of hair behind his ears. He wore a neat grey suit and carried a bulky brief case, and he looked prim and precise—like a fussy business-man with his yellow leather gloves.

Hardy saw him begin to fumble with the brief case he carried and the first thought that crossed his mind was that there was a gun in there and that the old man was just about to pull it out. Hunching his shoulders, he started shouting.

"Hurrah for Murphy," he yelled and the other students around him, not hearing what he was shouting in the hubbub, started pushing too. For a brief instant, he saw Robert Boderin's startled face and angry eyes across the tossing heads, then he was swept away, and as they surged forward he saw the old man with the brief case stagger back, brushed aside by the press of young bodies, and he caught a climpse of Cellini thrusting his way through.

Souprosse saw General Boderin at almost the same time as Cellini and Hardy, and he and a group of policemen began to force their way in a solid wedge through the shrieking students.

"Quickly," Souprosse panted. "Surround him."

Then someone shouted. "He's not coming this way!" The voice was shrill with disappointment. "He's getting straight into the car!" And Souprosse realized the students had spotted the different arrangements that had been made.

"The other gate," Hardy yelled, and there was a massed rush from the lounge. Several of the banners and placards were thrown down and trampled on, and he saw General Boderin stagger as though caught by a gale. Across the room, he saw the brief anger on Robert Boderin's face as he was bundled unceremoniously against the wall, then a student fell and, in a second, there were half a dozen of them sprawling on the floor. Someone shrieked as he had his fingers trodden on and a girl screamed and fainted.

"My God," Hardy said. "What have we stirred up?"

Nicole looked pale and unhappy, but there was little he could do to help as they were swept up against an elderly American sergeant who was jammed in a corner muttering to himself in a monotonous string of curses.

Hardy saw the car pause for a moment by the gate, and began to wave.

"Now's our chance," he shouted.

As Robert Boderin pushed forward after his father he saw the figure of General Murphy quite clearly within reach in front of him, then he was flung aside, almost as though he were a feather, by the hurtling crowd of students, and slammed against the wall. He almost fell and by the time he had recovered himself, the students had streamed round the car, between him and Murphy.

Souprosse and his men reached General Boderin at almost the same time as Cellini.

Cellini saw the old man open the brief case and thrust his fist inside. As the yellow-gloved hand came up, he made a grab for it, just as Souprosse snatched the brief case away. In a moment, General Boderin was surrounded by policemen who were hustling him, Souprosse and Cellini, all still clinging together, towards the wall, Cellini still gripping the old man's wrist. Schneider appeared, brushing people aside, and stood alongside them, tall and military-looking, waiting for them to make their search.

The crowd, no longer interested in Murphy, turned to watch this new little drama, and Cellini was aware of startled eyes and open mouth. The old man's hat fell off and disappeared under the scuffling feet, then they had him with his back to the wall, spreadeagled there by half a dozen policemen.

Souprosse was staring into the brief case and Cellini saw the look on his face change to surprise. He lifted the old man's hand and stared at the object he held in his thin fingers, a thick wad of cheap pink paper, tightly printed in small type.

Across the top in larger letters he saw the words *L'Erreur à Percéval*.

He snatched at the papers and stared at one of them. "*The mistake at Percéval*," they announced, in large type. "*France demands a re-trial. France demands that this miscarriage of justice be set right*."

Then there was a mass of small type in which he saw Murphy's name recurring and the names of several military units. Finally, there was a small crude map, and a signature written with all the full flourish of pride—"*Nicholas Jean St Omer de Lespinasse-Boderin du Crest, ancien Général de Brigade, commandant à Percéval, Les Bligues*."

Souprosse was fishing more sheets of the same sort from the brief case, scattering them like snow about the floor, in his hunt for a weapon. Then he straightened up, his hands full of paper and stared at Schneider.

"Pamphlets," he said in bewilderment. "Pamphlets. That's all."

PART TWO

★ I ★

THE news of General Boderin's arrest reached Paris even before the newspapermen had freed themselves from the crowd and rushed for the telephones.

Long before the big black police car had pulled up outside the glass doorway of Orly, long before they had pushed the old man inside it, still protesting, still puzzled, a car had vanished from the airport and was hurtling back towards the city.

Pulling up at a bar on the Villejuif road, its driver descended and ordered a beer. Leaving the counter before it arrived, he asked for the telephone and dialled a Paris number.

"Listen, Edérède," he said as soon as he heard the voice in the earphone. "He didn't do it! He didn't do it!"

"He *didn't*?" The voice sounded startled. "What happened? Did the police get to him?"

"No! He just didn't do it."

"Why? Hadn't he got a gun?"

"This'll make you laugh. He wasn't going to use a gun at all."

"What? What then?"

"A horsewhip! He was going to horsewhip him."

"A horsewhip! My God! I thought they went out with the Second Empire."

"He'd got it under his coat. I saw it. Only there was a whole bunch of students demonstrating. I've never seen so many. The whole of the Sorbonne must have been there. They completely covered Murphy. *Nobody* could have got near him. They arrested the father. *He* had a brief case full of pamphlets."

"What do we do now, then? Do you think he'll try again?"

"I think he will."

"Find out. We've got to get hold of him. He might be tempted to use something better than a horsewhip next time, and assassins don't grow on trees."

There was a long pause then the voice came again, low and wondering. "A horsewhip! Holy Mother of God!"

Souprosse's office seemed to be crammed with people. Nicole Boderin sat quietly on a bench alongside her father, not speaking, not moving, apparently not even seeing. Cellini was smoking quietly in a corner, staring over his shoulder from time to time at the others. Hardy had stretched out on another bench, reading a newspaper.

General Boderin was mutttering over a few papers he held, and there was a policeman by the outer door and another one outside Souprosse's room. They all knew there were other policemen in the corridor. The old man's brief case stood on a table in the centre of the room—alone, as though it were a deadly weapon— the crumpled pamphlets that had been picked up from the floor at Orly by perspiring officials, stacked on the table alongside it.

"I must think clearly," the old man was saying, half to himself, and it was obvious he was still concerned with his own affairs and not at all certain why he was there. "I must get it quite clear in my mind. General Murphy's bound to take up my case. For all his faults, and he had many, because he wasn't a man of much background, he tried hard to be fair. He didn't see my point of view at Percéval, he never did—but I have to admit he *tried*."

"Father"—Nicole turned to the old man and spoke to him in a sharp demanding voice—"what did you intend to do out at Orly?"

General Boderin swung towards her, surprised that she didn't understand. "But I've told you," he said. "I wanted to make the injustice of my case known to everyone. I wanted General Murphy to be made aware of what I've suffered from this stain on my honour. I must try to see him," he went on thoughtfully after a short pause. "I must speak with him. I must try to ask him if he remembers the exact order of things that day. My own memory's becoming a little confused after all this time."

He sighed and looked round at her. "I always had a good memory before," he said, as though he were puzzled by his own failing capabilities. "You remember that speech I gave at the cavalry school in 1931, Nicole, on the mistakes of 1914. There were many figures and dates in that and I had to keep them all in my head. It was an exceptional feat of memory. The applause was tremendous. The Commandant himself congratulated me. You must remember, Nicole."

She shook her head. "No, Father, I don't remember," she said shortly.

"No, of course not." He shook his head. "You wouldn't have been born. It would be Etienne or Jean-Michel."

He prattled on for a little in his flat monotone, but no one answered and the room became oppressively still, and even Hardy, in spite of himself, was aware of a terrible sadness as he watched the old man. He was pathetic in his childish satisfaction, not recalling his speech as a great achievement, but remembering the pomp and circumstance of its delivery, and the applause that had greeted it.

For a long time, they remained silent, while the old man sat alone, muttering occasionally, then the door handle clicked and Souprosse appeared with Schneider.

Schneider crossed at once to the brief case that lay on the table and, picking up one of the pamphlets, studied it before he spoke. Finally he turned round and faced the old man.

"Who was with you out at Orly?" he demanded abruptly without any preliminaries.

General Boderin, who had been watching him with bright-eyed interest, looked surprised.

"Who was with me?" he said. "Why, nobody!"

"Of course there was somebody," Schneider insisted. "There must have been."

The old man smiled, untroubled by any sense of guilt. "There were a great many students," he said. "I saw them myself."

"I don't mean the students," Schneider said more sharply. "I mean, was there anyone else concerned in this idea to throw pamphlets at General Murphy?"

General Boderin frowned and looked angry. "But, of course not," he said sharply. "Who else could there be? There's only myself and my daughter and my son left who're the slightest bit concerned with my troubles. Why were there so many police out there? Why was General Murphy so closely guarded? Why was he hustled away before anyone saw him?"

"We thought there might be more than just pamphlets," Cellini said over his shoulder.

"More than just pamphlets?"

"We thought there might be a gun," Souprosse interrupted harshly.

"A gun?" The old man looked startled, then hurt and angry. "So that's why you hustled me about so much! That's why I was arrested. That's why I was dragged pellmell into a police car. You thought I was there to *murder* General Murphy?"

Schneider and Souprosse nodded together.

"You haven't much idea how the minds of the Boderins work," the old man said contemptuously.

"On the contrary"—Schneider spoke sharply—"perhaps we have a *very good* idea. If you had no intention of doing him any harm, then what have you done with the pistol you kept at your apartment at Chartres?"

"Pistol? What pistol?"

"You had a Belgian automatic, which you purchased several years ago."

The old man nodded, his eyes veiled. "Of course," he agreed. "I bought it at a time when my life was in grave danger."

"What sort of danger?"

"I made many enemies at that time," the old man explained. "Perhaps, now, they've forgotten me, but at that time not long after the war when feelings were running high, there were many people who felt we shouldn't upset the Americans. France had cut her losses and my feelings were only a small item in the debit balance. There were others who agreed with me, of course, but I can't deny there were some who thought I'd disgraced France. I'd received threatening letters. I thought it wiser to obtain some sort of defensive weapon."

"Why? You already had a British-made Smith and Wesson revolver. You were issued with it by the British army. You retained it after the war. That was a far more dangerous weapon."

Boderin stared at Schneider with a faint trace of arrogance. "Have you ever tried to carry one of those monstrous British revolvers in your pocket, Monsieur?" he asked coldly. "Its size would quite have ruined the cut of a suit. I decided instead to

obtain something smaller and lighter that I could carry, which
would not inconvenience me."

"Where is it now?"

"I don't know."

"Did you ever use it?"

"Of course not!" The words were snapped back indignantly.

"Why not?"

"Because no one ever made any attempt to waylay me!"

General Boderin suddenly seemed to sag and his face became
grey. "Under the pressure of other events," he said slowly,
"under the pressure of a collapsing series of governments when
there was little order in the land, under the pressure of a new
fear of the Russians and the arrival of the atom bomb, my
demands for a re-trial were put off again and again. It was a
tremendous disappointment to me and to my supporters."

Schneider looked up quickly. "Your supporters? Who were
your supporters?"

"I had a few," Boderin said proudly. "I still have. You saw
them today. Out there at Orly."

Schneider turned away and stood at the window. "School-
children," he said over his shoulder. "Who were your supporters
at the time you're talking of?"

"Resistance men. Men who'd had the honour of France close
to their hearts."

"There were all sorts of Resistance workers," Schneider
pointed out, turning. "Of all creeds and political colours. Some
of them working more for their own political future than for
France. Which group did they belong to?"

"They called themselves the *Partie des Abandonnés*. Later they
changed the name to the Society of the Friends of Truth."

"They were Communists, according to my account."

"They didn't call themselves Communists."

"That's what they were, nevertheless. They were using your
personal misfortune to create trouble for the Americans. They
were fishing in troubled waters as usual. Let me refresh your
memory. When you took up with them, you were dropped by
your army friends who'd supported you and by the Right
Wing politicians who felt you might have had a case. Isn't
that so?"

The old man shook his head, as though he were faintly dazed by Schneider's knowledge.

"I'm not a Communist!" he said. "I've never been a Communist!"

"I never said you were. But you allowed the Communists to make a great show of your case, didn't you? The best stories were always in *Franc-Tireur*, *Libération*, and *Front National*—all of them near-Communist papers. The biggest outcry of all was in *Humanité* and *Emancipation*, both Communist. *Huma's* dropped it since but I notice *Emancipation's* still trying. They brought the case up whenever American leadership was mentioned—at the time of the cold war, and the Berlin airlift and Korea and Indo-China, as a reference to the untrustworthiness of American leadership. You never objected."

"I'm an old man," Boderin said wearily. "I'd already grown tired. I had other supporters."

"Who?"

"*L'Hirondelle* never failed me. Héloîse Lamballer always took my part. She was no Communist."

Schneider looked quickly at him and said nothing, his closed police-face expressionless, and Hardy saw that the old man had stiffened and grown distant, as though he had brought up this new name and suddenly decided he preferred not to discuss it after all. Schneider seemed to sense he had withdrawn into himself again and he didn't pursue the matter.

"Did you meet anyone since you came to Paris?" Souprosse asked.

"Who, for instance?"

"A man by the name of Edérède. He's on our list. He was prominent among the Friends of Truth."

"I don't remember any such person." General Boderin was looking defeated now. "I stayed in the apartment Sergeant Blot had found for us in the Rue St Hyacinthe. You can ask Blot."

"Who told you of this place?" Schneider asked.

"Blot."

"Who told Blot?"

"Some Army friend I don't know." The old man was growing fretful and harassed now and all his pride was gone.. "Blot never tells me anything. In fact," he added peevishly, "he never says a word except when he goes to do the shopping and then he never seems to stop. The meals are always late and always hurried because he's wasted time with the shopkeepers. He's only fit to cook for farmers' boys."

Schneider turned to Souprosse. "Have we checked this place in the Rue St Hyacinthe?" he asked.

Souprosse nodded. "Nothing there," he said. "It's just as he says. Owner's a widow. Husband was killed at Abbeville during the war. There are no known affiliations with any political party."

"What about Blot?"

"He was with me at Percéval," the old man interrupted quickly.

Souprosse waited for him to finish before he spoke. "He's all right," he said to Schneider. "He's been checked."

Schneider paused, thinking, then he turned again to General Boderin. "Why did you choose this place in the Rue St Hyacinthe instead of staying with your son?" he demanded.

The old man shook his head, looking up with the weary glance of a very tired man. "My son has his affairs," he said. "I have mine. He never did approve of mere pamphleteering. He favoured stronger action."

Schneider looked quickly at Souprosse before he went on. "What about your daughter then?" he asked. "Why didn't you stay with her?"

"Because she's young. She also would have disapproved of what I intended to do." In his words there was the scent of misery, of a disrupted and broken family.

Schneider rubbed the desk with his hand. "Did you know your Smith and Wesson revolver had disappeared, too?" he asked.

The old man looked up. "It can't be missing," he said. "It was locked up in my desk."

Souprosse glanced at Schneider then back at General Boderin. "Did you know the drawer could be forced without the slightest trouble?" he asked.

Boderin looked up sharply. "No," he said. "I didn't know that. Who told you that?"

Nicole looked up. "I told them so," she said firmly, as though she were used to defying him. "I discovered it when I was still small. I used to take things at times. Cigarettes, for instance."

"That was dishonourable." The old man looked at her with a hurt and disapproving stare that made her drop her eyes.

"The revolver was there when I left," he said quietly. "I went to the drawer for some papers from which I might write my pamphlets. I saw it."

"What about the Belgian automatic? Where's that?"

General Boderin raised pale disinterested eyes to Souprosse's face. "I don't know," he said firmly.

Souprosse paused, then glanced at Nicole. "Who else knew about that drawer?" he asked.

Nicole shrugged. "No one," she said. "No one but myself and my brother Robert. We used to joke about it. We used to regard it as a sort of secret——"

She stopped speaking as she realized Cellini was staring at Hardy, and that Schneider had picked up the telephone and was speaking softly into it. The room had become silent, and Souprosse's gaze was fixed firmly on her.

For a long time her eyes flickered from one to the other of them, then, shocked by the thoughts that had come into her head, her mouth opened a little, and her eyes settled on her father. "Robert," she breathed. *"It was Robert who took the guns. Not you."*

When he discovered the mistake he'd made in trying to meet General Murphy at Orly, Master-Sergeant Sligo picked up one of the blue airport buses and returned to the air terminus near the Pont Alexandre III. All the way back, he smoked thoughtfully, deciding he'd been wasting his time. Thinking it over, he realized his scheme hadn't had much chance right from the beginning.

He left the air terminus with its groups of harassed tourists trying to find taxis, and walked along the river bank until he found a bar. Then he sat down and ordered a beer. Over the beer, he decided the only sensible thing to do was to go along to the American Embassy or back to the Information Bureau on the Champs Elysées to try to find out just where General Murphy might be. His leave was limited and if he had to return to Achensee without managing to throw up that salute he so dearly wanted to offer, he knew he never would. Certainly never as a serving soldier.

He swallowed his beer quickly and picking up a taxi, had himself driven to the American Embassy.

The reception for Murphy was over and the guard of honour had dispersed. There was a woman receptionist just inside the door, grey-haired and immaculately dressed, who immediately left her desk and appeared at Sligo's side.

"Can I help you?"

Sligo felt a little ill-at-ease in the entrance hall. It all seemed so much larger and more lavish than he had expected, and the woman receptionist, middle-aged, immaculately turned out, had the effect of making him nervous. After a lifetime of army installations, Master-Sergeant Sligo wasn't used to the sort of ostentation to be found in an embassy.

"Well," he said uneasily. "I guess I'm actually trying to find out where I can contact General Murphy. The cop outside said he was in here."

She frowned. "That's right," she said, "but I'm afraid he's really nothing to do with us."

"He might be, Ma'am, if you tell me where he is," Sligo said.

She paused. "Well, as yet," she pointed out, "General Murphy's plans are a little vague. As far as I know, he'll be a few days before he actually takes over out at Versailles."

"Well, where can I find him in the meantime, Ma'am?"

"He had an apartment in the Avenue Foch put at his disposal. Perhaps you can find him there."

"Will he be there now?"

"Well, no." The receptionist hesitated. "As a matter of fact, he's still here. He's upstairs."

Sligo's heart leapt. "Well, see here, Ma'am, can't I see him here?"

"I'm afraid not."

"Look, Ma'am"—Sligo decided to lay his cards on the table— "I've been chasing General Murphy round the world for thirty years or more. When I was in the States he was in the Philippines. When I was in the Philippines he was at Pearl Harbour. When I got myself a posting to Pearl, the Army had posted him back to the Philippines. Once I missed him by a fortnight. A fortnight, Ma'am. No more. Guess how I felt. And, Ma'am, I'm only a serving soldier; I can't afford to go jaunting round the world in the hope of coming face to face with him one day. I had to go where the Army sent me and hope it'd eventually be somewhere near where he was. I'm due to be retired in a few weeks and I thought I'd never make it but then, all of a sudden, he's sent over here, see? Well, Ma'am"—he could see the receptionist was listening with interest now and warmed to his theme—"I got me a pass to visit Paris. I went out to Orly to find him, but there were so many god-damn people there—begging your pardon, Ma'am!—that I never got within a mile of him. So now I've come here to find him. And you tell me he's upstairs. Ma'am, let me try to catch him. I'm throwing myself on your mercy. You want, I catch him. You don't want, I goof."

The woman looked doubtful for a while, then she spoke quietly. "There's a lift along there," she said. "Tell the attendant to take you up to where General Murphy is. He knows where he'll be. I warn you though, the place's still full of policemen and news-papermen. You might not even get near him. That part's up to you. I can't help you there."

Sligo grinned happily and saluted. "Ma'am, thanks," he said. "I'll take a chance on that. I sure am obliged to you."

In the big reception room on the second floor, Franks waited by the door while Murphy talked to the press. Most of them were Americans but there were a few Frenchmen among them, too. They'd reached the point when they were pressing Murphy hard about the *Affaire Boderin*. Franks had missed most of it with some business he'd had to attend to outside and had only arrived in the middle of the conference.

Murphy was speaking now, answering a stubborn questioner, with Lancy just behind him ready to object at once if anything cropped up which he considered couldn't be answered.

"No," Murphy was saying. "I didn't expect any demonstration against me when I arrived. In fact, I'm not sure yet how much notice to take of it. They were all students, I noticed."

"Will you let it distract you from what you've come here to do, General?"

Murphy paused. "No," he said. But Franks knew he was

making a mental reservation inside himself that if it were simply and solely his own unpopularity with the French, as distinct from their objection to the job he was there to do, that was causing all the trouble, then someone somewhere must have been wrong in sending him.

"Did you know, General," someone was asking, "that General Boderin was at Orly with a lot of pamphlets he was hoping to throw?"

"No, I didn't."

"What would you have done if you had?"

Franks sighed. The questions grew more fatuous with every day, he thought.

Murphy was more patient, however. "I wouldn't have done anything," he said. "What would you expect me to do?"

"We've heard, General, that General Boderin had hopes of meeting you. He hopes to force a re-trial. He's counting on your support to see that he gets one."

Franks saw Murphy's mouth grow tight and his eyes grow angry. It seemed to him, too, about time to start getting tough. He saw that Murphy had decided to make his position clear here and now and stop anybody getting any false ideas.

"The Boderin case as far as I'm concerned," he said firmly, "started in August 1944. My part in it was finished in September the same year. I wrote a report on what happened and submitted it. My actions were upheld by General Eisenhower, who was then my commanding officer. I was never asked to review it until 1947 when General Boderin was court-martialled at his own request. By then I was back in the States. I was asked to provide a report, which I did. There was a lot of to-ing and fro-ing, and I was asked to answer a few supplementary questions before a lawyer. This I did. That, as far as I know, completed my interest in it."

"He's put a lot into it, General."

"I'm sorry about that," Murphy said sincerely. "I'm sorry for General Boderin. But don't quote me on that or some guy'll go and say I'm on his side. I'm not. I know what happened and if it happened again I'd act in just the same way. But this is 1957 and it's not my business to get involved in French politics. The people who sent me over, and the people here who agreed to me coming over, knew of my part in the affair, but they obviously decided the whole business was over and done with and that I was no longer part of it. That, gentlemen, is just how I intend it to be. It's none of my concern now."

Nobody seemed to want to ask any more questions and the group broke up. As they left, Colonel Franks appeared at Murphy's side.

"The police picked up the old man," he said. "General Boderin."

Murphy frowned. "I hope they didn't rough him up," he said. "What was he up to? No bombs? No house bricks? No guns?"

Franks smiled. "No guns," he said. "They're picking up the members of his immediate family now. They've got his daughter but they've not managed to find the son yet."

"Maybe he's gone fishing. The French are great fishermen."

Franks didn't smile this time, and went on to remind him of his engagements, determined not to let the Boderin Affair involve him too deeply, on his first day in France.

"Better think about moving on," he suggested. "There's the reception at the Elysée Palace now."

Murphy sighed. "Hell," he said. "I wish people would remember I'm supposed to be a soldier, not a diplomat. Will you be there, Prof?"

"I'll follow you up. Van Anders from AGARD's on his way round here. He's been on the phone. He's in a hurry to see AMRA working. I'll have to see him."

"O.K. I'm off then."

"You can go through the door there," Franks pointed out. "There are a few odds and ends in the corridor hoping to meet you, and you can dodge 'em if you go that way."

Sligo went up in the lift with a light heart, feeling he was beginning to get somewhere at last. As he stepped out, however, he knew it wasn't going to be as easy as he'd thought. There were several officers standing in the corridor, talking to a group of men in civilian suits who looked like policemen.

One of the civilians turned and approached Sligo the moment he appeared.

"You're on the wrong floor, Sergeant, I think," he said gently.

Sligo glared, angry for the first time. "How do you know I'm on the wrong floor?" he said. He knew he was being foolish. Now wasn't the time to antagonize anyone, but the other man obviously took him for a dumb soldier looking for information.

The civilian stared and his face grew harder. "You're even in the wrong building," he said. "The place for information's the Centre up on the Champs Elysées. It's not hard to find."

"I don't want any information."

The other man began to look angry. "Well, what *do* you want?" he demanded. "This is the Embassy. Not a club. This isn't the place for soldiers."

"Well, what are *they* doing here then?" Sligo indicated the two or three officers standing talking farther along the corridor.

"They're on General Murphy's staff."

"Well, they're just the guys I want to see."

The other man looked hard at him. "You'd better let me see your papers, Sergeant," he suggested.

Sligo produced his identity card and his leave and travelling pass. The civilian stared at them.

"They look all right," he admitted grudgingly. "But I can't let you up here. We're here to see that the General's not bothered."

"I don't want to bother him," Sligo snapped. "I just want to see him, that's all. For ten minutes. No more. I won't trouble him."

The other man planted himself squarely in Sligo's path. "I'm a detective," he growled. "And I say you *can't* see the General. You're in the wrong joint, bud. I've told you once."

"They sent me up from downstairs."

"Who did?"

Aware at once that perhaps someone had taken a liberty with the rules. Sligo promptly withdrew. "Oh, some guy down there," he said. "Told me the General was up here and I might get to see him."

"Well, he told you wrong. You can't."

One of the officers talking near the door turned and approached. "What's the matter, Lieutenant?" he said to the plain-clothes man.

The detective turned, angry and bristling. "Colonel," he said, "this guy wants to see the General. I told him he couldn't."

The officer stepped up to Sligo who saluted smartly, relieved to be on familiar ground. "My name's Franks," he said quietly.

"I'm on the General's staff. I make a lot of decisions for him. In fact, one of my jobs is to take a lot of unnecessary weight off his shoulders, and decide who ought to see him and who oughtn't. What's the trouble?"

Once again, patiently, one eye on the detective whom he regarded with a faint sense of embarrassment, as though his request were a little childish, Sligo put forward to Franks all that he had planned to do, and all the reasons why he had not been able to do it.

Franks thought for a moment, rubbing his nose. "Pity you didn't come ten minutes earlier," he said. "You just missed him."

Sligo sighed. "How about tomorrow, sir?" he asked.

Franks paused. "See here, Sergeant," he said. "It's going to be hard—in fact, it's going to be impossible—to see the General today, tomorrow, or even the day after. He's full up."

"Hell, sir"—Sligo looked hurt—"I only want ten minutes of his time."

Franks smiled. "Sergeant, you don't realize what a request that is. How about coming back in a month or two? I'll personally be glad to arrange an interview with you. I know the General won't mind."

"Sir"—Sligo was getting desperate now—"there may not be another time. I'm sweating on being sent home, and if I get sent home, I might *never* manage it. It's here and now in Paris, or not at all."

Franks's eyes were amused. "Is it *very* important, sergeant?" he asked.

"It might not be to the General, sir. It might not be to you. But, sir, it sure as hell is to me."

Franks thought again, his sensitive intelligent face understanding. "See here, Sergeant," he said. "It's impossible now. I know it's impossible. He's gone to the Elysée Palace and he's already an hour late." He began to write down an address on a slip of paper he tore from a notebook. "See that?" he said. "That's where the General will be staying. It's temporary but he'll be there for a while. Come along there. You'll feel at home. There'll be a sergeant on the door and a couple more inside. One'll be the General's driver. One'll be his servant. One'll be a clerk. I'll be there myself. I'll try to see that you get ten minutes with him."

"When, sir?"

Franks frowned. "That's the problem, Sergeant. It won't be tomorrow. It won't be the day after. That I can promise you. Try the day afterwards."

Sligo threw up a salute. He was pleased to be able to offer the gesture and he put all he had into it.

"There's just one thing, Sergeant," Franks concluded. "It might still not come off. You've got to be prepared for that."

Sligo's face dropped.

"That's his first free time," Franks said. "But that doesn't mean that someone with more stars on his shoulder—or more medals on his chest—someone more important than you or me or the General himself might not take it up. The General's still pretty much at everybody's beck and call. He's being snatched up by everybody who wants to meet him, from the Commander-in-Chief himself to the President of the Republic and the military representatives of half Europe. You've just got to take your chance."

Sligo saluted again. "O.K., sir," he said. "I'll do that. If it's not possible, I'll just keep trying."

Between them, Souprosse, Schneider, Hardy, Cellini and Nicole, together with a couple of uniformed men and a plain-clothes detective seemed to fill the apartment near Père Lachaise.

The journey out had been a depressing affair, all of them jammed into a big police vehicle, with General Boderin fretfully demanding explanations and apologies and claiming his right to be allowed to go free. In the end Souprosse had refused to allow him into the apartment on the grounds that he would distract his men, and he was now outside in the car, sulking, watched over by a detective.

Schneider left most of the work of searching to Souprosse and the uniformed men, and stood with his hands behind his back, gazing at the photographs on the wall.

"*Formidable,*" he said dryly, half to himself. "The apotheosis of the family De Lespinasse-Boderin du Crest. The mirage of the past. The cult of the martyr. As usual, we are living on our dead bodies."

He moved slowly about the apartment then he spoke briefly and quietly to Souprosse, and turning their backs on the rest of the room, they stared out of the window as they muttered together. After a while Schneider straightened up and turned to face Nicole.

As he approached, she moved closer to Hardy and he felt her fingers groping for his, as though she felt he would know what to do. In that moment she seemed simple and uncomplicated and lacking in that defiant pride that always made her so hostile, and his sympathy and pity flowed towards her, warm and encouraging, and she seemed to sense it. As Schneider began to speak, he felt her fingers tightening on his and he gave her hand an answering squeeze.

"Were you aware," Schneider asked, "how highly your brother appeared to regard this—this"—he gestured with his maimed hand, searching for the right word—"this history, mademoiselle?"

Nicole nodded without speaking.

Schneider turned away and the place became silent again, except for the movements of the searching men. Then Souprosse stopped in front of Schneider.

"Nothing here," he said, shrugging. "Nothing to indicate where he might be?"

Schneider's hands tapped together behind his back then, as though on an impulse, he crossed to the telephone.

"Where else might I find him?" he asked Nicole.

"You might try where he works," she said wearily. "Benet et Compagnie. Boulevard Haussman."

Schneider stared at her for a second, then he began to paw through the telephone directory, flipping through the pages with the noisy clatter of thin paper. After a while, he paused, stared more closely at the small type, then slammed the book down and dialled a number.

For some time, he stood rubbing the edge of the table with his crippled hand, thoughtful, his eyes distant, then they heard the quick chatter of a voice in the earphone and the life came back into Schneider's eyes at once.

He spoke quickly into the mouthpiece and they heard the thin voice at the other end again.

"Well, do you know where I might find him?" Schneider asked.

Again they heard the high-pitched chatter in the earphone, then Schneider put the instrument down. There was an odd look on his face.

"What sort of a man is your brother," he asked quietly, speaking to Nicole. "What does *he* think of the *Affaire Boderin*?"

"He considers the Americans let my father down."

Schneider nodded, then gestured at the pictures on the walls. "I notice that, almost without exception, the males of the Boderin family went into the army," he said. "In fact, I happen to know there's quite an impressive list of them who were killed fighting for France. Why wasn't your brother a soldier?"

"He was rejected on medical grounds. An American lorry knocked him down during the Liberation. The driver was drunk."

"I see," Schneider nodded. "What about during the war?"

"He was only a boy then."

"I'm aware of that," Schneider said. "But I imagine he wouldn't be satisfied to remain on the sideline. Not being a Boderin."

To Hardy there seemed a faint sneer in his voice, but Nicole didn't appear to notice.

"All my brothers fought in the war," she said with a trace of pride. "One of them was with the cadets of Saumur. One was shot in the Avenue Hoche. You can see the plaque for yourself if you wish to look. Etienne——"

"It's Robert I'm interested in," Schneider reminded her gently.

She stopped, her eyes large and round and afraid for the first time.

"He was only a boy," she said again, almost apologetically, her fingers working nervously in Hardy's. "He joined an organization in 1941 that was pledged to fight to the end. There were all sorts in it. Sick and injured. Boys and old soldiers no longer fit for the army. The Men of Honour they called themselves. There were a lot of students, and they had a few hidden weapons. Robert was an excellent shot. He always was. Before the war my brothers all did a lot of shooting. We had a house then near Amiens and they shot every week-end."

"What happened? Did these—er—these Men of Honour join up with the Maquis?"

"No. They decided to wait for the liberation of Paris. Because they were Parisians, you understand."

"And then? When the Liberation came, what did they do, these—these Men of Honour?"

"Nothing." Nicole shrugged and spoke flatly. "They just talked. Robert got furious with them and went off to find the Maquis. But he was very young. He never quite caught up with the war. It was moving too fast just then. He was like the rest of them. He talked too much and walked too slowly. He never did *anything* in the end. Why do you ask all these questions? What do you want with my brother?"

Schneider paused and began to stuff tobacco into the short briar pipe that gave him such an oddly English look. Nicole stared at him for a second, then her eyes flew to Hardy's and back to Schneider's.

"Robert wouldn't do anything," she said quickly, breathlessly. "You can't believe that."

"I've discovered," Schneider said, "that it's never a good idea to jump to conclusions. I'll wait before I form an opinion. In the meantime, however, I'm afraid we shall have to put a guard on this apartment."

Nicole swept the room with her hand. "But a lot of things here are mine," she said indignantly.

"The pictures, mademoiselle?" Schneider asked gently. "The weapons?"

"They belonged to my father. They belonged to the family and I must look after them. But I kept things here too. My own place isn't large enough."

"I'll give you a permit that will carry you past the guard," Schneider said. "But we must have someone here, you understand, in case your brother returns. The guard will make a note of anything you remove. I'm afraid I'll have to insist on that."

She looked troubled and wary. "Why are you waiting for him?" she asked. "What has he done?"

Schneider was more chilly, more stiff, more English, than ever. He removed his pipe and seemed to stand at attention.

"Nothing, mademoiselle," he said. "It's not what he's done that worries us. It's what he *might* do. I think we'd better try to find him. He hasn't put in an appearance at his office for four days."

By the time Franks got round to the Elysée Palace to pick up Murphy, the papers were carrying the story of the demonstration at the airport.

In the Chamber of Deputies, the Communist member for Hénault-Supérieur, claiming—despite the fact that he was far too young to have taken any active part in the war—to represent the National Federation of Deportees, Internees, Resistance Men and Patriots, had managed, in spite of opposition, to raise the question of Murphy being in France. Why was it, he had asked, that an American general who was such an anathema to the soul and honour of France had been appointed to a NATO position in Paris, and what steps had been taken to see that he was removed? There had been an immediate uproar and, following the fashion of French deputies in debate, several groups had attempted to exchange blows. No one had been seriously hurt but the member for Hénault-Supérieur had been removed from the Chamber and his bitter complaint was in all the papers.

There had been Communist meetings in several of the northern suburbs and an abortive attempt by the Friends of Truth to start a protest march from the Place de la Nation to the Place de la République. In every case, the subject of the *Affaire Boderin* and General Murphy had been dragged up by the speakers. Obviously it was a concerted effort, and the United States Command, sensitive as always to reactions of other people to the members of its forces, had carefully collated all reports and phoned a summary of them to Franks.

General Murphy looked tired as he appeared on the steps between the casqued and sabred guards, who looked as though they'd stepped straight out of the ranks of Ney's cuirassiers at Waterloo. He was with a British general whose red collar gorgets seemed to glow in the half-light and they stood for a moment chatting before they exchanged salutes and Murphy walked slowly down to the car.

"How did it go?" Franks asked as he sat back.

Murphy lit a cigarette. "Well enough," he said. "The President remembered me, or said he did."

The car edged forward and joined the line of limousines waiting to pass through the great gates into the Rue du Faubourg St Honoré.

"Anything happened while I've been in there?" Murphy said.

Franks nodded. "Van Anders came round," he said. "He sure is raring to go. There was one other thing, I fixed it. I thought you'd like me to."

"What was that?"

"An old comrade of yours called round to see you. He missed you by ten minutes."

Murphy looked up, interested. "Old comrade?" he said. "Who?"

"Master-sergeant. By the name of Sligo. Eddie Sligo. At present stationed in Achensee in Germany."

"Sligo?" Murphy frowned. "I don't know any Sligo. Only Barney Sligo. He was with me in North Africa. But he's out of the army now. He's the only Sligo I know."

"I think you know this one," Franks said. "He says you once saved his life from drowning. On manoeuvres, I think he said, in Virginia. About 1924."

Murphy's face lightened. "Goddammit, yes," he said cheerfully. "I remember the guy! Master-sergeant, eh? Well, I'll be —I always thought that kid had got what it takes." He paused, dismayed. "My God, Frankie," he said, "that makes me old. It wasn't so long after the Argonne."

"That's what he said. He's no kid now."

"What's he want?"

"Nothing." Franks grinned. "At least, no favours. Nothing like that. He just wanted the pleasure of thanking you."

Murphy looked puzzled. "A guy doesn't need thanking for saving somebody's life," he said. "If it'd been the other way round, he'd have saved mine, I guess. Besides, as I remember it, he *did* thank me. He wrote me from hospital."

"He wants to do it personally."

"He sure is determined. It must be all of thirty years ago."

"That's what he said. He say's he's been trying to catch up with you ever since."

"And he *still* wants to thank me?"

Franks grinned, tickled by Murphy's delight. "He says—to use his own words—that he's saluted every lousy officer in the U.S. Army and he's never yet had the pleasure of saluting the one he admired most of all, the man who saved his life. You."

"Well, what do you know about that?" A slow smile of pleasure spread across Murphy's Irish face. "That sure is a story, isn't it? If I were the kind of guy who went in for publicity, I'd get my camera boys and my newshounds and get a nice posed shot of this. Best profile. All my medals. And all his. He's got a few, I suppose?"

"Quite a lot. Two, I noticed, for bravery or distinguished service. And a Purple Heart. Just the story for the army magazines. It crossed my mind that I might contact 'em."

Murphy swung round. "Don't you dare," he said. "If a master-sergeant with thirty years' service can't meet a general without a battery of goddamn newspapermen—even army newspapermen —hanging around, then I reckon it's time they lowered the boom on the both of us."

"That's what I thought you'd say," Franks grinned. "That's why I didn't contact 'em after all."

Murphy slapped Franks's knee. "I know now, Prof," he said, "just why I've enjoyed having you along all the time. What are we doing for Sligo?"

Franks shrugged. "I couldn't promise anything," he said. "He's due home soon, but I told him to come along to the apartment in two-three days' time. I thought we might fit him in then. Give him a drink. Make him feel at home."

"That's a good idea." Murphy's face clouded. "I only hope to God somebody doesn't snatch me up that day. Hell, if he's been chasing me round the world for thirty-odd years I guess he's entitled to succeed."

"That's what I thought." Franks paused and handed over the slip of paper containing the summary of the news. "By the way, here's the press reactions to us."

Murphy glanced at it quickly. "Not so bad as it might have been," he commented. "Not so good either."

"How did the press conference go? Did they bite?"

"Not too deep." Murphy tapped the paper. "We'll see to-morrow when we get the papers. I'd like another summary like this. I'd like plenty."

"O.K. I'll see you get them." Franks gestured. "How much did they go for the *Affaire Boderin*?"

Murphy sighed. "I think they'd like to start the goddamn' thing all over again," he said. "Dammit, Frankie, it's only sensation they're after. They don't care two hoots whether that poor guy Boderin gets justice or not. They just want to give their readers something to chew over. I think they'd like the Commies to start a few riots like they did in 1946. So they'll have something to write about."

"I hope they don't," Franks said.

Murphy looked up. "Why not?"

Franks stared at Murphy. He'd never been one of the Americans that the French had hated so much after the war, the generals who were prepared to go to any lengths on the Conti-nent, safe in the knowledge that their own homes and families were separated from danger by three thousand miles of ocean.

"I'd hate to see you driven home," Franks said simply. "I think you're the man for this job, and I'd hate to see some politician push you out of it just for a bit of cheap publicity and a few lousy votes."

The apartment that General Boderin had rented in the Rue St Hyacinthe was a shabby affair alongside a laundry and the wet smell of steam seemed to find its way up the narrow-gutted staircase to the little set of rooms at the top.

Inevitably, the table was covered with documents and Sergeant Blot seemed almost to be on guard over them.

"There's a lot I have to do," the general said, apologizing to Hardy for the confusion as he showed them inside. "I have so many maps to study. I might even pay a visit to Percéval and take another look at the ground."

He was still clearly obsessed by the need to put himself right with the French nation which had once judged him. What had happened or what might have happened at Orly seemed to have slipped entirely from his mind.

He offered them drinks but Nicole refused, merely begging a cigarette from Hardy and standing by the window, toying with it, her face pale and angry, her finger fidgeting with the edge of the black leather coat she wore.

Outside the apartment at Père Lachaise, Cellini had taken Hardy on one side, while Schneider and Souprosse, aided by the girl, were still trying to calm the fretful old man in the car.

"Look after the kid," he'd said, taking out a handful of notes and thrusting them into Hardy's hand. "I've got to stick to Schneider. There's a hell of a story breaking here and I'm way ahead of everyone at the moment. Take care of her. She's a nice kid and she's had a nasty blow."

Nicole had seemed bewildered and shocked into a mute rage as the police car had dropped them, and her father had stamped hurriedly up the stairs to his rooms, full of apologies, full of urgent requests for them to join him for an apéritif, shouting for Blot and dropping his papers in a confused pile as he fumbled for his keys. All the petulant arrogance that had been in her when Hardy had first met her seemed to have changed to thwarted anger, as though her father irritated her to the point of fury.

"I want to go away," she said softly, so that her father shouldn't hear her. "I want to go away from here—I want to go away from Paris." She had repeated it again and again, like a litany, bitter and unhappy, as though blaming all her anger on the city she lived in.

She'd recovered a little now but still seemed unable to bring herself to speak calmly. Her father seemed indifferent to her distress and Hardy suspected that in his obsession with his honour he had *always* been indifferent to her.

"It was such a waste of time," he was saying indignantly. "All those ridiculous questions. Why couldn't they merely take my word? I'm a gentleman. I wouldn't lie. All that stupid business at police headquarters. As though I were a common criminal. I'm tempted to go to law against them. If there were any good lawyers left, I might." He lit a cigarette with trembling fingers and turned to face Hardy. "It's put me behindhand," he explained. "And, if I'm to visit General Murphy, I must have the facts exactly right. It would be pointless trying to get General Murphy to consider my case without having it clear in my own mind."

Nicole turned to him at last. "Father," she said, her voice harsh. "You can't go on with this."

The old man swung round on her. "Why ever not?" he demanded. He pushed a sheet of paper into Hardy's hand, ignoring her. "That's the plan of the action," he pointed out. "You'll notice I've coloured it to make it simpler to understand. The French troops are the blue blocks there on the right. I used blue because it's symbolic of our traditional uniforms though, of course, at the time we were wearing your dull English khaki. The red blocks are the Germans. I used green for the Americans because I thought it again was symbolic. Compared with the French and the Germans—and, I suppose, the British," he added grudgingly, "the Americans were new to the art of war. Compared with the European armies, they were green troops."

"This is where I was." He jabbed a finger at one of the blue blocks. "I was just behind Gallifet's post. There—at the intersection of these two lines—AA and this one KK. Good man, Gallifet. Presumptuous, but good. He might have given evidence for me at the court-martial but unhappily he was caught by a mortar bomb late in the afternoon."

He paused and his washed-out eyes became faraway. "I could see right over the top of the position," he said slowly, reminiscing. "The sun was in my eyes, I remember, and there was quite a bit of mist in the hollows that made it difficult to see what the Germans were doing. I was in a jeep, an American jeep which General Murphy had given me. Later in the day, it passed over a mine. The driver was killed. I remember thinking I'd have to ask for another jeep and another driver."

He prattled on, his mind years away in front of Percéval, his hands skating nebulously over the map, always looking for something that permanently eluded him, something he wouldn't ever find.

"I've still got my orders somewhere," he said vaguely. "Gallifet got them out. We took them off his body and I preserved them. Unfortunately, the prosecuting counsel claimed they had nothing to do with my case. That's why we must get fresh witnesses. Our case must be impregnable." He gave the papers a sudden hopeless shove and sat down, his eyes lost and defeated. "One of these days," he ended vaguely, "I shall have to get you to help me sort

134

these papers out, Nicole. I never seem to have the time these days."

For a moment, he sat brooding, then he sighed. "If General Murphy would say only one word in my favour," he said, half to himself, "it might be the means of having my case reopened, and then I might receive my pension at last. Not that the pension matters, you understand. It's the accusations that were levelled at me. Those are what I care about most."

"He can't reopen the case, Father," Nicole said suddenly.

"Why not? Why not?" The old man's head lifted in a quick birdlike movement.

"He can't give opinions on French domestic cases," Hardy explained when he saw she wasn't going to answer. "He's here to do a job for the United States. If he once wanders into French politics, he's a dead duck."

Boderin heard him out then he stiffened pridefully. "General Murphy's a soldier," he said. "He would understand. Brave men always understand each other."

"I'm not so sure," Hardy said. "There've been cases of brave men behaving in damn' funny ways off the battlefield."

The old man's face seemed to crinkle with distaste and he turned away, losing interest, absorbed in his papers once more. There wasn't much point in remaining to argue with him and, while Nicole was collecting her few belongings, Hardy called a taxi and directed it to the apartment in the Rue Jacob.

Her hand in Hardy's, clutching it fiercely as though she were afraid of her own fury, Nicole sat in silence most of the way and it wasn't until they reached the Boulevard St Germain that she spoke.

"Stop the taxi," she said abruptly. "Stop it here!"

Hardy stopped the vehicle at once, and they got out.

"I don't want to go back there," she said at last. "They all know my name's Boderin by now. They all know what happened out at Orly. They were all there. I don't think I could stand all their stupid questions."

Hardy shrugged. "O.K.," he said. "Where are we going then?"

She looked at him frankly, her eyes steady. "Sam, I think I'd like to go where you're going."

"I'm going home."

She looked at him, unmoved. "I'd like to come too," she said.

They stared at each other for a second, and there was a sudden piteous appeal in her eyes he'd not seen before. "Just for a while," she pleaded. "I won't bother you, I won't get in your way. I just want to sit there quietly. It would seem so—so sane."

The Rue des Prêtres de St Séverin was quiet in the purple darkness of the evening. The caged linnets were quiet now, but the piano accordion was still going and the music had a dream-like disembodied quality.

For a moment, Nicole stood staring up at the old flat-fronted houses, then she took Hardy's hand and pulled him inside the church.

The interior was dusky with the evening and there was only a solitary group of candles burning, and he waited at the back of the church while she crossed herself and knelt down in the back row of seats.

"*Saint Père*"—her words were only a whisper but he could hear quite plainly—"*sois compatissant pour la plus malheureuse de Tes servantes——*"

He turned away in the dusk that was scented with the peppery smell of incense, feeling as though he were witnessing something that should have been hidden from him, and stood with his back to her, pretending to examine the notices at the rear of the church, all the little yellow papers giving the dates of festivals and pardons, then he saw her rise and drop some money into the offertory box and take a candle which she lit and set up alongside the others. Briefly she stared at it then, crossing herself, she touched Hardy's hand again and went outside.

Still a little uncertain of her, Hardy offered her a drink but she refused and he moved uneasily about the apartment, apologizing for its state, trying to pick up the things that made it untidy, the scattered papers and open books that he'd put down and forgotten, faintly disturbed by her silence. She didn't seem to notice, however, and sat down on the divan, her brows drawn down, deep in thought. After a while, he sat down alongside her.

"You need a button sewing on," she said abruptly, touching his jacket.

"Yes, I do." He nodded. "I'm beginning to look a bit like a rag-picker's mate."

"I'll do it for you."

He went down the stairs to borrow a needle and thread, and watched her as she sewed, aware of the quick swell of tenderness as their hands touched, and the warm glow on her skin; and he realized that behind that prickly pride of hers there was warmth and joy, and that underneath that shapeless olive jersey she chose to wear there were arms that could be lifted in love.

She bit the thread off and sat winding the cotton round the spool for a moment. After a while, she put it down and looked up at him frankly.

"I was afraid," she said clearly. "I was afraid to go home."

"That's all right. You can stay here as long as you like."

"I think it was finding out that Robert's the same as him——" her voice had grown cold with loathing, as though she'd suddenly seen her father through different eyes, as though her whole unstable family had been paraded before her and found wanting. "And all that about Héloïse Lamballer coming up like that. It seemed to come from so far away. It made me feel as though I'd got lost in the darkness and was never going to get back to the light."

"Who *was* Héloïse Lamballer?"

Nicole turned. "She was a journalist—a political journalist. She was famous before the war. A bit like Geneviève Tabori and a few others. She was discredited when the Germans arrived and everything that she'd said couldn't happen, did happen. A lot of them were caught that way. After the war, she tried again but somehow, like Tabori and the others, she never caught on."

"The public's pretty fickle," Hardy said.

"It wasn't that. It was wishful thinking. Nobody wanted a war so she told them one wouldn't come. She was wrong. But so were all the others. But *she* had put it in writing and that made it worse. She was even wrong about my father."

"Why did she support him so?" Hardy asked. "When no one else did?"

Nicole shrugged indifferently. "She was his mistress," she said.

"That's why she gave him her support as long as she could. The *Affaire* finally discredited her too, and the newspapers eventually dropped her one after the other."

"When was all this? I mean, when was she his mistress?"

She shrugged. "As long as I can remember," she murmured. "He used to take us to meet her at week-ends. We always ended up at her flat. It overlooked the Arc de Triomphe. Father liked to take binoculars so we could read the names on the Arc. We could see De Lespinasse's name and he liked that. You got to it from the Rue de Tilsit. It's over a hotel. The place's empty now, but we used to think it was wonderful. We used to have tea with her and admire the Place de L'Etoile. There were always wonderful things to eat there. She was a wealthy woman."

"What happened to her?"

She shrugged again. "You know how it is. People forget. The importance of my father's case died away. The politicians found they could get nothing out of it. There were all those strikes and all that fuss when we all thought the Russians were coming." Her eyes flashed and she looked defiant again, as though challenging him to dispute the indisputable excuses she was putting forward. "France was an unhappy place to live in. No government seemed to last more than a few weeks. There were accusations and counter-accusations and people called each other collaborators and the courts were full of libel actions. You can't imagine what it's like to live in a country that's been occupied by the Nazis. You can't torture someone for four years and not leave scars."

"Go on. What happened?"

"She fought to the end for him. Even when he grew petulant about it, she went on fighting. It finished her."

"And what about them? Your father and her?"

"They just stopped seeing each other. I still visited her occasionally. She bore no malice. She always went on behaving to me as if nothing had happened. My brother still went to the apartment from time to time to study—even when she was away, he went. But my father stopped. She stopped encouraging him. I think she decided in the end that what they accused him of might have been true after all."

Hardy glanced quickly at her. This was the first time she had admitted there might have been truth in the allegations against her father.

"He became obsessed with it," she said. "He lost what little dignity he had left by accepting the Communists and lobbying the politicians. I think she began to realize he wasn't after all a big man who'd been wrongly accused of something, but perhaps rather a small man who might even have done what they said of him. She went to live in Nice. She's old now and we hardly ever hear from her."

"What about your brother?" Hardy asked. "Could that be where he is?"

"I don't think so. It's all over, though they always got on well together. When he first came to Paris to the University, he lived at her flat for a while. He spent his week-ends there. He used it to study. He always had his own key and came and went as he pleased. She was very good to us. Particularly to Robert. Perhaps she saw something in him that wasn't in my father." She paused, her eyes on his face, troubled and large. "Do you think Robert's all right?" she asked.

"I don't know," Hardy said. "Honestly, I don't."

"I suppose you disapprove of all this—this mix-up. Of Héloïse and my father, and of me."

Hardy touched her hand. "Disapprove? Why should I disapprove?"

She was sitting very straight beside him, hiding her uncertainty with anger, and he wanted to grip her shoulders tightly, feeling her flesh and bones through the thin fabric of that shapeless green jersey, trying to pour some of his own indestructibility into her.

"Somehow, it was just like Robert," she said. "It was so futile, so childish. It was like that demonstration. What good does it do? They'll never go through it all again. All that old evidence's like reading the epitaphs on so many old tombs, that's all. Nobody's concerned with one old man trying to win back his honour. It was all so long ago, and waving banners and placards and shouting slogans will never make any difference now. No more than throwing pamphlets or using guns. There's a new generation grown up. They just don't care any more. There's nothing quite so dead as the past.

"There's nothing left in Paris for me," she ended bitterly, her voice harsh with disillusionment. "Take me with you when you go away. Take me to London."

Hardy gestured helplessly. "If I could, I would. But I can't. I haven't a bean."

"*I* have."

"That won't work, Nicole," Hardy said with a rueful smile. "You've come to the wrong man. It's the Cellinis of this world you have to appeal to, Nicole. They're younger and better off. All I've got is a sense of humour and my strong right arm. But what I have got—which isn't much, God knows!—is yours if you want it."

She was still trembling with anger but behind her eyes there was a suggestion of profound doubt. He touched her hand to calm her down, but she clutched his fingers fiercely, and brought his hand up to her lips, holding it there, hugging it with both her hands.

Then she released it and sat staring at him, her eyes dangerously bright and challenging.

"Well," she said. "What are you waiting for?"

It seemed the most natural, the most inevitable thing that had ever happened to him.

★ 3 ★

As soon as he had left the airport buildings, Robert Boderin had hurried towards the little red Dauphine he drove and jammed the horse-whip down between the seats. Blot had long since disappeared. Boderin had last seen him hurrying shamelessly for the exit and he had guessed he had not been able at the last moment to face up to what they'd planned.

He had started the car savagely and driven like someone demented for the city, past the flat, stubble-covered fields and the blocks of new flats. There had been a lot of lorries along the Avenue d'Italie but he had cut in and out of them, hooting madly whenever some old woman stepped off the pavement from among the market stalls along the wide sidewalk. Going down the slope alongside the overhead Métro at Corvisart, a dog had run out from under a clothing stall and he had had to brake sharply to avoid it.

A man had shouted at him—*"Salaud! Assassin!"*—but he had ignored the cry and driven on, his eyes burning, a hollowness in the pit of his stomach, the sickness of disappointment in his throat.

There'd been an accident near the Pont Alexandre III, and the damaged horn of a car had got stuck and blared interminably, to the annoyance of the police who were disgustedly beginning to stop the traffic, but he'd managed to sneak past before all the cars finally came to a standstill, and had roared into the bright whirl-pool of vehicles circling the obelisk in the Place de la Concorde.

Outside the American Embassy he had dragged the car to a stop under the horse chestnuts and started to run. He could see a line of policemen and inside the tall gates a group of soldiers pre-senting arms. For one brief instant, he had caught a glimpse of Murphy—his second glimpse that day—and there had been wild ideas in his head of rushing forward, pretending to be a news-paperman, anything; of just getting within reach of him to land that one blow with the whip that he had hoped would echo round the world. But with a sickened feeling of uselessness, he had then remembered he'd left the whip in the car.

The weight of metal against his leg had reminded him of the heavy Smith and Wesson he'd taken from his father's desk at Chartres and stuffed into his pocket in case some hothead had got in his way at Orly, and his fingers had tightened momentarily on the weapon in a sudden impulse to use it, but then he remem-bered he'd unloaded it in case it had gone off by accident and someone had been hurt. It had suddenly hardly seemed worth all the trouble he'd taken to steal it, all the waiting he'd had to endure before he could get past the concierge and into the apartment, the lies he'd told the police and Nicole about it; and as he paused, sickened by his own inefficiency, he saw Murphy disappear, surrounded by officials and men in uniform, into the Embassy.

He had stood for a moment, one hand in his pocket on the revolver, panting heavily, then he had turned and limped slowly and unsteadily back to his car.

There was a story in the papers the next day to the effect that Robert Boderin was believed to have taken his own life by throw-ing himself into the Seine. His car had been found parked on the

Ile St Louis, just behind Notre Dame, and, an inquisitive policeman, checking up on it, had made the discovery that it belonged
to General Boderin's son.

Emancipation went to town on the story, to the disgust of
Colonel Franks. He did his best to keep the paper from the eyes
of General Murphy but some well-meaning idiot pointed it out
to him, and Franks saw his face grow sombre at once.

"Frankie," he said at lunch, "I didn't come over here to start
a wave of suicides."

As a matter of fact, though, in spite of the bargees and the river
police and the reporters waiting for the body to float to the surface
down at the Pont d'Issy, Robert Boderin had done no such
thing.

It hadn't taken him long to realize that the police would be
anxious to interview him. He'd seen them take his father away
and he knew that the dossier of the affair at Percéval that they'd
worked on in their spare time for so many years would inevitably
be examined. And when it was, it would be found that most of
the handwriting in it was his own.

As a lawyer, he knew very well that the police had powers to
place in custody anybody who might bear malice against visiting
officials and heads of state, and keep them there just as long as
they wished. If there were no relatives who could guarantee good
behaviour, they even had the power to guarantee it themselves—
by the simple means of a trumped-up charge and the turning of
a key in a lock.

At the very least, the police would be eager to question him
and he didn't feel like answering questions. Inevitably, too,
they'd try to keep him under observation, which was also something he had no desire for. He had recovered from his first
disappointment by this time and wanted to complete what he'd
started. His failure at Orly had in no way put him off.

Brooding over the imagined slight against his family, his
failure had only increased his hatred. Perhaps, he'd decided, he'd
been trying to do too much. Perhaps the whole idea had been
wrong. The more he thought about it, the more the presence of
General Murphy in Paris became a challenge to him. He had
spoken so often of his hatred of the Americans in general and of

Murphy in particular, he knew he'd never be able to face his friends again if he didn't do *something* as a protest.

Not only had he harangued Blot on the need for action, but he'd also boasted to others. He'd even once, he remembered uneasily, bragged of a non-existent conspiracy to do away with Murphy and had been humiliated by the laughter with which his words had been greeted. There was more than a little need for face-saving in his desire to do something drastic.

Baffled and furious, he had turned away from the American Embassy and had driven round and round the city for the rest of the day. Somehow, with his desire to show the people who had jeered at him just how wrong they were, the idea of using a horsewhip had seemed suddenly childish and melodramatic— something that belonged to the third-rate plays he'd once acted in, something that went with false whiskers and dark glasses and lacked the first elements of dignity. He could imagine them discussing the incident in the bars and the offices and the clubs with an air of boredom and smiling contempt. Suddenly there had arisen the need for more positive action.

For a moment, he had wondered if he could possibly kidnap Murphy, but, with only the wretched Blot, who was completely untrustworthy, to help him, he couldn't see himself pulling it off. It would need chloroform and several men but, in spite of all the hints he had ever dropped to his friends, no one had ever shown any answering enthusiasm.

Only once had he been offered help. When the story of Murphy's appointment in Paris had first appeared he had been approached in the Cemetery of Père Lachaise by an odd-looking little man carrying a shopping basket who appeared to be engaged in studying the Boderin family vault with the mild interest of a tourist. His first words, though, had told Boderin he was no visitor.

"I hear there's a move to get General Méfait at Orly," he had commented, jerking the copy of *Emancipation* he held in his hand.

Boderin had looked up, his face angry, afraid at the knowledge that other people were interested in General Murphy, too.

"They want to shoot him, I hear," the little man had continued. "I've heard they're expecting a man with a gun."

Boderin's nostrils had twitched nervously. How could they have heard anything, he had thought. No one knew of his plan but himself and Blot.

"Mind you, nobody would worry about seeing General Méfait dead." The little man's tone had been busy, fussy and conversational but it hadn't deceived Boderin. "There are too many Americans in this world, anyway. I often wonder how a man would go about a thing like that. Where he'd get his weapons. How he'd do his planning. He'd need friends to help him, you know. Powerful friends."

Boderin had said nothing and the little man had flipped his *Emancipation* and stared pointedly at it for a second.

"There *are* people, you know," he had continued conversationally, "who'd be only too glad to help. They could provide the right weapons, the right plans. It wouldn't be hard to contact them either."

Boderin had half-turned, nauseated. The thought that other people, cheap people, could use his pride and his family's honour for political ends had revolted him.

"I've seen you here before, haven't I?" the little man had concluded. "I come in here often. I usually find a seat near the Chapel and read my paper. You can always find me there, comrade."

He had smiled benignly and shuffled off, and Boderin had stared after him, his gorge rising. The meeting had left him cold and afraid, with a fear that came back to him now as he drove. In his vanity, he was afraid of others getting into the act.

His own emotions went deep down to the glory of France, he felt. There could be no world, he had told himself a thousand times a day, where France was feeble, and the presence of American soldiers on her soil had always been to him an indication that she was weak.

He had felt many a time as he had stood in front of the great red marble block in Père Lachaise, that he was reaching right back to the soul of the nation, through the disgraces of the Third Republic and the Second Empire to the great days of French courage when the French spirit had been borne aloft on massed banners, and the shrill cry of massed trumpets could be heard at every street end, with the thunder of massed drums, and the earth-quaking crunch of massed feet. That was France, he had thought often with a painful nostalgia for something he'd never known, not the shabby intrigues of the governments which had followed one after the other ever since. They needed the old cry of *La Revanche*—Revenge!—to stir the hearts, something bitter as aloes to bring them to their senses.

Americans couldn't smear his country's honour with disgrace as they had in the Bligues and when they'd treated with the Vichy government instead of with Free France. To save lives, they'd said at the time, but more likely, he'd long since cynically decided, because they'd known that Free France was composed of the strong and the sane-minded who refused to truckle to anyone.

Confused by the thoughts churning in his mind, his aims kept becoming lost in his hatred for French political ineptitude, which with true French Chauvinism he chose to blame on others, and Murphy and the United States merged into a single symbol of his detestation.

It was while he was still debating with himself, that he realized his hand was resting on his father's heavy Smith and Wesson and suddenly the answer stared him in the face. Blot had once put it into words when they'd first started discussing plans for the affair at Orly. "Horsewhips!" he'd said, horrified at the act he was being forced into. "Yesterday it was slapping his face. Today it's horse-whipping him. Tomorrow it'll be assassination!"

Suddenly Boderin felt uplifted and his eyes shone. Assassination! That was the one thing in which he might reasonably expect to succeed. That was the one thing for which he needed no accomplices. He was used to guns and he was a good shot. Assassination had been at the back of his mind all the time, he realized, but he had constantly unconsciously rejected it because it was a crime.

Now, however, he saw he must accept it as a crime, together with the consequences that might follow. He must place himself outside the law, consoled by the knowledge that he, at least, knew what it was all about. Perhaps, he thought, he could devise some scheme, write some treatise and send it to the newspapers, so that it would be known why he had done what he intended to do; so that there should be no feeling that he had done it in a mere frenzy of hatred, but in a cool, premeditated desire for justice.

There was no hatred in him, he told himself, no jealousy or envy. His reason rested solely on the need for the honour of his family to be restored. And, since it couldn't be done by legal means, it seemed suddenly that murder might somehow prove that an injustice had been done. In the instant blinding clarity of his thoughts, in his new exalted state of mind, he couldn't conceive of other people recoiling from him in shame or disgust or horror.

His first need, he felt, was for a suitable weapon. The Smith and Wesson was too clumsy for an act such as he was contemplating. It was dangerously inaccurate, particularly in crowds, and in his twisted way, Boderin liked to consider himself a humane man who didn't want to hurt anyone. The obvious answer, since he was an excellent shot, was to use a rifle.

He had been on the point of heading towards Père Lachaise to pick up the hunting rifle he knew was kept locked up at the apartment there, when he had realized that inevitably the police would be watching the place. The answer seemed to be to acquire a new one. So, remembering a little gun shop on the Ile St Louis, behind Notre Dame, where he had more than once bought fishing tackle, he drove there, parked his car under the trees and went inside.

The old musty interior smelt of gun-oil and grease and the scent of new canvas and leather. All around him were stacked rifles and fishing rods and cases of hunting knives. On one counter was a display of small Belgian automatics and boxes of ammunition and a notice, *If you are in the habit of travelling alone, or returning home late at night, or camping in remote spots, why not be prepared to defend yourself against footpads?*

For a while, with the assistance of the proprietor, he inspected the rifles, weighing them in his hands, then, as he turned, he saw a policeman standing outside in the road alongside his car, rocking on his heels. Immediately, he took fright. He had almost decided on a British-made rifle with a telescopic sight, but he abruptly pushed it away from him with the excuse that he would return later and consider it again.

"But, Monsieur—" The proprietor, who had been congratulating himself on an easy sale, looked disappointed. "It's such a perfect gun."

"I have no money on me just now——"

"We'll accept a cheque, Monsieur, with pleasure——"

"I've forgotten my cheque book!"

At the *ting* of the doorbell, the policeman looked up and Boderin lowered his head, pretending to look into the shop window. Hurrying towards the Métro subway, he decided to return later in the day to pick up the car.

When he reached street level again in the Gare d'Orléans on the other side of the river, he was struck by the number of police on duty and, assuming they were looking for him, he promptly turned round and descended into the Métro once more. For a long time, he rode round the city heedless of where he was going, before hunger finally drove him to the surface again. He emerged this time near Montmartre and, finding a small restaurant in a back street, ate there.

There was a wireless blaring on the counter and the proprietor, the waitress, and a couple of customers were listening to a commentary on a match between Rheims and some Spanish team.

"Leblanc s'avance"—the harsh voice of the announcer made it difficult for him to concentrate, anxious as he was to form some sort of plan—*"Il controle le ballon très facilement."*

The waiter and the proprietor slapped their thighs.

"A Mattea, à Billadola, à—mais non, Evergne l'a pris——"

He ordered a steak and wine and decided to put off making his plans until he had time to think. The match finished and the proprietor reached behind the tired plants that surrounded the Marie Brizard and pernod bottles, and switched to a thunderous musical programme. Back-slapping men appeared, to discuss the result of the match, and the proprietor, a toothpick between his lips, joined in the hilarity as he busied himself behind the Espresso machine.

Fighting to shut out the noise, Robert Boderin tried to decide where he'd gone wrong at Orly. To succeed next time, he must know where they'd failed.

He'd been so careful, he thought. He and Blot had stood in the airport entrance on several occasions as the planes arrived and departed, watching the passengers and working out just which way Murphy would go, and just where a man might stand to be near him.

He had been trembling with excitement and fear when he had finally taken up his position, and had had to make a tremendous effort to quieten his nerves. He'd been able to see well and no one, not even police or aides-de-camp, could have interfered. He might even have gone almost unnoticed, he realized, and one blow of the whip would have been enough. It would have been in every headline in the country by evening and would have flown across the world in no time.

"GENERAL BODERIN AVENGED!"

He started abruptly out of his glowing daydream. It hadn't gone like that! There'd been no blow, he remembered bitterly, and no headlines.

Sitting in his little oasis of silence in the noisy bar, he reproached himself that he had not been clever enough. It should have been so easy to step up to Murphy as he passed. The thing should have been over before anyone could have stopped them. He had felt dedicated and martyred, he remembered, thinking of the things he'd given up, of the life he'd tried to live for the improvement of his family's fortunes.

He had written a note to his father, vaguely explaining what he'd intended to do, so that the old man would know there was one Boderin at least to whom family honour mattered. He had even paid his tax dues and cleared up all his affairs. He'd never before felt like paying taxes to the half-witted governments that ruled France, but he had wanted everything to be clear at that moment because he'd fully expected to end up in gaol.

He had even written to the girl at Vincennes ending the affair between them completely. There had been a terrible scene when she had come to see him, and it had been difficult to explain to her, without going into details, that it wasn't because he'd grown tired of her. She'd even threatened to shoot him and herself too, though he'd suspected that was only a little Gallic drama.

He still felt vaguely fretful about the way people had reacted. He suspected, in fact, that Blot had privately laughed at his ideas in his dull, peasant way.

Blot was stupid, narrow and despicable, he decided. He was

perpetually frightened of the authorities—because, he suspected, he had no honour and was occasionally on the wrong side of the law. He had joined in Boderin's activities originally as a joke and had even sworn the dramatic oath Boderin had pushed on him as a joke too, faintly embarrassed and awkward. Boderin would almost have preferred him not to be in the plot, but he had needed a companion, not so much to provide help, as to explain his ideas to, so that if anything had happened to him—in case some hot-headed policeman had drawn his pistol—there would have been someone who could explain what it was all about. He had even written a will in case of accidents.

Everything had seemed so straightforward—but for the students. He had never dreamed there would be so many.

He had all along been faintly irritated, he remembered bitterly, by the discovery that the students had planned a demonstration for the one day he'd chosen for his own great coup. There was about student demonstrations a sort of hysteria that didn't go with the exaltation he'd wished to feel.

He had even worked up his emotion over a matter of days visiting the red marble tombstone in Père Lachaise with all its aura of history and sense of sacrifice. He had even visited the Invalides and stared at Détailles's spirited paintings in the Musée de l'Armée; and gazed down beneath the great brassy dome that dwarfed the whole of the Quartier St Germain, on the red catafalque of Napoleon, caught by the sense of timelessness in the names of Moscowa, Marengo, Austerlitz, Wagram, Friedland, Jena and Rivoli that circled it; feeling somehow that the great Emperor, flanked by the tombs of Turenne and Foch and the King of Rome with their hooded marble mutes, would somehow have understood how he felt.

The noise in the restaurant grew louder, interrupting his brooding, and after a while, he could stand it no longer and he hurried out and took the Métro east towards Père Lachaise.

Even as he turned into the Rue du Douleur, he saw Blot standing on the corner, combing his hair one-handed as he smoked. As soon as he saw Robert Boderin, he threw away his cigarette and hurried towards him, smiling nervously in a way that infuriated Boderin.

Blot was still suffering from a strong sense of guilt. He knew he'd deserted at the crucial moment, but the sight of Souprosse's wedge of policemen advancing across the entrance hall had destroyed the last vestige of enthusiasm he'd managed to feel for the operation and he had turned and fled. Outside, a taxi had just been turning and Blot had fallen into it, shouting to the driver to get him into the city as fast as possible.

"You can't go home," he said quickly as Boderin approached, taking his arm in an over-friendly ingratiating way that grated on Boderin's nerves. "The flics are hanging around. They've been questioning me on and off half the day. They don't know about the whip. They think you want to shoot him."

"I do."

Blot ignored the words, thinking he'd misheard, and took Boderin's arm again, pulling him aside, offering cigarettes and matches, talking nervously all the time at full speed.

"What happened?" he demanded. "Where've you been all this time? Where's the car?"

"I had to leave it. I've been riding round in the Métro all afternoon."

"Well, you can't go home. It was awful, wasn't it? And I thought we'd got it all safely tied up."

"There were too many of those damned students of Nicole's."

"What about your father? Did you know the police have got him?"

"He'll be all right," Boderin muttered. "They can't do a thing to him. He only had pamphlets. Pamphlets!" he said bitterly. "Holy Mother of God, what good do pamphlets do?"

"What good does horsewhipping do?" Blot said gloomily, wishing he were free of the whole business.

"None at all," Boderin said quietly. "None at all."

Once again, Blot thought he had misheard and took no notice, and Boderin walked away, galvanized into action, his resolution hardening all the time, his thin figure taut with nervous tension. "Suppose they ask him questions?" Blot asked, running up behind him.

"He knows nothing about us." Boderin flung the words over his shoulder. "We've nothing to be afraid of." He stopped abruptly and swung round on Blot who backed away quickly.

"For the love of Heaven," he said, "that's in the past. Why worry about that? I've got to find somewhere to go. I can't afford to have them arrest me. They've got the stations watched. I've seen them. I can't leave the city. What about your place? Can't I hide there?"

Blot had stopped dead, his eyes wide, his jaw dropped.

"My God!" he said. "Not likely! Martine would never let you stay there. You know what she's like. She'd make life unbearable."

"I've got to have somewhere." Boderin looked at Blot, suddenly desperate, his eyes wild, his manner urgent and afraid. "For God's sake, Blot, show some intelligence. Don't you know anywhere? You're a house agent. You must know of some small hotel in the city that no one uses. Don't tell me you've never taken a girl to some place where you can't be found."

Blot looked uncomfortable. "There's a place in Montparnasse," he said. "It belonged to a friend of mine. It's in the Rue du Maine. It's only small, but it's safe. No one'll ask questions. I've been there once or twice when—well, you understand." Blot looked sheepish and Boderin knew that he'd been there with girls. "You can lie low there as long as you like."

"You'll have to keep me supplied with food," Boderin said.

"All right. All right. But, let's get going." Blot looked nervous, half-hoping that when he had safely deposited Boderin in Montparnasse he might be able to bow himself out and have nothing further to do with his fantastic schemes.

But Boderin seemed disinclined to let him forget them.

"I've not finished, Blot," he said harshly.

"I know that."

"I shall try again."

"That's all right. Only shut up and let's get away from here. Let's pick up a taxi."

"You're a good friend, Pierrot!"

Blot looked nervous. "I need to be," he said. "With all the flics looking for you like this."

Boderin managed a smile. "They're not looking for me now," he said. "I left my car by the Seine. They'll think I've thrown myself in. They'll not bother us any more."

Major Schneider stared through his window to where he could see the sun falling on the square towers of Notre Dame. It was late afternoon and the white of the midday glare had vanished. The sun was reaching now to the west, and as it sank the amber hues grew stronger.

He sat smoking slowly, holding his cigarette awkwardly in his crippled hand. On the desk in front of him, a file was open and he was staring at it from time to time, as though to refresh his memory. Opposite him, Souprosse sat, stooping slightly, his thick fair hair standing up on his bullet head, his heavy shoulders hunched like a great bull's.

"He obviously wasn't intending to commit suicide," he was saying slowly. "Wonder why the devil he left his car."

Schneider turned, unbending, his back still straight as though he were on a parade ground, staring with a faint contempt at Souprosse's slouching shoulders and thick neck, the unruly stiff hair, the plain artisan's face so much in contrast to his own moulded features. Schneider was never quite certain whether to be contemptuous of Souprosse for his working-class background or to admire him for his shrewd brain.

He reached across to the file and pushing papers aside, he extracted a document and slid it across the desk.

"This girl out at Vincennes," he said. "Name of"—he paused, leaning over to consult the paper—"Jacqueline du Largy. I think she was his mistress, though she won't admit to it. He broke it off a few days ago without giving any good reason." He withdrew another sheet of paper and skated it over the desk. "That's a report from his bank," he said. "He drew about nine hundred thousand francs a week ago from the Société Générale in the Boulevard Haussmann. It looks very much as though he intended to flee the country."

He considered the folder in front of him for a moment. "Better have a man watch the girl's apartment," he said. "He might try and get back to her. Put one on the sister's apartment in the Rue Jacob, too, and one on the place where the old man's staying. We can't take any chances. There was a note to his father, by the way. It turned up at Chartres."

He began to read.

"*Dear father,*" he said. "*What I am about to do will be mis-*

interpreted by most people but I'm sure that you at least will understand. I trust you will forgive me and believe that it was done for France—Robert."

"That all?" Souprosse's eyebrows rose.

"That's all."

"Not much, is it?" Souprosse seemed unimpressed. He had a titbit of news too, and he had been saving it up. There had always been a competitive spirit between them to see who could unearth most and, whenever they worked together, they behaved a little like schoolboys, Schneider the senior prefect, Souprosse the junior who enjoyed shaking his dignity.

"Did you know we found a will?" he asked.

Schneider looked surprised, but he recovered quickly and shrugged. "Inevitable, I suppose," he said coolly. "Where?"

"Deposited with other papers at his office. It makes everything in favour of his father and his sister. It's not inconsiderable either."

"The Lespinasse breweries brought quite a bit of money to the Boderins," Schneider commented. "Anything special in it?"

"No. Quite straightforward. There's a sum for the Lamballer woman." Souprosse looked up. "You noticed, of course, how the old man dried up about her? Was she his mistress?"

Schneider nodded coldly. "Of course," he said. "France nearly died in 1940 because of political busybodies like her. I had the Nice police look into her. She no longer has any interests round Paris. She sold up all her property here some months ago. Go on about the will."

"Nothing to it," Souprosse said, "except that it indicates he was quite serious about making this attempt against Murphy and was prepared to die for it if necessary."

Schneider ground out his cigarette in a large ashtray bearing a St Raphael advert.

"We've found the printer who set up those pamphlets for the old man," he said. "He didn't report it until he read the paper today. Why should he? He's always printing pamphlets of one sort or another. France has always suffered from too many words."

"Any others involved?" Souprosse asked.

"Could be. I think we ought to pick up anybody who was even

153

faintly connected with the Friends of Truth. What's the name of that damned man———?"

"Edérède."

Schneider nodded. "Try him first," he said. "Have you anything on him we can use to hold him with?"

Souprosse grinned. "Not likely. He's too clever. Like his name. Whichever way round you turn him, he still looks the same."

"We'll have to find something," Schneider said absently. "It's a pity we had our sights so firmly fixed on the father we failed to see the son. You have the stations watched, of course?"

"Naturally. *And* the roads."

"Think he might try to get to Algiers?"

Souprosse shook his head. "Why should he? He's in no trouble. He made no threat to Murphy. He hasn't been found in possession of a gun. All we know is that his father's guns are missing, that he's written a letter and hints at some action he's careful not to describe, and that he's now disappeared from his home, and from his work. If we find him, what are we to charge him with?"

"Doubtless the Prosecution Department could find something," Schneider said coldly. "We can't take a chance on him having another go."

"Another go at what? He hasn't had a go at anything yet."

Schneider looked faintly irritated and extracted another sheet of paper from his file. "It might interest you," he said with the air of a chess-player producing his queen, "to know that I've found a report on this young man. Eighteen months ago, he became involved in a brawl with an American student whom he found with his sister. He went to horsewhip him."

Souprosse grinned. "He seems to have a penchant for horsewhips. Did he get away with it?"

"No."

"That's the worst of these Americans," Souprosse said. "They're so damn' big. Go on."

"There was quite an uproar," Schneider said, his nose wrinkling as though anything as undignified as a scene revolted him. "There was an assault charge and Boderin's advocate put up a defence on the grounds of emotional instability. He offered a

154

psycho-analyst's report on him. Here it is. Dr André Sif-Guédella."

"Any good?" Souprosse asked.

"It shows us what we're up against." Schneider studied the paper and began to read. *"Nicholas Robert Jean de Lespinasse-Boderin du Crest,"* he quoted out loud. *"Father*—we know about him"—there was a polished irony in his voice. "In fact we know about the whole family." His lips moved again as he read half-aloud for a moment. *"Mother, daughter of a soldier with a strong military background. Died in Amiens after the Liberation. Son at school under the Germans."* He looked up, lowering the paper. "That, my dear Souprosse," he said, "was the first seed of resentment." His eyes fell to the paper once more and his lips moved again. *"Brothers dead . . . leg broken . . .* There's your sense of inadequacy, Souprosse . . . *joined anti-H-bomb movement . . . fired from his job . . ."*

Schneider looked up again. "Here are some of Dr Sif-Guédella's comments," he said, continuing to read. *"Unless under strain a young man of unusual warmth and charm. In general, kind, unobtrusive, law-abiding and serious—too serious, in fact. Hot-tempered when motivated by resentment or imagined grievances chiefly stemming from various brushes with Americans."*

"Of such things are assassins made," Souprosse said ponderously.

Schneider nodded and continued to read. *"Politically vehement, but never belonging to any subversive organization. Merely unstable, flitting from one creed to another! Self-centred, easily moved by hate or love."* Schneider raised his eyes. "There is, it seems, a taint of insanity in his family," he said. "Very lightly marked, of course, but it's there."

He lifted the paper once more. *"In a more or less depressed state from time to time,"* he continued, *"particularly since the accident which prevented him following his family profession. He had a tendency to unbalanced opinions and to the creation of morbid and delusive projects. A tendency to misinterpret affairs of a complex nature, which he managed to connect with himself, the starting point being the exaggerated self-feeling of the morbid egotist."*

155

"You couldn't want better evidence than that," Souprosse commented dryly.

"In short," Schneider concluded, "all distinct paranoidal indications. All these delusions of grandeur, this sense of being conspired against, this over-emphasizing of his family's importance, this feeling that the Americans are against him. A rebel, without the normal aim of a rebel—to upset the framework of society and replace it with another one. His aims are satisfactory to himself alone, though he seems to think they would benefit France. All distinct psychopathic tendencies. And, when you think of it, what else were his father's?"

"Perhaps we *had* better pull him in on some excuse," Souprosse admitted ruefully.

"I've studied assassins," Schneider said, clearly enjoying himself. "They're invariably small men with big notions, with personal animosity as an ingredient. Their country's always important to them and the possibility of the gallows at the end of the road makes no difference. Their causes are always transcendent and they're invariably in the grip of a delusion. With the exception of a few—the assassination of Alexander of Yugoslavia at Marseilles, for example, and the murder at Sarajevo— they're invariably lone operators."

He put his finger tips together as though giving a lecture. "It's our duty," he said, "to protect the President and members of the Government—even though sometimes I'd like to pull the trigger myself against some of them—together with important foreign visitors. General Murphy comes under that heading. I think we should talk to him. In the meantime, we'll go along with the newspapers and let people think young Boderin *has* committed suicide. If he thinks we're no longer looking for him, it may make him careless."

Cellini looked tired when he appeared at Hardy's flat and his mouth was sour with too many cigarettes.

Vigueur had demanded a special on the Boderin Affair and he had been up half the night pounding his typewriter, telephoning contacts and finding photographs. He'd tried to play the story down as much as he could, his newspaperman's instincts struggling hard against the desire not to give pain to Nicole, but he was still uncertain and unhappy. It only needed an over-enthusiastic sub and a slap-happy picture editor to destroy all the balance he'd tried to give to the story.

Nicole was standing by the window when he arrived, staring at her face in the mirror, while Hardy sat smoking on the divan bed.

There was something veiled and obscure in Nicole's expression, and Hardy suspected she'd lived so long and unnaturally with her father's obsession that in her life there hadn't been much room for kindness and normality, and she was now seeking them both with a fierceness that was angry and abnormal.

He had been startled by the ferocity of her love-making, the urgent desires of someone who had been thwarted of warmth for half her life. She had turned to him again on waking, passionate, demanding, and in her glance now there was something of shame and fear, and plea to him to keep it all to himself.

While she finished putting the make-up on her face, he and Cellini went downstairs to the little bar below and Cellini bought them coffee.

"Did she stay here all night?" Cellini asked quickly, his voice sharp with anger. He seemed faintly shocked and desperately disappointed.

Hardy nodded. Cellini swallowed. "What about you?" he demanded thickly. "Where did *you* sleep?"

"I went along the corridor," Hardy lied. "There's a striptease artist lives there, who works near the Bobino and she's always willing to put on private performances."

Cellini frowned. He had a headache with worrying about the story he'd written and Hardy's blank face irritated him.

"You kidding?" he said bitterly.

It was on Hardy's lips to tell Cellini the truth. He knew Cellini regarded him as a failure and he felt a great temptation to boast. But then he thought of Nicole, shivering from reaction and misery, tormenting herself with a feeling of guilt and rushing to Hardy's arms again because she needed reassurance. He wasn't certain yet of his own feelings, because there was a nagging feeling in him that he had taken the easiest way out when he should have resisted; but they had needed each other and he preferred to remember her warm and passionate and glowing with the knowledge that she was wanted.

157

"Yes," he said, nodding. "I'm kidding. I went to see Ernestine at St Denis. I've just got back."

Cellini seemed doubtful but satisfied. "I've got to find her somewhere to go," he said. "She can't go on living alone in that damned place in the Rue Jacob."

"What's wrong with here?"

"Well——" Cellini looked embarrassed. "I guess I'm not sure that this is the best place for her. This district. This apartment, Sam—you know what I mean——"

"Sure, I know the trouble. Me."

"Hell, Sam——" Cellini looked unhappy. "I was only thinking of the girl. She needs security."

"Security's a habit," Hardy said dryly. "Like insecurity. I wish you wouldn't try to sound like God, or even His representative in this *arrondissement*."

"Everybody needs security," Cellini persisted sharply.

"Sure. People'll do any kind of dirt for security—kill, thieve, marry even."

Cellini frowned, goaded to stubbornness by Hardy's bland mockery. "I think she ought to get away from Paris," he said. "It's too full of memories. Every time she goes past the Arc de Triomphe or the War Ministry or the Ecole Militaire it's bound to hurt a bit. I'd give anything to break that damn' family's stranglehold on her. I've already compromised my professional reputation trying to play down a story I've written. It seems such a damn' shame to put more on her than she can stand. This blasted family of hers seems to pervade every one of these god-damned apartments of theirs."

"All the more reason why she should stay here," Hardy suggested. "You could hardly call this dump redolent of glory."

"Maybe you're right at that." Cellini still looked doubtful. "It was the brother, of course, who took the guns from Chartres. I think he intended to kill Murphy yesterday out at Orly."

Hardy seemed unimpressed. "He may have intended to kill himself and drop dead at Murphy's feet," he said. "You know how the French like to make gestures."

Cellini nodded gloomily. "Could be," he agreed. "Did you know I've been checking army records? That driver who hit him with a lorry wasn't drunk at all."

158

"I never thought he was."

"He was a sergeant with a first-rate record of sobriety and common sense. He's still serving, as a matter of fact. He's a captain now. And deservedly so, it seems. My people found him and spoke to him. The boy was so busy cheering at the lorry in front, he never saw the lorry behind. It's all in his own mind, this business about the driver being drunk. It's just an obsession against Americans." He paused. "This kid, Nicole, she's had a hell of a time, I reckon."

"So I gather," Hardy said dryly. "However, I think you'll find her rather more pliable and helpful now—far more of a Lager Lespinasse than a Boderin or a du Crest."

★ 4 ★

GENERAL MURPHY and Colonel Franks weren't quite sure what to make of Schneider and Souprosse when they arrived. The two Frenchmen in their turn, knowing how much they were paid to look after General Murphy and what sort of home it provided, were faintly resentful at the lavishness of the Avenue Foch apartment.

"*Formidable*," Souprosse breathed as they paused outside the door.

"So many times," Schneider murmured as he jabbed at the bell with the mouthpiece of his pipe, "I've heard them say 'Why does no one like us in Europe?' But one's only got to look around. No one likes anyone who lives better than he does himself. If their purses were only half as fat, if their clothes were only half as good, if their men were only half as tall and their women only half as handsome, they'd find that *everybody* liked them. The British have never been so popular in France as they are now that they're no longer the leaders of the world. We have a common sympathy here in Europe with poverty."

With his natural antipathy to Transatlantics, he was already half-decided to dislike Murphy, but he found himself completely won over by the General's natural friendliness, and by Franks's aristocratic charm.

"We don't think for a minute"—Schneider came to the point

159

at once—"that Robert Boderin has destroyed himself at all. We don't think his body will ever appear in the Seine."

"Neither did I," Murphy said with a smile.

Schneider looked surprised. Somehow, it had never occurred to him that the Americans would be reasoning along the same lines as himself and would reach the same conclusion.

"Why didn't you think so?" he asked, interested.

"You forget," Murphy said, "I knew his father. I knew him well, and I gather the son's very much the same type. I would say that neither of them would make a somewhat shabby gesture of this kind. If they were going to make a gesture, they'd do it in style. The Boderins don't like darkness."

Schneider nodded, accepting that Murphy was no fool.

"I think you're right," he said. "Though I reached *my* conclusions by a different route: We've heard that about the time when he must have first left his car on the Ile St Louis, he was considering buying a British rifle with a telescopic sight from a shop there. In the end he left without it. There was a policeman nearby and the proprietor thinks he may have taken fright."

Murphy raised his eyebrows and Franks looked worried, but neither of them spoke.

"The proprietor's come forward," Schneider went on. "At first he didn't connect the two things, but gradually he began to wonder if the man who came into his shop could possibly be the man whose name's been mentioned so often in the papers. Somehow, the attempted purchase of the rifle seemed sinister, and, in the end, he felt obliged to walk along to police headquarters and report it. I think we can accept that the man who did, in fact, attempt to buy the rifle was Robert de Lespinasse-Boderin du Crest."

Murphy smiled. "Major," he said. "That sure is a mouthful. I can quite imagine anyone with a name like that getting to worry about it. With a name like that, it wouldn't be beyond the bounds of possibility that he'd take a notion to shoot someone just for missing off a few syllables."

Schneider, whose name, when he was at home with his family at Mülhouse in Alsace, was François-Pierre Harcourt D'Appeli-Schneider, didn't smile.

"Furthermore," he went on, "now that we've had the time to

make investigations and people have had time to think about it, several others have come forward who've heard him speak angrily of the American nation from time to time. It's clearly an obsession that he's made no attempt to hide. There's a barman at the bar he frequented on his way home from his office, a friend of his near St Cloud, and a girl with whom he was—er—connected, who lives in Vincennes."

Murphy nodded, his face sombre, and Schneider went on soberly. "We have also had a man come forward by the name of Achille St Martin. He's an actor of sorts, and an acquaintance of Boderin's. He says Boderin lent him money from time to time when he was in difficulties. Some time ago, Boderin asked him if he were prepared to join a conspiracy to horsewhip you."

Murphy glanced quickly at Franks. "Horsewhip?" he said.

Schneider nodded. "Horsewhip," he repeated firmly. "In fact, I have begun to wonder if that isn't what he actually intended at Orly. We found a horsewhip in his car."

"My God!"

"However, don't let us underestimate him," Schneider went on. "I don't think for a moment that horsewhipping is what will be in his mind now. It seems he did a great deal of talking to the man St Martin and there was once even reference to assassination." Schneider screwed a monocle into his eye and consulted his notebook.

"At first he called it a business deal and asked the man St Martin if he were interested. When the man St Martin said he'd be interested in anything that would bring him money, Boderin told him there wouldn't be much money in it but a great deal of honour. Asked for details, Boderin hedged and muttered, until the man St Martin begged him to speak out, and he then announced that he was engaged in a conspiracy to horsewhip General Murphy."

Schneider looked up at Murphy who was sitting unmoved. "The man St Martin was startled."

"I guess I'd have been startled too," Murphy commented.

Schneider hesitated for a second then went on in the same monotonous voice as he read his notes. "He was not *unduly* startled, however," he said, "because he had on other occasions heard Boderin talk even of crossing to the United States for this very purpose and had not put much faith in the suggestion. Now, however, Boderin said, '*You wish to join me in this?*'

"The man St Martin replied—in fun, you understand, of course—'*Why not shoot him and have done with it?*' Boderin's reply to this was '*That's an idea. Will you help?*' The man St Martin immediately told him not to be ridiculous."

"Good for the man St Martin," Murphy said.

Schneider didn't seem amused. "The man St Martin," he continued sombrely, "made an excuse and tried to leave, but Boderin insisted on talking, and they stood for some twenty minutes arguing. In the end, Boderin extracted a promise from the man St Martin that he would not betray him and, thinking that Boderin was a little drunk or ill, St Martin gave the promise. Although he discussed it with his wife, he thought no more about it until he saw the papers which made reference to General Boderin's attempt to pamphletize you, and the absence of Robert Boderin and the fact that two guns were missing. On learning this, he immediately came to see the police and was brought to me."

Schneider snapped his book shut. "It's because of this very thing," he said briskly, "that I'm anxious to have your permission to have you guarded at all times."

"No!" Murphy barked the word at once and Schneider looked startled. "No, Major. I'm not going to have a squad of cops following me around. Neither yours nor ours. I've made up my mind on this score—for reasons of my own. I'm not afraid of being shot at. In fact, if I *am* shot at, it might give me the answer to a few questions that have been worrying me. I'm not being stubborn. I'm not even being difficult. I've just made up my mind that if the French people want me so little that they're prepared to kill me, perhaps I shouldn't be here."

"Robert Boderin's not the French people."

"I'll have to accept for the purposes of argument, that he is."

Franks joined in. "General, how can you take that view? Young Boderin's obviously obsessed by what he considers an injustice done to his family. I know, you know, the major here knows, I'm sure, that it was *no injustice*."

Murphy seemed to pause. "It's an unfortunate thing," he said gently, "but a soldier's pay's often disgrace. I've nothing against General Boderin as an individual. He merely suffered because the system's what it is. If he'd been a civilian and wavered or failed, all that would have happened to him would have been that he'd have lost a lot of money and probably gone bust. A civilian can be a coward or brave—or just ordinary—and he remains what he is, a boss, an executive or merely a worker. A soldier has to face up to the possibility of dying or being responsible for other people dying, and the few seconds out of his life when this occurs can stamp him for ever. If he loses his nerve, it's not just a ticking off he gets from the boss or the loss of a few profits. It's disgrace, and for the rest of his life. He wears it round his neck like a collar. And if he's a general and important enough to get his name in the papers *the collar's made of lead*."

"That's not your fault," Franks said.

"No, I guess not. If he failed in that system, maybe it's because he should have belonged to another system, or because too much was expected of him all his life. But when we think this way, we're starting to complicate matters. Let's just say that for me, young Boderin represents the French people. Let's let it lie and see how the French nation reacts. It won't be difficult to see what they feel about it. I guess they'll give us their answer in the end."

"There are many subversive societies on my files," Schneider said. "I might say in confidence that I even know of one composed of fanatical anti-communist officers of the French Army who have sworn to assassinate Khrushchev if he ever sets foot in France. We feel you should be protected."

Murphy shook his head. "Let's just let it slide," he persisted.

Schneider and Souprosse rose. In the corridor outside, Franks touched Schneider's arm. "The General's a very humble man," he said. "In spite of his high office, Major, he doesn't consider himself very important."

"I quite understand," Schneider said. "However, we have our job to do. I assume he has no United States troops with him when he moves."

"He won't hear of it."

"Then we'll endeavour to see that he's shadowed, unknown to him, wherever he goes. I think that can be arranged, eh, Inspector?"

Souprosse nodded and Schneider turned to Franks.

"I assume that you, personally, wouldn't object to that, Colonel?"

Franks smiled wearily. "Personally," he said, "I'd be very happy about it. I happen to think a great deal more about the General than he does himself."

Back inside the apartment, Murphy looked up from his desk as Franks entered. "Don't tell me you've been up to something secretive with those guys, Prof," he said.

"No," Franks lied. "I haven't. You said not, so that's it, as far as I'm concerned. If you want to get shot to hell and gone, that's your affair."

"Don't let it burn you up, Frankie."

"Well, hell, it's so goddam' silly—you've got to move about the place."

Murphy's eyes fell on a newspaper on his desk and Franks could see he was looking at his own name in the headlines. He was frowning now but this time it was only a frown of weariness.

"Frankie," he said. "Do you think it would be a good idea if we saw this guy, Boderin, after all? Had a chat with him? Gave him some gum? Sent him home happy? I get tired of all this trouble."

Franks shook his head. "No, general. That would be wrong."

"Even to have the guy in for a drink?"

"Even to give him a drink. All sorts of things might be read into the gesture. Weakness. Bribery. Cunning. God knows what. We can't afford gestures. We've got to think NATO-wise. Out at SHAPE we're not American, English, French, German."

"It doesn't seem much to do for the poor guy, all the same."

"I quite agree. It occurred to me, too, and I contacted the Embassy."

"No dice?"

"They thought it would be very wrong. They want it all to be forgotten. There's too much publicity of the wrong sort coming your way. There's even talk of——" Franks paused and Murphy looked up.

"Of pulling me back home?" he asked.

Franks nodded unhappily. "It can't go on," he said.

"No, I guess not." Murphy frowned. "I might be a NATO

164

officer, but I'm still an American and with all this mud-slinging going on, a bit of the dirt's bound to stick in the wrong place. After all, I guess there aren't many people who really know it's an international force with international officers and men. To most people, I'm still an American."

Franks gestured. "They were right, you know," he said indicating the door through which Schneider and Souprosse had gone. "About protection, I mean. This Boderin can sit on almost any corner where you're going to be and take a pot at you. You've got to move about. For instance, in case you don't know, you're going down to Percéval in the Bligues for a start."

Murphy looked up, delighted. "Prof, you fixed it already?"

Franks nodded. "Yep," he said. "I fixed it. There's a letter from Chatelin de Bruneval. The man you mentioned."

"No? Say, that's nice."

"He's got a few others round him. Marchand was one you mentioned, I remember. And two or three others. He wishes you to meet them."

Murphy began to smile. "That's nice of them," he said.

"It's more than you deserve," Franks said bitterly. "All this refusing to have someone keep an eye on you."

"Go on, Prof," Murphy said firmly.

"They suggest that they'd like you to accompany them to the battlefield and lay a wreath on the war graves and take wine and food with them afterwards. They've informed the local newspaper."

"Oh, hell, these Frenchmen, they sure like to play it big, don't they?"

"Well, that's the way it is," Franks said, "and in view of the press you've been getting, I'm going all the way with them. You meeting all these old boys with their medals should be just the thing to shut the newspapers up."

Murphy nodded doubtfully. "I'm glad to go, of course," he said. "Not just because it'll give me a better press. But because these guys fought with me. I thought they were the tops and I still do. If the French Army had been officered by men like those guys instead of the stiff-necked stuffed shirts they did have, there'd have been no 1940. Go ahead, Frankie, I'll do as you say."

Franks smiled. "Well, I'm glad that's fixed without much effort," he said. "Because you're already late for your meeting with the Air Force."

"Those two cops," Murphy explained sheepishly.

"You're a general," Franks said severely. "You're expected to *enjoy* meetings. Besides, SACEUR'll be there. Let's see you off. I've got the car waiting."

"Are *you* coming?"

"Not if I can help it. I've got things to attend to. CINCENT for one. They want me over there. These old gents from Percéval for another. You'll have to find someone else to talk to today."

Murphy smiled wryly. "O.K.," he said. "I'll try." He paused. "Isn't it today that Eddie Sligo's coming in to see me?" he asked.

Franks nodded. "I hoped you'd forgotten that."

"Why?"

"Because *I* hadn't forgotten it. And when this damned summons came to meet the Air Force I knew I'd have to put him off. It worried me. I was just hoping it wasn't worrying you."

"Well, I'm sorry to disappoint you: It is. Look, Frankie, we've go to do something for this guy. When have I got a free hour?"

"You haven't. Not till you come back from Percéval."

Murphy thought for a moment. "Well, look," he said. "We can't let the guy down. This is a guy who's done his country proud. He's a right to expect a few favours. Fix something, Frankie, or by God, I'll get you posted to Alaska."

Franks smiled. "I'll think of something," he said. "Leave it to me."

He watched Murphy disappear in the direction of the lift, then he returned to his desk and, picking up the letter from Percéval, started to draft out a reply. He was happily engaged in working this out, when the door opened and a sergeant put his head round.

"Sir," he said. "There's a guy here called Sligo. Says he's got an appointment to see the General."

Franks sighed. This was going to be difficult. There'd been no way round it. Murphy had had to go. He'd practically received an order.

"Show him in," he said.

Sligo came in smartly, in civilian clothes. For a moment,

Franks thought he was going to salute, then he seemed to change his mind, and Franks held out his hand.

"Sit down, Sergeant," he said. "Have a cigarette?—cup of coffee?"

Sligo accepted the cigarette but shook his head at the offer of coffee. "No thanks, sir," he said. "I don't take much coffee these days. Kinda gives me indigestion. Guess it's a sign that it's time I retired."

Franks nodded and lit a cigarette himself. "Well, Sligo," he said. "I've got some bad news for you. The General isn't around."

Sligo's broad honest face—very much the same type of Irish face as the General's, Franks decided—lengthened considerably.

"He's not here?" he said, and Franks could hear the disappointment in his voice. "When *will* he be here sir? Shall I wait?"

Franks summoned up his courage. In face of Sligo's disappointment, he felt all his resolve turning to water.

"I'm afraid, Sergeant," he said, "that that would be waste of time. I can't tell you when the General's due back. It's as I warned you: Someone with more stars on his shoulder wanted him—the Supreme Commander himself."

"I don't mind waiting, sir."

"I know that, Sergeant, and if it were sensible to wait, I'd try to make you comfortable, or at least tell you when to come back." Franks scratched his head, uncomfortable in front of Sligo's unhappiness. "But, listen, the General was most insistent that we fixed something up. He was keen to meet you. And I'm not just kidding you along, not just telling you that to please you. He really was."

"I thought he might be," Sligo said simply.

"It doesn't give me much pleasure having to disappoint you, Sergeant," Franks went on. "But things have cropped up. He's got to go to Percéval in the Bligues. The French there want to meet him. *Want to*. And, in view of the bad press he's been getting, he's got to go. He's got to start getting some *good* press. I'm sure you see that."

"Yeah. Sure, sir." Sligo tried hard, but he still felt that maybe he was more important than a few Frenchmen. However, he tried to go along with Franks.

"That'll only take two days," Franks continued. "But he's going to be away from here for two days, and while he's here those two days away are going to crowd the rest of his time. If you could come back after it's all over, I'm sure there'll be no snags. I promise you that. I want you to believe that we're doing our best for you—not army-wise, but between friends. Don't give up."

Sligo grinned. "After thirty years of trying, sir," he said, "I guess I can go on trying a bit longer."

After Sligo had gone, Franks stared at the door for some time, then he got up and began to prowl about the apartment, smoking, restless and uneasy. He had high hopes that the meeting with his old comrades at Percéval would help General Murphy a lot, but, somehow at the back of his mind, he had a feeling that, good as the idea was, it left the General far too vulnerable.

He wandered over to the window, where there was a pile of newspapers and magazines on a table, placed there for the General's benefit. He picked them up one after the other and stared at them. On his right there was a glimpse of the greenery of the Bois de Boulogne and on his left a side view of the Arc de Triomphe. But Franks had no eyes for the beauty of the city, absorbed as he was in the newspapers and their reports of the press conference.

Figaro had run a story to the effect that General Murphy's intention was purely to concentrate on his job. *Paris Soir* had stated quite simply what Murphy had said, that the *Affaire Boderin* had been closed for twelve years and that he had not arrived in France to reopen old wounds. Unfortunately, however, they'd put it in a box, in heavy type and surrounded by thick leads, so that, intentionally or not, it looked vaguely like a mourning paragraph. *Emancipation*—which had not even been present and had obtained its facts second-hand—strove for malice with an appeal for justice for General Boderin, then by clever cutting of Murphy's speech, made it appear that he had said point blank that he considered Boderin guilty as charged and that he was washing his hands of the whole business.

Murphy didn't come very well out of that one, Franks decided with a frown. It made him seem tough and hardboiled and transatlantic—the sort of American officer that *Emancipation* liked to present to its leaders.

He tossed the paper down in disgust, wishing he'd told the press about Sligo without giving the General a chance to object, and picked up *Vigueur*. They'd featured the story too, and inside there was a picture of Murphy in battle-dress sitting in a jeep surrounded by his staff at Percéval. There was a similar one of Boderin taken at Sidi Ifna. Then there was a composite of odd de Lespinasses and Boderins and Du Crests, and a screed that went with them that indicated how well the family had served France in the past, and finally a photograph of Boderin and Murphy together, both in battle-dress and backgrounded by a wrecked German Tiger tank and a group of smashed houses, shaking hands and surrounded by smiling members of their staff. The heading was 1944. *Amis: Maintenant*——" 1944. *Friends: Now*——?

Cellini had tried hard to be fair to Murphy without being cruel to Boderin and he hadn't completely succeeded in either aim, and the enthusiastic sub and the slap-happy picture editor he'd feared had completed the ruin.

Franks slammed the magazine on the table and stared bitterly out of the window, hoping against hope that nothing would go wrong at Percéval, that no interfering busybody of a journalist would see in it an opportunity to make copy of the wrong sort.

It seemed to Colonel Franks just then that General Murphy was badly in need of a break.

★ 5 ★

IT was pure whim that decided General Boderin to go to Percéval after Murphy—the culmination of a chain of events which had originally never seemed likely to lead there.

He had gone out to drink coffee in the Rue St Honoré and had picked up a *Vigueur* which someone had left behind. For a while, he glanced through it, unconcerned, drowsy, his mind occupied with the maps he'd been working on ever since the incident at Orly, then he sat up abruptly as he saw his own face staring at him from the glossy pages.

169

There was a wrecked Tiger tank in the background and some ruined houses, and himself and Murphy standing in the middle of the foreground, smiling. For a moment, it seemed to carry him back to the shrubby hillsides near Percéval. Gallifet was there, slight and wiry, his arms full of papers as they always were, ready to advise and make suggestions, and just behind him Devéria, a dark swarthy little man from the Jura who'd started his career as a private in the Legion. Even now, Boderin could remember his rough speech, very little improved with the commission they'd given him.

For a long time, he stared at the picture, then he slowly turned the page. There was a two-column photograph there of the Minister of War just leaving the Ministry, followed by a staff officer whom Boderin recognized as an old comrade but could not give a name to.

The Minister, said the caption, *is debating whether consideration should be given to General Boderin's request for a re-trial. It is believed in some quarters that he has great sympathy for General Boderin's suffering and feels that the time has come for reparations to be made. Because of the trouble in Algeria, the country needs officers of the calibre of General Boderin.*

The sub that Cellini had feared had gone in for sensation; and the picture editor, with the joyous irresponsibility of French journalists, had written into his captions something that wasn't even true. To the old soldier, his mind already obsessed with his imagined betrayal, it seemed like a shaft of light in the darkness.

Surely, he thought, if the Minister were considering it, now was the time to make another attempt to convince him. By tomorrow, he might have changed his mind under the influence of some shallow political manœuvre. General Boderin knew how these things worked. He'd already been sacrificed, he felt, to the single-mindedness of the Americans. At the moment, however, with the newspaper tide running against the United States, it seemed that the Government was inclined to be generous, and it suddenly became imperative that he should go at once to interview the Minister.

He glanced quickly at the date on the magazine, checking

how old it was, then he called the waiter and gave him a hundred-franc piece to order him a taxi.

As the taxi moved along the Rue de Rivoli in the shadow of the Louvre, General Boderin glanced upwards at the gallery of statues along the wall. Ney. Lannes. Masséna. Lassalle. Murat. Every one of Napoleon's marshals and a great many of his generals, each in his own niche and snow-capped by the pigeons. Then, as he shot past the Place des Pyramides, he caught a quick glimpse of the gilt statue of Joan of Arc. He was in good company, he thought.

By the time the taxi had reached Concorde, he was glowing with optimism. The Minister was considering his position. It said so in the magazine. With the naïvete of a man divorced from reality, he was already imagining himself restored to his rank and fortune. No more of that damned apartment out at Chartres. No more back-street cafés where he wouldn't be recognized, no more of the bitterness of his son that wearied him so much and made him feel so old. He'd soon be able to take his place again and hold up his head, looking in the eye those people who'd hummed and hahed every time he'd asked their help over the last fifteen years.

Outside the Ministry, in the Boulevard St Germain, a couple of students heading towards the Boul' Mich' spared him a quick glance, but took no further notice of the thin, erect old man in his out-moded clothes as he sat down on a bench for a second and with a handkerchief flicked the white dust of Paris from his shoes. Feeling smart and rejuvenated, he marched boldly into the Ministry, feeling that he might see there the first signs of a new interest in him, but the clerk on duty behind the big counter in the main entrance didn't even recognize him and was quite indifferent as he inquired his business.

"I want to see the Minister," General Boderin said peremptorily. "Is he in now?"

"I'll find out, Monsieur. You have an appointment?"

"No, I haven't."

"Then, Monsieur, I'm sorry——"

General Boderin frowned. "An appointment won't be necessary, I think you'll find," he said.

He extracted a card from his wallet and wrote beneath his name "*ancien général de brigade*" and added "*affaire pressante*".

The clerk eyed the card doubtfully, then took another look at the straight old man in front of his desk, recognizing him at last.

"Monsieur, I'm not sure——" he began, but General Boderin gestured irritably, reassured by the story he'd seen in the newspaper, his manner brusque and commanding.

"Please be good enough to send my card up to the Minister at once," he said.

The Secretary to the Minister was in a breezy mood when his assistant brought in General Boderin's card.

"Now what, Robineau?" he asked cheerfully. "What have you got there?"

The assistant hesitated, staring at the card in his hand. "Well, I'm not sure that it's important," he said.

"Everything's important in this ministry," the Secretary said. The Minister had not long been in office and there was a new-broom look about his personal assistants. "You know what the Minister says: 'Attention to detail must be our motto. Too often France has suffered because this particular Ministry failed to attend to details.' What is it?"

The assistant offered the card, by this time well thumbed. "It's only this," he said. "I thought perhaps I ought to let you see it; Major Nadauld says he's downstairs and not being very helpful."

The Minister's Secretary held the card at arm's length, squinting at it, then he reached across the desk for his spectacles.

"I've plenty of time at the moment," he said. "Even for people who are making a nuisance of themselves. Thank God I've got that damned artillery schedule off my hands at last. Let's see, who's this? *Nicholas Jean St Omer de Lespinasse-Boderin du*——"

He stopped dead and stared up at Robineau. "Here," he said quickly, thrusting the card back. "Send him away. I don't want to be mixed up in this business. Tell him I'm sick, I'm dead. Tell him what you like. Give him a drink. Give him a lottery ticket. Just get rid of him, that's all."

The telephone rang and he grabbed for the instrument. "No," he said at once, without even thinking, "Major Proust will *not* change dates. The Minister's already given a decision on that."

When he put the receiver down, Robineau was still standing by his desk, and he looked up cautiously.

"What's he want?" he asked.

"Nadauld's spoken to him. He doesn't want to talk to anyone but the Minister."

"The Minister's busy. He's always busy. You ought to know that. He's no time to interview crackpots."

"He insists."

The Secretary frowned. "What's he want?" he demanded angrily.

"I don't know."

"Well, find out."

"We can't. He wouldn't tell Nadauld, but Nadauld thinks it's the same old thing."

The Minister's Secretary moved the papers on his desk irritably. "The French Army's always had too much reverence for elderly generals," he snapped. "That was the trouble in 1940. We can't change the ruling just for him."

The Minister's Secretary shuffled irritably in his chair but his assistant remained stubbornly rooted to the spot.

"He doesn't want a ruling," he said. "I think he came originally expecting you to reconsider his case, but he's been kept waiting about the place—you know how long it takes—and I think he's getting bored or tired. He's started to change his course. Nadauld says he's been doing a lot of thinking and now he says that in view of the emergency in North Africa, he's prepared to alter his demands. He's willing to forget the past and accept re-employment in a lower rank. He realizes how short we are of officers, and he's quite prepared to forgo his seniority and accept employment under someone else—even, if necessary, as a regimental officer."

The Minister's Secretary stared. "Regimental officer? Re-employment? He's too damned old for employment, even on a lines of communications job. There's no place in a modern army for old men. Besides, he's out, he's finished. He was sacked. And if I——"

He paused for a moment. "What *did* happen at Percéval,

173

Robineau?" he said thoughtfully. "I never did read it. Pass his file over. We had it out the other day for the police to look at. That's the one with the red binding."

Robineau passed the file over and the Minister's Secretary opened it out on his desk. The first words that met his eyes made him raise his eyebrows. *Definite disobedience to written orders* . . . the summary in the first paragraph seemed to leap out at him . . . *no excuse for behaviour* . . . *Entirely—repeat entirely—unsuitable for further employment in any responsible command* . . .

"My God," he said slowly. He read a little more, then he slowly put down the file. "Well, he certainly asked for all he got," he commented.

"Shall I send him in?" Robineau asked.

"No, you won't! Make him wait a bit longer. This makes interesting reading. Why hasn't anyone ever drawn my attention to it before?" The Minister's Secretary settled back and picked up the file again. "I never realized *this* was what was at the back of all that damned nonsense in the newspapers. How long did you say he'd been waiting?"

"He's been hanging about for two hours now. I think he's getting pretty impatient."

"Well, he can wait a bit longer," the Minister's Secretary snapped. "At least until I've finished this lot. Or, better still, *you* deal with him. There's to be no nonsense, though. No telling him to come back another day. From what I can make out, the answer will always be 'no'—a complete and unequivocal 'no' to anything he might demand—now or at any time in the future—absolutely anything. We're to have nothing to do with him in this department. I'm beginning to wonder what all the damned fuss is about, in fact. He deserves all he got, as far as I can see."

General Boderin had grown a little exhausted and confused by the time his card was returned to him. He felt completely lost, and was startled at the youth of all the officials around him. They made him feel older than ever and more conscious of the weariness of his legs.

He was very glad of the chair that was offered to him in Major Nadauld's room. He felt he'd been shifted from department to department and from official to official half the morning. He was growing weary, bored and frustrated, and was even beginning to wish he hadn't come.

Nadauld was glancing at the hieroglyphics he'd scribbled on his blotter, resentfully taking note of the fact that Robineau had pushed his problem smartly back into his lap. It was all very well, he thought bitterly, to say the answer was an unequivocal "no" but Robineau wouldn't have to deal with the resulting scene.

He glanced up and saw that General Boderin's face was white and drawn and, in spite of himself, he felt sorry for him. He coughed softly to attract the old man's attention, and Boderin looked up eagerly in a way that made Major Nadauld feel as though he were about to strike a favourite dog.

"I'm sorry," he said. "But the Minister's engaged at the moment. He's got to attend a meeting and he's already on his way."

"Then his personal assistant——"

"Gone with the Minister," Nadauld said immediately. "However, they've asked me to say that your generous offer will be put on record and brought to the Chief of Staff's notice. And if the occasion arises when we feel we can use your services, you will be informed immediately. Perhaps you'll drop us a line and let us know where you can be found."

He stood up as General Boderin rose wearily, and waited until the door had closed behind him, then he reached for the internal telephone.

"That you, Clavel?" he asked. "Well, look here, this chap Boderin—he damn' near got as far as the Minister just now. He's not to be allowed through again."

When he left the Ministry, General Boderin stood uncertainly on the pavement for a moment, watching the traffic streaming past towards St Germain, then he stopped the first taxi that approached him.

He felt he hadn't succeeded in achieving much, but having set off with the intention of buttonholing someone, he was determined not to go home without having done so.

"Take me to SHAPE headquarters," he said to the driver.

The driver stared. "That's at Versailles," he pointed out.

"That is so."

"It's a long way."

"I'm prepared to pay."

The driver shrugged, threw away the shredded stub of his Gauloise and let in the gear.

As he stood in front of the row of vivid flags that fronted the prefabricated offices just off the Versailles road, General Boderin realized he had made a great mistake in paying off the taxi and sending it home. They were refusing to let him in without a pass and he now looked like being stuck out there without any means of getting back to Paris.

He felt old and hot and badly wanted to sit down. The young American with the white patent-leather pistol holster and Sam Browne, and the white laces to his calf-length boots, was very friendly and went to a great deal of trouble on his behalf. He was tough, in spite of his youth and his helpfulness, a symbol of a new generation, a new country, a new way of life, all of them foreign to the old man. With his fresh face and his immaculate khaki drill and the enormous SHAPE brassard on his arm, the young soldier made him feel desperately tired and wishing he could just give up the whole thing. But if he did, he felt, Robert would give him no rest with his talk of family and pride and his bitterness towards the whole American nation, which the old man, even in his worst moments, had never quite managed to feel.

The young American was returning now from the offices across the apron of concrete where he'd gone to make inquiries.

"I'm sorry, sir," he said when he returned, "but it isn't possible to see General Murphy."

General Boderin sighed. "But if I could have just a few minutes——" he began.

"I'm sorry." The young American shrugged. "The General's not here at the moment. He's just left. You've just missed him."

"His assistant perhaps——"

"He's gone with him."

"Then someone else. They *must* know who I am."

The young American, remembering the panic that had ensued among General Murphy's staff when they had discovered who was wanting to see him and the distinct and unrelenting "No"

176

that had been given to him, did his best to make it as easy as possible.

"They say they don't," he said. "They say they've never heard of General Boderin."

As they talked, the old man could see the cars moving in and out of the gates, past the American and British and French service policemen on duty. The flags made a gaudy spectacle that stirred his heart but, curiously, not as much as he felt they ought to, and he reluctantly put it down to the fact that he must be older than he'd realized and had probably got a little past being stirred by flags and military sounds and sights.

"Where *is* General Murphy then?" he asked.

"Well, I heard he's off to Percéval or some place. He's gone there for some ceremony."

"Percéval? The battle? But I was there with General Murphy during the battles round Percéval."

"Is that so?" The young man's eyebrows rose slowly. He was trying hard not to be too unhelpful. "That's sure interesting. I guess he'd be glad to meet you."

"Yes, no doubt he would." An idea, a wild idea, had begun to creep into General Boderin's stubborn, obsessed mind. "When is this ceremony?"

"Day after tomorrow, I heard. On the battlefield, or something. I dunno. It was all in the papers this morning."

"Where can I get a paper? From the stall there?"

"Well, no, sir. That stall's reserved for SHAPE personnel."

"Perhaps you'd be good enough——"

The young American stared at him for a moment, beginning to be weary of the old man, then he shrugged. "Oh, well," he said, "I guess so."

He bought a paper and Boderin took it from him. "Now, perhaps, if you'll call me a taxi——"

"Look, sir"—the youngster was growing angry—"I'm not here to call taxis. I'm supposed to be on duty. And in any case, sir, there aren't all that many taxis come out here. Everybody's got their own cars."

The old man's brows knitted fretfully.

"Well, how am I to get back to Paris?" he demanded.

"You can use the SHAPE bus, if you want." The American

indicated a dark green vehicle in the distance that looked ominously like one of the police camions that were always waiting in the Pigalle area.

"I'm not accustomed to using buses," General Boderin said sharply.

"Well, that's all there is. Maybe you could thumb a lift."

"No, thank you." The old man seemed to shudder. "Perhaps I'd better take the bus after all. I'd better hurry if I'm to catch a train to Percéval."

Inevitably, the newspapers made much of the story of the meeting that was to take place between General Murphy and his old comrades and, for a while at least, his press improved.

Colonel Franks was delighted, but his joy was short-lived because in *Emancipation* he came across a statement said to have come from some association called the Friends of Truth which claimed that the men in Percéval had been paid with American money to arrange the meeting solely for the benefit of General Murphy's reputation.

Franks sighed. It seemed it was going to be difficult to produce *anything* that wasn't going to have its meaning twisted. He considered for a moment calling another press conference and trying to explain, but the more he thought about it, the more he came to the conclusion that perhaps the wisest thing to do would be to let things take their own course.

General Ridgway in his term of office at Versailles had survived a most unfortunate soubriquet and had even managed to gain popularity. Surely, Franks thought, Murphy ought to be able to do the same, by virtue of his own quiet commonsense and intelligence. Oh, hell, Franks thought, it stuck out a mile that there wasn't much wrong with General Murphy!

In the end, he just decided to let things slide and see what he could do with the ceremony at Percéval. He was determined this time to see that the press had the full story of what happened there, and he was going to make damn' certain that any flattering remark made about the General was going to reach the editorial offices undiluted.

Cellini was in a state of considerable excitement when he met

178

Hardy in a *café-tabac* in the Boulevard St Michel near to the Church of St Séverin. He had a bundle of newspapers under his arm and he seemed in a hurry.

He seemed surprised to find Nicole still with Hardy, but he clearly tried very hard not to comment on the fact. Hardy could see the objections trembling on his lips but he managed to bite them back, though his eyes never left Nicole's face.

She sat reading a newspaper and smoking, apparently unheeding, though occasionally her eyes caught Hardy's and her gaze dropped quickly. She had calmed down considerably since the uproar at Orly and a lot of the anger had gone from her, almost as though her contempt for morality had begun to die and with it the fires that burned inside her. She was cool now but oddly aloof, as though Cellini's gaze worried her and brought a sense of guilt.

Hardy watched her, troubled. Her face seemed suddenly so much older and yet in a way so much more poignantly young than when he'd first met her. As she answered Cellini, even though she spoke casually and with apparent indifference, he felt jealousy sharpen and become a pain, and all the feeling for her, all the earlier contempt, all the anger he'd felt at her obsession with her family, became hot and possessive as he saw Cellini trying to catch her attention.

He had taken a sly delight in the last few days in keeping her out of Cellini's way, pretending to himself and to her that he was merely making things difficult for the efficient American. They had sat and smoked among the screaming children on the dusty statued pathways under the chestnuts of the Luxembourg Gardens, and walked in the Bois de Boulogne. They had eaten together in dark little restaurants, and he had taken her to the Opera, going there himself for the first time in his life.

He had even bought her flowers, spurred by some whim that sprung from a desire to please that startled him, and unexpectedly she had blushed and accepted them quietly, kissing him on the cheek, gently, lovingly but without passion, demure and young and kind again.

Cellini seemed to sense the difference between them and he kept talking all the time, nervously almost, as though he couldn't bear their silences, which were deep and curiously intimate, and

Hardy found himself resenting the American's concern. The knowledge that he should be interested in Nicole at all irritated him, starting a small sharp feeling that he was intruding on something that was personal and private. Then the feeling changed and grew deeper and warmer as he watched her, swelling into a hard knot of needing her, a fear even of losing her, and he was aware of a tremendous sense of relief at her indifference to Cellini's questions.

"Did you know," Cellini was saying, "that the police don't believe he committed suicide at all?"

"I never thought he did," she said, shrugging.

"Why not?"

"He hasn't the courage."

Cellini glanced quickly at Hardy, then back to Nicole, his expression unhappy. "Do you think he'll try again at Percéval?" he asked.

"I don't know," she said. "Somehow, I don't think I care very much. I've lived all my life with the Boderin honour and the Boderin temper, and suddenly, I'm not interested any more. I'm not even thinking about it."

It was obvious that Cellini was shocked by her attitude. He had thought her original ardour for her family's cause misplaced but now he seemed to feel she was being disloyal, and he clearly suspected Hardy's influence.

"If anything happened, it could make your brother a murderer," he said earnestly. "Surely you can't mean that you don't care."

She shrugged again. "I'm suddenly tired of pride and families," she said angrily. "I just want to live a normal life."

"Where do you think your brother's gone then? Try and help us, Nicole." Cellini's tone was pleading.

"I don't know," she said. "Perhaps out of Paris. Probably to Algiers, or to England or Spain. I don't know."

Cellini glanced at his watch. "I think," he suggested, "that I ought to be seeing you home."

"I don't want to go home," she pointed out coldly. "I'll stay in Sam's apartment."

Her answer was unequivocal and suggested that she had no intention of offering explanations or apologies. Cellini frowned, unhappy at her unhappiness, unsettled by her instability. He guessed there was more than a little defiance in her attitude and he didn't know what to say to her. She appeared to have thrown over for good the family obsession which had held her, and no longer had even that anchor in her whirling world.

Hardy smoked quietly, almost in the background, suddenly confident and sure of himself as he watched the expressions flit across Cellini's face as his thoughts chased each other through his mind.

"You can't stay in Sam's place," the American burst out finally. "It just isn't right!"

"Then where shall I go? I'm not going to my father or to those awful places at Chartres or Père Lachaise. I've been wearing them round my neck all my life."

She seemed to lose interest in the argument, and walked to the bar to buy cigarettes and a magazine. While she was browsing over the counter, Cellini leaned across to Hardy.

"Sam, we've got to do something for that kid," he said earnestly.

Hardy shrugged. "What can we do that we're not doing already?" he asked. "She seems to be responding to treatment."

"We've got to make her forget these damn' relations of hers. She's had enough."

"Jimmy, you do-gooders have a habit of failing to notice when the patient's cured. She's doing all right, I tell you."

Cellini stared at him with narrowed eyes, accusations hovering on his tongue. "That's not enough, Sam," he said. "We've got to bring her back to life. She needs fun."

"I can give her fun. In fact, I think I am doing."

"Yeah, but what sort of fun?"

"What sort would you like her to have?"

"Her sort. Not seedy night clubs."

"For Christ's sake, Jimmy," Hardy snapped, "don't be so bloody smug! Any minute now you'll start talking about democracy." He paused and went on slowly. "We haven't spent all our time when you've not been around sitting at bars drinking pernod. I think she's as sick as I am of boys who wear beards and berets like open wounds. We went out to Bougival and had a meal there in that place by the bridge. We just talked. You'd be surprised, when I'm in my Proust mood, I'm quite an orator. She doesn't have to go to a church social to be saved. It's just the way we do things over here and if you don't like it, for Christ's sake, go back to your automats and office parties! All's fair in love and war."

As he turned away, Cellini leaned forward again. "Hell, Sam," he said. "I'm sorry. I didn't mean to be offensive. It's just that I think she needs more than that damn' decaying honour of theirs."

"She's getting it."

Cellini looked up quickly, searching for hidden meanings in Hardy's words, then he sighed. "Yeah," he said. "O.K. Maybe she is. Only we've got to look after her. That's all. She's got enough to think about already. Damn it, Sam, have you ever seen her smile?"

"Once or twice."

"You're lucky." It was Cellini's turn to look young and vulnerable now. "I haven't."

When Cellini had gone, Nicole sat staring at her glass, and Hardy watched her for a while. "Well?" he asked. "Where do we go from here?"

She continued to stare into her glass. "Take me home," she said softly. "Take me home with you."

Hardy stared at his fingers for a moment, uneasy and, in spite of himself, troubled by what Cellini had been trying to say. "Jimmy's right, you know," he pointed out gently. "You ought to be going back to your own place."

She looked up quickly. "I can't," she said, and he could see all the fear of loneliness again behind the defiance in her face. "I can't go back there. I've been cutting lectures at the University and they'll all want to know why. They'll want to know all about Robert and my father and you. I couldn't face that. You know I couldn't.

"I've been listening to stories about that stupid affair all my life. I've been listening to theories and trying to find excuses for it. I even used to sit outside the War Ministry with my father while he tried to lobby some general," she said bitterly. "Even when I was big enough to be embarrassed by their refusals. I've even been to Percéval with a tape measure, measuring distances and making notes. 'St Roth was burning,' he would say, 'and the smoke was filling the valley. I couldn't possibly have seen the Germans, could I?' And I'd agree and say, no, he couldn't. Then he'd go on to prove to his own satisfaction that he was innocent and ask me if I didn't think so too. And I'd say, yes, of course he was. And I'd come home feeling as though I'd told a lie, because I didn't really know. I was just trying to keep hope alive when inside myself I knew there was no hope. That's how I've been living for twelve years—going over and over and over that ridiculous battle, again and again, trying to decide what it was that made him do what he did."

Hardy was startled by her outburst. Somehow it didn't ring true and he wondered if it were only a sudden desire to live her own life by her own standards instead of her father's.

"Do you think now that he *did* do what they accused him of?" he asked gently.

She shrugged and he saw her eyes had filled with tears—the first he'd ever seen. "I don't know," she said wearily. "Probably. Very likely, in fact. It may have been because he'd been wounded. It may have been because he was tired. It may have been because he'd lost a lot of men. It may have been just because he wasn't a Lespinasse after all or even a Boderin, but just a Du Crest. Perhaps that was the reason. Perhaps it was just that streak that runs through all of us. Perhaps that's why Robert's as he is, and why I dress like this and put too much make-up on and drink things I don't like. Because we're all a little bit stiff-necked and unreal and theatrical and all pretending to be something we aren't at all."

She began to cry softly, suddenly frail and feminine again and needing him once more, and he put his hand on hers.

"Everything seems so hopeless," she whispered. "They'll never have a re-trial now. It's nothing but a mirage. At first I was so enthusiastic. It seemed so important to put things right. To make my father happy. It seemed important to me that the country should see things his way. After all, most things have a reason and if he behaved wrongly, then he must have done so for some reason. It was important to me that it should be explained. It was important to me for twelve years. Now—now"—she seemed to have been hollowed of emotion, as though all the spirit and fire that had ever been in her, had been scoured out by wretchedness—"now, it suddenly isn't important any longer."

She sighed and pulled the black leather coat closer, as though she were cold. "If I felt we were being honest," she said, "I'd still go on struggling, but somehow, now, I've begun to feel we're just hanging on to something that didn't even exist. Perhaps he *did* run away. He was never very stable. He was never able to endure much. His whole life was one of shifts—Robert's the same—and I think he's reached the point now when he no longer really knows what happened. He's convinced himself that what he'd like to have happened *did* happen, and he's come to accept it as fact. If someone showed him something completely in-disputable—some evidence that he'd *have* to believe—I think he'd just die. He's made it so much of his life. If they took it away there'd be nothing left to live for."

She stared at Hardy, blinking rapidly to keep back the tears, trying hard to hold her head up, striving still for defiance.

"I want to get married and have children," she said. "And I want them to grow up thinking in terms of the future not the past. There are many mistakes that I wouldn't want them to make." She paused. "They'd have so much that's good in the way of example if they looked."

Her eyes glowed for a second, and Hardy saw that she had not completely thrown off her family and probably never would. The instinct ran too deep.

"I should tell them only about the good Boderins," she went on slowly, her eyes far away. "The bad ones can be thrust out of sight. There are quite enough of the other sort to live with."

Hardy's eyes were troubled as he watched her, the jealousy coming again, not for Cellini this time, but for all those genera-tions that she couldn't put aside.

"I want to live a normal life," she was saying slowly. "To be loved by someone because I'm me, not because I'm someone who might help sort out some puzzle which ought to be dead and gone."

The bitterness had returned abruptly to her voice and she paused and stared around her at the hurrying crowds, and the lights that stretched all the way from the rust-stained fountain of St Michel, with its stone dolphins and its moss-dripping cornucopia, up to the Luxembourg gardens at the top of the hill, at the big American cars like darts, the gendarme directing traffic near the Musée de Cluny; the waiter sweeping the cigarette ends and scraps of paper from among the chairs.

"I don't think I like it here, Sam," she said quietly. "There are too many people. Please take me home."

"Oh, hell!" Hardy began to fiddle with his glass, restless and troubled and searching for words. "Listen, Nicole, we can't go on like this."

"Don't you want me?" she demanded fiercely.

Hardy paused. "I want you more than anything else in the world, Nicole," he said finally, his voice firm, pronouncing the words slowly so that there should be no mistake about them, either in her mind or his.

She stared at him, as though what he'd said had come quite unexpectedly.

"But I'm right, Nicole," he went on. "We can't go on in this way. It's complicated as hell. Love isn't girls in pink peignoirs in grubby rooms. I think decency's got a lot to do with it. There's nothing to hold us together and I find I *want* something to hold us together. I'm sick of St Germain and the Institute all of a sudden. I'm sick of students in Toulouse-Lautrec moods carrying books about books. It's all a bit shabby really. You can't go on for ever rolling round the Latin Quarter till you look like the Phantom of the Opera and no one wants to know you. I'm growing too old, I find."

She sat silently, her eyes on her hands, her brows frowning, as though she were steeling herself to hear something unpleasant. She looked so young, so pale, Hardy smiled and touched her hand.

"I thought I was content here in Paris," he said slowly. "I thought I didn't ever want to leave. But when you asked me to take you away, I started to see things differently. I've decided now that it doesn't much matter where I am, what I do, so long as you're there too, Nicole."

"Sam!" She looked up quickly, her eyes startled and suddenly happy, and Hardy stumbled on, groping for the right phrases to express what he was feeling.

185

"I'd always regarded this marriage business as a bit of a sweat," he went on, labouring a little with unaccustomed sincerity. "Perhaps I got off on the wrong foot last time. Perhaps that's the trouble. But I don't think it is really, do you, Nicole?"

She shook her head, her eyes shining and fixed on his, unwavering.

"In the short time I've known you, you've become part of me, Nicole, part of my life. I don't think I could stand not having you about the place any more. I always regarded myself as something left over from the Roaring Forties, but I discover I was wrong after all. As a man, I think I've been a complete flop and it's time I did something about it. I've got to get down to things, that's all."

He grinned, suddenly feeling better, suddenly delighted with himself in his new role. "Hard work and application and eye on the ball. That's what I need. I'll have to learn not to answer back when someone's rude to me. That way you can earn lots of money, I'm told." He looked up, serious again. "We can't go on making love in a dim grey ugly room, Nicole, and thinking it's beautiful. I've got to find somewhere decent for us. And that means nose to the grindstone. It's going to take some doing but, if you'll just be patient, I think I'll manage. If I go down, at least I'll founder with all flags flying."

She took his hand in both of hers. "Sam," she said softly. "Take me home."

Hardy grinned, excited and laughing now. "Hell, this isn't what Cellini told me to do when he said I'd got to look after you." He stood up and pushed his chair back and she rose alongside him, her sleeve brushing his, her eyes never off his face. He was aware of the softness of her breast brushing his arm and the trembling response of her body.

"All right," he said. "I'll take you home. I'll sleep on the kitchen floor."

But he didn't.

In the little room he'd rented off the Rue de la Gaiété in Montparnasse, Robert Boderin felt quite safe because he'd given a false name and he'd never been in the district before. No one knew him and no one expected him to be there.

The days were wearisome but Blot kept him supplied with newspapers and liquor and food, and occasionally even, after dark, they slipped quietly out to a small dark Chinese restaurant in the Rue Delambre, where they could find a small shaded table and eat with safety.

He waited eagerly as he heard Blot's feet on the stairs and snatched the papers from his hand almost before he was through the door, scouring the columns for news of Murphy and references to himself. Blot brushed the rain off his clothes—the roofs were wet outside the window and there was the whisper of water along the gutterings—then he flung himself down on the bed and, lighting a Gauloise, picked up one of the newspapers. *Pamphlets for NATO General*, said the headline. *Frenchman Still Sought. Police of 5* Arrondissements *Throw Out Net.*

"By the way," he said casually, "he's going to Percéval tomorrow. He's going to visit the battlefield."

Boderin nodded, his eyes racing over the print.

"It says so here," he said. "I'm just reading it."

Blot looked at him nervously and gestured with his cigarette. "You're not still thinking of going through with that silly horsewhipping business?" he asked. "Not after Orly?"

Boderin shook his head. "No," he said. "I've finished with that."

Blot gave a sigh of relief. "Well, that's something. I always did think it was a lot of damned nonsense. We couldn't have done it. Too complicated. Too easy for it to go wrong."

Boderin stared at him contemptuously, and Blot gestured again. "I don't see how you could have been so certain as you were," he went on. "The police were there. You knew they were going to be there. Nicole said so."

Boderin looked down his long nose. "It would have been very simple," he said slowly. "I had a gun."

"*What?*" Blot sat up abruptly, suddenly scared. "A gun! Where did you get it?"

"I went to my father's apartment at Chartres and helped myself."

Blot got to his feet. "So you did take them," he said. "You told the police you didn't."

"I took that damned monstrous British gun. That's all. I've

187

got it still. I was looking for the other but it was missing. He must have got rid of it."

"Now, look here"—Blot's words began to stumble over themselves in his nervousness—"I'm not going to get mixed up in anything involving shooting. Get someone else to help."

"I've tried. I tried Achille St Martin. He was in that third-rate show at the Babylone. He was afraid."

"So am I."

Boderin's face darkened. "You promised," he said. "You swore to help me."

Blot gestured. "I wasn't thinking in terms of firearms."

"You swore an oath——"

"Yes, and a damned childish oath it was, too," Blot shouted, remembering the ceremony that showed more a spirit of conspiratorial play-acting than anything else. "I felt like a Boy Scout. All that nonsense about silence and seriousness. Switching off the wireless. The Bible."

Boderin stared at him contemptuously. He'd seen nothing unusual in the ceremony. "You swore——" he said.

"I swore to help you do all you could to humiliate Murphy. Then, it was only slapping his face. Now it's got to guns."

"The gun was to keep back anyone who tried to prevent me. That was all."

"There you are," Blot said bitterly. "See what I mean? You'd not thought about it. You'd got a gun, so you thought you'd be all right. Do you know the flics can pinch you for pulling a gun? And how could you have kept your eye on somebody who might try to stop you when you were watching Murphy at the same time? It wouldn't ever have worked. The plan was crazy. If you'd kept your eye on Murphy, someone would have grabbed you. If you'd kept your eye on everyone else, Murphy would have grabbed you."

"He wouldn't have dared. Not with a gun."

"He's got every medal under the sun for bravery. Dutch, British. Even a few of our own. I never liked the idea. And now I know about this damn' gun I like it even less. Martine would have played the devil if she'd known. Suppose he'd grabbed you?"

Boderin shrugged. He hadn't been afraid of being grabbed.

He hadn't even been afraid of gaol and perhaps almost welcomed the possibility. His trial would have given him the chance to speak, and what he had had to say would have been fully reported in all the newspapers. He had thought often about it and had intended it somehow to be in the shape of a call to honour, a clear indication of duty. He'd never clearly worked it out but he had intended to when the time came.

"Then he'd have grabbed me," he said flatly. "As it happened, he didn't. It didn't happen that way. Next time it'll be different. And then perhaps they'll all think differently about honour. If I'd succeeded at Orly, he'd have felt some of the pain my father felt in 1944. If the story had got into the papers, he'd never have been able to hold up his head for the laughter that would have rung round France."

"Only you didn't succeed," Blot pointed out bluntly.

"I *shall* succeed, don't worry." Boderin nodded thoughtfully, pausing before he continued. "There's a train from the Gare de l'Est at midnight," he said. "I've travelled on it before. You have to change at Nancy."

"You thinking of going to Percéval too?" Blot demanded.

Boderin looked quickly at him, the colour flooding up from his throat.

"Yes," he said. "I'm going to Percéval too."

Blot's eyes widened. "What for?" he demanded in a voice that was almost a neigh.

Boderin stared at him, wondering how he could possibly put it all into words so that this weak-kneed oaf could understand it. To himself the thing seemed to grow more simple with every day. Alone and brooding in the shabby little room in the Rue du Maine, the obsession had grown on him until he could now see no other reason for living.

It wasn't merely Murphy that he hated now, but what he stood for, the wealth of the New World that had crushed his father, the naïvete that tried to impress its politics on France, which, having lived for so many years with tragedy, knew how to deal with it. Murphy wasn't just a general, famous though he might be. He was as much the symbol of the United States as the American Eagle. He had become the man who had broken Robert Boderin's leg with a lorry, he was the American tourist

189

who had first complained about his rudeness, the American student he had found in his sister's bed.

He was no longer sure where the hatred had started. In fact, he was hardly aware any more that it existed. It had grown, flowering like an ugly weed, and Murphy had no more than to breathe to make himself be hated more each day, and his presence in Paris was a sustained insult directed personally at Robert Boderin.

"I'm going to Percéval because I must," he said, and in his words there was all the obsessive and unhealthy stubbornness of the unbalanced.

"You're not thinking of trying it on at Percéval?" Blot had got to his feet and, when Boderin didn't reply, he stepped nearer and went on hurriedly. "Look here, Robert, Percéval isn't Paris. They're *for* Murphy there. They're not interested in political reputations. They think there that your father was wrong. They'd tear you limb from limb if you tried to horsewhip Murphy at Percéval."

"Who said I intended to horsewhip him?"

Blot stared at him for a second, then he relaxed. "Oh," he said. "I thought"—he turned away then swung round again, suddenly afraid—"well, why *are* you going to Percéval if you're not going to horsewhip him?"

"Because I've changed my plans," Boderin said. "I've finished with all that childish nonsense. I'm going to do the thing properly this time. I'm going to *shoot* him."

★ 6 ★

CHIEFLY due to the expert efforts of Colonel Franks, Murphy only managed to reach the Bligues without being recognized. No one noticed the sturdy man in civilian clothes, and it was not until they reached Toul and stopped for lunch that Murphy spotted the two men who'd been riding in the big black Panhard which had trailed them most of the way.

They were sitting at the other side of the dining-room, glancing from time to time at Murphy. They had chosen a position where they need not take their eyes off him as they ate, and Murphy watched them for a long time, an interested smile on his face.

"Those guys following us, you reckon, Frankie?" he asked at last.

Franks looked up innocently. "I guess not," he said.

"They wouldn't be some of these assassins you're scared of, would they?"

"They look harmless enough to me."

"They wouldn't even be detectives that you've arranged to sit on my tail, would they?" There was a gleam of amusement in Murphy's grey eyes, and Franks began to wish that French detectives could manage, as detectives in other countries did, to look inconspicuous. These two, one of them even to Franks's horror in a black leather coat, seemed to have little to say to each other and as they finished their meal, they sat smoking Gauloise after Gauloise, rarely taking their eyes off Murphy.

"Not to my knowledge they're not," Franks said.

As Murphy went back to the car, Franks stopped in front of the two detectives. One of them immediately jumped to his feet.

Franks signed to him to sit down. "Please," he said, "can't you manage to look more like ordinary travellers? Stop staring at the General."

"Who were they, Frankie?" Murphy asked innocently as Franks reappeared. "Russian agents?"

"Commercial travellers," Franks said shortly. "It just happens they're going to Percéval too. They're travelling in ladies' underwear."

Murphy looked sideways at him. "I've never known drummers travel in pairs," he observed slyly.

Franks pretended to be busy with a cigarette and Murphy laughed. "I might almost imagine," he said, "that you'd let that guy Schneider put a couple of watchdogs on me—if I didn't know you, Frankie."

When they got to Percéval there was an unexpectedly large group of elderly men waiting outside the Mairie, holding a gold-fringed tricolour, and a small girl to hand over a bunch of flowers.

Surprisingly, Murphy didn't seem to mind. He always seemed

to be infuriatingly at ease when you least expected him to be, Franks decided irritatedly. He was shaking hands all round, smiling his wide smile, and jabbering away in that appalling French accent of his which seemed to delight everyone. Then the Maire led the way into his office, and wine and vermouth appeared.

"Or do you prefer *le Scotch, mon général*?"

"Negative," Murphy said. "There are enough people at SHAPE all trying to drink other people's drinks. Frenchmen drinking Scotch, Americans drinking pernod, Englishmen drinking Bourbon. I'll drink wine."

Sergeant Blot managed to acquire a taxicab as they came out of the station. It had been raining a little and General Boderin's feet made only a soft pad-pad on the wet grass under the trees. Somehow, he didn't quite remember Percéval looking like this, he thought gloomily. The whole place seemed bigger, though the square was exactly as his old maps showed it, drab, provincial and unimpressive. There was the Grande Place with its scattered plane trees and the inevitable World War I memorial, with its heroically-posed *poilu* frozen for eternity in stone, the usual Hotel de la Poste and Banque de France, the usual lounging old men and the smocked children on the way from school.

It looked drabber somehow, though, and oddly different from what he'd expected. Still, he reflected, it was a long time since he'd seen it, in spite of his interest in the place, and in those days twelve years before, his eyes had been seeking out strong points and fields of fire, not the shuffling crowds round the market stalls and the crowded Citroën vans and the coloured umbrellas. He'd been looking for safe roads and speedy routes to move his men, and he remembered with a twinge of the irritation he'd felt then, that they'd all been obscured by the confusion that had existed. Batteries of ack-ack guns, grey and ominous and long-snouted, were being held up in the square by a string of great green-brown lorries, hurried on by anxious officers who'd been afraid of being caught without their weapons in position. A file of weary American and French soldiers had been threading between them, cursing the traffic and the heat and the harassed police who were trying to clear a pathway for his own dusty vehicle.

"You'll have to get round to the east," Gallifet had said, he remembered. Gallifet had met him in the square and was riding on the side of the jeep, clinging on for dear life as he tried to explain where the Germans were, gesturing with a hand that was bandaged where it had been nicked by a shell splinter. "They're trying to get round there," he'd said. "You've got to get guns up that way or it'll be too late. I've found a good spot. I've marked it here, look, with a cross. Right opposite this wood. You'll recognize it by a broken stone wall. There's a big house you can use for your headquarters. It's got a slate roof and a weathervane like a cockerel. You can't miss it. I'll meet you there."

But Gallifet never had met him, General Boderin remembered sadly as he watched Blot stuffing the brief cases of maps into the taxi. He had seen him later, lying in a ditch, pulled off the road by the side of his wrecked jeep, his bandaged hand tucked underneath him, scraps of dried leaves sticking to the blood at the side of his dead mouth, no longer able to encourage and advise as he had done all the long way up from Equatorial Africa, strong, indifferent to danger or to weariness, careless of what people thought, the son of a Picardy farmer, motivated only by his hatred of the Germans and untouched by thoughts of military glory or family honour, and at that moment without even a blanket to cover his smashed corpse.

It was from that moment, Boderin remembered wearily, that things had started to go wrong. It had seemed as though a prop had been snatched away from under him and he'd begun to realize just how much he'd relied on Gallifet. In his weariness, signals had not meant as much to him as they had to the tireless Gallifet and there'd seemed to be no life in him to stir the men around him to courage.

He felt some of the sense of despair he'd felt then, at the heat and the weariness and the everlasting dust that had been with them ever since they'd landed in the South, the stench of hot oil and rubber, and the stink of sweaty uniforms, and the stale smell of tired, frightened men.

Sergeant Blot packed him into the taxi and they set off, the mist blurring the windscreen, General Boderin feeling curiously frail and ill-at-ease, suddenly beginning to wish he'd never returned, but still with somewhere at the back of his mind the firm feeling that if he could only meet Murphy on the actual field of battle, on the spot where the affair had taken place, he'd be able to explain things to him, and show him just where he was wrong and just where he, Boderin, had been right. Somehow, in that court martial after the war, things had never come out. They'd never let him explain properly just how things had happened.

He stared through the windows as the taxi threaded its way through the wet streets out of the town. There was nothing to see now of the confusion of those last days of the war beyond a few chips off the stonework round the station where bullets had hacked a line across the façade, and a spatter of stony dents on the marble pillars of the entrance.

As they passed the Mairie, he caught a glimpse of tricolours and, wondering if they were for Murphy, he turned to question the taxi driver.

"Is Murphy here today?" he asked.

"*Comment?*" the taxi driver raised his head, his shredded Gauloise hanging from his lip. "Murphy?"

"General Murphy?"

"Who's General Murphy?"

"You remember, he fought here in 1944, against the Germans."

"Oh, this American in the papers!" The taxi driver shrugged. "I didn't know he was here," he said. "I'm from Provence. I only came up here when I got married."

Boderin leaned forward, persisting in his questions, reaching backwards uncertainly for something from the incident twelve years before that would be familiar and encouraging.

"But you must have heard of the battle," he said. "I was in command of the Fighting French. I held on at St Roth. You must have read of it."

The taxi driver shook his head. "Monsieur, it takes me all my time to read the papers. I prefer the television. All I know about St Roth is that our lot let it go without a fight and the Germans nearly got back into Percéval. It was a damn disgrace, I'm told. It would have been God help everyone if they *had* got back. They'd all put tricolours out and were dancing in the streets.

194

My father-in-law told me. If it hadn't been for the Americans he wouldn't be with us now. They'd have shot him."

"No, no!" Boderin began to gesture. "You've got it wrong," he said. "That's not how it was. At least, I don't think that's how it was."

He stopped abruptly. After twelve years he wasn't certain any longer.

"You must have heard of me," he continued slowly, before Blot could stop him. "My name's Boderin."

"Which Boderin?" The driver's eyes were on the road and he was disinterested. "Something to do with the one who plays centre-forward for Rheims?"

"No, no, no!" The old man in the rear seat beat at the cushions in his irritation. "You must remember the court-martial."

"Which court-martial?"

"It was in all the papers at the time."

"When was that, Monsieur?"

"It's twelve years ago now."

The taxi driver spat his Gauloise dexterously through his open window and gave a short laugh. "Twelve years. That's long ago now and they were bad times. Things are better now. It's best to forget twelve years ago."

General Boderin sank back wearily, his sad eyes hurt, his mind confused and frustrated. Then Blot touched his arm and pointed, and he saw a grey-stone house with slates. There seemed to be something familiar about it, and he noticed the golden cockerel on the rooftop which shone in the grey light, motionless in the wet windless afternoon, and he remembered it all again vividly. This was the very road where he'd waited for Gallifet to meet him, he realized. This was the very spot where a frightened corporal had run through the hedge from the signals head-quarters, tearing at the brambles in his panic, to tell him that Gallifet was dead.

He swung round urgently and stared through the rear window of the taxi as they passed. That was the place where he'd stood in the thick dust, his boots white with a film of it like flour, and felt the whole world drop away from him, uncertainty starting already to peck at him.

He felt a little oppressed. The place seemed so small. In those days it had seemed so huge. For a moment he imagined he must be wrong after all, but then he recognized the line of trees on his right with a single tree on the hilltop beyond, twisted to the east by the prevailing winter winds, and the broken stone wall Gallifet had mentioned, behind which he'd seen tired men crouching, their faces dirty and drained of all expression except despair. Somehow, he guessed now—after all this time—that they'd been aware of his own hesitation, and the same sense of panic that had struck him had already touched them. They'd thought a great deal of Gallifet. More than they had of him, he knew. He'd never been able to unbend sufficiently to get their friendship as Gallifet had. Gallifet could swop jokes and cigarettes with them and slap them on the back and still not lose caste. If only that mortar bomb hadn't got him! Things would have been different if Gallifet had been able to give evidence at the court-martial. But then—in a curious self-destructive, perceptive flash—he realized that if Gallifet had not been killed, perhaps there'd have been no reason for a court-martial at all.

He climbed out of the taxi, feeling the shock of the drizzle on his face, and paid the driver while Blot unloaded the maps. He made arrangements to be picked up later and stood watching the taxi drive away, aware of the difference in the place. It was like the corpse of someone he'd once known, with all the flesh fallen from the face, something that had once been vividly alive for him but now no longer held much meaning.

"We'll walk across to the hill, Blot," he said, pointing with his stick and assuming an air of briskness to hide his depression. "The graves are there and that's where he's bound to stand. We can wait there and have a sip of brandy. Then perhaps we'll do a little measuring. We might as well have all our facts and distances doubly checked so that we can present them to him. You've got the dossier—in the big brief case—with all my papers setting out just what happened."

Blot nodded and they set off walking. It was cooler than they'd expected and, with the lane leading to the hill rough and muddy after the rain, General Boderin began to realize that the years were weighing more heavily on him than he'd cared to realize. The rubber shoes he'd put on to keep the damp from his rheumatism seemed more clumsy than they should have done and the ruts jarred when his feet slipped in them. Also, he was certain that the hill was steeper than it had been when he'd last walked up it.

There were a great many bushes round the base of the hill—more than he remembered—and he looked at them distastefully as they brushed wetly against his clothes, wishing again that he hadn't come. Uneasily, the thought began to steal across him that perhaps it was all a waste of time, after all. He'd managed to live in peace for the last five years since Robert had left Chartres to live at Père Lachaise. It had become easier merely to sit and think about other things than to trouble his mind with the past. Nobody else seemed to be worried. They were all like the taxi driver, all with too much to do, all too worried about the future to be concerned with the past.

However—he sighed—perhaps Robert *had* been right. Perhaps it *was* still important. It was wrong that they should go on thinking he was merely an amiable if taciturn old gentleman with a bee in his bonnet who spent all his time in libraries trying to find some clue that would unlock all the doors that had been closed to him for so long.

After today—with luck—they'd stop sneering at him and point him out in the street with a certain amount of pride. "That's Boderin. You've read about him in the paper. They've just upped him to Major-General and given him the Grand Cross of the Legion of Honour to make up for all those years of disgrace. They've proved he was right at Percéval after all." There'd be salutes again, and smiles, and people seeking his friendship, his advice, his company, after his long years in the wilderness.

He had almost reached the dreamy state of reinstatement, when his mind jarred back to the present as his foot dropped unexpectedly into a pothole with a jolt that rattled his teeth. He stopped and stared up at the hill in front of him again, fretfully—aware for the first time of the fact that he didn't really care much any more about meeting Murphy, or even about pride or reinstatement.

"We'll sit down," he announced, trying to hide his weariness and pointing to a log with his stick. Blot, sweating under the brief cases, was only too pleased to obey.

"Get out the brandy, Blot," he said. "It's cooler than I expected and I feel I need something. This damned place seems different from what it was."

As he sipped the glowing spirit, he took out the map and spread it across his knees, more for the look of the thing than anything else, and stared at the crimson arrows marking the path he'd tried to take that day, and the violet ink crosses that indicated where he'd found the German batteries.

He frowned and forced himself to concentrate, trying to imagine it all again. But somehow, with the drizzle brushing at his cheeks and the chill against his back, his mind was reluctant to conjure it up. It was easier merely to stare at the map, half-dozing in spite of the damp, reluctant to get to his feet again, wishing somewhere at the back of his mind that he was in a chair with his feet up, with Blot fussily anxious to see that he got his afternoon nap. Try as he might, he could manage only brief mental glimpses of men digging frantically, smashing down the hedges in their haste, and the smell of dust and trampled undergrowth and stale sweat, and officers shouting orders, and the burn on his hand from the barrel of a rifle he'd grabbed, his mind set on making a gesture of resistance.

He tried hard to concentrate on the map, his eyes on the words *Checked, '49*, inscribed in Robert's handwriting, and the distances between two points marked alongside in green ink, but he found it easier merely to sit and admire the work of many years, his own handiwork, in a melancholy sort of pleasure, than to try to put it into hard facts and translate it into slopes and pictures. He even began to wish that Blot would stop rattling the papers and disturbing him. Then he remembered just why he was there and forced himself once more to think.

"We have to visualize the position as it was," he said, and Blot nodded and sighed with the weariness of a man who had heard it all thousands of times before. "My striking forces had been much reduced by the attack the day before—when I was wounded, you remember. There were barely enough of us to hold the place, and the Germans had got enough batteries to blow a way through to Percéval. That's where they were—though we didn't know it then —those purple crosses behind the yellow line. These are the woods here. Murphy himself said in his memoirs that the

Germans weren't reduced in artillery at all, and von Martienssen said he expected to be back in Percéval before nightfall. They read his sworn testimony at the court martial. It did me a great deal of harm, you remember. It was very accurate, of course. That is, except for that ridiculous statement he made about knowing that we'd give. Damn it, how did he know we'd give? You were there, Sergeant. Did you see anything to indicate we'd give?"

Blot shook his head, occupied with pouring himself more brandy and indifferent to the old man's questions, and Boderin went on fretfully.

"It was a sound line I'd chosen. They couldn't have taken us in the flank and we had a good view over the Cortambert Valley. You must remember, Blot."

"Yes," Blot said stolidly. "We could see all right."

"They must have been at least a kilometre away from us. Don't you agree?"

"Yes. At least a kilometre."

"I can see no reason at all to suggest we'd give. Can you?"

"No. None at all."

The old man stared at Sergeant Blot, irritated by his unhelpful answers.

If it hadn't been for Gallifet going down, he thought, St Roth might have turned out a brilliant holding action. As it was, von Martienssen had been right. They *had* given and the line *had* dissolved into ragged bunches of shouting men diving for the cover of the trees and streaming back down the road towards Percéval where the guns had got them again as they crossed into the open. Only Murphy, coming up at the last moment, had saved them.

He tried hard to remember just what Murphy's orders had been to him. He'd never been able to recall that Murphy had told him there'd be artillery. It must have been Gallifet who'd been told and he'd failed to pass it on. Or one of those damned staff officers who came up to him afterwards and reproached him so bitterly for letting them down.

He found he'd grown stiff and cold with sitting and he got to his feet abruptly, turning up the collar of his coat. "We'd better move up, Blot" he said, staring at the hill with distaste. "We've got to be there when he arrives."

Blot sighed and began to stuff away the maps and papers. The old sergeant's enthusiasm had long since smouldered to ashes.

"There's a path through the trees there, if I remember," General Boderin said. "I remember going up it for a look the night before. We'll take that one." He spoke as though he'd be glad to get it all over and done with.

They'd not gone more than fifty yards through the trees when Blot jerked a hand to his right, and Boderin caught a glimpse of a man walking stealthily through the bushes in the same direction as himself, pushing them aside cautiously as though he didn't wish to be seen.

Even as he became aware of the other figure, he heard voices speaking in English somewhere up on the slopes ahead of him. The sound carried down to him on the thin breeze, and he guessed it must be Murphy's party already ahead of them and probably in position.

"We must hurry," he said.

He glanced again at the man among the bushes and realized there was something vaguely familiar about him. Then he saw that the man was limping and carried something in his hand which gleamed dully in the filtered light that came through the trees. Almost in the same instant that he realized the object was a heavy revolver, he recognized the other man as his son.

"It's Robert," he said at last in astonishment. "What's *he* doing here? And what the devil's he doing with that gun?"

He was on the point of shouting, then he decided it would seem nervous and cheap and vulgar, and he gestured instead with his walking stick. "Fetch him over here, Blot" he said quietly, "Put the cases down. Get over there and see what he's up to."

As Sergeant Blot put the cases down and started to crash through the bushes, Boderin saw his son stop dead and turn. For a second, he saw a white face with a set expression of taut anxiety. Then Robert turned abruptly on his heel and ducked away into the bushes, and General Boderin saw his head bobbing as he limped away frantically, back towards Percéval.

"Stop!" he shouted, raising his voice for the first time, but the bobbing head seemed to duck lower, and a moment or two later it was out of sight.

Sergeant Blot stopped and turned round, as though seeking instructions, and while they were still staring at each other, startled and uncertain, they heard bushes being thrust aside, and two more men appeared from the slopes above them, one of them in a black leather coat, then behind them two or three policemen in uniform.

* 7 *

THE Paris newspapers and magazines descended on Percéval like a pack of wolves. By the time they arrived, however, General Murphy had disappeared again and General Boderin had already been whipped back to Paris under escort, and there was little left for them to see or hear beyond the old men who'd fought in the hills round the town. And they, warned by the Maire to hold their tongues, had very little to describe beyond the simple ceremony at the war graves, which nobody could hide anyway, because it had been seen by several bigwigs and more than one newspaperman.

Nevertheless, someone, somewhere in the pattern of things, was indiscreet enough to drop a hint of what had happened out of sight in the woods of St Roth and the reporters clamped down on it at once. In the absence of eye-witnesses, they were unable to gather much in the way of details, but it didn't stop them developing the story to the best of their abilities, and all the good that might have come from the comradely nature of Murphy's visit was undone by the appearance of the inevitable irritant in the shape of General Boderin, all the warmth and good spirit of the meeting between Frenchmen and Americans obscured by the gleeful revival of old hatreds.

Emancipation began to hammer away again at the *Affaire* as though it were all a new and joyous scandal that might pull down the government, and they reported it with glee and gusto and mostly quite wrongly.

It is understood, they claimed, *that General de Brigade de*

Lespinasse-Boderin du Crest, the chief figure in the regrettable affair of twelve years ago, journeyed specially to the Bligues on Wednesday with the express intention of conferring with General Murphy during his visit. It was General Boderin's intention to present maps and diagrams concerning the battle fought there in 1944, and to offer for the American's perusal a dossier of documents concerning the affair which ended in his court-martial. The American, it concluded maliciously and quite incorrectly, *refused to see him.*

Vigueur, with less malice but an equal amount of gay indifference to exactitude, stated: *General Boderin, accompanied by his servant, ex-Sergeant Blotte, made an attempt on Wednesday to confront General Murphy on the hill at Percévalles where the affair which led to his removal from command in 1944 took place.*

The American general, who was accompanied by Colonel Francis, his chief of staff, was not aware of General Boderin's presence because the police intercepted him as he made his way forward. General Boderin resisted and he and the servant, Blotte, were conveyed from the scene by police car. In Paris, they were interviewed at Police headquarters by Inspector Souprosse and Major Sender, of the Special Branch.

There was a great deal more in the same strain, most of it wrong. *Figaro* made the telling comment that a great many people were making a great deal of fuss about an affair which had been terminated twelve years before. *Unless,* it said, *the Affaire Boderin is another Affaire Dreyfus, which it isn't, there can be no reason why General Murphy shouldn't meet General Boderin amicably and clear up the whole thing. This nonsense of the General meeting the soldiers of the Bligues in the hope of distracting the attention of Frenchmen from the fact that, if nothing else, an old soldier's pride is being toyed with, does not hide the fact that General Murphy has acted very foolishly. A friendly meeting could clear the air so simply.*

Only *Le Monde* took the trouble to use Franks's hand-out at any length and even then it made the comment that *General Murphy seems to be trying very hard to win the good will of Frenchmen but it seems that he is being very badly advised. A meeting with the old soldiers of the Bligues can never obscure the fact that sections of the public feel that France's pride has been touched.*

Schneider stared down at the newspapers on his desk with a weary air, feeling a great deal of sympathy with General Murphy. It was very hard, he thought, to be misunderstood so completely.

There was a curious atmosphere of repetition about Souprosse's office above the Quai des Orfèvres when Cellini and Hardy and Nicole entered. The two policemen were sitting at one side of the desk—Souprosse, thick-set, spectacled, his hair *en brosse*, his face friendly and encouraging, and Schneider, his complete opposite, tall, slender, pale, his thinning hair brushed flat against his dome of a bony skull, his eyes bright and sharp and shrewd under the greying eyebrows, his maimed hand inevitably polishing the edge of his chair.

Sergeant Blot sat comfortably by the window, alongside a policeman, his face wearing an expression of self-righteousness, as though he were still a non-commissioned soldier acting under the orders of a superior officer.

General Boderin was perched on the edge of his chair in front of the desk, gesturing at Souprosse as they entered. "In ten minutes I could have got from General Murphy all that I required," he was saying. "If I hadn't been interrupted, I could have cleared up all this long unhappy mistake and gone some way towards clearing my name."

Nicole returned the old man's embrace indifferently.

"They wouldn't let me see Murphy," he complained in a high fretful voice as they all sat down. "All I wanted to do was show him the map I'd drawn. It had all the disputed points marked quite clearly on it. I've never since had the opportunity of showing it to him on the very spot where it all took place."

Nicole touched his arm and he subsided. Schneider passed cigarettes round but the old man pettishly refused them and lit one of his own.

"Why have they taken all my papers from me?" he demanded, putting the matches down on the desk in front of him, his thin bony fingers toying nervously with them in an irritating rattle the whole time.

"It's taken me twelve years to get all my papers together," he

203

said almost in a whine. "All my measurements and photographs are in that file. Everything I shall need when we get the re-trial."

"You can have them all back very shortly," Souprosse said gently, with a beaming smile that showed brown and broken teeth. "They have to be examined in detail. They'll be brought in, in a moment or two."

"Why do you have to examine my papers anyway?"

"It was your brief cases we were examining."

"But why? What for?"

"In case you had a weapon in there, monsieur," Souprosse said sharply.

The old man's head jerked round. "Weapons? What is all this? This is the second time you've searched me for weapons."

He spoke sharply in his high angry voice, almost like a spoiled child, and to Hardy he seemed suddenly older and oddly un-balanced, as though he had abruptly passed the peak of his life and had begun to descend into the querulous valley of old age.

"What do you suspect?" he was saying. "Why can't I be allowed to see General Murphy?"

Schneider's sharp tones stopped him dead.

"*Monsieur le Général*," he said, almost as though *he* were the general and Boderin the difficult young major—"General Murphy has behaved with a great deal of generosity. He's insisted that we don't put any restrictions on you. He only asks that you promise not to bother him again."

"But I'm *not* bothering him."

Hardy shifted uneasily in his seat as the old man burst out again. He had entered into this fantastic *opéra bouffe* for money and he was now caught up in it beyond the point when he could back out, in love with Nicole, sorry for the pathetic old man, sorry even for Souprosse and Schneider and for Murphy, and sorrier still for Robert Boderin, with his hurt body and the twisted mind that had hatched this hatred that obsessed them all.

"I'm not bothering Murphy," the old man was saying shrilly. "I only wish to speak to him about my case. I only wish to bring to his attention a few facts——"

"If it were possible to do anything for you," Schneider pointed out sharply, "General Murphy would do it. He's said so. But he's a busy man and he must first have proof that his time won't be wasted. Perhaps a lawyer——"

"I've been to the lawyers!" Boderin gestured angrily, waving his cigarette and rattling the match box on the desk top with an infuriating regularity. "They all say the same: *'It's twelve years since.' 'Too much has changed.' 'Too many people have died.' 'Too many have forgotten.'* They're nothing but third-rate mortgage dealers. The law's become the dustbin for the riffraff of the country all out for a quick franc. Now, if Gallifet had not been killed——"

"Perhaps you should try another adviser," Schneider interrupted quickly, before he could launch into another of his interminable diatribes. "Perhaps another advocate."

Nicole spoke abruptly. "There are no more," she said. "There are no more who'll even look at the case."

Cellini leaned forward and touched her hand. "I'll find someone, Nicole," he said impulsively. "There's bound to be someone who'll try. Maybe I can find an American practising over here. Don't worry. We'll get someone."

"I beg you not to be too optimistic," Schneider said.

"Why?" Cellini seemed suddenly young and aggressive. "Have you heard something?"

Schneider shrugged, toying with a long envelope. "I should hate you to be hopeful," he said, "when there was little to be hopeful about."

Cellini stared at him for a second then he turned again to Nicole. "Leave it to me," he said eagerly. "I'm sure I can fix it. I can fix a lot of things if you'll just give me a chance, Nicole. I can find you a job—either with our outfit, or some other American outfit here in Paris. It shouldn't be difficult."

She flashed him a grateful look and Schneider stopped playing with the envelope to sign to the policeman waiting by the wall.

"Perhaps the General will wait next door," he suggested gently.

"Why? Why must I?" General Boderin got to his feet, trying to push past the broad figure of the policeman who was ushering him inexorably towards the outer office.

"Because we have orders," Schneider snapped, standing up. "And we must carry them out."

205

The words seemed to invoke an old instinct for obedience, and General Boderin nodded abruptly. As he went out, Sergeant Blot rose awkwardly to his feet and followed.

Schneider waited until the door closed then he indicated the chairs again. Nicole sat down between Hardy and Cellini, her face taut and wary.

"Messieurs, mademoiselle," Schneider said. "We must talk a little."

"Wouldn't it be easier to get Murphy to agree to a meeting with General Boderin?" Cellini said aggressively.

"It isn't possible," Souprosse said. "General Murphy's willing to do all he can to help but his own position dictates these things and we'd be wasting his time if we couldn't provide anything fresh."

"Maybe if it were all properly investigated," Cellini said, "something might turn up." He seemed to be trying to impress Nicole rather than Souprosse, and his eyes kept flickering in her direction—almost as though he resented Hardy's influence and was trying to break it.

Souprosse, however, was unmoved. "I doubt it," he said.

"We've no right to condemn him."

Souprosse shrugged and spread his hands. "It's not for us to argue about that," he said. "That's a lawyer's job. But so far as we can see—and we've had advice on the matter—there's nothing to warrant taking up General Murphy's time."

"Perhaps Murphy doesn't want to see the old boy," Cellini said bitterly.

Schneider spoke now, in his cold, hard, arrogant voice. "General Murphy's a generous-minded man with nothing to hide. He's acted frankly and always correctly. I can assure you you're wrong."

"So what do you want us to do?" Cellini said, his face hostile.

"We wish you to extract a promise from General Boderin that he'll make no further attempt to pester General Murphy. If he should find fresh evidence and feels he has good reason to bring his case before General Murphy, he must first convince a lawyer. We've put our law department at his disposal."

"We'll get our own lawyer," Cellini said. "I'll find somebody."

206

Schneider shrugged. "If you wish it. I personally will be only too happy to help. I was a soldier myself once, monsieur, and I had my own career cut short when it looked like prospering." He held up his maimed hand. "I know how it feels."

Hardy watched the two officers, deciding they were a bit like Tweedledum and Tweedledee in the way each kept taking up the story as the other left off. They even seemed to speak alike.

"If we can't get a promise," Souprosse said, "we'll be compelled to take steps to make sure that your father, mademoiselle, *is not allowed to leave his home.* We might even take stronger measures and we've no wish to do that."

"I expect we can get a promise," Cellini said in a flat, defeated voice. He glanced at Nicole, as though expecting gratitude, but she sat stony-faced, indifferent to him.

"I'll go and live with him," she said, speaking for the first time.

They all turned towards her but her face showed no emotion. It was devoid of expression even.

"No, Nicole!" Hardy said at once. "You can't do that!"

As he spoke, he knew he wasn't so much interested in her reactions to her family as to himself. He was oddly scared at the thought of being lonely again, without the sound of her voice about him, afraid of the silence again, afraid that what they'd built up together would fall apart without her near.

"Nicole," he persisted. "You can't do this."

"I can't help it." She seemed to be speaking to Schneider instead of to Hardy. "There's no alternative. We must retain some pride. We'll move him to the apartment at Père Lachaise and I'll join him there at once."

Hardy opened his mouth to protest again but there suddenly seemed to be no point in arguing with her. She was accepting her duty as a Boderin, shouldering the family's burden in just the same stubborn way that they all did. He glanced at Cellini for support, surprised that he didn't object also, then he realized that Cellini preferred having her immured in her own family history to remaining with Hardy. Doubtless, his mind was already working, with its sharp newspaperman's precision, on the problem of curbing her family's influence.

"I guess we can get the promise you want," he was saying to Schneider. "I'll talk to him myself, in fact."

"It must be in writing, monsieur," Schneider pointed out. "I've hesitated to make it legal, knowing that the General is a graduate of St Cyr and a man concerned with his honour, but alas, I've no alternative. Did you know he'd been out to SHAPE headquarters in an attempt to buttonhole General Murphy there."

"He doesn't intend harm," Cellini said loudly. "Hell, you can see that for yourself!"

"Monsieur Cellini," Schneider said coldly. "I can see nothing. We're policemen, not psychiatrists. How do I know where the dividing line lies between an angry old man and someone who'll take up a missing gun and use it? He's been trying to get in touch with the Minister of War. They've given instructions that he must not go there again. They've been in touch with us, and I must pass the request on to you. *We must have this promise.*"

"I expect it'll be all right," Cellini said heavily. "I'll see you get it." He glanced at Nicole for her approval. "Is that all?"

"I'm afraid not. Not quite." Schneider pushed an envelope across to Nicole. "For your information, mademoiselle," he said, "and with the Minister's consent, to clear up many things."

She touched the envelope, picking it up hesitantly, looking doubtfully at Schneider as he spoke.

"Because I know what you must be thinking of us," he said, "I've been able to extract information from the secret files at the Ministry. It may help you to understand our position. This is from your father's own dossier, compiled by Frenchmen, not Americans. It was specially kept because of the court-martial. Normally, no one's allowed to see this file, but under the circumstances, and so that you'll be able to understand why we have to be so adamant, I've obtained permission to copy a summary of your father's character from it. It's in that envelope. It's for your eyes alone, mademoiselle. For your father's sake, please don't let him see it."

Nicole nodded and Cellini rose. "Is that all?" he asked again and Schneider made a gesture of apology.

"I'm afraid not, monsieur," he said. "There's one last point and this one's even more important. Mademoiselle's brother was also at St Roth on the day that General Murphy was there."

Nicole's eyes had flown to Schneider's face. "My brother?" she said.

"Yes, mademoiselle. As you know, we've been wanting to interview him for some time. In the circumstances, every suspicious action has to be investigated, and your brother's been acting very strangely."

There was a long pause, then Souprosse took up the story.

"We've established that he was at Orly when General Murphy's plane landed," he said bluntly. "We know he attempted to buy a rifle. We believe he was outside the American Embassy on one occasion, hoping, doubtless, to waylay General Murphy. And now we find he was at Percéval. We rely on your help if you should learn where he is."

Cellini seemed to be shocked into silence at last, and picked up his hat without a word. Hardy touched Nicole's arm and turned towards the door. For a second, she stared at Souprosse and Schneider, her eyes flickering from one to the other. She seemed to be on the point of questioning them, then she blinked rapidly as though she were shaking off the effects of a blow, and turned abruptly on her heel and followed Hardy.

After the door had closed behind them, Schneider and Souprosse remained silent for some time, Schneider staring out of the window towards the towers of Notre Dame, Souprosse still hunched in his chair staring at the desk. After a while, he reached out to the corner where General Boderin had been sitting.

"He left his matches behind," he said slowly.

Schneider turned. "I shouldn't worry," he said grimly. "He's lost much more than his matches today."

* 8 *

IT had not been possible to return at once to Paris after the fiasco at St Roth. Even as he was running through the wood, Robert Boderin had decided it would have been hopeless to return to Percéval to pick up a train. The police would have been there before he was.

Fortunately, he had blundered out of the wood right on to

the main road to the west, and, even as he sat down to get his breath back, he saw a *Nicolas* wine lorry rolling towards him.

He stood up, combing his hair and straightening his tie. There was a small Rénault parked by the roadside, and when he tried it and found it was locked, he guessed it belonged to the young couple who had sat up among the undergrowth, dishevelled and sheepish, as he had almost blundered on to them in his race for the road.

Quickly, he walked back towards the car and stood alongside it and, as the lorry approached, waved the vehicle to a standstill.

"My car," he said, gesturing vaguely at the Rénault. "Can you give me a lift to the next town? Then I can telephone my firm and arrange for a tow."

He made some vague generalization about being the representative of a Paris firm with branches in the Bligues, and the driver opened the door and he was on his way north from St Roth within ten minutes of seeing his father. In the next town, the lorry pulled up in the main square and he slipped to the ground, remaining motionless until the lorry had gone so that the driver shouldn't notice his limp. As soon as the vehicle was round the corner, he hurried from the square and found there was a bus just due to leave for Bar-le-Duc, and he bought his ticket quickly and climbed aboard.

When the bus dropped him off at Bar-le-Duc, he found he was too late to catch the train to Paris, and for a while he stood in the station entrance, listening to the voices of the porters echoing under the roof and wondering whether to catch a night train or the next morning's so that he would arrive in Paris when the streets were crowded, instead of at night when any alert policeman would find his task of looking for him easier. In the end, chiefly because a policeman took up his post near the station entrance, he walked away and eventually found a small hotel where he took a room for the night.

He was up early the next day and caught a slow train just before midday. Descending at Meaux just outside the city, he caught a bus to the Métro at Pantin. At the Gare du Nord he was relieved to find there'd been a surprise strike on the Clignancourt-Orléans line and the crowds were thick, and he was able to get by without being noticed. Before dark, he was back in the little room at Montparnasse.

Blot was already there, waiting for him, nervous and surrounded by newspapers and cigarette ends. There was a brandy bottle by the window and a dirty glass.

"You didn't manage it," he said at once, jumping to his feet, the relief showing in his face like a beacon. "Thank God for that!"

He began to clear up the newspapers and the cigarette ends and the brandy bottle, and Boderin watched him, quite calmly, indifferent to the show of loyalty, taking it for granted as he'd always taken for granted everything that Blot had ever done for him.

"Suppose they'd caught you!" Blot straightened up and faced him, red-faced and relieved but curiously ill-at-ease before the abnormal tranquillity of the other.

"I'm not worried." Boderin's face was expressionless, and he was self-assured in a way that worried Blot far more than his normal passionate anger. "I expect them to, of course—*in the end*."

He was moving about the room, putting his things in order, picking up the newspapers Blot had tidied and staring at the headlines. "But they'll never dare to question me in open court," he said, glancing at Blot. "If they do, I'll make Murphy look a fool. Remember, I'm a lawyer. And if they don't question me in court, it'll make him look a coward, as though the Americans have used their influence to keep me quiet. We have friends on the newspapers, Pierrot, who'll be glad to pick up a story like this."

Blot looked unhappy. "They've not been so friendly in the last few years," he reminded him. "I think they've forgotten. It's a long time ago. Still, thank God, friends won't be necessary. Nothing happened. I never did think you'd get close enough. It was all decided too much on the spur of the moment. You hadn't even bothered to think what you were going to do."

Boderin whirled on him, his calmness gone, angry, contemptuous of Blot's nervousness. "What else was there to do," he snapped, "except to point the gun and pull the trigger?"

Blot grinned. "All the same," he said. "You didn't. You thought better of it."

Boderin shook his head. "My father was there," he said bitterly. "He saw me and shouted out. The police came. He's becoming a nuisance. This is the second time he's got in my way."

"I read about him in the evening papers," Blot said slowly. "But there was nothing about you, so I just thought you'd decided not to do it. You're not going on with it now, of course?"

"Of course I am."

Blot's face fell with disappointment. "What? After two failures?" he asked.

"I'm more determined now than ever. I need your help."

"No!" Blot backed away at once, but Boderin stepped after him, his face darkening. "You promised you'd help," he snapped.

"That was only when you were thinking of horsewhipping him. I've told you—I didn't mean shooting!" Blot's cry was almost a bleat.

"I shall hold you to your promise. Many times in the past when you've been in need of money for your wretched gambling and women, you've come to me and I've always let you have it, because our families were so close, because your father meant something to my father. Now, you're too much in my debt to back out. You can't refuse to help me."

"I've helped!" Blot wailed. "I don't want to get involved!"

"Don't be ridiculous!" Boderin sneered. "I'm not asking you to commit any crime. I'm only asking you to obtain things for me that I shall need."

"Such as what?"

"I don't know yet. I must sit down and think. My ideas weren't good enough. I must think this time of something really sound, something that won't depend on mere chance."

Although General Boderin was still arguing, he was very subdued by the time they'd got him established in the silent flat at Père Lachaise. His complaints had subsided to a depressing whine that wearied them all.

The streets had the sultry look that Paris often wore on

summer evenings, and they were all a little tired and angry, and sick of the old man's self-pity.

"I'm sorry it looks so shabby," he said sadly as he ushered them in. "We got it as long ago as 1914, you see. My father, you will remember, was killed just before the Marne. He and his troops had been thrust back almost to the gates of Paris, and he considered it his duty to do something about it. He led one of the last cavalry charges of that war. They brought his body out of the battle——"

"How did the battle go?" Hardy asked sharply, almost sourly. "Did he lose many men?"

Boderin shook his head. "Unhappily, he lost most of them. But the situation was saved. He was buried in Père Lachaise with full military honours. His uniform was given to the Musée de l'Armée. It's in the Invalides to this day—War of 1914-18 section. You can see the holes the machine-gun bullets made." He nodded proudly, almost as though the rents were decorations. "We took this flat at my mother's request because she wished to be able to tend the grave. The district's fallen back a little since, I'm afraid to say."

He shook his head and sat down, stiffly encased in his own despair. "And now, it seems," he went on flatly, "I'm to be virtually a prisoner here. I might as well be in the vault across the road."

While Cellini busied himself fetching drinks, helpful to Nicole and completely ignored, Hardy was wandering round the flat, staring at the pictures and the framed scraps of message pads which bore out the Boderins' claim to fame, and the old-fashioned furniture which didn't have the quality of antiquity and was only heavy, sombre and oppressive. There was a stagnant smell about the place, as though it stank of lost hopes.

Nicole's face was expressionless and she seemed deep in thought. In spite of the apartment, Hardy decided, the Boderins hadn't yet quite taken over. There was a curious aliveness behind her eyes and the blank despair he'd seen there when they'd been summoned to the Préfecture had gone.

She had glanced once in the car on the way back at the sheet of paper from the envelope that Schneider had given her, sitting silently while she read it. At first she had gone white, then somehow she had seemed more cheerful and Hardy had suspected that whatever it contained, it was final enough for her to see some hope of normality behind it.

She had read it through, without speaking, then without offering it to Hardy or Cellini to read, had jammed it hurriedly back into the envelope and stuffed it into the pocket of her coat. For the rest of the journey she had said nothing.

Hardy could only guess at the contents of the paper but he suspected it contained the views of someone important at the Ministry of War on the character of General Boderin, and he guessed it was unanswerable and irrevocable. That could be the only meaning of the new life in her eyes.

Old Boderin, unaware of what she knew, was prattling on. "I might just have caught him there on the hill," he was saying gloomily. "If I could only"—he paused and shrugged—"but, of course, I've given my promise and, as a man of honour, I must abide by it."

Hardy glanced at the black leather coat where it lay over the back of a chair, aware of what it contained—the old man's death warrant, so to speak, the end of the road for him, the iron curtain on all his hopes—and he wondered if she'd ever have the courage to tell him about it.

"Why did you send Robert after me?" General Boderin was demanding now. "There was nothing he could do that I couldn't do. Now *he* seems to be involved in some way. I tried to contact him but he hurried off. Now why did he do that? He must have recognized me. He must have seen Sergeant Blot."

As Nicole handed him a drink, he began to mutter to himself and disappeared into the other room, fishing in his pocket for a pencil.

"You must forgive me a moment," he explained to Hardy. "I've just recalled something and I must write it down while I remember. I've so many things to bear in mind. But I noticed at St Roth that the trees obscured the valley from the hill, and I wonder if that could have been why I failed to be aware of the German artillery. Probably I couldn't see. I must check it at the library. Perhaps I can get permission later when this is all over to go back to Percéval again and have another look."

He disappeared, and for a long time there was no sound but the

214

shuffling shoes of Sergeant Blot on the carpet as he passed the glasses round. They could hear drawers opening and shutting in the other room and once the thump of a heavy book on the table as General Boderin became absorbed in what he was doing and forgot them.

Standing at the window, staring over the tops of the sepulchres of Père Lachaise, Hardy began to wish that Cellini would go and leave them alone. There seemed to be so much he had to tell Nicole. He had written to his wife, asking for a divorce, and he wanted her to know. She was talking to Cellini now, asking about her belongings, and Hardy grew desperate. There was so much he had to say, but Cellini was all smiles and confidence at the thought that he'd get her out of Hardy's flat at last, and when she had left the room he turned angrily on the American.

"Well," he asked. "What happens now?"

Cellini glanced at him, resenting the note in his voice but unable to keep the triumph out of his eyes.

"We go and fetch Nicole's belongings from that place in the Rue Jacob," he said.

"You're enjoying this, aren't you, Jimmy?" Hardy asked. "The Great White Right triumphing over the Powers of Evil."

Cellini pretended not to understand. "I don't know what you're getting at, Sam," he said calmly.

"You wanted her out of my place, didn't you?" Hardy sensed that he was being petulant and schoolboyish but he couldn't help it.

Cellini shrugged. "It was wrong, Sam," he said earnestly. "It wasn't as it should have been." He paused and drew a deep breath. "Listen, Sam," he said. "I could love this girl if she gave me half a chance——"

"Cut it out, Jimmy. You sound like Gregory Peck."

"I could, Sam." Cellini's face was hard and hostile. "And if I get the breaks I will. You're always talking about all being fair in love and war. O.K. So it is. Let's face it. And I think it was wrong for her to stay in your place. You've no right to her."

"I'm going to marry her. Doesn't that give me a right?"

Cellini stared. "You're married already," he accused.

"I'm getting a divorce."

"I don't believe you."

215

"I'll show you the letter I wrote to my wife."

"I'd rather see the one she writes back. Suppose she says 'no' again. She always has done up to now. Until I see that, I'll do all I can to keep Nicole away from you, Sam. I know you. I've known you a long time. She's better here with her father."

"With the Inter-Continental News Agency to keep an eye on her?"

"Yes," Cellini snapped. "With the Inter-Continental News Agency—me—to keep an eye on her." He paused. "I guess she seems a lot happier now that I've promised to find a lawyer for her," he ended.

"I don't think she gives a damn about your lawyer, and I don't think you'll find anyone willing to touch it with a barge-pole—not even an American."

Cellini stared aggressively at Hardy.

"You think us Americans are a lot of fools, don't you?" he said.

"Not really," Hardy said wearily. "I often envy you your ability, in fact. It's just that I think you're all too kind—too optimistic. Why should you be able to do better at this than the people who live here?"

"You can do a lot if you've got a bit of faith to start off with," Cellini pointed out.

"Nobility's rather tedious," Hardy said sourly. "I seem to remember when I was a kid thinking that Sir Galahad was a bit of a drip."

Cellini began to get angry. "You don't like us, do you?"

Hardy looked up quickly. "More than you know," he said gently. "You're a hell of a lot nicer than your popular writers ever let people think."

Cellini seemed mollified and ready to be friendly again. "I know you English think we're a lot of suckers," he said slowly, "and I know we're comparatively new over here, but people started helping each other long before the United States got into the business. Jesus Christ started it, remember?"

"My God," Hardy said, beginning to get angry again. "How smug can you get?"

"'Smug's' a word," Cellini retaliated, "that's used by the discontented to describe the contented."

"Touché!" Hardy's anger died and he stared affectionately at

216

Cellini again. "Are you in love with Nicole, Jimmy?" he asked, suddenly gentle.

Cellini met his eyes frankly. "I guess I would be if she ever looked at me," he admitted. "I feel damn' sorry for her."

Hardy turned to him earnestly. "For God's sake, don't get involved in this damned affair through pity, Jimmy," he begged. "This is nothing. The French army's shaken to its foundations by scandal once every generation. Keep out of it."

Cellini gave him a wry smile. "I'll look after myself, Sam. We're not really barbarians, you know. I know you and the French think we are and maybe we are at that—I know we often envy you your age—but, Sam, even barbarians learn and grow civilized."

Hardy grinned, unable to quarrel long with Cellini. "O.K., Jimmy," he said. "At least you're honest. What's the next move?"

"I'd like to find young Boderin before the police do. Maybe we could get him examined by a psychiatrist. Maybe we could get him put away. Anything rather than letting him do what he's intending to do. Are you still willing to help?"

"I've got to eat."

Cellini pulled out his wallet and took out several large-denomination notes. "I'll pay your expenses, as usual," he said flatly.

When Nicole came into the room, they had settled their differences, and, even if they weren't in agreement, they weren't openly hostile to each other.

"All set?" Cellini grinned, obviously making a great effort to cheer her up. "Let's go collect your things."

She nodded and he took her hand, just as Sergeant Blot appeared from the other room, carrying an armful of books and papers which he spread out on the table before shuffling back into the kitchen.

"I've just discovered an interesting point"—General Boderin's voice came to them from the other room—"I've got a new map here that I bought the other day. I notice there's a bunch of trees marked on it. They stand right in front of where I set up my headquarters, and they aren't on the older maps. Now, I wonder if it could have been that my maps were wrong. I wonder if that could have been the reason I never saw the German artillery."

Hardy eyed Cellini, and Cellini jerked his head towards the door.

"Nicole"—the voice rose imperiously and she half-turned—
"perhaps you'll bring me that file of documents in there. You'll
find a green folder. We might find some reference in my notes to
trees obscuring my position——"

Cellini pushed Nicole quickly and firmly towards the door.

"Come on," he said. "Let's go!"

"But my coat—I'll need my coat!"

Cellini edged her nearer towards the door. "Let's go," he
insisted, "before you get caught up. It's warm. There's a coat in
my car you can borrow if you need one. Besides"—his soft voice
sounding chiding—"you ought never to wear black. Black's not
your colour."

She glanced up, the trace of a smile on her face as she let him
pull her towards him.

"Why not?"

"You're young. You're pretty. You need something
brighter."

Hardy grinned slyly and gestured with the notes Cellini had
given him. "I'll buy you something, Nicole," he put in quickly.
He knew Cellini had been working up to a suggestion like that
and it gave him an immense pleasure to forestall him. "I've just
come into some money. I can afford it."

He could see the protest on Cellini's lips, but the American
bit the words back.

"Sure," he said gallantly. "I'll help. Let's say it's a present from
the both of us."

As they disappeared, General Boderin came into the room,
his arms full of papers.

"Nicole! Nicole——!"

His voice rose fretfully, then he stopped and turned, realizing
the room was empty.

"Odd," he said aloud.

He decided comfortably that perhaps she'd grown tired of his
old battles at last. Everybody else seemed to have. Even Sergeant
Blot. And she seemed to spend a great deal of her time with the
two young men, he'd noticed. Perhaps she was in love at last.
Perhaps she'd settle down. Perhaps——

He shrugged his thoughts aside and sat down at the table with his maps and papers, absorbed with a new enthusiasm. He had a great deal to do. The discovery of the new map had set him thinking along a thousand new lines, and all the weariness, frustration and boredom he'd felt on the hillside at St Roth had vanished in this new erratic burst of optimism.

There must have been a good reason for what had happened that day, he thought. There must have been. Although he'd given with great reluctance his signed promise not to worry General Murphy again, in that curious over-optimistic way of his that pushed unpleasant facts to the back of his mind, he had a feeling that even that problem would sort itself out in time. He would inevitably unearth new facts if he tried hard enough, and then they'd have to withdraw their ruling.

He heard the clink of bottles in the kitchen, then Sergeant Blot stumped past him towards the door, carrying a shopping bag. He nodded gaily and the old sergeant returned his smile with his normal expressionless stare.

As he heard the door slam, Boderin turned again to the papers before him, suddenly feeling young again. Blot would be back soon with a meal and a good bottle of wine. That and a cigar would be a good way to start his new life. Caught by hope, he began to shuffle the papers before him, trying to force his mind to feel alert.

It should have been obvious to him, he thought, that the Germans had had concealed guns near St Roth. He couldn't understand why he hadn't thought about it at the time. Somehow, he had the feeling that someone had warned him about it—perhaps Gallifet or Devéria or even Murphy himself—but he could never understand, if they had, why it should have slipped his mind. Then he remembered how angry he'd been that day when Murphy had refused to let him lead the attack against St Roth, and he unexpectedly found himself wondering if in his anger he had overlooked it. The thought came with a startling shock—ugly and cold and uncomfortable. In the whole twelve years that he'd been thinking about it, that possibility had never occurred to him before. Anger! The black Boderin anger! Could it have been that?

He shrugged irritably, as though shaking off something unpleasant. No, he thought, it couldn't have been anger. He was a trained soldier, drilled to think calmly and without panic. It was part of his background.

But he had to admit to himself that he remembered reading somewhere that if his father had taken the trouble to move cautiously at the Marne instead of putting his head down and charging bullheaded at his enemy, he might have succeeded in what he was attempting and remained alive to enjoy the glory. He'd seen it in some history book, but he couldn't remember where now. Then there'd been the Boderin who'd lost a hundred and thirty-five men in some stupid affray in Algeria, because he'd not troubled to find out where the enemy was. Rumour had it that he'd been confronted the night before by his captain over some woman and was still black with rage from the quarrel. It wasn't in any of the history books but the story had been passed down from generation to generation in the family and all the Boderins knew of it.

When he thought about it, calmly and dispassionately, he realized the Boderin temperament wasn't the easiest in the world to get on with. His own rages, when everything seemed to go black and blank, and rational thought disappeared, had died away now, because he was too old for them, but Robert obviously still suffered from them, and he wondered briefly if that was what had happened at St Roth.

It was odd, he thought, that it had never occurred to him before. He had considered every other possibility but never this one. Perhaps it was that he was growing more inclined with age to self-examination. He could never remember thinking before that it might have been his own fault. With true French arrogance he had never indulged in soul-searching, had never done anything but seek to lay the blame elsewhere.

The thought disturbed him and he sat back in his chair, staring at his papers, feeling as though he'd like to sweep the whole stupid lot into the waste paper basket. Many times he'd felt the same way before, but whenever he'd talked of giving up, Robert had always bullied him—yes, *bullied* him, he realized now—into continuing. Suddenly assailed with doubt, he wondered if he'd been wasting his time for the last twelve years.

Other men had suffered disgrace and had accepted it and had watched the world forget while they went on to make themselves happy in other spheres. He remembered a major from Sarthe who'd been accused in Algeria of selling arms to the Arabs. He'd been found guilty and not only dismissed the service but sent to prison as well. Ten years later, Boderin had bumped into him in Marseilles, obviously sufficiently benefiting from his experience of buying and selling to have set himself up as an importer and exporter, with a charming wife and three children, and a mistress with the sort of beauty that took your breath away, all his misdeeds forgotten in a community that hadn't even known him in his days of disgrace.

But that, he decided bitterly, would never have been possible in the Boderin family. If a man were disgraced, that was the end of him. If there were doubt, his pride, his honour, forced him to fight back to the last breath, to the last centime, as he had done himself after St Roth. But had he been honest with himself? With a frightening clarity—the clarity of an old man looking back on his life for the first time with unafraid eyes—he realized he might have been making life miserable for a lot of other people besides himself, purely because he'd refused to face facts. He'd probably simply forgotten the instructions about the guns. Murphy had always insisted he'd given them to him and had produced documents to prove it. He'd never been able to dispute them, although he'd never admitted until now that they might have been genuine.

He sat back, feeling frail and futile, and badly in need of a drink. Rising, he poured himself a brandy and sat sipping it, his mind feebly mulling over the facts.

After a while, he began to feel better. For the first time he told himself, he was facing up to things, and he felt strong suddenly, and younger, as though this facing up to facts had helped him to put them behind them, as though at last he could stare the future in the eye.

His washed-out eyes brightened with a new pride in himself that he'd not been able to feel for years, a different pride from the stiff-necked arrogance that he knew he'd always worn before, and he felt that from that moment he could be gentler, kinder, more understanding, a new Boderin, a good Boderin taking his place among the best of the long line of widely diverse characters who made up his ancestors.

221

He took out a long cigar, thinking he'd enjoy sitting back and appreciating this new Boderin he'd become, but he found to his annoyance that he hadn't any matches, and he remembered he'd left them on Schneider's desk.

"Blot," he called fretfully, forgetting his new character at once in his irritation. "Blot!"

There was no reply and he remembered that Sergeant Blot had gone out to get the wine for the evening meal.

He pushed himself out of the chair and angrily began to search the house for matches. There were none in the kitchen and he pawed about, his hands quick and clumsy, among the papers on his desk. Then he saw Nicole's black coat and felt in the pocket, expecting to find matches there.

Sure enough, he found cigarettes and matches, and tired and breathless and annoyed with himself that he'd let his new self elude him so easily, he was about to light the cigar when he noticed a buff envelope with a piece of paper sticking from the inside pocket, as though it had been hastily read and hurriedly pushed back again.

He was about to turn away when he noticed his own name along the top of the paper and with trembling fingers he took out the envelope. The new courageous feeling he'd experienced faded quickly as he felt frightened of what he might read. He had no idea what the paper contained, but he guessed it was some private information on himself.

He knew it was dishonourable to pry into other people's affairs, and if the paper was in Nicole's pocket, it couldn't be any concern of his and it was mean and ungentlemanly to touch it. But, with his new feeling of self-honesty he tried to believe it didn't matter any more what he did. If it were about himself he felt he ought to face it.

As he unfolded the typewritten sheet, he saw his whole military life listed in front of him, from the day when he first became a cadet at St Cyr, until the last date in Paris, which marked the end of his court martial.

He turned the sheet over and immediately the summary of his career hit him like a blow between the eyes.

Definite disobedience to orders . . . no excuse for behaviour . . . unbalanced to the point of suspected cowardice . . . entirely

*—repeat entirely—unsuitable for further employment in any
responsible command whatsoever* . . .

His startled eyes saw that they had even set out his family background. His father's gallantry at the Marne, which had gained him
a medal and an early death, was summarized as *unnecessary
impetuosity*. They had even gone back as far as Sedan to quote
his great-grandfather. The whole family weakness seemed to be
laid bare before his eyes.

*Unbalanced. Too obsessed with pride. Old family, too con-
cerned with honour to be realistic*. The words seemed to burn in
his brain and he felt the room whirling about him. It was there in
front of him in black and white—exactly what everyone thought
of him, what Murphy had known all along and had never been
cruel enough to tell him, what the army thought, what the people
in the know thought, what perhaps even Nicole and Héloïse
Lamballer had guessed in the end.

With the knowledge that what he had hidden from himself was
already known to everyone else, he began to admit to himself
again what he had never been able to admit before. He *had* been
in a black rage that day at Percéval, and that and that alone had
been the cause of the disaster at St Roth. He had led his men
blindly into the trap that Murphy had warned him about, from
sheer arrogance and, having found himself caught, had lost his
head. He remembered now the splitting headache that had started
—the headache that always came with his tempers—which
seemed to cut off the sense from his brain. He had panicked and,
when Gallifet had been killed, he had no longer seemed to have
the power to control events, and had joined the frightened men
streaming back towards Percéval.

For the first time in his life, he truly faced the facts, and he
found them terrifying.

He glanced at the sheet again and the whole unhappy business
came back to him, his protestations of innocence; the questions
at the court-martial that the lawyers wouldn't let him ask; the
long speeches on French honour and French pride by men who
had never had to face an enemy bullet; the dreary waiting in
silent ante-rooms; the long hours of cross-examination, when
they had made him say things he hadn't intended to say; his own
frantic pleading—*"M. L'Avocat,* I can't remember. I was tired.

I'd been wounded"; and then the headlines—*General Boderin Cashiered. Court-Martial Returns Guilty Verdict.*

He remembered wondering if they'd disgrace him with all the ghastly ceremonial of a hollow square. But they hadn't. They'd merely allowed him to leave—as though they were glad to get rid of him—and sent on to him in a buff envelope like this one the information that his services were no longer required. He could still see the sidelong glances of the officers as he'd walked out of the court, the silence that had greeted him in the corridor outside, the turned backs, the starkness of the words on the single sheet of notepaper.

He could still remember the gendarmes who'd hurried him through the gaping crowd, and the booing, and the flash of photographers' bulbs, the long wait in a shabby waiting-room several miles down the line where, to avoid political disturbances, the Army had thoughtfully arranged for the train to stop instead of having the uproar on the main station. He could still remember that train, and sitting huddled in a corner in the darkness with the blinds drawn, pretending with a newspaper over his face to be asleep, fearful lest someone would get in who recognized him, the dark glasses he'd worn to fool the newspapermen who'd later insulted him by offering him sums of money for his life story.

The whole thing came back with a pain that cut like a knife—a pain he had carried ever since like a splinter under his ribs—because he knew he was being discussed in every bar and music hall in France, at every shabby political meeting, with wild statements by the Leftist press that the whole thing had been stage-managed by political tricksters who were truckling to the Americans. But it hadn't been stage-managed. He admitted now it hadn't. There'd been no trickery about it, and no truth in the statements that the witnesses had been bribed. Even Devéria had spoken against him, reluctantly, but forthrightly because he was honest and wanted to see justice done. In the end, all the story of trumpery had died down and there'd been only his own voice whining alone in the wilderness; and all the indignities he'd suffered from his own foolish desire to satisfy his pride had been forgotten—except by himself. Suddenly he knew that if he lived to be a hundred, he could never forget that he had brought it all on himself.

He stared at the papers on his desk, and started again on the long dreary course of memory, striving in his stubborn way to prove to himself that he must be wrong after all. Then, he stopped and folded the paper again and replaced it in the envelope which he then pushed back into the pocket of Nicole's coat. He still had the cigar in his hand but he put it down now, and laid the matches alongside it.

All his resolution to face the future squarely and boldly had slipped away from him. There was no future. It seemed to have been lopped off as though by a knife by the slip of paper he'd read.

For twelve years he'd been struggling unnecessarily while all the time everyone had laughed at him, knowing what he didn't know himself. The thought shocked him, and he felt he could no longer put his face outside the room. He couldn't face decent men any more.

After a while, he sat down, grey-faced. He lit the cigar and smoked it slowly, his mind working, his face expressionless and dead. The apartment was stuffy with the stagnation of age, and silent except for the creaks of the woodwork that came like the tapping of a woodpecker's beak, and he suddenly realized how much he hated the place with its scent of lost hopes, and always had done.

Rising quickly, he put down the cigar, thanking Heaven that Blot was inclined to be talkative when he went to do the shopping and hadn't returned yet. He went to the locked drawer of his desk, unlocked it, and took out the little Belgian automatic that he'd pocketed at Chartres. For a while, he stared at it, reflecting that he'd even lied about that. While Schneider had been looking for it, he'd had it safely hidden away under the carpet beneath the desk in the flat he'd rented in the Rue St Hyacinthe. In case he needed it to finish his own life. He remembered the despair with which he'd bought it—not to protect himself as he'd always claimed, but to do away with himself. At last, he seemed to feel the need for it.

He quickly stubbed out the cigar, and locked the door. Then sitting carefully in the chair in front of his papers, he raised the little pistol to his head and blew his brains out.

PART THREE

★ I ★

INEVITABLY, General Boderin's suicide was splashed across the front of every paper in Paris. They hadn't been having a circus for over a fortnight without deciding to make full use of its end.

General Boderin, Martyr des Americains, announced *Emancipation* with glee, as it raked over all the muck of 1944 and 1947 to make sure that everyone should know what was in the old man's mind when he had taken out the little automatic and pulled the trigger. *Was it a broken heart?* asked another one, and recounted all his struggles to have his case reviewed. There were pictures of Nicole and Robert Boderin—*who has been missing ever since the arrival of General Murphy in Paris*—and there were newspapermen's cars parked along the grass verge outside SHAPE headquarters, and photographers waiting to get a picture of Murphy as he came out.

"As I said a while back, Frankie," he said to Franks. "I didn't come over here to start a wave of suicides. The old guy must have been sorely troubled to do this."

Major Schneider put it differently. For a long time he studied the newspapers on his desk, then he looked up at Souprosse who was standing at the other side, grave-faced, ugly, sombre.

"Suicide's an acknowledgment," he said slowly, "of the incapacity to make a job of living. He died as he always lived—a sous-lieutenant just out of St Cyr."

He lay the paper down carefully and arranged it neatly with the others in a fan on his desk top, thoughtfully pushing them into place.

"This isn't going to make our job easier," he said slowly. "If anything, it'll stoke up the fires. Get Edérède, Souprosse. We must have Edérède."

Souprosse looked up. "We can't go around hauling everybody

in," he said bluntly. "It looks so bad and doesn't help General Murphy."

"Never mind, haul him in. On any pretext you like. But get him. We've got to talk to him. We've got to find where this wretched boy is and Edérède may have tried to contact him. Have we heard anything?"

"Nothing," Souprosse said grimly.

"The papers have had a description of him. Hasn't anyone been in?"

"Only the usual procession of madmen who think there might be a reward. All of them useless. God knows where he might be now. He might be in Algiers or Italy."

"Or back here," Schneider said slowly.

He stared down at the newspapers again and the three-column pictures of General Boderin that were plastered all over the front pages with the inch-high letters of the headlines.

"*Nicholas Jean St Omer de Lespinasse-Boderin du Crest,*" he read out slowly, enunciating the syllables as though they were indictments on a crime sheet. "He made a mess of most of his life and, like the stiff-necked purblind imbecile he was, he took care to make of his death the occasion for still another mess."

When Blot burst into his room, Robert Boderin was still asleep, lying on the bed with his hands under his head. In his depression after the failure at St Roth, he had finished the brandy that Blot had brought and had fallen asleep in his clothes, and he sat up now, startled and unshaven, his clothes rumpled, as the door was flung open.

Blot was agitated and nervous and was sweating profusely. The previous night he had been cornered in a bar opposite the Gare du Nord by a shabby little man carrying a bag and holding a copy of *Humanité* as though it were an identification card. There had been a lot of talk in glib terms that made it quite clear, however, that there were other people as interested in Robert Boderin's anxiety to remove General Murphy as he was himself. Although money had been mentioned, Blot had been reluctant to listen at first, but the amount that had been finally suggested as his own share had been staggeringly big enough to make him change his mind.

228

However, in spite of the wad of notes that had been handed over, he had promised nothing and had left the bar in an uncertain mood, torn different ways by his greed and an instinctive loyalty towards the Boderins. He had returned unwillingly to his rooms, afraid lest the source of his increased wealth should be questioned, but Martine had been tired too, and in a waspish mood. She had been waiting with a bag ready packed and had announced as soon as he was through the door that her mother was ill and that she would have to go to Bordeaux for a few days to look after her. Blot had returned from accompanying her to the station, depressed and lonely, appalled at the thought of spending the night on his own. He had spent some of the money on drink but had slept badly in spite of the brandy he'd consumed. He had risen reluctantly to go to work, stupefied, with a headache and unwilling to face the day.

As he tried to tie his shoe-laces without leaning too far forward, he had stared sourly round the shabby set of rooms where he lived, aware of the scent of drains that came up to him from below, the chatter of women from the street and the clang and hammering and the shriek of steel on steel from the motor repair yard whose rear wall backed up against the other side of the courtyard. For all his new wealth, he was in a surly mood, and, with his headache, ready to back out of anything.

At the bar on the corner, he was standing at the counter, ordering coffee and croissants for his breakfast, when he had glanced up and seen the headlines on the newspaper held by a man alongside him.

General Boderin, Martyr des Americains, he read gloomily, and wondered what they'd raked up now. Then the word *suicide* caught his eye and he craned nearer.

With all its usual gleeful attention to detail, *Emancipation* had described fully what had happened, with all the gory details of the scene when the body was found. They had spelt Nicole's name wrong, and Cellini's name, but there was no doubt about the photograph of his own father explaining to reporters how he had returned to find the body. As he stared shocked at the newspaper, its owner began to turn the sheet, and Blot had snatched it from his fingers, holding him off for a second with one hand while he finished the story. Then he had jammed the crumpled sheets back into their startled owner's hands and run from the bar, while the waiter sprawled across the counter bawling after him that his breakfast hadn't been paid for.

Running down the hill, holding his splitting head with one hand, he had stopped long enough to buy a newspaper and scan it quickly to make sure he hadn't been seeing things, then he had grabbed a taxi across the river and hurried into the little apartment block in the Rue du Maine where he had installed Robert Boderin. Pounding up the stairs, he flung open the door and almost fell across the bed, holding his head again and moaning. Robert Boderin sat up at once, dark-chinned and ugly with anger.

"Look!" Blot panted. "Look! It's your father! The old fool's shot himself!"

Boderin snatched the newspaper from his shaking hands and swung his legs from the bed. His face had gone ashen-white.

"It's all over," Blot said wildly. "There's nothing left now!"

Boderin sat staring at the paper. The cause for which he had worked and suffered so long and so earnestly, had gone. There was nothing left to get worked up about, nothing to put right. No review of any court-martial could ever bring back his father now. He had committed the final dishonour by shooting himself and in his death there was a tacit admission of guilt.

By this time, however, Robert Boderin's obsessions had grown beyond the mere desire for revenge, and even before he spoke, Blot knew his father's suicide had only strengthened his decision to continue.

"Now, more than ever, I'm determined," he said slowly. "Murphy is only the first stone from under the feet of this American colossus. We must make plans."

"Well, don't include me," Blot said quickly. "I've got a headache and I'm not going to join any conspiracy."

Boderin shrugged. "I don't want conspiracies," he said harshly. "They smack of evil. What *I'm* planning is for the sake of the soul of France."

Blot backed away. "You're not getting along very fast," he said sarcastically.

"My time will come. Even without the help of wash-outs like you, Pierrot."

230

Blot flushed with anger, then he remembered the little man in the bar with the copy of *Humanité* and the wad of money in his back pocket, and he was consumed with the desire to show that he was clever too.

"A friend of mine was talking to me today," he announced. "He said you were going about it all the wrong way."

Boderin whirled. "A friend? You've told someone?"

Blot laughed nervously, afraid to say too much. "Lord, no," he added quickly. "I told him about it as though it were a story I was reading, you understand. He said you hadn't got a hope of pulling it off. He said you have to have organization. He said that anyone wanting to kill anyone as important as Murphy would need help."

Boderin sat up. "Why?"

"He'll be too well guarded. That's why! Especially after St Roth. You'd need some sort of diversion to get the flics away from him."

There seemed to be sense in what he was saying and Boderin nodded. "That seems reasonable," he said.

"You've not achieved much alone," Blot pointed out bluntly. "You've failed twice. But if you're still wanting to do it, a word in the right ear could make it easier. It's merely a case of kicking up a rumpus nearby so that it would leave the coast clear for you. Besides, you'll never get close to him after St Roth. You want a better weapon."

"I'll get a rifle. There's one at Père Lachaise."

Blot laughed jeeringly. "Do you think the police aren't watching the place?" he said. "They're not fools."

"I'll buy one then."

"They'll have contacted all the gunsmiths. The minute you went in, they'd show you a couple of guns to keep you busy then nip round the back to ring the police. And then, bang, you're caught, and probably so am I."

"Then how do I get a rifle?"

"This friend of mine——"

Boderin turned sharply. "This friend of yours," he snapped. "We hear a lot of him. Who is he? Is he Right Wing or Left? Is he Fascist or Communist? What's his interest in helping me?"

Blot backed away, holding his head. "Not so loud," he said

weakly. "Not so loud. As a matter of fact, he's just a man who loves France and believes in justice as strongly as you do." He began to feel better as he saw Boderin's growing interest and even began to consider himself rather clever. "He believes in a strong France," he went on. "He believes in France not being dependent on Wall Street."

"I don't want a conspiracy, I tell you," Boderin said. "I want to do this alone."

"You needn't worry," Blot said, airily making promises. "He and his friends aren't anxious to get involved in any publicity. They're only too pleased to keep in the background."

"Are you in the pay of these people?" Boderin's eyes narrowed.

"Me? Not likely. I just happen to know one of them, that's all. I've not told him about you, of course. It's just that we were speaking generally. But they have means of acquiring apartments in the right places, you know, and means of getting hold of a rifle, and means of getting it into an apartment disguised as something else. They know, for instance, where Murphy's going to live. He's been looking at houses in the St Germain-en-Laye-Le Vésinet area. Did you know that?"

"Did this friend of yours tell you all this?"

"Well, not all of it—just some of it. But it's all true. They can provide these things. They've got contacts. They know where you can get a little quiet practice with a rifle, for instance."

"I don't need any practice! I'm a crack shot. All my family are crack shots."

"Well, there you are, then." Blot spread his hands. "With a good rifle and a telescopic sight, you can't miss."

"I don't know." Boderin hesitated. "I want to do it at the right place. Sarajevo was never a worthy location for such a sacrifice. I want this to be a gesture for France. It would have been, at Orly. At the moment he set foot in France. It would have been at St Roth. On the very ground where he started it all. An official occasion is the time for it."

"You haven't a hope," Blot said, losing his temper suddenly, as his head started to throb again. "You'll never get within forty metres of him! My way's the only way."

"No." Boderin snapped the word. "I refuse to shoot him down

232

on his own balcony in front of his wife. That's personal. If I do it elsewhere it's official. It's different."

"Is it?" Blot said flatly. "It doesn't seem very different to me. As far as I can see, he's dead either way."

With Cellini in a frenzy of work, it was Hardy who had to take Nicole to the inquest on her father. She wore the old black leather coat again, he noticed, and had tied a scarf of black chiffon round her hair, and he thought how French she looked, how provincial.

Her hands had toyed for a moment with the little white mackintosh they'd bought for her. It was only a cheap thing, for she'd refused to allow them to pay much, but she'd obviously thought a great deal about it, almost as though it were a symbol of her emergence from the wearisome Boderin past into the light. She'd been humbly grateful for the step forward and, when Cellini had finally gone, they'd eaten at a little restaurant in the Rue de Seine and gone to Hardy's flat, forgetful at last of the grey-bearded old nincompoop at Père Lachaise. She had made love eagerly, then he had taken her back to the Rue du Douleur and they had found the place full of policemen, with Sergeant Blot, silent and wooden-faced, and Schneider and Souprosse, and Jimmy Cellini, bitter and reproachful and accusing.

She went through the ordeal of the inquest blank-faced, wearing the old black coat and scarf indifferently, no make-up on her face, as though she were unconcerned about her appearance.

Later, outside the cheerless police office, with its grey paint and cinder-stained tricolour, she had rejected Schneider's offer of a car to see her home. The Métro was busy but she seemed to prefer it that way, as though she were clinging to the company of other people. She had lost her gaiety. The family she had tried so firmly to put aside still wouldn't let her go, and she seemed afraid to be alone again with all the crowding Boderin history about her.

As they returned to the apartment in the aptly named Rue du Douleur, Hardy walked slowly up the stairs behind her. At the top, she turned and paused by the door that stood behind her, inscrutable and curiously menacing like the shadow of something evil.

"I'd like to be on my own, I think," she told him.

He nodded, trying to understand. "That's all right," he said. "But wouldn't you like to leave this damn' sepulchre, Nicole? Wouldn't you like to come back to my place? There's nothing to stop you now."

There was a hint of desperation in his voice. The apartment in the Rue des Prêtres de St Séverin had seemed so big and cold since she'd left, dark and cheerless and offering nothing in the way of comfort.

"I'll come back," she said. "But not now. Soon. I must stay here for a while. I've got to close everything up. I'll be all right. I'm not superstitious. There'll be no ghosts."

He nodded, not knowing what to say.

"I think it's because it's all finished now," she went on. "So completely. So irrevocably. There are no ghosts now because he can't raise them any more."

"I'll stay here with you if you like," Hardy said.

She shook her head. "I'd rather be alone. I need to think a bit. You can't conceive what it's like to discover your father's a coward after all. I think he always was. I think Robert is too. Neither of them was ever capable of facing facts."

Hardy paused. "I wanted to talk to you, that's all," he said. "I thought you might like to know. I've heard from my wife."

She managed a faint wintry smile, her face haunting him with its white weariness. "I'm glad," she said.

"I didn't mention it before," he went on, "because it didn't seem to be the time to. But—well, now, you're free, and it seems that so am I. She's surprised us all—herself, most of all, I suspect. She says she's willing to give me a divorce. I gather she's met another man. It comes to us all in the end. I thought you'd be pleased." He tried desperately to see some sign of enthusiasm or pleasure in the blank expressionless face.

"But I am."

"We can go ahead now," he said.

"Yes."

"We can make our plans as we wish."

"Of course."

"Can't I come in?" he asked again.

She pushed the door gently towards him. "I'd like to think," she said again.

For a moment, he thought of pushing it open, but the occasion didn't seem to call for strong methods just then, and he turned away and walked slowly down the stairs.

Colonel Franks was in the lowest possible spirits by lunch time. The press, which had reacted well to the proposed visit to the Bligues and Percéval and had given General Murphy the first decent break he'd had since his arrival in France, had now swung, with true French inconsistency, into a completely opposite mood. General Boderin was being presented as a martyr dying for his country.

Most of the newspapers had touched on him in their leaders and, though most of them were guarded in their comments, the feeling seemed to be that somewhere at the back of him there had been American pressure. Franks wondered if they couldn't sue or something, and even spoke to the Embassy about it. The Embassy, however, were inclined to let it go, on the grounds that action would only stir up more trouble.

By the time the late mail arrived, Franks was suffering from a heavy depression and had snapped at everyone within reach. He'd already seen General Murphy and he knew that Murphy, too, was suffering from the same sort of feelings. It was nothing to do with them that General Boderin had moved true to family form and, unable to stay the course, had removed himself violently from the running, but it was hard all the same to feel detached—particularly with the telephone going all morning, and invariably with a newspaper at the other end of the line. Once, it had been the voice of some crackpot who had shouted in English, "Americans, Go Home" and then rung off without further explanation. In the end Franks had had to insist on all calls being checked before being put through.

He wasn't looking forward to the mail. It seemed to be full these days of letters from lunatics and lunatic organizations. It consoled him a little to realize that no one with any sense of responsibility had yet had anything to say against Murphy, but he knew it wouldn't be long before someone did. Some opportunist politician, seeing a chance to promote his own ends, would inevitably make some pronouncement before long, and that would be the beginning of the end, for it wouldn't take long, then, before they were all at it.

The incident had now got into the German and British papers, he'd noticed, and in fact, one of the less reputable London dailies was suggesting that Murphy's appointment was a bad one and that the British Government had not been consulted. The Embassy was beginning to get worried about it now, Franks knew.

"John F.'s having the bad breaks," he'd been told at lunch only that day. "A few more and they'll have to pull him back home, whatever they feel about him. After all, it isn't just Murphy they've stuck up in the pillory. It's the United States of America."

The argument was sound enough, Franks had to admit, but it still struck him as an example of the unfairness of fate. Of them all, Murphy had behaved with the greatest dignity. Not once had Franks heard him blame anyone.

He was in a deep depression when the sergeant clerk appeared.

"The mail, sir," he announced. "And there's that guy Sligo again," he added.

Franks frowned. Sligo certainly had a habit of picking the wrong day to look in.

"Show him in," he said sadly.

The sergeant placed the mail on the desk and Franks started going through it.

Sligo was in civilian clothes again when he arrived, and Franks indicated a chair.

"At ease, Sergeant," he said. "Sit down." He pretended to paw through his diary, though he knew perfectly well there wasn't going to be a cat in hell's chance of fitting Sligo in. Although Sligo had said ten minutes would be sufficient, Franks wanted to make it longer and he knew that Murphy would want him to make it longer.

"Sergeant," he said, wondering just how he was going to put it. "How about Thursday week? I can guarantee that day. I know he'd meet you that day."

Sligo sighed. "Sir, I'll be back in Achensee then, waiting for my ticket back to the States."

Franks frowned and flipped the pages back again. "It's a hell of a——" He paused and rubbed his hand over his eyes. "Sergeant," he said wearily, "he's just full——"

He stopped once more, deciding it was useless trying to say it couldn't be done. He wanted the sergeant to meet Murphy as much as Sligo and the General did. It had *got* to be fitted in.

Sligo was watching him unhappily, aware of stresses he knew nothing about, and he began to see all his hopes withering under the pressure of great events.

"How about before breakfast?" Franks said slowly. "Hell, no," he went on quickly. "That's no time to meet anybody."

As he spoke, he realized he had been holding in his hand a letter headed *Les Vieux des Bligues*, and while he was thinking of Sligo, he scanned it briefly, expecting it to be nothing more than a formal "Thank you" for Murphy's visit. But, as he passed the fulsome opening paragraph, his eyes lit up and he suddenly thumped the desk with a gusto that startled Sligo, and gave vent to an expression that he'd probably not used since he'd left high school.

"Hot dog!" he yelped.

Sligo looked bewildered and Franks grinned.

"Sergeant," he said. "I think we've got it! Damned if it hasn't just come up in the mail!"

He paused, reading quickly, then he looked at Sligo again.

"See here, Sergeant," he said. "How about this? The General's going to lay a wreath on the Tomb of the Unknown Soldier. He doesn't know it yet but he is. He's going to meet a lot of Frenchmen who fought under him at Percéval."

"I thought he'd just met 'em, sir," Sligo said, puzzled. "At least, he did in my paper."

"That's right," Franks said. "He did, but he's going to meet 'em again. Only more of them this time. And listen, they'll be drawn up round the Arc de Triomphe and there's bound to be a small detachment of our boys with the General. I've got an idea. How about you joining them? You got your uniform with you?"

Sligo grinned. "Sure have, sir," he said.

"Well, see here," Franks leaned forward. "I think that with a bit of string pulling, I might get you put along with that detachment. How'd you like that?"

"Sir, that'd be better than ever."

"Then you can salute him, not with your own arm, but with the rifles of all the boys behind you."

Sligo was grinning now, reassured and happy. "Sure, sir," he said. "That sounds fine."

"And I'll see that he knows you're there and I'll see that he inspects the detachment and I'll see that he knows just where you're standing. How about that?"

"That'll do me fine, sir."

"What's more, if I can fix it, there's going to be a reception for these French guys. I reckon they deserve it for their loyalty to the General."

"The General produces loyalty, sir," Sligo said simply.

Franks looked up for a second, then he nodded. "Yes, Sergeant," he said. "I guess you're right at that. Well, I'm going to see that there's a proper reception and that he gets a chance to talk to 'em all properly. That affair at Percéval was a bit hurried because he had to get back. And if you're there in an official capacity, I'll see you're invited too. Then he'll get to talk to you. How does that sound?"

"Fine, sir. Fine."

"It's the best I can do, Sergeant, but if I know General Murphy he'll make quite an occasion of it."

"I'd like that sir."

"Good. Well, look, I'll have to go into this a bit more. I'll have to find out who'll provide the detachment and arrange it with their C.O. It shouldn't be difficult, though. Thank God, this is a democratic army. You'll have to meet them and join up with them. O.K.?"

"O.K., sir."

"Good, well, give me your name and address and I'll get in touch with you. Any trouble with your pass—when it starts to run out—come and see me. I'll fix that too."

When Murphy returned later in the day, Franks followed him into his room.

Murphy picked up a file as he entered and pretended he'd been reading it, but Franks's quick eyes had spotted the newspapers spread across the desk.

"Hi, Prof," the General said slowly.

"General Murphy," Franks said, addressing him with a mock formality, "we've had a break. At long last, we've had a break."

Murphy pushed at the papers in front of him. "Yeah, this," he said heavily.

"No, not that." Franks grinned and drew a deep breath. "General, have you ever laid a wreath on the Tomb of the Unknown Warrior under the Arc de Triomphe?"

Murphy looked up quickly. "No, I haven't," he said. "You know damn' well I haven't."

"Well, you ought to," Franks said. "Every important visitor who comes here seems to do it."

"Well, let's say that this is one who isn't going to."

Franks looked disappointed. "Why not?" he asked. "Have you some objection?"

"Hell, no!" Murphy shrugged. "For all I know, the guy underneath that slab's probably someone I once spoke to in 1918. I was over here in that shindig too, remember? So, why should I object? But, for God's sake, let's be sensible. It's ostentatious for me to go and lay a wreath on the tomb of the Unknown Warrior. I'm not that important. I'm not SACEUR. It helps nobody. It throws the police department into chaos. Special cops. Special traffic arrangements." He looked up, suddenly suspicious. "Say, what *is* all this?" he demanded.

Franks grinned again. "You've got some good friends, General, and, thank God, they're not afraid to say they're your friends."

Murphy looked puzzled.

Franks waved the letter at him. "Look," he said. "It's from an organization called *Les Vieux des Bligues*. It's a veterans' organization."

Murphy stared. "What is it, Frankie? Give us the dope."

"What it amounts to is that the Veterans of the Bligues—the Resistance boys and the troops who joined you and fought with you at Percéval—not our boys, not just your pals, Marchand and Bruneval de Catalin—the lot, Frenchmen, Boderin's men as well —well, they've been reading all this goddamn nonsense in the press, and now they want to join in the fun too."

Murphy looked bewildered.

239

"They think someone's gravely misrepresenting the case," Franks continued. "They say they have no complaints about how you handled the French troops at Percéval. They hadn't then and they haven't now."

Murphy began to smile. "Say, that's nice of them to go to all that trouble."

"This isn't just from friends of yours, either. That's the point. They're very anxious to point out that it's official. They go further. They're so concerned at all the publicity that's been given to the affair, they're anxious to meet you again—here, where everybody can see, not at Percéval. They had a big meeting about it, it seems—all the local branches—and they're prepared to turn up in numbers—let's see, they talk here about four hundred and that's a hell of a good turn-out. They've asked to meet you, feeling that the very fact that they want to meet you ought to kill for ever any rumours that there was any resentment against you among the Frenchmen you commanded."

Murphy nodded. "That's damn' nice of them," he commented.

Franks nodded. "Listen," he said and began to read. "*The Veterans of the Bligues, having read the accounts of the suicide of General Boderin and seen the reactions of the Paris press, are anxious to prove to the world that they, at least, do not conform to the general pattern of thought.* Blah, blah, blah. There's a bit more of the same sort. Then they go on: *They have, therefore, decided to ask General Murphy to join them in some sort of ceremony in Paris where they can affirm their trust in and affection for him.*"

"Hell, that's nice of them," Murphy said again. "Those old guys must have liked me for some reason, and it sure helps to know it. You remember what Ike said: *'It doesn't matter if there are three thousand demonstrating against me if there are three thousand demonstrating for me.'* I feel the same way. Say"—he paused and jabbed a thick brown finger at the letter—"are those guys from the Bligues wanting me to lay a wreath?"

"That's it," Franks smiled. "They feel that they'd like you to. And they're all in it. Bruneval and Marchand, all the branches of the organization, a few assorted *Maires*, and a lot of others who were there who don't belong to any organization and picked themselves in just for the hell of it. They've even got the necessary permission from the Ministry already, it seems. They certainly work fast. All they want is your consent."

Murphy looked thoughtful. "Well," he said. "If I've been drafted, I can't see what I can do about it. I thought *you'd* been fixing it up and I'd invited myself just to get a bit of good press."

"I can go ahead then?" Franks asked. "I can tell 'em you'll fall in with their plans?"

"I guess so," Murphy said doubtfully. "So long as it's cleared in the right places."

"I'll get on with it right away."

"Let me know what gives."

As Franks left his office, Murphy was hanging up his hat. He was staring in front of him, his face wondering and grateful.

"I always did think those guys from the Bligues were good joes," he said, half to himself . . .

Back in his office, Franks was happily engaged in contacting the necessary departments when the door opened again. General Murphy had a newspaper in his hand.

"I see they fixed the funeral, Frankie," he said.

"What funeral?—oh, Boderin! Yes, I saw that."

Murphy tapped the newspaper. "I guess we can't go along, can we?"

"I guess not."

"No, I thought not. Well, maybe we could send some sort of wreath. After all, the guy was someone I once fought alongside of and, up to St Roth, he did all right. And when you've fought a battle or two with a guy, that's something, believe me."

Conscious of the absence of warfare in his own desk record, Franks nodded.

"I guess so," he agreed and Murphy nodded.

"I've tried all my life to understand the other guy's point of view," he went on soberly. "I've tried to judge Englishmen by their own standards and Frenchmen by theirs. Maybe that's why I've still got a few friends among 'em. I've never condemned Boderin for what he did, although it was wrong. I just decided that maybe he did it because he was French and had been brought up differently from me. So I'd like to think I'd remembered an old comrade. There's nothing political about a guy when he's dead."

Franks sat up abruptly and hurriedly pushed sentiment aside. "There is in France," he pointed out.

Murphy's jaw grew hard. "Yeah. Maybe there is at that," he agreed. "But I'll take a chance on it all the same. See that one's sent, Frankie."

They buried General Boderin with the usual French solemnity in Père Lachaise, dark bowed figures among dark bowed trees. They were unable to get the hearse into the old part of the cemetery, which had never been built for motor vehicles, and the coffin had to be carried on the backs of the undertakers' mutes from where they had to park the hearse.

An elderly uncle from Bordeaux, a frail retired major, who looked like a replica of old Boderin himself, had turned up the day before and insisted on a military funeral and a squad of men to fire a volley over the grave, but the Ministry, by this time tired of General Boderin and anxious to be rid of him as quickly as possible, let it be known that they would prefer the funeral to take place with as little ostentation as possible. They made it quite clear that there was to be no gun carriage or any kind of army vehicle for a hearse and that they would be happy if the whole affair were carried out as quietly and quickly as could be arranged.

There were no serving soldiers present. Obviously sensing which way the wind was blowing old comrades of General Boderin had decided it would be wiser if they did no more than send discreet notes to the family, and there weren't very many of these even. The elderly uncle managed to produce a tricolour and insisted on the dead man's medals being displayed on the top of the coffin, together with his gold-laced képi and his sabre in its shabby scabbard, for which Hardy had found himself making a special journey to Chartres in Cellini's car. The whole ceremony, in fact, was an odd mixture of styles, with the dramatic simplicity of the tricolour and the medals and the sabre strange against the black-and-silver curtains of the civilian motor hearse and the absence of any uniforms whatsoever.

In spite of the haste with which the Ministry had proposed to dispose of General Boderin, Souprosse had laid on a cordon of police in the Boulevard de Ménilmontant by the main gate of

Père Lachaise in case of trouble. But Schneider had kept the time out of the papers and, as it was cold and inclined to rain, the civilians who gathered to watch were few and far between.

Apart from the newspapermen and photographers who had got permission to attend, there seemed to be no one interested beyond Cellini and Hardy, and old Blot stumping silently behind the coffin as the cortège wound between the cypresses and the lopsided tombs. There were a few relatives, of course—heavily-veiled bent old ladies for the most part, and straight-backed old men who carried their walking sticks as though they were sabres. Nicole walked silently by Hardy's side, with Cellini just behind, followed by Sergeant Blot, and his son, who even there managed to look curiously cheap and out of place.

The elderly uncle made an oration by the opened tomb, attributing to the dead man all the virtues everyone knew he was most glaringly deficient in—his strength of character, his calm nature, his humility—but since it was not only the normal thing to do but necessary to satisfy good manners and decency, no one seemed to think it odd.

The weather, which had been threatening all day, broke as he finished and the rest of the ceremony was conducted with indecent haste, in the grey and pitiless rain that stitched their backs and set the tops of the tombs and the mountainous breasts of the stone angels shining, and dripped off the horse-chestnuts in great tears that were whipped away in a sudden searching wind.

General Boderin was laid to rest as he had gone through life, muddled, confused and disorganized, the only spectators of his end the handful of relatives, a couple of cemetery officials, and a large group of people wearing red badges who appeared from nowhere towards the conclusion, filtering belatedly through the grey tombs as the priest was droning to a stop. One of them wanted to make a speech, but the elderly uncle shut him up at once without ceremony. There was a little unseemly scuffling between them, but nothing much, certainly not enough to warrant the numbers of police who were posted at various parts of the cemetery in case of trouble. With the exception of a few windy Left-Wing politicians and the press, everyone in the rest of Metropolitan France seemed to remain as indifferent to the

243

troubles of General Nicholas Jean St Omer de Lespinasse-
Boderin du Crest in death as they had been in life.

When Blot went round to the Rue du Maine the following
morning to report on the funeral, Robert Boderin was melancholy and disinclined to talk. He had been drinking again and
his face was dark and angry.

"What was it like?" he asked at once.

"Oh, it was all right," Blot said lamely.

"What happened?"

"Nothing much."

Boderin whirled and grabbed Blot by the lapels. "Listen," he
said bitterly. "I sent you round there to represent me, to tell me
all about it, and I want to know. That was my father they were
burying, a man who'd been hounded to death by the enemies
of his country, and I want to know how people reacted."

Blot stared at him with frightened eyes. It seemed to him just
then that Boderin was less interested in the funeral of his father
than in the reactions of the mourners and his own emotions.

"Well," he said. "My father was there. Nicole was there too,
with the Englishman and the American reporter."

Boderin turned away and stared unseeingly through the
window. "You'd have thought she could have found someone
better than that," he said in a low voice. "I'd have preferred
anyone rather than an American or a potato-faced Englishman.
Who else?"

"The priest. A few relatives. The press were there. And there
were a lot of people from the Society for the Friends of Truth."

"Is that all? Wasn't there anyone to represent the Army?"

"None that I saw. One of your uncles made a speech, though.
Said what a fine soldier he'd been."

Boderin turned away. "Never mind, never mind," he said
bitterly. "I can read all that in the papers. Didn't anyone
demonstrate?"

"There was a bit of a shoving match between your uncle and
one of these chaps from the Society for the Friends of Truth.
Nothing much, though."

"No one had the courage to speak out for my father's martyrdom?"

244

"It was raining."

"Raining!" Boderin gestured bitterly. "It was raining, so France stayed away."

"Well, it was throwing it down in the end."

Boderin jabbed a quivering finger at Blot. "France needs a shot in the arm," he said. "The whole political stew's foul-smelling and unwholesome to a degree."

"Yes, I suppose so," Blot agreed lamely.

"They need something to stir them. It's a dreary rotten collapsing world, Pierrot. France's suffering from an abscess that needs lancing."

Blot listened disinterestedly. He could always gauge Boderin's mood by the luridness of the words he used.

"But amid the nauseating stench of defeat," Boderin was saying, "there's hope, Pierrot. We're not alone. There are others who believe as we do."

"Who?" Blot asked with disconcerting frankness. "I've not met them."

"You will. They'll rise up when the time comes. It's always easier to fill Paris streets than empty them. We'll strike a blow that'll set the whole city roaring with the intoxication of a successful riot."

By this time Robert Boderin had lost his melancholy in his exaltation and Blot had an uneasy feeling that he had formulated some concrete plans at last and that he, Blot, was going to be asked to assist. He was right. Dead right.

Boderin tossed the newspaper over to him. It was folded into a small square, and Boderin, obviously brooding, had marked a short article with a pencil.

The Veterans of the Bligues had not wasted any time in passing on to the press the information that they were to be in Paris for the express purpose of laying a wreath on the Tomb of the Unknown Warrior in company with their *old friend and wartime comrade, General Murphy,* and there was an interview from the Maire of Percéval, who had made it very clear that this visit had not been made on the suggestion of anyone but their own members. It was probably one of the best write-ups Murphy had had since he'd landed in France. Blot looked up quickly at Boderin.

"You've got to find out when it is," Boderin said.

Blot nodded sullenly. "What are you going to do?" he asked.

Boderin's eyes were far away. "This will be my opportunity," he said.

"What?" Blot gave a shrill yelp of alarm. "At the Arc? You couldn't do it."

"I could. Easily." Boderin fished in his pocket and brought out a bunch of keys. Carefully he selected one. "I have a key to an apartment overlooking the Arc. I've had it for years. You know how one carries keys for ages after they've ceased to be useful. Everything's playing into our hands, Pierrot."

"You'd never do any good from a window."

"This window is right opposite the Arc. It's in an apartment that belonged to Héloïse Lamballer, Pierrot. You must remember her. It's over an hotel that lies between the Avenue de Friedland and the Avenue Hoche. It's been closed for two years and the rooms have been empty. But I've still got the key, Blot. All we have to do is get in."

"That's easy, I suppose," Blot said sarcastically, comforted a little by the apparent impossibility of the project.

Boderin seemed not to notice his words. "The last time I went past there," he said, "there were workmen in the place. They're converting it into offices, I'm told. They've been there months now. All I've got to do is get past them."

"And then what?"

"The apartment's got a magnificent view of the Arc. I know that because I used to sit on the veranda as a boy and read the names on the pillars. Our own name's on the south-east pillar. I've seen it often. Getting into the place shouldn't be difficult. After that, it's simple. Police protection's based on the assumption that an assassin's a lunatic with a clumsy close-range weapon like a bomb or a revolver or a knife. They won't be looking for a long-range shot from a rifle held by an expert."

Blot watched him, fascinated, completely under his spell. Robert Boderin's eyes were bright and glittering and underneath his melancholy there was a strange excitement that swept Blot along, too, in spite of himself.

"I shall need a rifle," Boderin continued. "A good rifle. You must get it for me."

246

"Me?" Blot yelped. "Where'll *I* get a rifle?"

"You can buy them. We have money. We must get a move on though. We've a lot to do. I've failed twice and I can't afford to fail again. The apartment's Number 4, top floor. I want you to take the key tomorrow and try it."

"Me?"

"You can say you're a house agent and that you're checking up on all the flats. Nobody'll ask questions. They're only a lot of stupid painters and workmen. You'll be all right."

"But I——"

"I'd like you to do this for me, Pierrot." The calm insistent voice overrode all Blot's objections with a blank tranquillity born of obsession. "And as you come away, I'd like you to find out just how far it is to the Tomb of the Unknown Warrior from there. You can pace it from the railings in front——"

"Pace it? Through all that traffic?"

"Listen, Blot," Boderin snapped, coming to earth abruptly. "Are you in this with me or not?"

"I don't want to be incriminated. I don't want my name mentioning."

"Who wants to mention your wretched little name? I'll take full responsibility. I'll be proud to. But you said you had ideas, that you wanted to help. Well, you can do this for me, then. Pace it off. At night or early morning before the traffic starts. I know the height of the window. I measured it once with string when I was a boy. I even knew just how far it was from that window to the name of my ancestor carved on the south-west pillar. I took pride in it but I've forgotten it since. All I can remember now is how the names on the pillars go and the names of the battles round the top, and that it's forty-nine metres high and forty-five wide. You find out the rest for me and I can work out to a centimetre how far away he'll stand."

"You still haven't worked out how to get into the building," Blot complained.

"We shall do. One of us. You or I. This is better than shooting him down in his own back garden when he's sitting with his wife. This way he'll be in uniform and wearing all his medals. This way he'll be the true symbol of the United States. Your way, Blot, is murder. My way, it's for the name of France."

WHEN Blot returned the next day Boderin was standing by the window of his room and the ashtray showed just how much he'd been smoking. His manner seemed nervous and strained, but he seemed sure of himself and more certain than ever of what he intended to do, and there was an intensity in his manner, an ice-cool sharpness, that frightened Blot.

He put down a slip of paper and a key on the bed and stood as near to the door as possible, almost as though he preferred to be where he could make a quick getaway.

"*J'arrive*," he said nervously.

Boderin turned slowly and Blot indicated the bed.

"There's the key," he said. "It fits. Nobody worried me. I looked the part." He laughed nervously. "I had a brief case and a lot of papers in my hand and a lot of keys, just as you suggested."

"What did it look like?" Boderin's eyes were far away, years away, melancholy again, as though he were reaching back towards happier days. "How did it seem?"

"Just like an apartment," Blot said blankly.

"My God!" Boderin's distant expression vanished at once and he spoke viciously. "You've got the soul of a pile of sand, Pierrot. *Like an apartment*. My father's funeral was '*all right*'. '*Nothing much*' happened. There was only half the press of France there. There was only a scuffle between my uncle and some damned half-baked Jacobin. There were no troops. My sister was with an American. All this I had to drag out of you. Now you say the apartment just looked like 'an apartment'. The one sincere supporter my family ever had, the one person who never abandoned us, lived in that apartment. You can see de Lespinasse's name on the Arc de Triomphe from that apartment. You can see all the majesty of the Empire from that apartment, the whole soul of France. And it looked to you just like"—he made a gesture of disgust—"like an apartment. Did the sun shine into it, man? Did it look neglected? Did it look lost and unloved?"

Blot's jaw worked. To him, it had looked like a set of empty rooms, painted in white and with fading wallpaper on the walls.

There had been bare boards and empty fireplaces, and resounding echoes. It had looked to Blot just as he had described it—"like an apartment".

"I used to sit in the window," Boderin went on dreamily, in his melancholy mood again, "I used to recite the names that ran round the top of the arc, where all the tourists stand with their cameras. They used to sound like a poem. *Valmy. Jamappes. Fleurus. Montenotte. Lodi. Castiglione. Arcola. Rivoli. Pyramides. Aboukir. Alkmaar. Zurich. Marengo. Hohenlinden.* I know them all. My father used to give me his field-glasses to read them." He paused and seemed to start out of his reverie. "Come, did you get the measurements I asked for?"

Blot nodded towards the bed. "They're on the paper there," he said. "I nearly got run over."

"A pity you didn't," Boderin retorted. "It might have given you something to think about."

"I still don't see——" Blot almost shouted the words, then he stopped and stared nervously at Boderin. "I still don't see how you're going to get in there," he said. "There are bound to be police about. And how are you going to get a rifle in? You can't tell me you can just walk into a place like that—even an empty place—with a rifle. The police are bound to be on the look-out."

"I've thought of all that," Boderin said complacently. "What's to stop me walking in looking like a workman?"

"All right, all right," Blot said agitatedly. "So you'll look like a workman. But workmen don't carry rifles. I tell you, I don't like it. I didn't intend to get mixed up in all this. Suppose they start asking questions afterwards——"

"I'm quite prepared to give my life," Boderin said simply.

"Well, *I'm* not," Blot yelped. "I never said I would."

"I don't want you to," Boderin said coolly. "I don't expect a Blot to be willing to make the same sacrifices as a Boderin."

"Oh, all right." Blot said sullenly. "But I still don't like it. And I still don't see how you're going to get a rifle inside—even as a workman."

"Suppose the workman was complete with tools and a piece of lead pipe. Suppose he carried four or five five-foot planks of wood, all carefully tied together with cord for neatness."

"I still don't see——"

249

"Neither does anyone else." Boderin smiled and the smile seemed to Blot the very essence of evil. "In fact, *nobody* sees, because only the outer two planks are complete. The inside ones are merely ends and sides screwed to one of the outer planks. The centre of the five planks is hollow——"

"And inside?——"

"Is the rifle."

Blot suddenly couldn't help smiling, in spite of his nervousness. He had to admit that Boderin was certainly thinking of everything.

"Well, that *sounds* all right," he said. "Where are you getting the rifle?"

"*You're* going to get it," Boderin said. "You're going to get some of those precious friends you've talked about so much, to get it for you. They'll probably show more sense than you would and will know where to find it without questions being asked. All you've got to do is produce it, and have the bundle of planks made to fit it. They may also be able to do that for you, too. See that it's packed carefully with waste or rags and that it's clean and loaded. Then I shall want a bag of tools—not a new one, an old one, so that no one will look twice at it—and a length of lead pipe. A short length would be better, then if necessary I can use it as a weapon. And a suit of overalls. They're not to be new either. You'd better buy them from a second-hand dealer. You can do all that?"

"I suppose so," Blot said uneasily. "I don't like it though. I'm getting involved."

"You're getting afraid, Pierrot," Boderin said silkily. "You swore to help me. You swore you'd help to avenge my father."

"You *made* me swear!" Blot's voice rose.

"Nevertheless, you swore," Boderin shouted.

Blot's protests dissolved in a wail but Boderin seemed to dismiss the problem of his disaffection from his mind.

"You'd better start now," he said calmly. "Leave me. I've work to do. I can work out to a centimetre now just what the range will be. Oh, arrange to hire a car too, will you? Not a big one. Not a fast one. Just an ordinary car."

"Oh, all right." Blot went sullenly to the door.

"I'll expect you this evening to report that everything's all arranged. And while you're at it, bring me some more brandy and some newspapers and magazines and writing paper. This damned room's driving me crazy."

Blot stared back sullenly, trying to indicate defiance, but Boderin was already sitting at the table among the litter of papers and cigarette ends and was working out figures on the back of an envelope, completely engrossed, expecting and assuming Blot's whole-hearted support with the blind self-interest of a megalomaniac.

There was a subtle differing in Nicole when Hardy returned to the flat at Père Lachaise.

He seemed to have spent the last three days mostly on the Métro. He'd unearthed one or two shabby political friends of Robert Boderin's, but his questions hadn't yielded much. Most of his contacts had got one eye firmly cocked in the direction of Police Headquarters on the Ile de la Cité.

He'd spent a long time also in and out of the bars of the Boulevard St Germain and Montparnasse, looking for students and artists who'd know Robert Boderin, but none of them had been able to help much either, and the young solicitors who'd worked alongside him were thinking for the most part of their careers and had no desire to get mixed up with the *Affaire Boderin,* which had been the breaking of more reputations than General Boderin's already. He'd approached old girl friends, using some of Cellini's money to buy them drinks. He'd had his coffee and croissants at little bars and his meals at brown little restaurants full of middle-aged businessmen preoccupied with their secretaries and their stomach pills.

He had gone to the apartment at the Rue des Prêtres only to change his clothes, and had been caught on one occasion by the telephone and the unhappy voice of Ernestine, begging him to return to her.

The conversation had been difficult, and she'd been hard to put off. He'd made excuses and vague promises he'd no intention of carrying out, and ended with the uncomfortable feeling that he'd not been firm enough and that she'd be right back again.

He found himself oddly tensed as he got off the Métro and walked along the Boulevard de Ménilmontant past the big half-circular entrance of the cemetery. Cellini had arrived at the apartment before him and was already in the old dark lounge with its lingering smell of age, a dusty nocturnal smell that came even through the scent of wax from Sergeant Blot's furious furniture polishing. He was sitting well back in an armchair and to Hardy he had about him a disconcerting look of comfort and secure establishment.

"Who's looking after the Inter-Continental News Agency?" he asked sourly. "Groszwicki again?"

"Groszwicki's a sure-fire boy," Cellini said calmly, strangely certain of himself. "He doesn't miss any moves."

"Neither do you, come to that," Hardy snapped.

Nicole handed him a drink. Her hair was piled neatly on top of her head and she looked cool and efficient, and Hardy wondered what she'd be like in a modern apartment, with the sun on her, instead of in this dark mausoleum of a place.

Cellini smiled at her and she smiled back, then Hardy noticed she'd discarded the olive-green jumper she'd always worn and had on instead a bright yellow one that suited her dark complexion.

"I see you've been talking to Nicole," he said to Cellini when she was out of the room.

"Sure," Cellini nodded. "Why not?"

There was a faint gleam of triumph in his eyes. Cellini was a trier, Hardy decided uneasily. He was tougher than he looked.

"Get a solicitor?" he asked.

Cellini shrugged. "I couldn't," he said. "Still"—he sat up, briskly, as though determined not to be beaten—"I got a promise from a friend of mine who's over here that he'd look it over."

"You're wasting your time, Jimmy. It's as dead as old Boderin himself." Hardy paused and went on maliciously. "By the way, it might interest you to know I've spent up. I've nothing left."

Cellini permitted himself a smile. "Well, I guess the job's finished now, anyway," he pointed out.

"I thought that would be coming," Hardy said. "Get Sam back to work and out of the way."

Cellini frowned. "I'm not sure if I understand what you're getting at, Sam."

"You're a fool if you don't. And you're no fool, Jimmy."

Cellini shrugged, looking faintly guilty. "The job's finished as

252

far as I'm concerned," he said. "I've stopped looking. The old man's dead. Robert Boderin's not in Paris. He'd have turned up if he were."

"I hope you're right. But I don't think you are. What does Souprosse say? And that cold fish, Schneider?"

"They're not saying one way or the other."

"You bet they're not. They've got their eye on the ball. They've not suddenly discovered that they've got other fish to fry."

Cellini got to his feet slowly. "What are you getting at, Sam? Let's have it out in the open. Do you object to me being here?"

Hardy shrugged. "I was chasing girls round Paris while you were still in short pants," he said. He lit a cigarette, and blew the smoke out noisily, then he nodded. "Yep," he said frankly. "That's about it. Maybe I do."

Cellini's face looked concerned and he rose and put a hand on Hardy's shoulder. "Hell, boy, I'm sorry, but all's fair in love and war. You say so yourself."

Hardy shrugged his hand off. "Oh, keep your bloody wise saws to yourself," he said. "Was it you who suggested she put her hair up and tried a different-coloured jumper?"

"I guess I did suggest something of the sort."

"I must remember that. It never occurred to me to want her different. She was all right for me, just as she was. Still, maybe for an all-American boy like you, Jimmy, it wasn't quite the thing."

"Cut it out, Sam!"

"I can see I'll have to regard you as a serious competitor. You're such a decent clean-cut type. I bet you use after-shave lotion and take chlorophyll tablets. I bet you played end—or is it guard or wicket-keeper?—for your college football team. You're just the sort of man these Continental girls are looking for. A ticket to the New World. Security."

Cellini's big fists doubled and his eyes flashed. "I'll knock you flat on your back in a minute, Sam."

Hardy waved a hand. "O.K.," he said. "Go ahead if it'll help. Boy, how you Americans do fall! You complain about the way your own women treat you, then you come over here and start getting the French girls in the same frame of mind."

"Nicole's not that type!"

"How many times have I heard that before?" Hardy opened

253

the door. "You'd better be going, Jimmy," he said. "I'm sure the Inter-Continental News Agency's calling. Groszwicki's on the ropes. You're neglecting him. That'll never do."

The two of them faced each other, eyes angry, Cellini's fists clenching and unclenching.

"Suppose I say I'm not going," he said fiercely. "What happens then?"

Hardy shrugged. "Nothing! You're bigger than me. If you say you're staying, you're staying, but I don't like it. There's suddenly too much domestic bliss around here for me. It reminds me of my wife. I prefer the barricades."

As he began to close the door, Cellini put out a hand and stopped him.

"O.K.," he said. "Don't worry, I'm going. It's better that way." He picked up his hat. "I'll go, Sam," he said. "Not because you scare me but because I wouldn't want Nicole to get involved in any quarrel between me and you. You've got the draw on me this time."

"I'm a dirty fighter."

"But I'll tell you this about yourself——"

"Don't hang back."

"You're not the man for Nicole," Cellini said gravely. "I know it. You know it. She knows it. She'll realize it too, one day. Your way of life'd never do for her. And, as soon as I can, I'm going to see that she's taken away from it and from you. O.K.?"

"O.K. You've laid it on the mat pretty squarely."

"Right, Sam. I'm off. I'm sorry it's come to this. In spite of the arguments we've had, I've always enjoyed knowing you. But we're on opposite sides of the fence just now." Cellini held out his hand, still under control, still trying to be friendly. "No hard feelings?"

"Keep it," Hardy said. "There are quite a lot of hard feelings on my side."

Cellini shrugged. He put on his hat silently and turned away down the stairs, and Hardy stared after him for a moment, conscious of having been boorish and childish, conscious of fear and a dread of loneliness, and the certainty that he couldn't win.

As he slowly shut the door and turned away, Nicole appeared from the kitchen. "Where's Jimmy?" she asked.

"He had to leave," Hardy said shortly. "He left his apologies. He'd got work to do."

She stared at him for a long time.

"Did you drive him away, Sam?" she asked in a quiet voice.

Hardy lit a cigarette. "Yes," he admitted. "I did."

"Why, Sam?"

"I—oh, hell, I don't know! He's got so much. I've got so little. He makes me want to throw things. He's in love with you. Did you know?"

She looked up quickly. "Well, what's wrong with that?"

"There's not room for two of us."

She ignored the comment. "He wants me to get a job," she said. "He says he can find me one with his firm."

"I suppose he can. It's more than I can do. And if he doesn't? Shall you stay here?"

She shrugged. "I'm growing used to it," she said calmly.

He stared. "Growing used to it! To this mausoleum?"

"I'm staying here because someone must stay here," she said quickly. "Someone must look after it."

"There's nothing to look after! Only a lot of dusty weapons and fading press cuttings! Nicole, for the love of Heaven, come away from this place before it gets you too!"

He stared at her, scenting defeat. She'd accepted, as the last member of her clan, the responsibility for the family's history that her father had been unable to bear. She'd shouldered the burden of custodianship as naturally as breathing, now that there was no one else to carry it.

"For God's sake," he burst out. "Come away! There's nothing here but decaying honour. The place's full of shabby banners that refuse to float in the wind, and moulting eagles and battle honours bare of gilt."

She seemed to draw herself up and her eyes grew hot and angry.

"I can't Sam," she said. "Don't you see? There are two hundred years of my family here. I can't put them aside just like that."

"My God, Nicole," he burst out. "I hate your damn family! It's become a religion—a miracle of fortitude and despair—

regarding the living only as potential dead. I prefer flesh and blood to that kind of duty."

"Sam!"

"It's no good, Nicole. It's not normal. Come away with me. I'm free and you're free, and there are forty million years of the future ahead of us, and only two hundred years of this flag-wagging past. For God's sake, let's leave it, while we can!"

She stood stubbornly by the window, not answering, and he turned to the door.

"So long, Nicole," he said heavily. "I'm going to get drunk, I think. I'll be round again when you've thought it over. If you change your mind before then, give me a ring."

He closed the door behind him, half expecting her to follow him, but she didn't, and he slowly walked down the stairs to the bottom. Standing there, in the hall, he lit a cigarette and drew a few puffs from it, then, with a violent gesture, he snatched it from his mouth and flung it away from him with an oath.

The concierge, who had been watching him from his little room by the door, looked up, his head at the little ticket-office hatchway, like a booking clerk on a railway station.

"Something wrong, monsieur?" he asked.

Hardy managed a lopsided grin. "Yes," he said. "I think I just got wind of the smell of burned boats."

★ 3 ★

YOUNG Blot was feeling better when he returned to the room in the Rue du Maine. He had been so busy for two days that his wretched little mind had not been able to dwell on what might happen to him after it was all over.

The sun was out and the streets of Montparnasse were hot, and the children playing in the little railed playground off the side of the road were kicking up the dust as they scuffed a football around.

He had been drinking steadily for some time now but, although his head was still none too clear, at least the liquor had the effect of giving him courage. The minute he set foot inside the shabby little apartment house, however, he was aware of a sinking of

256

his spirits, as though the shadowy interior, smelling of cooking and noisy with the sound of babies and at least eight wireless sets, all on different stations, reached out to him at once and depressed him immediately.

Boderin swung round as the door opened and Blot slipped inside, remaining near the door as he always did these days. There was a dark dangerous look in Boderin's eyes, a sullenness that came with waiting and boredom and nerves.

"Well?" he said at once, and Blot backed nearer to the door.

"I fixed everything," he said. "I've got a car. It's a little Citroën. I'm to pick it up the night before we want it. I've got you some clothes, too. They're at my place now. I got a big size so that you can slip them over your own clothes, then get out of them afterwards. That way, you'll be harder to spot, if they're looking for you."

Boderin nodded. "It sounds as though you've been using your brains at last," he said. "What about the rest of the things?"

"The tools will be in the car, together with the clothes and the lead pipe."

"Never mind the tools and the clothes. What about the weapon?"

"I've got that."

"Where from?"

"I got it through a friend of mine."

Boderin's lip curled. "These damned friends of yours. Political, I suppose? Jacobin?"

"Well," Blot bleated. "*I'm* not going into a gunsmith's buying you a rifle. This way, no one knows where it came from."

"All right. All right. I suppose we'll have to accept it. Is it all prepared?"

"I've done it all myself. I had to buy the wood and a saw and a ruler. I did it in my rooms. Thank God Martine's away. It took me ages to clean the mess up."

"And the rifle?"

"That's in the middle. The magazine's full. It's a British army rifle, they said. I expect it was picked up during the war. They fitted a telescopic sight." Blot fished in his pocket and passed an envelope across to Boderin. "There's some data here. And a target to show how it fires. Apparently over long ranges it swings a bit to the left."

"That won't matter at this range. Where is it now?"

"It's in my rooms with the tools and the clothes. And damned glad I'll be to see the back of them. Martine'd never rest till she knew what they were for. It'd be no good me trying to pull the wool over her eyes. She always knows when I'm lying."

Boderin wasn't listening. He was standing erect, almost at attention, his eyes unseeing, his face glowing.

"Everything's quite straightforward now," he said. "The ceremony's timed for two-thirty, I noticed in the papers. You'd better be here first thing in the morning."

"Me? Why me?"

"I shall need help."

"Oh, all right," Blot said unwillingly. "But why first thing? What'll we do all morning?"

"We'll wait. Suppose something were to go wrong with the car? We'd need to put it right. Suppose the crowds were thick? I've got to give myself plenty of time. I wish I could have tried the rifle first, but I suppose it's not possible."

Blot hesitated. "Er"—his jaw worked uneasily—"I gather there's going to be a bit of a demonstration down in Concorde, starting about two o'clock."

Boderin swung round. "What sort of demonstration?"

"Oh, a bit of shouting. That sort of thing. 'Down with Murphy.' 'Justice to Boderin.' You know the way it goes."

"Your friends, of course?" Boderin sneered. "Taking advantage of the situation, I suppose."

"Well, something of the sort."

"I don't want demonstrations. I don't want to be connected with your filthy friends."

"They got you the rifle," Blot complained.

"It's been paid for, I suppose."

"Well, no, they wouldn't take payment."

"So, because they wouldn't take payment, they think they can share in what I'm going to do. I don't want them to share. This is my affair. Mine alone."

"They don't want to share," Blot wailed. "They're only trying to help."

258

When the idea of a demonstration had been put to him, he had thought it would be applauded. He had not allowed for Boderin's obsessive desire for loneliness of action.

"I thought you'd be pleased," he complained. "If there's something going on down in Concorde, the flics are going to imagine there'll be a rush across the bridge towards the Assembly. They always go for the bridge. It'll draw them away from the Arc."

There seemed to be sense in what Blot was trying to say and Boderin nodded. "All right, then," he said condescendingly. "There can be a demonstration. It might contribute to success. They might even think, if they're expecting anything, that the blow will come as he leaves the Embassy instead of up in the Place de l'Etoile."

Blot nodded eagerly, snatching at his acquiescence. "That's it," he said quickly. "You'll probably find it easier to get into position. Everybody'll be looking the other way."

"Good." Boderin nodded. "Then we're all set. I'll expect you round here about nine on Thursday."

Blot gave him a military salute. "I'll be there, Captain," he said.

He slipped out of the room and scuttled down the stairs as fast as he could go, glad to get away from the intensity of the atmosphere in Boderin's room. At the corner, he stopped in a bar and bought himself a brandy.

As he picked up his change, he stared at the glass, deciding it might be a good idea when it was all over to do a bunk out of the country. He'd been promised enough money if it succeeded, and the fact that Martine was away would contribute considerably to the ease of his getaway. There were plenty of other women.

"Ah, well," he said to himself, as he drank. "Here's to Thursday at nine a.m. It's going to be easy."

On the Ile de la Cité, Inspector Souprosse and Major Schneider were making their own plans. They were unconcerned with France's pride or even with Murphy's bad press. Their job was to see that Murphy came to no harm and they had set about it in the same way that they had tackled all the other similar big jobs which had come in their direction.

All possible persons who might be interested in an attempt against Murphy—or even against the United States—had been interviewed and quite a lot of them had been put under lock and key. Policemen had been posted near the homes of the odd few mental cases who'd been known to speak against the Americans in general or Murphy in particular, and there was one at that moment night and day in the Rue du Douleur.

At all the functions Murphy had attended the waiters had been screened and wherever one of them had been a recent arrival as a refugee from an Iron Curtain country he had been discreetly given the day off at Schneider's request. Even the letting of the house that General Murphy had chosen at Le Vésinet had been postponed on their instigation until they could screen the inhabitants of all the houses which overlooked it.

From the point of view of individuals, they had touched on every possibility, and they were concentrating now on the wreath-laying at the Arc de Triomphe where things had grown a little more complicated.

A British trade delegation, in Paris in connection with the European market, had heard of the ceremony and had expressed a wish to lay a wreath at the same time. The junior minister in charge had dropped into France to help the Resistance during the war and, being very conscious of publicity, he had decided it would do his delegation and his personal case a great deal of good to join in. Then, just when all that had seemed settled, information had come through that the Belgian Foreign Minister, who happened to be in the city, also wished to take part, and the ceremony had begun to grow out of all proportion to what had been originally planned. Schneider had been to see a worried Franks at Franks' request, and had been told that both embassies had thought it would be nice if their countrymen were supported by a squad of their own troops. So that now, in addition to the American troops, a squad of men had been sent from Belgium and a squad from a British base near Hamburg. Neither Schneider nor Franks had welcomed the additions to what was originally intended to be a ceremony chiefly for the benefit of General Murphy, but they'd been unable, without being undiplomatic, to object.

Schneider rubbed the edge of his desk with his maimed hand

and looked at Souprosse. He drew an immense amount of sour satisfaction, under the circumstances, from the decision he'd just made with Souprosse and Franks to have the ceremony postponed unexpectedly for twenty-four hours. No one—not even the press—were to be informed of this move until the last moment, in the hope that any arrangements that might have been made for an assassination attempt would be thrown into confusion. At least, Schneider thought, the Belgians and the British junior minister would have to do a quick double-shuffle. If nothing else, it would probably teach them not to muscle in on private arrangements in the future.

"What have we fixed, up to now?" he asked Souprosse, his face cold and aloof.

"We shall have men all the way round the Etoile," Souprosse said, running his hand over a wall map that was dotted with flags. "There'll be more on duty by the Arc itself. No one, except for screened newspapermen and these people from the Bligues, all of whom have been investigated, will be near enough to use a revolver or a bomb."

"What about longer-ranging weapons?" Schneider asked.

"They could only be effective from the windows of these buildings here," Souprosse said, running a hand round the plan of the Etoile. "But I've investigated every one. Unfortunately, the trees have only recently been trimmed, which gives a clear view of the Arc from the two top floors all the way round. However, all inhabitants of apartments and offices on these two floors have been or are being screened. At the top of the Avenue Hoche, there are a group of apartments over a former hotel. At the moment it's empty and being converted, but the men engaged in the work have no access to the rooms overlooking the Etoile. However, for safety, I can have a man posted there."

"What about the apartments themselves?"

"I'll have another man at the top of the stairs so that no one can get up without being seen, and we'll inspect the apartments on the morning of the ceremony. In addition, I'll have men on top of the Arc with instructions to watch the windows of empty apartments and offices. I shall be in touch with them at the bottom of the lift. I shall have a telephone and a radio. As far as I can see, we've thought of everything."

261

"Intersections?" Schneider said, mentally ticking off the notes he carried in his head. He'd been through all this so many times, on other occasions, he no longer needed a note book.

"The route will be lined as usual," Souprosse said. "With extra men at every intersection so that the car can't be held up."

"We mustn't take any chances."

Souprosse shrugged. "I don't think there's anything we've left undone," he said. "There's always the human element, of course. There's always the fool who'll do his job wrongly, but we can only counter that by picking the best men we can. After all, we can't do it all ourselves, can we? At least no one'll be near enough to use a short-range weapon, and long-range weapons are always a much more tricky affair."

"Did you know young Boderin's an excellent shot?"

"He'll never be nearer than two or three hundred yards."

"I've brought down a deer at a thousand."

Souprosse shrugged. "Every window will be under inspection with field glasses," he said. "The mere sight of a rifle will set a dozen men on to its owner."

"I don't like it," Schneider said uneasily.

Souprosse's eyes were hard. "Neither do I," he admitted. "If young Boderin's gone to earth as he has, it isn't because he's modest."

Schneider nodded. "The tightest security in the world's completely useless against a man willing to sacrifice his life. Did you know there's to be a Métro strike on the day of the ceremony?— as a token of the men's solidarity behind the honour of France, as expressed in the person of General Boderin."

Souprosse shrugged. "The trouble with them isn't honour, it's politics. Still, it'll discourage people from visiting the Champs Elysées. What difference does it make?"

"It might start trouble," Schneider pointed out. "There was trouble up near the Luxembourg the other evening, wasn't there? The station was closed, and someone started arguing. It took two vanloads of your men to stop it. It takes so little to start a riot in Paris, and there are bound to be shouts for De Gaulle. We don't want incidents, particularly as we won't be able to move men quickly to stop them. There'll be too many private cars out because of the strike."

"It takes a brave man to start trouble when we've got our people out in force," Souprosse pointed out grimly.

Schneider nodded. "I hope you're right," he said.

Much as he disliked the idea, it had been impossible for Robert Boderin to evade the fact that he couldn't achieve what he wanted to do entirely on his own. Twisted, warped, sickened by himself, he was still normal enough to realize that the Métro strike that had been announced and the proposed demonstration in the Place de la Concorde could do nothing but help.

He'd not welcomed the news all the same, because he felt vaguely that his own cause was becoming obscured by some sordid political movement that he knew he'd never have supported even if he'd known what it was.

He was aware of a deep melancholy, yet a satisfaction that, whatever happened afterwards, he would have demonstrated to France just what he felt and what he considered France should feel. In twenty-four hours it would all be over. He had no fear for himself, and felt no apprehension at the possibility of physical pain. He was far more concerned that the police might pick him up before he'd accomplished what he was setting out to do.

His only real worry was that the world might attribute to his deed mean intentions, when he himself was conscious only of the purest motives of honour. For this very reason, he wanted no help and the support of no political parties.

He had decided to write a letter—not a note such as he had written to his father before his attempt at Orly, but a long letter—a testament almost—that would set out just why he had done what he was now contemplating.

With the single-mindedness of the unbalanced, he wished his act to rank only as a gesture for France, and was anxious that there should be no mistake about it being recognized as such.

Right or wrong, he had set down in his sprawling handwriting, *for this I expect to be judged by God, not by my fellow men. Their judgment will come later.*

He had addressed the letter to the editor of *Le Monde,* not because he favoured *Le Monde* particularly, but because his family had been in the habit of reading it and it was the first name that had sprung to his mind.

He was thinking seriously in terms of his own death. No one knew him beyond his own family and a few friends, but he hadn't the slightest intention of failing to be identified in case he should die making his escape. He was going to carry his passport, and wear a bracelet with his name on it, and his letter was to add clarity. It was to let the world know that it was Nicholas Robert Jean de Lespinasse-Boderin du Crest who had cleared the stain from the family honour. He expected criticism of his act, of course, but someday, he felt, when anger had cooled, time would justify him and people would understand what was behind it all. His own family would understand immediately.

Though my action may be considered wicked, he had written, *my motive is good. I love life and I love honour and all the years when I have had to live under the shadow of a wrongful stain on the family honour have been years of suffering. There is no time for words. I write in haste. I know I shall be considered foolish by some for what I am about to undertake but I love justice more than life.*

For a long time, the pen scratched in silence, then Boderin reached for a fresh sheet of paper and commenced his peroration.

This is the country of Charlemagne and Saxe and Turenne and Napoleon, he concluded. *This is the country where men have always managed to distinguish themselves without help from the New World. I have always counted it one of the greatest blessings ever bestowed on us that we have the ability to rise from disgrace to greater heights than ever before. This has been so in the past. It will be so again in the future.*

My love is for my country alone, and for my family, endeavouring to hold its place in society. I am only a Frenchman doing his duty.

For a moment he hesitated before signing it, reading it again and again, pleased with his phrases. This was to be the document that would assure him of a place in the history books.

He signed the letter with a flourish, *Nicholas Robert Jean de Lespinasse-Boderin du Crest,* and as an afterthought, in smaller writing and with far less flourish added, the words below, *aided by Pierre-August Blot.* Then he put it into an envelope which he addressed to the editor of *Le Monde.* Now, whatever happened to him, his testament would be made public. He could just imagine the uproar it would cause. He could just see the leader columns upholding what he had done as the first stroke towards the re-birth of France. Whatever the newspaper's policy, it couldn't fail to uphold his action as a step forward by the strong youth of a strong France.

He folded the envelope containing the letter and put it into another envelope on which he wrote *Mademoiselle Nicole Boderin* and the address of the apartment in the Rue du Douleur. For a while, he sat staring at it, then he crossed out the name and wrote *Mademoiselle Nicole Christiane Françoise Lacquart de Lespinasse-Boderin du Crest*.

Satisfied at last, he blotted it and crossed to the window. The postman was just making the last collection from the blue box opposite and, as he disappeared, a khaki-clad *képi*'d figure bobbing among the passers-by, Boderin quickly walked across the road, his head down, and slipped the letter into the box. He was back inside his room within a few seconds. Nobody had even looked at him. He regretted the absence of a stamp but felt that when she knew what it was all about Nicole would forgive him.

He had just got back to his room and lit a cigarette, when he heard shoes pounding on the stairs, and he dived for his clothes and rummaged for his father's heavy Smith and Wesson. Before he could get it free the door rattled under a pounding fist and he heard Blot's voice.

"Let me in! It's me — Pierrot!"

He pushed the gun under the pillow and crossed to the door. As he slipped inside, Blot's face was pale and taut with strain.

"What the devil's the matter?" Boderin asked.

"They're on to us!"

Blot thrust the paper at Boderin, jabbing at it with a flat forefinger, and, as he snatched it away, Boderin saw the words, *Arc Ceremony Postponed*.

His eyes travelled swiftly over the printed words, and the blunt announcement that owing to the indisposition of General Murphy the wreath-laying would be held the following day.

"We'd better get moving," Blot said, panic-stricken. "They'll be round here soon. I'm getting out of Paris while I can."

Boderin gave him a shove so that he fell across the bed.

"Don't be a damned coward, Pierrot!" he snapped. "What

265

good would that do? Every road out of the city'll be watched. We'd be wiser to hide *in* the city."

"All right, then. Where can we go?"

"We'd better go to your place."

"My place!" Blot's words came out as a yelp as he saw himself being drawn deeper and deeper into something he had never wanted to belong to in the first place. "Not my place!"

"Where else can we go?"

"But if they know you're at my place, they'll accuse me of helping you!"

"You swore to help me!"

"Yes, I know. But I didn't expect to get caught up like this! I don't like it. I'm scared!"

Boderin swung him round. "For Heaven's sake, man, pull yourself together. Stop behaving like a hysterical girl! All we've got to do is keep our heads. Tearing out of Paris will only draw attention to us. They're already looking for us. Besides, I—I wrote a letter."

"A what?"

"A letter. I addressed it to the editor of *Le Monde*. Telling him all about myself and my intentions."

"What for?"

"It's my testament."

"Did you sign it?"

"Of course."

"But that'll tell 'em straight away who you are. We shall never escape now."

"Are you *worried* about escaping?"

Blot's eyes flickered. "You haven't put my name on it, too?" he asked.

"Didn't you want to be included?"

"I don't want 'em to know about me."

Boderin hesitated before he replied, then he shook his head. "No," he lied. "I didn't put your name on it."

"Well, that's something. What the devil did you have to set it all down on paper for?"

"Because there was no sense in doing what we've planned to do, unless they knew why. I'd have been branded as a common or garden murderer otherwise."

To Blot's scared mind, that was exactly how it seemed.

Boderin was thinking quickly. "Get a taxi, Pierrot. Bring it round to the door." He fished in his pocket and handed over a bundle of notes. "Here, take this money and pay for the rooms. Tell them I've had to leave. Tell 'em I've got a sick uncle to see. Anything. Then come back and tell me when the taxi arrives."

"I don't like it. What would happen if my father found out?"

"Your father fought for France," Boderin said, his head lifting. "He'd understand."

Blot wasn't so sure. "What about Martine then?" he asked. "She'll give me hell!"

"She need never know. You said yourself she's away for a couple of weeks. I'll think of somewhere to go by the time she returns. I'll find somewhere to hide. Now go and get a taxi!"

Blot stood with his back to the door, his eyes rolling, the sweat standing out on his face. Then he pulled a handkerchief from his pocket and, wiping his moist forehead, slid round the door like an alley-cat round a dustbin, and vanished from the room.

* 4 *

GENERAL MURPHY was angry. He looked at the note on his desk, paused to take out his spectacles to make sure he was seeing it correctly, then rang quickly for Franks.

Franks came in at once, knowing from the length of the ring that Murphy was angry and what he was angry about. There was a half-smile hovering about his face that Murphy picked on immediately.

"Take that damn' grin off your face, Frankie," he said at once. "What's all this nonsense here about me postponing this wreath-laying at the Arc because I'm indisposed? I'm not indisposed. Do I look indisposed? Hell, I never felt better! I've said I'd lay the wreath tomorrow, and I'm going to lay it tomorrow. What about those old guys from the Bligues? What about Sligo?"

Franks paused, waiting until the tirade was over. He knew Murphy was hot and tired. He knew he'd spent the morning with a lot of officials he didn't particularly want to see and after a quick lunch he'd spent the afternoon with a lot more.

Murphy was pawing about on his desk now. He extracted another sheet of paper and, tossing it across, brought his fist down on top of it with a bang. "And what's all this about me not being able to take up the lease of this house we want?" he snapped. "Lilian'll be on her way soon. It's near to General Axelrod's, and Lilian and Shayne Axelrod get on just fine. What's going on? Is somebody trying to hog-tie us? Don't they want to let us have the house after all?"

Franks smiled at him, unperturbed.

"Sure you can have the house," he said. "The police have just asked for a day or two to poke their noses round the district, that's all."

Murphy banged the desk. "I don't want the god-damned police round the place!" he snapped.

"Maybe you don't, but they've got to do their job just the same. They've *even* got a department specially organized to look after people like you. They only want to help, and they're only asking for co-operation. That's all."

"Well, *aren't* we co-operating?"

"Sure we are. That's why we're not taking over the house in too big a hurry."

Murphy looked up over his spectacles, his scowl fading. "Well, O.K.," he growled. "But you can tell 'em I don't want their men all over my house. Let 'em toothcomb it for hidden spies and microphones and then tell 'em to get the hell out of it! I've already cabled to Lil' to say it's fixed and she can come out. And you know the police always make her nervous. She's been scared of someone bumping me off ever since that madman took a shot at me in Vienna after the war."

"Mrs Murphy's got good sense," Franks said.

"She's the best. Hell"—Murphy looked up suddenly, smiling all over his face—"do you know, Frankie, she's enrolled for French lessons already? Do you know"—he leaned one elbow on the table and jabbed a pencil across at Franks—"Lilian could speak German like a native seven months after she arrived in Vienna. Well — not like a native, maybe, but good enough. What do you bet that seven months from now she'll speak French like a Parisian?"

"I hope she does," Franks grinned.

268

Murphy chuckled. "You don't catch Lilian getting the maid to do the shopping," he said. "No sir!"

"I've said often that I have the greatest admiration for Mrs Murphy."

Murphy grinned again. "You know, Frankie, you have the nicest way of saying things. We'd all get on a lot better if everybody were as easy as you."

"We'd get on a lot better if all generals were as easy as you," Franks said sincerely. "But, then, the same would apply to Russian and Chinese generals, too, wouldn't it?"

Murphy's good humour had completely returned now, and he turned cheerfully to his desk, then his eye fell again on the slip of paper notifying him of Schneider's change of plan, and his frown returned.

"And am I to assume that this switching of the wreath-laying's got something to do with the police, too? he asked.

Franks nodded.

"You are," he agreed. "Since the newspapers got hold of the story, Major Schneider felt it ought to be postponed for a day."

"Sure it wasn't because all these damn' frock-coats want to join in? This British trade delegation and the Belgian Foreign Minister. Hell, I thought this was a private ceremony. Between me and those guys from the Bligues."

"They don't mind," Franks said. "I've spoken to them. As for these other people, you don't like it, I don't like it, the Embassy doesn't like it, the police don't like it. But there's no alternative."

Murphy frowned again. "I reckon we're pushing these old guys from the Bligues around too much. Why should they share it with the Belgian Foreign Minister and a guy buying cabbages to feed the British?"

"The people from the Bligues have been informed," Franks pointed out. "They're in complete agreement. The Elysée Palace and the Ministry's been informed. In fact, I'm leaving it all to Major Schneider. There was nothing I could think of that he hadn't thought of already. Incidentally, he also asked if you could alter your route."

"No, I can't," Murphy snapped. "I'm not sneaking up to the Arc by somebody's back door to please anybody."

Franks laughed. "That's what I thought, General. I told them so."

"Bully for you, Prof."

"As a matter of fact," Franks said. "It's what Major Schneider thought too. He didn't hold out much hope that you would."

"Schneider's a good guy." Murphy paused then looked up at Franks. "What about Sergeant Sligo?" he asked. "How will it affect him? I thought you said Thursday was his last day."

"I've adjusted that, General. I shall see that his leave's extended."

Murphy stared at Franks admiringly. "You know, Frankie," he said, "I often wonder how I managed that affair at Percéval without you. I had a guy there who was all left hands and left feet. At least, that's the way it seemed to me then. But I guess maybe he wasn't so bad at that. Maybe he was just a bit anxious, like I was myself. What happens then? Same as before, but a day later?"

"That's it exactly. I've adjusted your programme for those two days. Major Schneider begged that there should be no publicity before the affair."

"So does General Murphy!"

"He said we could use it as much as we liked afterwards. In fact, he suggested it might be a good idea to give it everything we've got. It would be a good press for a change."

"Unless some guy starts a riot or a lot of those students from St Germain come out with their little placards again," Murphy pointed out dryly. "I'm not laying a wreath because I want my face in the paper, Frankie. Or even to please you or the people who get up at Elks's meetings and the American Legion Clubs on the Fourth of July to say what heroes we are. I'm laying it because it'll please a few old guys from the Bligues who once helped me to keep Hitler's boys back when they were needed most, and because they've had the common decency to stand up for me when everyone else was trying to knock me down. That's why I'm laying a wreath. So don't you get any fancy ideas into your head about dressing it up for the glossies to look like something else."

"No, sir," Franks said, making a mental reservation, however, that he would see to there being plenty of pressmen on hand, with plenty of hand-outs on the Veterans of the Bligues and the reasons for their presence, and plenty of hand-outs on Master-Sergeant Sligo, too.

Quite unaware that he was to be the ace in Franks's hand, Master-Sergeant Sligo sat in the foyer of his hotel in the Rue de la Gaiété in Montparnasse. Although he didn't know it and never did learn it, he was only a few hundred yards away from where Robert Boderin had been hiding. He had chosen Montparnasse because there he could get away from Americans and practise his French, though from time to time, finding the strain beginning to tell on him, he slipped down to the Champs Elysées area and relaxed in the big American-style drugstore which someone had opened with a great deal of foresight near the Arc de Triomphe. There, browsing in and out of counters, wishing he had someone he could buy gifts for, he pretended a faint contempt for those of his compatriots who claimed to have "done" Paris after walking from the Etoile to the Place de la Concorde, buying their drinks en route at cafés where they were addressed by French waiters with American accents. In secret, however—he wasn't even aware of it himself—he felt much more at home there, because his French wasn't good enough to enable him to get into conversation with anyone, and Sligo liked company and hated eating and drinking alone.

Once, he had met an old friend, another master-sergeant from Berlin, who had greeted him with noisy derision.

"What you want to stay out in that crummy district for?" he'd asked. "Nobody out there speaks English. Why don't you try this place I'm at. Handy for the Champs and all the sights. Not that I'm home much. Haven't slept in my bed for two nights. She's a hostess on one of these sight-seeing buses. Walks like Marilyn Monroe. You'd never know she was French from her accent. She was a G.I. bride till she got divorced."

Master-Sergeant Sligo had smiled and bought his friend another beer, but he hadn't changed his routine. Even if he'd wanted to move, it would have been difficult because the address in Montparnasse was the one he'd given to Franks and he had no wish to lose touch with him now.

He'd had a letter saying that there was to be some change in the arrangements and that there might be a postponement of the ceremony at the Arc. That had given Sligo some heart-burning because it meant that he'd be A.W.O.L. and Sligo had never been back late from leave in his whole military career and the thought of a first offence just when he was due for retirement worried him. With relief, he'd seen the postscript which had added that if his leave pass needed adjusting, Colonel Franks would be only too pleased to make the necessary arrangements, with the full consent of General Murphy.

Sligo had filed that letter away carefully to add to his treasured souvenirs, and had taken the SHAPE bus out towards Versailles. Franks had come personally to the great desk behind the flag-lined entrance to meet him and conduct him to his office. He had taken the pass, made the necessary alterations personally and got it stamped and re-signed.

"How's your money holding out, Sergeant?" Franks had asked.

"I'll manage, sir," Sligo had said.

"Because, if you're in need, I've no doubt we can make some arrangements for you to be paid—or even a loan."

Sligo sat reading his paper with the warm glow of a man receiving V.I.P. treatment. He knew now that the meeting with the General that he'd always hoped for would become a fact, so long as some fantastic situation nobody had thought of didn't snatch one or the other of them away before it could be accomplished.

The *New York Herald Tribune* that he was reading carried a small story about the ceremony at the Arc. There was no reference to the Veterans of the Bligues, chiefly because most of the citizens of the United States in Paris on holiday, had never heard of the Bligues, but Franks had privately assured Sligo that he had every intention of giving as much publicity as he possibly could, not only to the men from the Bligues but also to Sligo. "I'll see you get photos, Sergeant—all the photos you can carry—so you'll have something to look at in your old age."

He had produced a coffee for Sligo in his office and explained at length why it was important for Murphy to get a good press.

"You must have read of all this fuss about the Boderin Affair, Sligo," he said. "It must be obvious to you that it isn't doing the General a lot of good and it's up to a few of us who like the

272

General to do all we can for him. Because he's the sort of man who won't do it for himself. This is where you come in."

Sligo had leaned forward, feeling a bit like a conspirator.

"It's obviously a good story for the General to meet one of his former sergeants—especially one with such a good show of medals as you have—who's spent all his army career trying to thank him for saving his life. Sergeant, that to me, is quite a story. I have every intention of having plenty of pressmen around. The General has expressly asked that publicity should be played down but he won't be able to complain when the ceremony's started and I know he'll go along with us afterwards. He might even like it. After all, he's a human being and he can't fail to enjoy a bit of good press once in a while. He's no Douglas MacArthur, but he won't complain, I know."

It was only when they were settled in Blot's shabby set of rooms near the Place des Vosges that Boderin began to take stock of what had happened and started to see things rationally. Night was rising out of the river and creeping along the streets that converged on the Place de la Bastille, and he could hear the iron roll of corrugated metal blinds as they were hauled down over shop fronts, the sound carrying over the scurrying traffic in the Rue St Antoine. As it grew darker, he prowled restlessly round the shabby little rooms, nervous, irritable and impatient, choked by Martine's lower-class taste in cheap furniture and dreary pictures. There was a framed print of Millet's *Reapers* and a calendar showing the Promenade des Anglais at Nice, and a lot of battered brown furniture in imitation Provence style which might have pleased Martine's artilleryman husband when he was home on leave but only drove Boderin to the point of disgusted fury.

He was afraid, though not so much for himself as for his plan. The very absence of police activity, the very absence of news in the papers, seemed to indicate not that the police had lost interest in him but that they were ominously aware of him. From the minute he had gone to earth in Blot's shabby little rooms, he had been waiting for the sound of footsteps on the stairs and the thundering knock on the door. But neither had materialized and their very absence was worrying, a vague suggestion of disaster that was hard to brush aside.

273

It had been hard to put off his plan, but there seemed little hope of it succeeding now. The chance of overlooking Murphy at the Arc might never occur again.

As he prowled about the little apartment, touching things with vague contemptuous gestures, the bitter taste of failure sickened him to the point of nausea. He could hardly bring himself to speak to Blot, who sat, almost crouched, in a chair by the door, his feet twisted round the legs, smoking endlessly, one elbow on a little table by his side, his hat still on the back of his head, the picture of misery, watching Boderin continuously and emitting gusty sighs from time to time.

"For God's sake, Blot," Boderin snapped. "Pull yourself together."

"I don't like it," Blot said for the hundredth time. "I just don't like it."

Boderin had grown calmer now and he gestured with the newspaper he'd been reading, an angry irritable movement that jerked Blot to life. "Look," he said. "Suppose they're *not* on to us? Suppose they know nothing of us? There's nothing in the papers to say they do. It just says Murphy's indisposed. That's all."

Blot gave a great sigh that was almost like a wail. "I don't like it," he mourned.

Boderin stubbed out his cigarette viciously. "For God's sake, man," he snapped. "Stop saying you don't like it. I don't like it either, but I'm trying to be sensible and rational about it. Perhaps it's only an effort to frighten us off. Perhaps they thought that by postponing it, they could throw our plans out of joint."

"What about the letter you wrote?" Blot moaned without turning. "That'll tell 'em everything—*everything*."

"No, it won't." Boderin's heart felt lighter, as things seen more calmly began suddenly to seem less ominous. "I sent it to Nicole to be forwarded. Deliberately. She won't get it until tomorrow. Even if she posts it on at once the papers won't get it until the day afterwards. And that's still the day after the ceremony. We've still got a day to spare." His eyes had become brighter and even the dreary little apartment seemed to grow more cheerful.

"It can't stop us, Pierrot! Think about it! There was nothing

274

in it to say where we are. There was no address. We're quite safe!"

"I don't like it——"

Boderin stepped across to Blot who jumped to his feet immediately and put his back against the door.

"Listen, Pierrot," he said. "We've got a job to do. We can do it as well the day after tomorrow as we can tomorrow."

"I'm not sure I want to do it at all now!"

Suddenly Boderin found Blot's narrow, stupid face infuriating.

"Listen, Pierrot," he snapped. "Suppose Murphy isn't indisposed at all? Suppose the postponement's been made merely because they want to throw us all into confusion? In that case the best thing we can do is to sit tight and see what happens. It's probably only been done to bring us out into the open. To make us try to get out of the city. They can't know where we are—or they'd have been round here before. They're hoping to make us panic, that's all."

Blot's eyes rolled. "Suppose you're wrong?" he said.

"What if I am? We're no worse off. I've done nothing they can accuse me of. Neither have you. Not yet anyway. They can't do more than detain us."

The idea of being detained and of the whole thing falling through sounded like heaven to Blot, and his panic subsided at once.

"What shall we do then?" he said.

"Stay here, of course. If they come for us, all we have to do is deny everything. If we'd gone ahead with it and they'd picked us up, that would have been a different matter. If they pick us up now, they can't do a thing to us. And if they don't pick us up, we carry on as before, merely waiting an extra day."

Blot groaned at the thought. Then he brightened up. The possibility of being picked up seemed pretty strong and the prospect of a week or two in gaol didn't appal him any more. At least it might prevent a longer stay—or even worse—for what Robert was planning.

"Where shall we go then?" he asked.

"We'll stay here. Why not? It seems symbolic to me. It was near here that the first riot of the Revolution took place."

275

5

PARIS seemed to glow in the sunshine. There'd been an early mist along the Seine Valley, a light milky vapour all the way from Vincennes to St Germain-en-Laye that had shrouded the countless domes and spires of the city. Then, as the sun climbed into the brilliant sky, it had changed into a golden dust and finally dispersed, and the whole of Paris had become aflame with light.

The traffic in the Champs Elysées glittered like a necklace of jewels as it roared up the hill towards the Etoile, splintering off at the Arc de Triomphe and drumming between the trees to the outer suburbs where the pavements under the tall old houses were crowded with overloaded housewives with string bags, who thronged the dark interiors of old-fashioned *epiceries*.

Behind the Rue St Antoine, where workmen were still snatching a late coffee and *croissants* in the *café-tabacs* near the Métro, the air was still, but the tops of the houses around shone with an opal-like brilliance against the deep blue of the sky. The sound of the streets came up to Blot's little rooms with a gaiety that seemed doubly intense to the two men in there, one of them twitching with nerves and wretched with unhappiness, the other caught by a sense of drama that was heightened by the noise and the glare of the sunshine outside.

Boderin had put on rubber-soled shoes and was dressing himself with an air of dedication. He was quiet, intense and not inclined to talk. He had sent Blot out the night before to buy him a new white shirt and had spent the early hours of the morning pressing his suit. It was regrettable, he decided, that he must hide it all with the outfit of shabby washed-blue overalls that Blot had obtained for him, and he seemed to take pleasure in staring at himself in the mirror for a while before he put them on.

His handsome face was taut and pale, his fine, crazy eyes full of brooding self-admiration, not so much for his physical appearance as for the aura of tragedy he seemed to see around himself. Somehow, he felt, he looked the part. He *had* to look the part. When it was all over, he had every intention of getting rid of his disguise somehow, somewhere, whatever it cost him. If he were to die, there had to be something worth seeing afterwards, not just a shabby man in overalls.

He had bathed and shaved and combed his hair carefully. He had even contemplated the use of Blot's hair cream but, somehow, it had seemed cheap and over-scented and didn't go with the conception of a martyr that he had in his mind.

"I'll have the overalls now," he announced at last.

Blot rose sullenly from the chair by the door where he was still sitting and passed over the bundle of pale blue clothing. Boderin pulled the trousers over his own and slipped into the jacket. At once, it seemed, something was lost and he was tempted for a moment to put them aside and take a chance. But without them, he realized, he had no hope of getting into the apartment at the Etoile, much less of getting away afterwards. And, while he was prepared to die, he wanted to live because he was convinced that France would want him as the core of a new political movement that would be the backbone of a strong, proud country, independent of all foreign aid.

Reluctantly, he fastened the blue jacket and, feeling in his pocket for his passport, fingered it for a moment. Then he glanced at the silver bracelet on his wrist. In curling minute letters it proclaimed his identity—*Nicholas Robert Jean de Lespinasse-Boderin du Crest*. There could be no doubt, if he died, who he was and because of that there could be no doubt *why* he had died. Everyone would read his innermost thoughts at once and he could almost sense the exultant upsurge of pride that he felt would sweep through the capital.

Blot's eyes watched fascinated as he took the heavy Smith and Wesson revolver from the table and jammed it into the top of his trousers. In spite of his wretchedness, he was completely absorbed in the preparations and the strange suggestion of paraded martyrdom.

"Where's the car, Pierrot?" Boderin demanded.

"Round the corner." Blot jerked his head. "In the garage."

"And the rifle?"

"Inside the boards. On the back seat. There's a rug over them." Blot spoke wearily, his mind still occupied only with his desperate fear.

"The tools?"

"In the car."

"The lead pipe?"

277

"In the car."

"What provision have you made for getting the rifle out from between the boards?"

Blot's eyes looked startled. "Getting the rifle out?" he said blankly.

Boderin's dedicated calmness crumbled at once. "Yes, you fool! It's tied securely inside, isn't it?"

"Yes! Yes, it is! I made it secure in case it was dropped by accident."

"Then what about cutting the ropes? I can't struggle with knots. There may not be time."

Blot gaped. "I hadn't thought of that," he blundered. "It never occurred to me."

Boderin leapt across the room and grabbed his lapels, dragging him to his feet. "Listen, Blot," he snapped. "Listen to me! Pull yourself together and listen! Have you done everything correctly?"

"Yes! Yes, of course, I have! I thought of everything!"

"You didn't think of the ropes though, did you?"

"Well, no. I forgot that."

Releasing Blot with a contemptuous shove, Boderin crossed the room and taking a handful of knives from a drawer he tested them one after the other with his thumb. Selecting one, he studied it for a while, then rejected it for another which was pointed. "I'll take this one," he said. "I might need it."

Blot stared in alarm. "That's one of Martine's best knives," he bleated.

"I need it."

"What'll she say?"

"She'll never miss it."

"You don't know Martine. She knows where everything is. Besides, suppose the police find it afterwards?"

"There are millions like it in the city, you fool."

Boderin stared his companion down, commanding his obedience simply by his personality. "If you'd thought ahead a little," he said, "you'd have bought a knife. There's no time now. It'll have to be this one. Here, take it."

He thrust the knife into Blot's hand and stood over him. "Now, answer my questions. The car: Where's the car?"

278

"In the garage. Round the corner. It's full of oil and petrol. I rehired it for an extra day."

"Good. The rifle?"

"Between the boards in the back of the car." Blot's words came monotonously, automatically. "You can't tell it's a rifle. It looks like a bundle of planks. It's loaded."

"You're sure?"

"Yes, yes," Blot burst out, antagonized into rebellion. "I saw it loaded myself! Everything's all right! I swear it is! It's a good rifle. They'd tested it. They said anyone who could shoot at all couldn't fail to hit at that range."

"The knife to cut the ropes?"

"It's here."

"Put it in the tool bag. You understand? *In the tool bag.* You've heard me?"

"Yes, yes," Blot was almost in tears again. "I've heard you. In the tool bag."

"And where's the tool bag?"

"In the car. Everything's ready. I swear it is. Haven't I done everything you asked?"

"All right. Go and bring the car round. Bring some food as you return. And a bottle of wine. We'll eat before we start."

Blot heaved himself to his feet. "God knows what Martine'll say to all this when she finds out," he mourned.

"Go and get the car."

Blot opened the door, and Boderin turned round.

"And knock when you come back," he said coldly. "It may be that I shall be praying."

It was the number of police in the Place de l'Etoile that first began to attract the sightseers. Most of them were tourists who were anxious to find out what all the fuss was about. A few of them—a very small proportion—*knew* what was going on and had turned up, if they were French, to see the ceremony, or if they were American, General Murphy.

There seemed to be hundreds of blue-garbed men round the Etoile and more still down the Champs Elysées. They stood on corners or outside the huge black camions which had brought them from the Ile de la Cité, men in dark blue with flat-topped *képis,* fidgeting with their white belts, men in outriders' crash-helmets and red jackboots, their motor-bicycles propped against the pavement edges, men in riot hats, double-strapped so they couldn't be knocked from their heads, clutching their three-foot riot batons or swinging their lead-lined capes.

All round the Etoile and down all the boulevards, the black vans held more men, and there were clusters of them at every intersection, grouped round silver-braided inspectors, calm and confident, the men who'd broken a thousand riots in Paris.

Major Schneider paused at the top of the underground passage-way that led under the Place de l'Etoile to the Arc, nodded to the inspector in charge, then walked unhurriedly down the steps, tall, confident and calm with his walking stick and pipe and his curiously English clothes. As he came up the steps at the other end, under the shadow of the vast stone edifice, he could see the students who had grouped themselves at the top of the Champs Elysées, chanting *"Vive La France"* and *"France pour les Français"* and other popular five-syllabled slogans, without which no riot could ever be a success in Paris. They were holding a placard bearing a vast photograph of De Gaulle, monolithic in his arrogant incorruptibility.

One of the police inspectors standing by the Arc nodded towards them.

"And when they've got him, they won't want him," he said.

"We have a habit of raising old soldiers to political pinnacles," Schneider murmured, "and then complaining that we have to look up to see them."

As he spoke, he saw the police bunch together, then, under the direction of an officer, spread out in a line across the wide pavement, and advance towards the students.

"Down with the Politicians! De Gaulle to power!"

There were a few last shouts from the students as they began to march down the Champs Elysées, trying to look defiant and pretending indifference to the stolid policemen who walked in a line behind them, hurrying them along. A few tourists, realizing at last that wreath-laying ceremonies in Paris could be vastly different from wreath-laying ceremonies in New York and London, hurriedly scuttled into the entrances of shops and hotels and along the Rue de Tilsit into the Avenue Marceau.

Then one or two of the students stopped suddenly and shouted angrily at the policemen, refusing to be driven on, and Schneider saw the lead-lined capes swing. One of the students dropped a file he was carrying and a scattering of papers began to blow unheeded into the road, then they were running, still trying to look dignified and indifferent, still shouting "*France pour les Français. De Gaulle to Power*," pretending they were hurrying for their own amusement and not because the police were there behind them.

As they scattered into the Rue Galilée, the policemen came to a halt and the officer behind them gestured quickly. One or two policemen detached themselves from the line and vanished after the students, while the rest knotted together and walked in bunches back to the Place de l'Etoile, grinning and gossiping, far less disturbed by the incident than the students.

Schneider permitted himself a cold stare after the retreating youngsters. Nobody took much notice of students. They were always seeking inflammable catch phrases to shout at the Arc. *France pour les Français. Algérie Française. Non à De Gaulle. Pas d'armée pour les Allemands!* Schneider recalled with a feeling of guilt that he'd done it once himself before he'd gone into the Army. In those days it had been the Stavisky Scandal and the shouts had brought down the Government. All Paris students did it. One couldn't regard one's student life as successful unless one had run once or twice from the police.

But it wasn't the students that Schneider was worrying about now. There was a far bigger crowd in the Place de la Concorde where they'd closed the grilles across the entrance to the Métro for safety. There were Communists down there, and they kept trying to climb on to the pavilions representing the great cities of France that surrounded the square.

The National Assembly was sitting and if there were trouble, that would be where it would start. He'd seen the posters. *Non aux Américains. Non à Murphy. A bas la bombe.* They had sprung up from nowhere and meant nothing at the moment, but a nervous police sergeant, or a shaky line, could mean a surge across the Pont de la Concorde and up the steps of the Assembly.

But Schneider wasn't really concerned with the crowd down at

281

Concorde. A few tourists at the Crillon Hotel had complained that they couldn't get out and the American Embassy was concerned about General Murphy's car getting up to the Arc, but Schneider suspected shrewdly that the crowd at Concorde was nothing more than a feint. The Communists were anxious to make the most of the Boderin Affair and it had occurred to him that they were putting on an act down at Concorde merely to draw attention from what might happen up at the Etoile. Schneider had given strict instructions that no policeman was to be withdrawn from the Etoile area for the Concorde area whatever happened. Concorde could look after itself.

He paused on top of the steps as he saw Souprosse standing by a small table they'd erected near the lifts.

"Everything's under control," Souprosse said at once. "Don't worry about the students."

"I never do," Schneider said coldly.

"There's no sign of life anywhere."

Schneider jerked his arm. "What about the apartments across there?" he asked.

"Still empty. We inspected them this morning. There's no sign of forced entry. They were all locked. We had to get the keys from the concierge. I've got a man watching upstairs and one on the floor below, and another in the street with instructions to question anyone who looks at all odd."

"Good!"

Souprosse stared round the huge square and the smile he gave to Schneider was irritatingly confident.

"There's a big crowd," he said.

Outside Blot's apartment, Boderin was staring at the little Citroën with distaste.

"Did it have to be yellow?" he snapped.

Blot gaped at him, hurt and humiliated. The meal they had eaten had been like ashes in his mouth. He had had no stomach for food and had huddled wretchedly over his plate, his dulled eyes all the time on Boderin whose appetite was unimpaired and even, it seemed, improved by the situation.

It had been an unhappy meal, with Blot concerned only with his safety and Boderin indifferent to everything except the task ahead. They had hardly spoken to each other and Blot had answered morosely to the solemn toast that Boderin had offered.

As they had collected their belongings and gone down the stairs, he had shuffled sullenly behind, carefully locking the door of the apartment with true French concern for his belongings. Outside, the sun had made him feel better and for a fragment of a second he had managed to feel optimism, but the sight of Boderin staring disgustedly at the little yellow car had dispersed his cheerfulness at once.

"It was all I could get," he said.

"You couldn't have picked a more easily distinguishable colour!" Boderin's face was petulant, and his voice was irritable and peevish. "A grey would have been better. Or black. Or buff. Good God, Blot, there are ten million Citroëns like this in France and most of them are grey, black or buff! And you had to find a *yellow* one!"

"I tell you, I couldn't get anything else."

"I don't suppose you even gave it a thought. I suppose it was like everything else. You just didn't bother."

"I tell you——"

Boderin silenced Blot with a gesture. "All right," he said. "All right. It's too late to argue now. It'll have to do. Get in."

"Who? Me?"

"Of course."

Blot looked scared and began to back away. "Not me," he said. "I've done my share. I'm not coming with you."

"I'll want you to drive the car," Boderin pointed out. "Suppose I can't park. I don't want to be caught by some flic for parking just as I'm getting out of the car, do I?" Boderin advanced on Blot. "Damn it, Pierrot, you promised to help! Don't get lily-livered about a thing like this. It doesn't involve much. Nobody will even notice you."

"I don't like it."

"You'll be striking a blow for France!"

"I'm not so sure." Blot's voice began to rise in protest. "I've been doing a lot of thinking. I'm beginning to think the whole affair's just a lot of selfishness on your part. You're the only one who's bothered! Nicole couldn't care less. She's not bothered what happens to Murphy. And your father's no longer where he can be interested. It's only your own damned selfishness that keeps it going!"

Boderin leapt across the pavement and slammed Blot against the side of the car.

"Listen, Blot," he said quietly. "You swore you were in this with me—*to the end*. Are you in it? Or are you trying to back out?"

Blot was trying very hard to back out, but now, with Boderin's hand on his chest, and those glittering feverish eyes within an inch or two of his own, he found it very hard to put his desire into words.

"I'm in it," he muttered, unable to face the intensity of Boderin's gaze. "I'll not back out."

"You'll drive the car then?"

"Yes. Yes, I'll drive it. Only let go of me. You're crushing my tie."

They climbed into the car, and Boderin turned round and eyed the planks in the rear seat, the bag of tools and the short length of lead pipe. Then he glanced at the petrol gauge which read full.

"Well, at least," he said, "you seem to have done the other things properly."

He sat for a moment, lost in thought, and Blot thought he was steeling himself to the task in front of him. In actual fact, he was trying hard to achieve a feeling of exaltation, a feeling of dedication as though he were some ancient knight about to set off after the Holy Grail. Curiously, though, it didn't quite come like that. He felt nervous and his stomach seemed hollow, as though he hadn't eaten.

Eventually, however, he decided he had control of himself and turned to Blot. He was feeling magnanimous and forgiving suddenly, and he held out his hand with a gesture.

"Well, Pierrot," he said. "We've had our difficulties. But we've got over them. I think we'd better shake hands and wish each other luck."

Blot took the hand nervously, not certain what he was doing, his mind wandering everywhere like a moth and returning to the task in hand only with difficulty.

Then Boderin looked at his watch. "Very well," he said calmly. "It's time to go."

The shabby corridors of the Institut des Langues Européennes were crowded as everyone reappeared after the lunch break. Outside, the roar of the traffic came ceaselessly up the stairs to where Hardy stood by the window, smoking.

He'd firmly expected when he'd walked out of the apartment in the Rue du Douleur that Nicole would have followed him or, failing that, would have rung him in his rooms off the Rue des Prêtres. But she'd been stronger than he'd thought and much more of a Boderin, and the telephone call had not come.

She seemed instead to have nailed her colours to the mast and thrown her lot in with the other Boderins for good and all, to have sided with her father and her brother, and the grandfather who had died on the Marne and all those other Boderin martyrs of Algeria and Mexico and Indo-China and Sedan and Waterloo.

The only telephone call had been from Ernestine, pathetic in her pleas, and his first eagerness when he'd thought she was Nicole had taken some explaining away. Poor wretched Ernestine, he thought. Paris seemed full of rootless, unhappy people like her, seeking friendship and an anchor in a world that was too full of problems.

He had gone back to work at the Institute, unwilling and disinterested, hoping that perhaps Nicole might even turn up there looking for him, but she hadn't and he suspected that Cellini's ideas of finding her an English-speaking job had strictly excluded her from improving her languages at any school where Hardy taught.

There was a little bar opposite the window where he was standing and the pavement outside was littered with cigarette ends and matches and scraps of paper. The waiter, perspiration moist on his face, was irritably jerking tables neatly into position from where they'd been arranged in intimate groups by the students, and Hardy wondered sourly what it was that made Parisians claim to enjoy sitting on noisy boulevards with all the smell of petrol fumes and the heat from hundreds of hot engines polluting the atmosphere.

The students were filing back into the Institute rooms now,

shabby, poorer for the most part than the students at the University, threadbare boys from the Midi and girls from poor homes in poor jobs who were struggling to improve their lot. They pushed past Hardy, without seeing him, chattering and arguing and complaining, in shapeless jerseys and jumpers and concertina-creased jeans, black-skirted, rope-belted, sandalled, bearded, all of them impoverished and scornful, and it was while he was still staring at them that he saw Nicole hurrying up the stairs through the crowd, clawing indignant youngsters from her path.

"Nicole!" He started forward at once and there were knowing smiles on the faces of the students.

He pulled her to one side, waiting for her appeal to him, waiting for her to take up just where they'd left off, and because he wasn't expecting what she said, her first words struck him like a blow.

"Sam, you've got to help me," she said immediately, and he saw at once that it wasn't him she wanted so much as the help he might give.

He turned away, his face taut and hard, his eyes angry.

"Try Cellini," he said sourly. "He's more help to offer."

She caught his arm and pulled him round to face her again. "Sam," she pleaded. "I can't get in touch with him! He's not in his office," and he realized then that he'd been only the second string even when it came to help.

"Hard luck," he said. "He's up at the Arc de Triomphe, I suppose, seeing that the all-American hero, General Murphy, gets the ovation he deserves."

"Sam, don't talk like that!" There were tears in her eyes and her voice was trembling. "I need help." She held out a letter. "Look, this came this morning! It's Robert's writing."

He tried to turn away again, but her eyes held his. "Well, now at least you know he hasn't thrown himself in the Seine," he said brutally. "At least he's alive."

"Sam, it's postmarked Paris. He must be still in the city."

"Well, I'm not going to help you look for him, Nicole," he said harshly, hurt and ready to quarrel with her. "I've already got myself too involved with the Boderins and their half-baked affairs. I'm busy."

"Sam, you don't understand. Look what's inside it. There's a

286

letter! It's in an envelope addressed to the editor of *Le Monde*."

Hardy turned towards her. "What's that?" he said.

He took the envelope from her, studying the crease where it had been folded. "The editor of *Le Monde*, eh? Listen Nicole, I'm going to open this."

He tore at the flap of the envelope and, unfolding the sheets of paper, stared at the sprawling handwriting.

Right or wrong, he read, *for this, I expect to be judged by God, not by my fellow men . . . though my action may be considered wicked, my motive is good . . .*

His eyes flew over the careful phrases that made nonsense of the writer's claim that there was no time for words. Robert Boderin had obviously sat up half the night composing it. It shrieked of his need to set himself squarely in the limelight.

"Nicole," he said quickly. "I think he must be going to try to kill Murphy—today—at the Arc. Schneider ought to see this." He glanced at his watch. "My God," he said. "We've only got half an hour!"

He lifted the envelope and stared at it for a second, his resentment gone in a sudden chill of panic. "Nicole, where the hell can he be? He'd never get near enough to Murphy to do any harm. The Etoile's too wide and the Arc's too far away. He couldn't see him and we'd never find him in that crowd. There'll be policemen all round the place—Nicole!"—he stopped dead and swung her round to him—"didn't you once tell me that you used to visit an apartment that overlooked the Arc? That woman's—the newspaper woman's——"

Her eyes were wide and puzzled. "But she's been left there for two years now."

"But didn't you all have keys? Didn't Robert study there? He came and went as he pleased, you said. How do you know he still hasn't got a key? Nicole, I'll bet that's where he is. We'd better get there. Quick!"

Murphy stared through the high windows of the Embassy at the people outside among the trees.

"There's a hell of a crowd, Frankie," he commented. "I don't like it. What do they think I am? A goddamn' circus or something."

He fidgeted uneasily, very conscious of his best uniform, and Franks chuckled. Murphy's dislike of ceremonial was well known.

"This damn' strike on the Métro," the General went on, his voice rumbling in his throat in a low-pitched growl. "No wonder there are a lot of people about. The poor bastards can't get away even if they want to. They've got to stand and see John F. Murphy laying a wreath at the Arc whether they like it or not. I bet their dogs ache. I bet they're wishing they'd stayed home and watched it on the TV. Tell those camera boys not to come too close," he muttered. "I'm no John Wayne."

"It's all arranged," Franks placated him. "Just forget about it."

"How about Sligo?"

"He's up there now. I imagine he should be in his place already."

"I hope so. Frankie, if something goes wrong, you're to bring that guy home for coffee or something. Even if we have to stand up SACEUR and AMRA and the lot. Wouldn't he rather do it at home," he asked hopefully.

Franks grinned. "I think that now he'd rather share in the houpla at the Arc," he said. "It'll give him something to remember all the rest of his life."

"Say, has he got a job to go to when he retires?" Murphy asked suddenly.

"I haven't asked. But I did gather that he isn't looking forward to it."

"I'll have to fix something," Murphy said. "Surely, we can find him some sort of stores job—somewhere where he can smell rifle oil and hear *Taps* once in a while. Hell"—he rubbed his hands together—"how much longer have we got to wait?"

"Quarter of an hour."

"I wish it were over."

"So do I." Franks suddenly looked anxious. "I don't like it."

"Cheer up, Prof." It was Murphy now who was being encouraging. "Didn't Schneider ring up to say they'd picked up that guy they were after—Edérède or something."

"Edérède's a politician," Franks pointed out. "Or he says he is. I'd be much happier if they'd picked up young Boderin."

"Come to that"—Murphy admitted slowly—"so would I. I'm a sucker for threats really. What's that noise?"

288

Franks glanced at the window. Through the fringe of the trees he could see men running across the Avenue Gabriel.

"I think the crowd's spilled over a little," he said quietly.

They were shouting "A bas Murphy" now near to the American Embassy. Most of it came from small noisy groups of men who clung together in little knots of anger and most of the rest of the crowd didn't seem to know what it was all about. There'd been a little good-natured shoving at first, then someone had knocked a policeman over and someone else had kicked him and a few of the policeman's friends had lost their tempers and retaliated a little more ardently than they need have done. A few innocent people were rolled on the floor, and the rest of them started to flee up the Avenue Gabriel and flow round the Elysée Palace.

The Palace sentry under the high, spiked railings in the Rue de l'Elysée, uncertain what to do and nervous at the noise, pulled his plumed shako over his nose and stood with his back to the wall, his frock-coated uniform rubbing the grey stone, his rifle at the ready, his eyes wary. But no one took any notice of him. They were all far too much concerned with getting away from the police, who weren't over-anxious to arrest them anyway—it was always much easier to get them on the run than round them up—and they clattered past him, pausing only for a moment while a man with a red flag flung a spanner through the high glass windows backing up to the rails. The sentry whirled, bringing his rifle up, but the crowd were off again before he could do anything, scattering into human splinters that vanished among the astonished bystanders in the Rue du Faubourg St Honoré. More of them ran through the gardens and flower beds towards the Rond Point, knocking over the heavy little iron chairs that were scattered among the trees, and making the women who were resting their feet after shopping in the Avenue Roosevelt scream in fear at being caught up in something they hadn't expected. A coloured G.I., who emerged from a bar to watch, had to make a bolt for it, and a couple of reporters running from the steps of the office of *Figaro* to see what it was all about had to step smartly back again to avoid being knocked down. There was a sudden screeching of tyres as brakes were applied and cars began to come to a sudden stop. A few café chairs were flung and a few tables bowled over.

More men had climbed now on to the pavilions of Bordeaux and Strasbourg and Marseilles in the Place de la Concorde and on the statues by the Solferino Bridge, and others were scattering into the Tuileries gardens, turning up the steps above the Métro station to jeer at the police from the stone balustrade there.

Fortunately no one threw anything there and the police cordon across the entrance to the Pont de la Concorde leading to the Assembly wasn't even approached. The square began to empty as the crowds edged back, leaving a few hats and shoes lying in the roadway and a few red flags. The noisy little groups of agitators were holding their own now, shouting as much at the other people in the crowd as at the police, trying to get them roused. But there seemed a singular disinclination to be excited and the crowd, instead of shouting with them, were shouting back.

The guard outside the American Embassy, looking incredibly tall in their uniforms, presented arms as Murphy appeared in the doorway. With him was Colonel Franks and behind them officials and men in morning coats.

"Come on, Frankie," Murphy whispered, half-turning. "Let's get a move on. The longer we stay here, the worse it's going to get. The crowd's getting thicker."

In spite of the uproar at Concorde, the crowd round the Place de l'Etoile had remained good-natured and were indulging in shouting pleasantries at the police. *"Remboursez-nous,"* they yelled. "Give us our money back"; and once when a single motor car full of police officials hurried up the length of the Avenue, there were a few cries of *"Bis"* and *"Encore"* and some wag started to wave. *"Il y en a meilleur,"* he yelled. *"Mais il est est plus cher.* We've got better, but it's too dear."

In every side street, cars were parked and Boderin's eyes were glittering with rage.

"For God's sake," he snapped. "Park this damned car!"

"I can't," Blot wailed. "There's nowhere to put it."

"We shall miss him! For God's sake, find somewhere!"

"It's not my fault," Blot shouted back. "We left it too late."

They had been driving round the western end of the Avenue Hoche for almost ten minutes looking for a space to leave the car, but with the Champs Elysées blocked by policemen, the traffic was almost at a standstill, and everyone who had sensed that something was happening at the Etoile, had parked his car hurriedly and started to walk.

Both Boderin and Blot were in a state of nervous exhaustion. Boderin's feeling of magnanimity and forgiveness had vanished again now and he was edgy and irritable and inclined to explode into a temper, venting his fury on the wretched Blot who was unable to escape and drove round desperately, his eyes flickering along the kerb for a place to park.

"Park it, you fool," Boderin snapped.

"I can't," Blot almost screeched. "The police'd have me in a minute."

"What does it matter? For God's sake, set me down! It'll soon be too late!" Boderin glanced at his watch hastily. "He must be almost setting off."

"Stop getting me upset," Blot whined. "I'm doing my best, aren't I? There was a big crowd down at Concorde. That's bound to hold him up."

"Never mind the crowd at Concorde," Boderin almost shouted. "Find somewhere to park!"

"The police'll get me!"

"Damn you, what if they do?"

"How'll you get away afterwards if they impound the car?"

"I don't want to get away! I don't care what happens to me so long as I succeed!"

But Blot's words quietened Boderin. In his heart he had no wish to give up life so easily or so soon. It would be a pyrrhic victory if he could only destroy Murphy at the expense of his own life. He wanted a court case and the chance to speak and the sound of applause. He wasn't afraid of death but it would be pleasant to savour a little of his triumph first.

As they pushed into the Rue de Tilsit for the second time, a car moved out ahead of them and he yelled suddenly.

"There!" He flung out a pointing hand. "There's a place!"

A man had just left an office and climbed into a big Citroën.

291

As they watched, the car's nose swung out and it rolled off, trailing a puff of exhaust smoke.

"Quickly! For God's sake, don't miss it!"

Hastily, Blot slid the little yellow car into the vacant space and sat breathing heavily. "Done it," he panted.

He sat back, mopping his brow, but Boderin's nagging voice was after him at once, like an angry terrier, goading him to movement again.

"Don't lock the car," he was saying. "I might be in a hurry. Just take the key out."

Blot nodded blankly and began to climb out, handing him the ignition key. Boderin pocketed it without a word, and they hurriedly began to unload their belongings from the rear seat.

It was only when he tried to pick everything up at once, however, that Boderin realized how clumsy he was with the heavy tools and the set of planks and the lead piping.

"You'll have to help me," he said. "I'll never get this lot through. Not with these crowds. And I'll need a hand free to get at the key of the flat."

"Leave the tools behind," Blot suggested, in a conspiratorial undertone, his eyes flickering nervously to left and right.

"Don't be stupid! The knife's in there."

"Well, take it out."

"Here? Where everyone can see? You're mad! Get hold of those tools and come with me."

Blot backed away. "Not me," he said. "I brought you here. That's what I said I'd do. Well, I've done it and now I'm off."

"You've got to help," Boderin said viciously. "And for the love of heaven, stop looking so damn' guilty!"

Moaning, almost in tears with fear, Blot picked up the heavy bag of tools, and shambled off alongside Boderin.

It was difficult pushing through the crowds, but Boderin moved ahead with a set expression on his face. There was a policeman at each end of the street, but they were looking for a young man in smart clothing who limped, not a plumber in blue overalls who was carrying what appeared to be five short planks and a length of lead pipe whose weight disguised his limp, and made him look as though he were bowed under his load.

The decision of the authorities to keep as quiet as possible the time of the ceremony at the Arc was aiding him rather than impeding him because all the people who might otherwise have been standing in the Champs Elysées were still in the Rue de Tilsit, and neither of the policemen stationed there got a good look at the two young men and neither of them, their eyes open for others, took any notice.

There was no one in the entrance of the old hotel and Blot hesitated. For a moment, Boderin paused, seeming to draw a deep breath, then he glanced at Blot and stepped through the door.

Inside the echoing, carpetless hall, he glanced up the well of the wide staircase to where he could see a few painters working. A policeman was standing on the landing just above them, leaning on the banisters, smoking, his back to them, and the sight of him came as a shock, for he hadn't expected a policeman *inside* the hotel.

"There's a policeman up there," he whispered to Blot, keeping his voice low. "We've got to get him down."

"I'd better be going," Blot said quickly, but Boderin grabbed his arm.

"You've got to create a diversion," he said. "Make a row. That'll fetch them all down, painters and everyone."

"No!" The word burst out in a shrill yelp and Boderin clapped a hand over Blot's mouth. Wide, frightened eyes stared back at him over the sinewy fingers.

"Anything'll do," Boderin insisted. "Pretend to fall down the stairs. Anything to get the policeman down."

Blot's head wagged desperately and Boderin shoved him away so that he staggered.

"They'll know who I am," Blot wailed.

"Tell them I *made* you do it. Tell them anything you like. I'll take full responsibility."

"No! I'm not going to!"

The wretched Blot leaned against the banister, limp and useless, all the strength gone from his limbs, and Boderin pushed him up against the wall, his eyes fierce and not quite sane. "If you let me down now," he breathed, "I'll shoot you. I swear I will. I've not come this far to have to turn back now."

Blot's eyes rolled in misery, and, as Boderin gave him a shove, he began to climb the stairs with dragging footsteps.

There were only three painters on the landing above and they didn't even look down as they drew nearer. Then Blot stopped dead, his face drained of colour.

"There are *two* policemen," he whispered, horrified.

They stood back against the wall, staring up the well of the staircase to where they could just see the flat-topped *képi* of a second policeman, almost out of sight.

"You said there was only one," Blot whispered. "What'll we do now?"

"Perhaps they'll *both* come down."

"Suppose they don't?"

"You've got to make 'em."

"What'll I do if they ask my name?"

"Give them a false one. Just keep them busy. That's all."

"I can't do it."

Boderin took one glance at the narrow, frightened face and wild eyes, and he knew that Blot couldn't, in fact, do what he asked. He stood with his back to the wall now, petrified with fear, incapable of movement.

"Come up to the landing," he begged, resorting to pleading. "Come up to the landing below the painters. That's all. Just help me carry the things."

Blot stared at him for a second, then crept unwillingly after him. "And stop crouching like that," Boderin hissed. "Walk normally."

"I can't! I'm afraid!"

Boderin swore at him, and on the landing above, he pulled Blot out of sight into the empty corridor where he propped up the bound boards which contained the rifle and took the bag of tools from Blot's nerveless fingers.

"Now, go on," he said sharply, his voice harsh and commanding. "You've *got* to do it."

"I can't, I tell you."

"You've got to! Nobody's seen us yet. If you go down there making enough noise, they're bound to come down to see what's happening and then I can slip past."

"I can't! I can't!"

294

Boderin suddenly grabbed Blot and wrenched his arm up behind his back in a bone-cracking heave, his eyes wild.

"Are you going to?"

"No! No!"

Disgusted and despairing, Boderin propelled the smaller man to the top of the stairs.

"Don't! Don't!" Blot pleaded in a whisper.

"Shut up, you fool! They'll hear you!" Boderin clapped a hand over Blot's mouth again and the cries died to a mumble. Then, revolted and sickened by Blot's craven behaviour, he flung him away from him with all his strength.

He had not intended what happened. He had hoped only that Blot would go down the stairs, willingly or not, and that his feet slapping on the marble, on the rails, on the wall, as he went down, heels over head, head over heels, would ring through the silent building as though he were bringing the whole place down on top of him.

But instead of falling down the stairs, Blot staggered, half-turned against the banister, his body bowed backwards into space, his hands flailing the air, searching for something to grab as his feet slipped away from him. Transfixed, Boderin saw his body pivot over the banister, sliding down it slightly as his feet rose, then his head went down. For one last wild second, he saw Blot's eyes on him, agonized and accusing, then he stepped back out of sight as the shriek, echoing up to the highest roof, rang through the silent building.

His back against the wall of the empty corridor, he winced as he heard the crunch of Blot's body striking the marble floor of the empty hall, then he heard cries from the landing above and heard the shoes of the painters clattering down to see what had happened. His eyes empty and suddenly merciless, he caught a glimpse of the two policemen following them and he flattened himself against the wall, holding his breath.

"What happened?" he heard someone say. "Where did he fall from?"

"Well, *he* can't tell you. That's a fact. He's on his last legs!"

Quickly, silently in the rubber-soled shoes, while they were still crouching over the body, Boderin picked up the bundle of boards containing the rifle and fled up the stairs. At the last moment, he decided to leave the bag of tools where it was because of its weight, and he took with him only the short length of lead pipe in case he needed it for a weapon.

"He must have fallen from the landing below us," he heard one of the painters saying. "He never came past us."

There was no one on the top landing, and Boderin stopped against the door of Apartment Number 4, wrenching at his pocket for the key. The hubbub of voices down below muffled the click of the lock and the soft thump as the door slipped back into place. Quickly, he locked the door from inside and, dropping the boards that contained the rifle, looked round for the knife.

Then he remembered with a feeling of despair that he had had it put into the bag of tools, ready sharpened, and that he had left the bag of tools down below.

Cursing and frustrated, muttering his fears out loud in his anxiety, he searched the flat for a means of breaking the rope. There was a thin discarded poker in the hearth and he managed to force it under the rope and wrench it upwards, but the rope was strong and tightly tied and it wouldn't give.

For a while, he picked at the knots, breaking his nails until they bled, panting in his nervous fear that he would be too late. Rising to his feet, his mouth agape, his eyes glaring, he hurried silently through the empty rooms, searching for something with a cutting edge. At last, underneath the kitchen sink, he found a scrap of rusty hack-saw blade with several teeth missing, that some plumber had left behind years before, and he hurried back and began to saw at the ropes, cutting his fingers as the missing teeth snagged, muttering to himself in terror that he would not be in time.

Hardy's taxi had come to a stop near the Place Vendôme. The crowds near the Place de la Concorde were spreading down the Rue de Rivoli and the traffic kept coming to a standstill.

"Come on, man," Hardy said to the driver. "For God's sake, get going!"

The driver turned in his seat and let out a volume of explanations at them, then an opening appeared in the massed cars in front of him and he stopped abruptly and, with a flick of the wrist, he put the car into gear and shot through the opening with an inch to spare on either side. The driver of another car, which had also been heading for the opening, stood on his brakes with a shriek of tyres.

The taxi driver grinned over his shoulder, still heading through the traffic, apparently without looking. "*Ça, c'est bon pour Père Lachaise,*" he said. "I'll get round into the Boulevard Haussmann and get up to Etoile that way."

They shot across the Place Vendôme and swung to the left. A couple of old ladies about to step off the road jumped back hurriedly as they went round on two wheels, and a lorry swerved into the back of a stationary car while the driver turned to swear at the taxi driver.

Hardy was beating softly on the door handle and Nicole was chewing at her handkerchief with impatience.

"If I have to go through it all again," he heard her saying aloud to herself, "I'll kill myself. I swear I will."

He stared at her, shocked and sick at heart. The old uncertain Boderin traits were too strong in her to be exorcized easily.

"Nicole——" he began to plead, then the taxi broke through the mass of cars and roared into the Boulevard Haussmann.

"Straight ahead now," the driver roared gaily, as though he had accepted a challenge. "Soon be there now!"

The hack-saw blade broke before the last strands of rope parted, and Robert Boderin scrambled across to the fireplace on his knees, reaching for the poker. Inserting it again underneath the last tie of rope with trembling fingers, he wrenched it upwards so that the strands gave at last and he fell back panting, exhausted both mentally and physically.

For a second, he stared at the rope then he scrambled to his haunches and, taking off the top board, lifted out the rifle with its shining telescopic sight. He pulled the bolt back and saw the bullets gleaming in the magazine, then with a click he pushed it hard home so that the first one slid into the breach. He was ready.

6

MASTER-SERGEANT SLIGO felt straighter and younger and taller than he'd done for years. His heavy shoulders held back, his stomach pulled in so hard it made it difficult to breathe, he waited for General Murphy.

They had formed up at the American Cathedral in the Avenue Kléber and had climbed into lorries there to ride down to the Arc for the ceremony.

About him now there was the smell of lilies and roses from the wreaths that were held by the stiff-faced men about him. The flame over the Tomb of the Unknown Soldier wavered and flickered towards the Avenue Foch in the light breeze blowing from the north, whipping away the black, oily smoke from the orange-red flame. He could see the lettering on the bronze plaque—*Soldat Inconnu* and the words on the other plates nearby paying homage to the Resistance fighters, to Indo-China, to the Republic of 1870, and the return of Alsace and Lorraine, the lost provinces, to France in 1918. The roar of the traffic in the distant streets seemed to come over the top of the houses to the little oasis of silence under the high arches that carried the names of the Grand Army—*Rodrigo*, he could see, *Almeidad, Smolensk, Montebello*.

There was a young French soldier opposite him, bearded in a way that seemed oddly effeminate to the stern Sligo, standing in the casual slouch of Latin warriors, with his trumpet on his hip. No less than young Boderin waiting just behind and above him, Sligo felt a sense of history as he stood there, aware of what the immense brooding mass of stone above him meant to the French people—all their victories, all their pride, all the magnificence of 1800 and the sturdy splendour of 1914.

With those men opposite him with their sober suits and black ties and decorations and the two or three gold-fringed tricolours with the words *Vieux des Bligues* and *Percéval* and *St Roth* written on them in gilt letters, and with the young unbemedalled troops behind, and the immense mass of the Arc over him, brooding silently across the years towards the distant sound of trumpets, Master-Sergeant Sligo felt he was a part of the ages.

There was a large old unpainted table in the kitchen that Robert Boderin remembered with a wrench at his heart. He had eaten his meals off it many a time in the past when he'd been a student. He'd been sitting at it as a boy when they'd told him his brother Raoul had been shot in the Avenue Hoche by the Germans. He could still remember the feeling of desolation and pride.

He carried the old piece of furniture into the lounge overlooking the Etoile and set it down by the window. He still hadn't opened the shutters, but a glance through the slats showed him that the space round the Arc still had no officials in it. Just a couple of lines of soldiers in khaki and a dark mass of men in civilian suits whose medals caught the sun.

He lay down on the table with the rifle, then, still dissatisfied, he moved across the room and came back with his arms full of old newspapers which he had found stacked in the corner of a cupboard. With trembling fingers, he placed them at the end of the table nearest the window. They made a perfect rest for the rifle and from the height of the table he could see clearly over the low stone balustrade outside. His face was tense and taut, his ears alert for the sound of the police on the stairs.

Then he heard the wavering note of an ambulance drawing nearer and guessed it was arriving to remove Blot. His eyes narrowed but he'd already dismissed his useless accomplice from his mind. He'd achieved what he'd set out to do and there was no point in considering Blot any further. He was dying, if not already dead. He'd heard one of the policemen say so. At least he could no longer draw their attention by his stupid chatter to Boderin in the flat overlooking the Arc.

He opened the window a fraction of an inch and reached for the shutters. He guessed there would be men watching from the Arc and he daren't open them far enough for him to be seen. The most he could hope for was a narrow slit wide enough for him to push the tip of the rifle through.

Dragging the table farther forward, he lay down on it again and pushed the foresight through the crack in the opened shutters, and as he put his eye to the telescope, the scene leapt forward to meet him.

He could see the crowds among the acacias and limes and

chestnuts that lined the circle of the Etoile, and the glittering paint and chrome of the mass of cars parked down the Avenue de la Grande Armée. There was a young painter doing surrealist drawings against the railings at the top of the Avenue Mac-Mahon, and a child in a blue smock playing skittles under the trees. Just below him there was a tall circular pillar with the sign *Qui Boit Vabe Va Bien* repeated endlessly round its peak, and the words *Sedan, Bière de l'Est* just below. An old woman was feeding the pigeons, her eyes full of love, and the male birds were showing off and, as usual, the females were remaining coolly unimpressed.

The sun was shining on the front face of the Arc where they'd removed the chains for the entry of the official cars. There was a group of French and American soldiers there and another group, Belgians and British this time, on the side of the Avenue de la Grande Armée. There was a group of men in civilian clothes, older men who could almost have been the fathers of the young men in uniform, men with thickening middles and lined faces and greying hair. They would be the Veterans of the Bligues, he guessed, and the younger men the troops of the guard of honour. There were a couple of officers with them, and a grey-haired sergeant in front with his breast ablaze with medal ribbons.

Above them towered the sombre square of the Arc, with Napoleon, crowned with the stone laurels of victory, staring sightlessly across the circle of the Etoile towards the reds and yellows and blues and greens of women's dresses that were bright among the massed black and navy of the policemen. He could see men with cameras—tourists—and a lump came into his throat as he thought of Paris as a circus where trippers from all over the world came to stare and flash their bulbs and click their shutters. The Arc de Triomphe was nothing to them, he thought bitterly, but a pile of brown-grey stone with a lot of names on it. *Aspern-Essling. Eylau. Austerlitz. Wagram.* Just names. No more. Not the history of France bursting out of the dead stones with the names of the men who had made it. *Lannes. Soult. Davout. Ney, Masséna. Murat. Berthier. Lasalle.* His own great ancestor, *Lespinasse.* He knew exactly where it lay—half-way down on the far pillar, the south-west pillar. It was the link that tied him to glory and gave him the right to make the decisions he had made, to be here, now, doing what he was doing. It seemed almost as though he could hear the cries of long-dead soldiers coming through the clamorous sound of those old battles, calling out to him to rid France of this plague of parasites that clung about her, seeking out in her all the Frenchness that they expected, the naked girls at the Folies Bergère and the Crazy Horse and the Lido, the shops with their froth and fashion, the richness and the softness that obscured the fact that France had a history—that Paris was the centre, the core, the root, from which that history sprang, and not merely the centre of a neon-lit playground.

As he stared, the sense of drama almost bringing the tears to his eyes, he saw one of the officers turn abruptly to his junior. Distinctly, he heard a shouted order and saw the troops come to attention. Murphy was arriving.

The procession of vehicles was moving slowly towards the Etoile now, reaching the bottom of the slope, and Murphy could see that all other traffic had been stopped. The dark uniforms of the police speckled the causeway edges among the trees, and he could see people stopping in their stride to stare at the big black cars as they moved slowly up the hill.

A few people had left their chairs outside the cafés and were moving towards the edge of the road, and an American, better placed than others to see, recognized Murphy and gave him a shout, and a thin accompanying cheer rose from the people along the pavement.

"You could never say the French get themselves all worked up about ceremonies," Murphy commented.

"They save it," Franks said dryly, "for their own popular heroes."

They could see a cluster of tricolours now at the base of the arch, gaudy and strikingly dramatic against the stone.

"Looks like they're ready for us," Murphy said. "I only hope it does some good."

"I hope it does."

Murphy glanced quickly at Franks. "You been up to something, Frankie?" he asked.

"No. Nothing special. The newspapers'll want a picture. You've no objection, I suppose."

"Looks as though it's too late now, even if I have."

The policeman on duty by the Etoile waved the cars onwards, and the outriders swung to right and left. The big cars followed the right-hand column and swung once round the Arc. Murphy could see men drawn up in two groups on the front face, the troops in drab olive-brown polished until they shone.

"I bet those boys are sick at their stomachs," he said softly.

Opposite the troops were the dark lines of the Veterans of the Bligues, silent underneath the bunched tricolours. Murphy could see masses of flowers and medals, and an American officer holding the wreath he was to lay himself.

Then the car had come to a stop in front of the Arc and a policeman was stepping forward to open the door. As he stepped out, half a dozen hands went up in salute and he saw the face of the Maire of Percéval split into a broad grin in spite of the solemnity of the occasion.

Murphy brought his heels together and saluted back.

The taxi driver turned round and gestured wildly at Hardy.

"I can't get past," he shouted. "Something's happened. An accident, I think. It's an ambulance."

"We'll walk." Hardy felt frantically in his pockets for money, saw that he hadn't sufficient, and humiliated, turned to Nicole. Without waiting for the change, she thrust a note at the driver and they hurried into the crowd that was filling the Rue de Tilsit.

"Oh, hurry! For God's sake, hurry," Nicole was saying.

Hardy could see the tears in her eyes, and shoved harder against the backs of the people who were lining the pavements, standing on the bumpers of cars, shouting to each other and offering advice to the police.

Then he heard doors slam and a whistle blow, and caught the wavering whine of an ambulance's siren, and a big black van broke away from the crowd and turned downhill away from the Arc.

Master-Sergeant Sligo's heart lifted as he saw General Murphy. He had a good view of the General, who looked just as Sligo had expected he would look. Strong, firm, understanding, and prosperous.

He saw Murphy move forward alongside a square-shouldered

little man in a blue suit, both of them holding wreaths bedecked with tricolour ribbons with gilt-lettered inscriptions. Behind them stood several other men, in dark suits, one of them, with a stiff British face, wearing a black coat and also holding a wreath.

Murphy glanced down at the square-shouldered little man alongside him, then, together they bent down and laid their wreaths with the other flowers at the foot of the tomb. Then Murphy was standing back, saluting. For a long time, there was silence, then the shrill sweet notes of a trumpet rang out again. Out of his eye-corner, Sligo could see an inspector of police in a silver-laced black uniform with British decorations, doubtless won in the Fighting French, also standing at the salute, and hats being doffed. And suddenly his eyes were blinded with tears.

From the top of the arch, the men with the field glasses were sweeping the windows of the buildings around them. They could see people watching from verandas, splashes of colour against the grey stone that was otherwise relieved only by the red or yellow of a drawn sunblind.

Suddenly, one of them on the east side, caught a glimpse of movement as a pair of greying, sun-bleached shutters swung open abruptly. Startled, he brought the field glasses up to his eyes and stared, and as the window leapt into his vision, he saw the long straight thread of light as the sun caught what was clearly the barrel of a rifle, half-inside the room and half-outside, and he called out aloud in alarm.

As the sun entered the room, Boderin was relieved to notice that it fell only slantwise across the window. It came nowhere near his face as he lay down on the table top.

He put his eye to the lens of the telescopic sight and the figures by the Arc sprang forward again. He could see the Veterans of the Bligues standing in stiff rows with their leader alongside General Murphy. The tip of the rifle moved infinitesimally, following the American as he moved along the rows, stopping to talk to individuals. Boderin could only see the top of his head now and he decided to wait until he stepped back or moved across to the other row at the far side of the Arc. He pulled the rifle closer, cradling the butt against his shoulder, keeping the sight on the spot where he could see Murphy's cap.

About the American, he could see the battle honours—*Ypres, Luxembourg, Breslau, Berg-Op-Zoom, Montebello, Oporto, Toulouse, Badajoz, Sarragossa, Ciudad Rodrigo,* and above them still the greatest of the names of the Empire—*Lodi, Castiglione, Arcola, Rivoli, Marengo, Hohenlinden*—strangely poignant and springing out of the brown-grey stone at him.

Now he could see Murphy's face quite clearly, stern, sombre and hateful, as he spoke quietly to the Frenchmen who had come from all parts of France in the face of newspaper opposition, to prove their blind misplaced faith in the American who had once been their commander.

The moving tip of the rifle stopped as Murphy halted to talk to a man who had stepped forward from the ranks. They were shaking hands and the Frenchman was staring up at the taller American, the fool's face full of admiration and friendship. Boderin felt a wave of disgust at the sight and had to restrain an impulse to pull the trigger there and then.

To his relief, Murphy reached the last man and swung towards the mixed French and American troops at the other side of the Arc, turning his face towards Boderin again. The line was drawn up directly pointing towards him, and Murphy was moving swiftly down the line now, stopping only occasionally to talk to one or another man. He could see Murphy plainly now and he knew he couldn't miss. He cradled the weapon more tightly against his shoulder, his finger curled round the trigger, the foresight steady on Murphy's breast.

His finger tightened as he felt for second pressure. Then, just as he squeezed, he saw the grey-haired American sergeant step forward.

★ 7 ★

THE traffic near the Arc had stopped completely and there was only the faint rumble from the streets around. For a second, there had been a silence, incredible for Paris, as the wreaths were laid. Then the movement and the susurration of feet and the chatter of tongues had started again as Murphy began to move along the lines of the Veterans of the Bligues.

There was still an echo of the silence hanging in the atmosphere, a strange sort of shadow over the growing sounds of the city's pulse, and the whiplash of the shot came clearly across the air. The pigeons among the dusty pebbles under the acacias leapt into the air as one, and whirled in a dark clattering crowd among the trees. For a second, everyone stopped, then assuming that the sound had come from a car backfiring, the movement of feet and the chatter of tongues started again. But a woman in the crowd on the pavement between the Champs Elysées and the Avenue Foch had seen that the grey-haired American sergeant who had been talking to General Murphy had fallen forward against him, his head down, his body sagging in the General's arms. She shrieked and at once a policeman leapt forward, crossing the empty roadway of the Etoile in great strides, and several whistles blew.

The sound of the shot came only faintly into the Rue de Tilsit where the traffic jam was just clearing. Hardy's head came up and he saw Nicole's eyes on his face, a question in them that neither of them dared to try to answer.

Most of the people around them didn't appear to have heard the sound and were still more concerned with going about their business, but to Hardy, who'd been half-expecting it, it sounded like a thunder clap.

"Come on, Nicole," he shouted. "I think we're already too late!"

Cellini had just turned to glance at something which had caught his eye, the minor detail of two old Frenchmen embracing each other. He was trying to do a broad coverage of the ceremony, trying to get the picture of it rather than the mere facts. Franks had held a conference of the American journalists in the city and, explaining the position, had asked them with all the charm at his disposal to help General Murphy as much as they could, according to their consciences and the demands of their papers and agencies—and Cellini, on Murphy's side, was doing his best to carry out Franks's wishes.

He was trying to fix it all in his mind's eye—the sombre stone above him, the stony stare of Napoleon on the face of the Arch, all the names of his generals and his battles on the plinths. He had worked out a rough plan for his story, trying to link the New World with the Old, the history of the United States with the history of France. He knew his editor would go for that in a big way.

But it wasn't *just* history he wanted now. He wanted colour. He wanted to catch the green of the acacias against the grey-white stone of the distant buildings, the sprinkled black and blue of the gendarmes, that vivid splash of brilliance where the tricolours were grouped.

His eyes were still wandering and, although he heard the shot, he didn't at first realize just what had happened. Then he realized voices were babbling alongside him and he saw Sergeant Sligo was stumbling forward on dragging feet. As Cellini watched, the square-built sergeant seemed to sag and leaned face-downwards across General Murphy's breast, and it was only then it dawned on Cellini that the one thing they had all been dreading but had never really expected had actually happened.

For a second, he stared wildly round, trying to decide just where the shot had come from. He saw Souprosse pointing, then all the newspapermen round him were moving forward, running, the photographers in the lead, to get better pictures, and he was running with them.

The echoes of the sound seemed to hang in the room like shadows, clattering back and forth against the walls.

Robert Boderin knew he'd failed even before he released the trigger. The big American sergeant had stepped forward just as he'd sped the bullet on its way.

He stared through the eyepiece of the telescopic sight and he saw him now leaning against General Murphy, almost face to face, as though they were embracing each other, and he could see the sagging knees and the spreading stain below the left shoulder. In despair, he pulled the trigger again, but he knew he was already too late. Unsteadied by the first failure, his shots were wild and Murphy was still on his feet, supporting the sinking sergeant. Boderin could see his mouth open as he shouted for assistance. Then he became aware of men running forward and policemen diving for the subway.

Someone took the sergeant from Murphy and for a second he

306

stood unprotected and Boderin worked the bolt desperately. He saw pebbles go flying as the bullets struck among the legs of the men assembled in front of the Arc, and the ranks crumbling as they ducked and ran for shelter.

Then he saw that an officer was in front of Murphy, trying to pull him away, and he knew his chance had gone, and he flung the rifle aside and reached for the lead pipe.

As he lowered Master-Sergeant Sligo to the ground, Franks saw Murphy standing erect and uncovered.

"Get down," he shouted, but the look that Murphy directed at him was contemptuous and irritated.

All around him, men seemed to be bolting for the far side of the Arc but Murphy stood beside the body of Sligo, shouting for help in his awkward French accent.

Twice, Franks saw the pebbles leap into the air just beyond where he was standing, and he could hear shouts and a woman shrieking. Inspector Souprosse was running for the subway, followed by an inspector of police and half a dozen men, all reaching for their weapons, then the shooting stopped and there was a second of silence before the shouts and the shrieking welled up again.

The inspector who had been sitting in the black van at the top of the Avenue Hoche, waiting in case Souprosse should call him up, heard the rasping voice of the radio break through the silence of the van, then he was leaping for the door, shouting for his men to follow him. He could see policemen running down the Avenue Hoche from all directions, all heading for the intersection of the Rue de Tilsit.

Hardy had leapt for the stairs and was tearing up them as fast as he could go, leaving Nicole far below. Just behind him was one of the policemen who had been on duty at the top of the stairs, still unaware of what had happened at the Arc and thinking of Hardy as an intruder. The other policeman had become involved with the cars and the crowds outside.

As he reached the top floor, the breath rasping in his lungs, the door marked 4 flew open and Hardy saw Robert Boderin standing there. At first he thought he was a workman because he was wearing blue overalls and a blue linen cap, then the fierce, frightened eyes met his.

"Stand back!" Boderin shouted and Hardy saw what appeared to be a length of lead piping in one hand, and a heavy revolver in the other.

The crack of a shot exploded in his ears and he heard the bullet whining down the stair well, then he managed to get a grip on Boderin's ankle as he passed, and brought him down. He heard a yelp of pain, then the whole weight of the lead pipe came down across his shoulder and he rolled away, his arm numbed.

The policeman, panting up the stairs behind him, dragging his pistol from its holster, tried to side-step the swinging piece of lead but he was too late, and he went spinning backwards down the stairs, his *képi* rolling and bumping after him.

"Stop him," Hardy yelled between the stone pillars of the balustrade, but his words couldn't be heard for the hubbub of shouting coming up towards them.

Boderin was running now—lopsidedly as though he'd hurt his leg—and as he saw the crowd, he swung round on the stairs and pointed upwards.

"There he is," he yelled, and Hardy saw him fling himself back against the wall, still shouting and pointing as the mass of people, coming in through the door, unaware of what had happened, boiled past him up towards Hardy.

He saw Nicole, standing on the stairs, reach out as Boderin started down again, but he swept her aside with a backhanded blow that flung her against the wall, her hair over her face. Then as he reached the hall, a flood of policemen came through the door and Boderin stepped back, pointing up the stairs, and they swept past him.

"Hold him!" Hardy shrieked, climbing to his feet, but his words were drowned by the din.

He saw Boderin slip into the crowd outside the door and vanish, then the first of the people coming up the stairs were on to him, grabbing his arms, his clothes, his hair even, pulling him backwards and forwards, and pummelling him with their fists.

There was a whole group of policemen and newspapermen milling round the supine body of Master-Sergeant Sligo. Several times Cellini had seen Major Schneider take Murphy's arm and try to pull him into the shelter of the subway under the Arc.

"Take your hands off me," Murphy had snapped. "I'm not leaving here—not yet!"

Sligo was lying on the shining stones in front of the Arc, attended by a policeman who had thrust his rolled cape under his head. There was a look of shock on all the faces around him, then someone called out, and a man with a doctor's bag came hurrying across the pavé from the subway, and a nun with a pale sanctified face and a mouth stitched with wrinkles, appeared and knelt down on the cobbles.

Murphy was wiping blood off his hands with his handkerchief and Cellini saw there was more blood on the front of his uniform and on the stones by Sligo. Murphy looked puzzled and unhappy but in no way shocked or afraid, and there was a look of bitter anger about his mouth as he stuffed away his handkerchief and bent down to Sligo again.

Franks looked round as Murphy knelt, then he stood up, and Cellini could see that he, too, had blood on his hands and a look of misery on his face.

"He's going, General," he heard him say.

As the crowd of policemen and soldiers round the body on the ground parted briefly, Cellini could see Sligo's face was grey—almost the same colour as his hair, it seemed. There was blood on the front of his uniform where the bullet had smashed its way through, and more blood about his collar that seemed to have come from his mouth.

As the General bent over him, Cellini saw the dying man raise his eyes. There was a faint hurt, grateful look in them as he stared up at Murphy, and Cellini looked round, wishing he had a cameraman to catch that look on his face, a look of faith and admiration and almost he could swear, of pride.

"Quits, sir," Sligo whispered. "They couldn't have been after me."

"No." Murphy shook his head. "No," he said, "I guess not." Sligo's smile was weak and lopsided.

"That's O.K., though, sir," he murmured. "Better me than you."

Cellini heard the words distinctly and he knew tears were

coming into his eyes. As he turned away, he felt his arm caught by a strong grip and he found himself looking into the face of Colonel Franks.

"Did you hear what he said?" Franks asked.

"Yeah!" Cellini nodded. "I heard."

"Did anyone else, do you think?"

"I guess not," Cellini said. "He said it in English. It wouldn't mean much."

"That's what I thought," Franks said. "Look, young man, between us we might be able to do something for the sergeant there. We can't save him, but we might at least let other people know about him. Have you got down what he said?"

"No, I guess I haven't."

"Well, put it down before you forget! Between us we ought to make Master-Sergeant Sligo the best known man in the United States Army. By God, he deserves to be!"

Nobody looked twice at Robert Boderin as he made his way into the Rue de Tilsit. They were all too busy staring through the iron gates of the former hotel to notice the blue-overalled young man who came out.

There was a curious sense of unreality about it all as he slipped into the crowd, almost as though he were experiencing it all in a dream. He felt none of the exaltation he had hoped for—only a flattened sense of failure and unreality.

"*Un assassin,*" he heard all round him as he pushed through the crowd. "The police are in there fishing him out now."

He had strained his knee in the struggle with Hardy on the stairs but fortunately the crowd was so dense no one noticed his limp. The pain made the perspiration stream down his face, though, and his hatred for the rubber-necking, gaping people who stared through the doors infuriated him as he pushed through them.

He scrambled through the last of the crowd and walked slowly along the Rue de Tilsit, his hand thrust deep down into his pocket where he had the revolver, forcing himself to walk slowly. He was prepared, if necessary to put his back against a wall and fight for his life, but he preferred to get far enough away to escape. He wanted people to know the high ideals under which he'd acted.

He wanted them to read the letter he'd written. He didn't want to be beaten into bloody insensibility or death until he had at least first savoured something of the resurgence of opinion against the usurpers of the soul of France that would make even his failure worth while.

Eventually, he tried to hurry, but the pain in his knee was agonizing and he realized he had wrenched it more than he had imagined. Fortunately, the car was still where Blot had parked it, but it was only as he reached it that he realized a lorry was parked awkwardly in front of it now. In his state of anxiety, it didn't seem possible that he'd ever be able to get away before the police started checking the vehicles in the neighbourhood.

He started the engine, panting and gasping more with fear than with pain, and by edging backwards and forwards, managed to nose the little Citroën into the middle of the street. But at that moment the singleted driver of the lorry in front chose to climb from his cab, and with a Parisian's happy indifference to the rest of the traffic, leaned on the open door to conduct a conversation with another man inside.

Boderin banged on the horn button in an agony of impatience, but the lorry driver ignored him and went on with his conversation. When at last he deigned to move, he pushed back the American Army issue cap he wore and treated him to a mouthful of abuse as he slipped past.

At the end of the street, a policeman had appeared. To Boderin's horror, he lifted his hand up and, thinking he'd been put there to stop him, Boderin reached for the gun. But the policeman was there only to keep traffic from crossing the road into the blocked street opposite and after a second or two, he waved Boderin on, downhill away from the Etoile.

It was only as the little Citroën picked up speed, that it came to Boderin's mind that he didn't know where he was going. In his eagerness to set up his plot, he had not thought of what might happen afterwards.

The first thing that occurred to him now was that he must get out of Paris, but he realized that already the police would be setting up blocks on all the roads that led out of the city, and he turned in the direction of the Gare du Nord, in the hope of picking up a train.

As he approached the smoky-grey façade of the station, however, he saw there were police cars waiting alongside the curb already and he guessed they'd been directed there by radio. The only hope for him now was to go to ground in the city itself. But police would already be calling at every hotel in every *arrondissement* looking for new lodgers, and everyone with a room to let would be interviewed. Within twenty-four hours, the owner of the garage where they'd hired the car would be in touch with the police asking them to trace it, and by this time, too, they'd probably have identified the wretched Blot. It wouldn't be long before they realized that the young plumber with the blue overalls whom they'd allowed to slip through their fingers was the man they'd been seeking for a couple of weeks.

It was only then that he began to realize with a sickened feeling of failure just how inept his plot had been. By sheer good fortune, he had managed to set the stage for it only to be thwarted at the last moment by sheer ill-luck. In his concern, his blind megalomaniac concern with his plot, he had not considered the efficiency of the police until this moment, but as he thought about it now, as the normal intelligence that he possessed—unclouded by obsession and fanatic hatred—began to act, he realized just how much he had underestimated everyone—except for himself, where he had erred on the side of optimism.

He was afraid now, though still not of what might happen to him. There was still sufficient bigotry in him to be unconcerned with his own fate. He was only afraid that in failing to do what he'd set out to do, people would not understand his motives. They would think him insane.

There would be no impassioned speeches now—just brutal indifference. Somehow, suddenly, with this last irrevocable failure, he saw his cause was lost for ever. There would be no flags, no trumpets, no drums, only an attempt to make him appear ridiculous, over-excited and hysterical—a stupid young fanatic who had got his emotions all mixed up. They would class him with the hairy-looking beatniks who inhabited the Left Bank bars. He would be just an overgrown student who had never outgrown his student passions into realism.

The rallying cry he'd hoped to shout had died stillborn. The trial at which he'd hoped to speak could never now be allowed to take place—not in the face of failure. Success might have ensured further success, but failure could only breed contempt.

There was only one place to go now, only one thing to do. The only thing left to him was to make the last despairing gesture that France, with her appreciation of gestures, might just understand.

Blindly, almost unseeingly, he turned the car into the Boulevards des Maréchaux and headed west.

It was fortunate for Hardy that the policeman whom Boderin had sent sprawling with the lead pipe managed to sit up and collect his wits just as the crowd reached him. They had driven Hardy into a corner by the open door of the apartment and rough hands were already grabbing at him. His jacket was torn and some madman was swinging on his tie, half-throttling him.

"Let go of me," he yelled. "It's not me, you bloody imbeciles! You've got the wrong one!"

Seeing the milling crowd at the top of the stairs the policeman, still half-dazed and stupid from the blow he'd received, decided he might rescue a little credit out of the debris of the day by capturing the man responsible for whatever had gone wrong—and knowing nothing of what had happened in the centre of the Etoile, he still wasn't certain exactly what *had* gone wrong—and he struggled up the stairs, hatless, weaponless, determined at least to have his hands on the man who had attacked him by the time his superiors arrived.

He tore at the people surrounding Hardy, thrusting them aside, shouting and cuffing and using his feet.

"*Attention!* Look out, there! Move over!"

He had already laid one hand on Hardy's shoulder when he saw at once that they'd got the wrong man, and he swung round, gesturing angrily and shouting his disgust. Dismayed, the crowd fell back, and the policeman, followed by the furious Hardy, began to run down the stairs just as Schneider and Souprosse arrived.

"It was Robert Boderin," Hardy snapped, as they halted in front of Schneider. "He's gone. All these bloody lunatics grabbed me and let him walk past them! He'd got blue overalls on and a cap. He looked like a workman."

"Which way did he go?"

313

"God knows! Only through the door. I was too busy trying to fend those bloody madmen off."

"We shall need you to help, of course, monsieur," Schneider snapped, already heading up to the top floor. "See that a description's flashed out, Souprosse, and watch out for any attempt to change his clothes. Send someone at once to the apartment in the Rue du Douleur and the one in the Rue Jacob, and contact the Chartres office and tell *them* to be on the look-out in case he tries to hole up there."

With the arrival of Schneider and Souprosse, the confusion began to break up, and organization began to appear. Souprosse sent a man at once to look for a telephone and sent instructions for the radio van to be brought nearer. Policemen appeared as if by magic and began to clear the hall, pushing the crowd back from round the door, and more policemen took up stations in the entrance and in the street. A car full of detectives pulled up and a whole host of men with cameras and equipment of various sorts began to hurry up the stairs after Schneider.

"Better find someone to get the lift working," Souprosse snapped to a uniformed officer as he stared up the well of the staircase. "We're going to be pounding up and down there a bit."

No one seemed to have noticed Nicole and she was still sitting on the stairs, sobbing, when Hardy reached her.

"Where is he?" She was whispering as he lifted her to her feet. "Have the police got him?"

"No. Somebody slipped up somewhere. He got away."

"Don't let the police get him," she begged. "You mustn't let the police get him. He only felt he was doing his duty."

"I'll find him," Hardy said. "I think I know where he'll be."

He stared for a moment at her moist face, twisted with crying, then he broke away and headed for the door. As he reached the street, Cellini appeared. He had telephoned the bare bones of the story to his office in the Place Vendôme and had just arrived to try to find Schneider and Souprosse.

"Nicole!" he said as he saw the girl on the stairs. "What's she doing here?"

"We were just too late," Hardy snapped. "Get her home. I've got a job to do. I know where he's gone."

"Where?"

"If I'm any judge of that damned morbid spirit that seems to motivate this entire family, he'll have gone to make communion with his ancestors."

"Where, man, where?"

"Père Lachaise. For God's sake, where else? If I can get to him first I might be able to talk some sense into him before he does anything stupid with that gun he's got. Can you lend me some money for a taxi?"

He had snatched the money from Cellini's hand before he could object, and the American stared after him as he pushed through the gaping crowd, then he turned briskly back into the hotel.

Nicole was still sobbing by the stairs and he took her out into the street and managed with the help of the police to get a taxi.

"I'll come out to your father's place as soon as I've tied things up," Cellini said, as he helped her in. "Keep the door locked and don't talk to anyone."

She nodded and he watched the taxi disappear. Then, as he turned away, he remembered what Hardy had said.

"If I'm any judge of that damned morbid spirit that seems to motivate this entire family, he'll have gone to make communion with his ancestors."

For a moment, Cellini stood with his hand on the banister, one foot on the dusty marble staircase, staring up to the top floor where he could see Schneider gesturing to a group of policemen.

"Turn out every *arrondissement*," he was saying. "Get in touch with every office. See that every road out of the city's blocked."

Cellini turned and stared back at the door, and the faces crowding at the other side, beyond the dark figures of the police there who were holding them back. *The morbid spirit that seemed to motivate the whole family.* Nicole could never live a normal life so long as she was in danger from her brother's vengeful soul. While ever he was free, there could never be any peace for her.

He glanced again towards the top floor then, making up his mind, he set off up the stairs after Souprosse and Schneider.

The clouds which had been gathering over the northern part of the city seemed to have closed in abruptly, as Robert Boderin stopped the car and made his way through the gates of Père Lachaise.

He limped up the Avenue Principale, towards the chapel at the top of the slope, touched already by the feeling of glory that always came upon him the moment he entered the vast necropolis.

The tomb of Alfred de Musset, with the willow growing out of the top of it, was the first to catch his eye, as it always was, and he thought wretchedly how few there were left of the wild eloquent spirits to whom words and meanings were more important than money and position.

As he turned off the Avenue Principale among the tombs, he noticed that the pain in his knee had grown worse, and his foot had started to drag small marks in the gravel as it trailed behind him. But somehow, suddenly, he felt at peace now and certain of himself again. Here, he felt, he would be understood. What he had done and what he had tried to do would have been appreciated by the uneasy spirits of the nineteenth century.

France seemed to have started dying at Sedan. Even the revenge she'd waited for until 1914 had been obscured by the long years of misery that had made her the breeding ground for the disasters and humiliations of 1940.

Out of sight of passers-by at last, he stopped among a huddle of ancient tombs and tore off the ugly overalls, moaning with pain as he dragged them over his injured knee. Tossing them into the doorway of a crumbling tomb whose ironwork had fallen away to dust, he started off up the hill again, among the dark trees and neglected shrubs, hoping, praying in that unhealthy, obsessed way he imagined was patriotism, that France would appreciate that he had at least *tried*, even if he had failed.

There'd be no son now to carry on his name, no more Boderins to carry France's banners to the wars. Perhaps Nicole would understand her responsibility to the family now and would accept it with pride. He thought of her with a sudden surge of affection that increased his misery.

He was in the older part of the cemetery now, among the rusting iron and rotting wood, his feet dragging on the damp earth under the trees that never felt the warmth of the sun, enveloped by the deep decaying silence where even the voices of the birds seemed to be stilled. But here he was safe, he felt.

Most of the families with graves in this part of the cemetery had long since ceased to exist and there was never anyone about. The sweat was pouring from his face in the stuffy heat of the day with the agony of his knee, and the uneven paths and steps and slopes made walking even more difficult.

In little shuffling runs, grabbing at the crumbling tombs to pull himself along, he tried to hurry, feeling that if he could only get to that red marble semi-circle where his forefathers lay he might see some meaning in everything, and disperse the confusion that kept clouding in his mind the clear truth of what he had tried to do.

It didn't take Schneider two seconds to decide that Hardy's guess was right. He ran down the stairs with Souprosse and Cellini and instructed the officer on the door to obtain a car for them.

"Get in touch with the Eleventh and Twentieth Arrondissements," he said. "We shall need men at every gate and along the walls. That's a devil of a place to hole up with a gun."

The officer nodded and half-turned but Schneider lifted his walking stick and laid it on his arm, halting him.

"Tell them to be waiting for us at the main gate," he went on. "Each group must be in telephone contact with the others. If there isn't a telephone at every gate, establish contact through café telephones. Take the place over if necessary. We can't afford to make a mistake. Tell them we'll be there in a quarter of an hour."

As the police car came to a stop with a shriek of brakes outside the door, Schneider turned to Cellini with a little click of his heels that was curiously more German than French.

"I'm obliged to you for your information," he said shortly.

As he made his way at a hurried walk up the slope from the gate of the cemetery where he had left the taxi, Hardy suddenly realized he had no weapon, not even a stick. It had never occurred to him to feel he needed anything beyond his own voice.

As he climbed the sagging steps among the drooping cypresses, he felt a sense of depression as the old tombstones and sepulchres closed in on him. The trees grew closer here, in the labyrinth of twisting paths, hiding the distance, and he began to slow down, aware that he mustn't blunder on Robert Boderin without a chance to talk to him.

He passed an old lady carrying a little pot of geraniums, heading towards the new cemetery higher up the hill, where all the monuments to the dead of Dachau and Ravensbrück and Malthaus lay, and she gave him a startled look as he turned to his right among the tombs and started to run.

The silence in the cemetery seemed intense and only the sound of his own feet on the gravel came back to him, deadened by the crumbling melancholy of the crowding tombs and overhanging trees. He passed the high column over Masséna's grave and the half circle of granite where Ney was buried, then he stopped, his breath loud in the silence. Over the trees, from miles away it seemed, he could hear the faint hum of the traffic.

He plunged between a sagging catafalque and a lopsided column from which the stone urn had dropped to the damp earth among the weeds, and stumbling through sepulchres broken apart by the roots of sprouting trees, their iron doors fallen away to nothing, their interiors collapsed and full of rubbish, he suddenly came upon Robert Boderin, crouched, still panting, one hand on his knee, on the red marble steps of his family's tomb.

At the sound of his feet, Boderin swung round, reaching for his pocket, and Hardy found himself staring into the barrel of the heavy Smith and Wesson.

"Don't be a damn' fool," he panted. "Not any more, for God's sake! Why don't you get out of Paris while you can?"

"There's nowhere to go!" Boderin's face was tense and desperate, his face drained of colour. "There isn't a single place in the whole world that I can go to now."

The police car that sent the gravel flying as it swung violently with a shriek of tyres into the half-circular entrance to the cemetery sent the half-dozen workmen who'd been sitting there eating sausage and drinking *pinard* in the heat scuttling for their lives. Almost immediately behind it, one of the vast black police camions rolled to a stop alongside the abandoned yellow Citroën, its siren dying away in a wail. As Schneider hurried through the gate, a policeman stepped forward and pointed out the telephone

and the group of uniformed men who had gathered inside await-
ing orders, watched by the staff of the cemetery.

The workmen from outside had drifted through the gate now
and were staring curiously, and people began to wander from
the cafés and bars across the Avenue de Ménilmontant to see
what was going on.

Schneider and Souprosse vanished into the gatehouse and for
a short while Schneider was engaged in telephoning to officers
at the other exits from the cemetery.

"He'll be in the Thirty-Seventh District," he was saying.
"That's where the family tomb is. He's armed. Get your men
along the wall and set off in five minutes exactly from now. Set
your watch from mine."

Souprosse, the policeman, stood back, a half-smile on his heavy
face, watching admiringly as Schneider, the ex-soldier, took
charge of the operation. The men from the black van outside
the gate, and several red-booted, crash-helmeted motor cyclists,
were standing in little groups now inside the cemetery, their
hands on their belts.

"Spread your men out," Schneider said at once to Souprosse
as he came out of the gatehouse. "We have two minutes exactly.
Every man must keep within sight of the next man. He must
not be allowed to slip between us."

For a second, he stood staring at his watch, then he nodded
at Souprosse and the inspector in his silver-braided *képi*.

"*Alors*," he said. "Let's go!"

Moving swiftly up the hill in a line that faced obliquely
towards the south, the men began to pick their way between
the tombs.

"Keep your dressing," the inspector shouted. "Watch the man
on your right! And don't straggle!"

Schneider moved quickly to the front, upright and arrogant,
indifferent to possible danger, stepping ahead with his walking
stick and pipe as though he were out for an afternoon walk in
the Bois de Boulogne.

At exactly the same moment, other lines of men were heading
west, north and east, advancing in a vast ever-closing square on
to the Thirty-Seventh District.

Hardy and Robert Boderin were still staring at each other over the broken stonework of the ancient tombs, Hardy half-crouched, one hand on a set of rusting iron railings, Boderin half-kneeling on the steps of his family sepulchre, the heavy revolver sagging in his hand.

"Leave me alone," he said in a voice that was sharp with bitterness. "Let me be. *C'est impossible me rendre avant d'être battu. Ce serait un déshonneur.*"

Hardy made a move forward, but the wavering gun came up again.

"For God's sake," he said, "why don't you get moving? Why the hell did you come to this damn' place anyway?"

Boderin made a gesture of pain, irritability and contempt. How could this shabby Englishman ever understand what had brought him to this spot? It was something the English could never understand with their moronic indifference to history. Only France could appreciate his mental processes now, he decided. Just then, to his obsessed defeated spirit, the whole of Paris seemed to reflect the same despairing mood, with her boulevards named for the great figures of history and the vast rhetorical monuments to long-forgotten triumphs.

"You don't understand," he gasped, his face drawn with pain. "You can *never* understand."

Hardy seemed indifferent, even scornful, trying to edge nearer, his face taut, his voice tense with disgust.

"Listen, you poor benighted fool," he snapped. "What do you hope to achieve by all this? For God's sake, get away, while you can!"

Boderin shook his head, his thin face stupid with a hundred years of pride. "Keep away from me," he said. "I'm not going. It would be a mistake. To leave alive would be wrong. It would be a dishonour."

Hardy took a step nearer and the gun jerked up again. "I don't give a damn whether you leave alive or feet first," he said. "I'm not concerned for you, but for Nicole. She's got to go on living after all this. Why the hell should she have you and your half-baked sacrifice hung round her neck like an albatross for the rest of her life? Give me that damn' gun and get out of the country?"

"She'll understand. All France will understand one day."

Hardy jeered. "France couldn't care less, you poor fool! France isn't concerned with you and your kind. A few newspapers'll make a fuss about it tomorrow, and then they'll forget it all."

The pain and misery he saw in Boderin's eyes made him hesitate from more cruelty, but he was driven on by the need to get the gun.

"All the rest of France'll go on eating and sleeping and making love and having children," he went on mercilessly, "and watching the television just as though you'd never existed. How many of them do you think will ever come and stare at your name on this bloody stone and brood over what might have been if you'd succeeded. It's all over, Boderin. It's all been over for twelve years and only *you* failed to see it. Nobody cares any more."

Boderin's eyes blazed back at him like a trapped animal's. "No," he said in a low voice, as though praying that what Hardy claimed should not be true. "No!"

"They'll read your potty name in the paper for a day or two and stumble over all those ridiculous syllables. Perhaps someone'll even be stupid enough to ask questions in the Chamber of Deputies. Then the price of jam'll go up or there'll be a strike on the Métro, and everyone'll be far more concerned with discomfort than dishonour. Raise their taxes and the whole damned country will rise, but not for your half-baked history. *Never for that!*"

His contempt was like a sword twisted in a wound, and Boderin's pale face became ghastly. "No," he said. "No! The young men of France'll understand!"

"Don't you believe it, you poor fool!" Hardy leaned closer over the edge of the tomb, his face thrust forward. "They're too busy picking a star in the back row of the cinema, or deciding whether to buy a disc of the Platters or Shirley Bassey." He gestured, reaching forward to express his contempt. "Don't flatter yourself that France'll put your tuppeny-halfpenny ideas of honour before what won the two-thirty at Longchamp. Nobody's bothered with glory these days. Brigitte Bardot's much more entertaining."

Boderin stared at him, his face agonized, hating him for the

321

truth that was in his words. In his heart he knew, too, that no one cared any more. In the same way that his father had come face to face with the truth in the last desperate moment, so did he now. Suddenly, it was clear to him that it had all been for nothing. In the demands of life, no one was concerned with the aftermath of death.

The whole bottom seemed to fall out of his world as he saw the pointlessness of his twelve years of hating, his twelve years of unhappiness. He had denied himself everything, feeling always that his sacrifice was worth while for the honour of his family and for France. Now he saw it as a personal thing, small, trivial, peevish, selfish, of no concern to anyone else, as Hardy claimed. Even the newspaper activity of recent days had not stirred people sufficiently to make them hesitate in their normal activities for one second. They'd read the story and dismissed it, and tomorrow when it was all over, they'd read it again and dismiss it in exactly the same way. In his wretchedness, his sudden emptiness, his tortured defeat, Boderin knew that the whole thing, the whole affair, had always been alive only in his own imagination.

His eyes clouded as he stared at Hardy. "No," he said brokenly. "No, I don't believe it."

As his head sank and the heavy weapon dragged his limp hand down, Hardy cleared the broken tombstone in one bound and landed half-sprawling across him, his fingers clawing for the gun.

Schneider's face was hard as he pushed between the crumbling edifices among the trees. His line of policemen had been broken up badly by the crowded sepulchres.

As they reached the narrow pavé road surrounding the Thirty-Seventh District, his hand went up and the line halted.

"Send someone to the intersections," he said to Souprosse, pointing with his stick. "We'll wait until the others have come up. We'll blow a whistle when we want the final move forward."

The policemen behind him halted, hitching at their belts and adjusting their caps. It had been hot work coming through the cemetery uphill and at speed.

Just then, a man in a dark suit appeared in front of Schneider, his face glistening with perspiration.

"I must protest," he said. "I must emphatically protest, Inspector——"

"My name is Major Schneider," he was told coldly. "I'm not a policeman."

"Then why are all these men here? This is the National Cemetery of France, one might almost say. The nation's greatest figures are buried here. How dare you indulge in this desecration?"

"We're searching for a criminal," Schneider snapped. "And a dangerous one."

The man in the suit snorted angrily. "As an official, I must insist that the *Bureau* should have been asked. If necessary we could have given permission. But we have a duty to protect these tombs——"

"We hadn't time for conferences," Schneider said. "This man is a murderer. There's at least one man dead and possibly others. We can't wait on the decisions of the Board of Management. I had to make the decisions myself."

He turned away, contemptuously ignoring the other, as two policemen came running down the winding path to report that the other side of the narrow district was covered by men who were ready for the final move. Schneider stared coldly at the still protesting official then signed to Souprosse.

As the whistle shrieked, the men began to move forward again, and the official began to shout. "Take care of the graves," he yelled. "Take care!"

The men were moving more slowly now, cautiously, half crouched, pausing momentarily behind the shelters of the stone slabs. Nobody spoke and there was only the shuffle and click of boots on stones.

As they came on the towering plinth that formed the back of the de Lespinasse-Boderin du Crest tomb, Schneider gestured with his arm and set the line hurrying forward. Ahead of them, above and between the tombstones and the trees, they could see the bobbing heads of other policemen all converging on the same point.

Then, quite distinctly, they heard the scrape of shoes and a voice, and they all began to run.

As he struggled, Hardy's foot slipped on the mossy surface of the stone, and Boderin, in spite of his injury, threw him aside as though he weighed nothing. He fell on his knees, and as he turned, trying to regain his balance, the revolver exploded in his ear and he saw the kick of the gun fling away Boderin's hand at the same moment that the heavy bullet punched back his head.

The weapon clattered to the ground as he scrambled to his feet. Boderin had taken two steps backwards before his stumbling foot failed and he fell heavily across the red marble slab, his head bouncing sickeningly on the stone, then the next moment Hardy was surrounded by policemen.

One of them swung at him with a cloak and the lead-lined edge caught him across the eyes, half-blinding him. He felt hands grabbing him, thrusting his aside, then someone punched him at the side of the jaw and he fell down and felt his fingers crushed into the gravel by a boot. At last he heard Schneider's harsh voice shouting orders and he was left blessedly alone.

As he blinked the sight back to his eyes, he saw Schneider just in front of him, and beyond him, Souprosse staring past him towards the tomb. Across the marble slab, which was still scarred by the crow-bars where they'd lifted it for his father's funeral, Robert Boderin lay sprawled, his headlong headstrong spirit stilled. The blood that bubbled through his snoring mouth had formed a little pool which was trickling into the indented words of the family name that had been chipped across the stone. *Famille de Lespinasse-Boderin du Crest.* It was almost as though with his life he was paying some sort of toll to the past.

★ 8 ★

IT was dark and the bats were zig-zagging among the trees before they let Hardy leave Police Headquarters. His shoulder had stiffened and grown painful where it had taken the full weight of the lead pipe and his eyes still hurt where the swinging cape had caught them. There was also a bruise over his jaw where he'd been hit, but they'd had the decency to dab the cut with iodine or something that stung, and Schneider had offered to have him driven home.

As the afternoon had drawn into evening, he'd sat on a neigh-
bouring tomb among the forgotten statues, the winged birds and
the stone mutes and the angels that were dark against the sky,
ignoring the policeman who had offered to lead him back to the
gate as he went to telephone for an ambulance, sitting with his
head in his hands while detectives and police photographers
arrived and the newspapermen with their flash bulbs; even while
the ambulance man came with a stretcher. He sat motionless, all
the strength driven from his body by the sight of young Boderin
crucified on the stone, nailed to the past, it seemed, by his own
history.

Then, as they took him away, a gardener had arrived with a
bucket of water and a rake and, urged on by the still protesting
official in the dark suit, had attempted to wash some of the blood
from the marble and level the footprints in the gravel around.

"Monsieur," Schneider had said gently as the little procession
began to move at last towards the gate where the little yellow
Citroën still stood forlornly, and Hardy had trailed behind them
through the mourning cypresses and the willows and round the
looping paths back to life and the busy noise of the streets.
Schneider had opened the door of a police car for him and he'd
climbed in without a word.

Down at Souprosse's office, newspapermen were waiting but
he noticed that Cellini wasn't there and he guessed he was with
Nicole. Photographers' bulbs flashed briefly, then the door was
slammed behind them, shutting out all the clatter of shouted
questions.

There was all the rigmarole of a report which, Schneider said,
had to be made. Brandy and cigarettes were passed across to him,
and he went step by step through the whole ugly business, his
hands toying with the pathetic testament that had been written
in the room in the Rue du Maine, absorbing all the feverish
obsessed spirit Boderin had thought was patriotism. The whole
shabby story was laid out before him now, for Blot had not been
dead when they'd found him, and had lived long enough in
hospital to make a statement.

"The inevitable note," Schneider said, staring at the sheets of
paper that Hardy passed across. "The inevitable explanation. It
isn't sufficient," he observed dryly, "that *they* should know why

they do what they do. It's essential to their ego that everyone else should know, too."

He paused to light his pipe. "Perhaps it was fortunate for you, Monsieur Hardy," he went on flatly, "that Monsieur Cellini told us where he was."

"Did Cellini tell you?" Hardy asked, looking up quickly.

"Of course. It's a good job he did. You might have been hurt. It was very courageous of you to grab him, but it was also very foolish."

Hardy opened his mouth to point out that he hadn't gone to Père Lachaise to grab Robert Boderin for Schneider and Souprosse and the Préfecture on the Ile de la Cité, but somehow it didn't seem important any more why he had gone there, and he let it pass, and he sat throughout the rest of the evening in Souprosse's office listening to the reports that came through on the telephone as Robert Boderin gasped out his life.

He hadn't even succeeded in making a good job of his own death. The bullet had entered his cheek, not his temple, and had taken out his left eye, smashing his nose and ruining his features. He had taken four hours to die, while the doctors worked over him, and the newspapermen, never far behind the wailing camions of the police, had besieged the cafés in the Boulevard de Ménilmontant, commandeering the telephones as they dictated their stories to the copy-takers.

"Why did he do it?" he said wearily to Schneider. "What could he hope to achieve?"

Schneider didn't say anything and Hardy sat holding his brandy, his eyes blank, his shoulders hunched. He hadn't had anything to eat all day and he was just a little drunk now.

"There aren't any blunders left to make," he said slowly. "Between them, the Boderins seem to have made them all."

He paused, toying with his glass, and quoted Boderin's words wonderingly, unbelievingly. " '*It's impossible to give myself up alive—it would be a dishonour.*' My God, what conceit!"

Schneider stared at him for a second, then he rose. He looked twice as straight suddenly, and twice as tall.

"The Three Musketeers would have been laughed out of conscience in England," he pointed out slowly. "But this is France, remember, and we're all condemned from the start by our origins. We're only occasionally saved by a favourable wind."

Hardy glanced up at him, startled, then he nodded. Just for a moment, Schneider had looked extraordinarily as though he might have been a Boderin himself.

"But what a waste of talent," he said, "What a waste of time and happiness!"

Schneider began to light his pipe with slow puffs.

"I'm not sure if you understand France as much as you say you do," he commented unemotionally. "I'm not sure if anyone does. We all tend to judge each other too freely and forget to make allowances for national character and the differences imposed on us by background. We French bear studying, I admit, but I doubt if anyone ever really gets to the bottom of us. Our country's been occupied many times, Monsieur Hardy, and that's why I shall always be different from you, however hard we try to understand each other. It's made us what we are and, in spite of our arrogance, we envy you your stability just as we envy the Americans their power. Make no mistake about that."

Hardy nodded. Everybody seemed to be envying everybody else just then, he thought. Even Cellini envied them in his own way.

Perhaps it was just a sign of an ancient, dissatisfied world. Or perhaps it was an indication of how easy it was for the people of one nation, working by one set of standards, to misjudge the people of another nation, working by another. They were all in the dark really, all groping towards the light, all needing each other; and old jealousies, old misunderstandings seemed suddenly to have no place in the pattern of things. It seemed to call, somehow, for patience and tolerance and a willingness to appreciate the differences that lay like a barrier between them all.

Schneider put down his matches carefully before he went on. "Boderin was a Frenchman," he explained, "and Frenchmen are born malcontents. Their intellectualism can border on stupidity, and liberty means so much to them that they're indisciplined. The curse of this country is that everyone thinks he understands politics." He shrugged. "France is an unstable nation, Monsieur Hardy," he went on. "She's the only country in Europe with one border on the North Sea and the other on the Mediterranean and it affects our behaviour. But young men like Robert Boderin are what France's made of. Whatever their follies, they stir the conscience and even in this sad world that's something that France can still do herself occasionally. She has the gift of being sincere even when she's misdirected. With France in the turmoil she's in at the moment, perhaps we need these young men—just as they are. We need their gestures—and *now more than ever*."

Hardy stared up at Schneider's hard handsome face with its deep-drawn lines of pain, then he saw that Souprosse was watching him too, and nodding slowly as if he agreed.

"I suppose you're right," he said. "I expect you are."

As he rose, Schneider shook hands. "Many thanks, Monsieur Hardy," he said. "I'm only sorry we were just too late."

Remembering Boderin crucified by his background, Hardy shook his head. At least, he thought, if Boderin were now in a position to know anything about it, he'd be highly satisfied with the gesture he'd made. It couldn't have been better and was certainly an improvement on the shabby business it would have become if they'd managed to bring him to trial, with all the advocates with their sharp legal brains making nonsense of his hopes and fears, jeering at him, making him seem only a squalid murderer with a twisted mind.

"No," he said. "I'm not. I think it was better the way it was."

The papers were out as he came into the square opposite Notre Dame, and he crossed the Petit Pont to the first Left Bank stall he saw and bought an armful of them. Then he stopped and bought a beer at a bar opposite the floodlit bulk of Notre Dame over the misty river. The *bouquins,* the little bookstalls of the river bank that sold everything from paintings to old Prussian helmets and sabres, were closed and the boxes had a grim coffin-like look about them.

For a while he read the headlines, half-stupefied by the brandy he'd drunk in Souprosse's office. The newspapermen seemed satisfied, he thought bitterly. They'd all be down like vultures on him at the Institute the following day, wanting the gory details for *Ici Paris* and *Dimanche Soir,* setting it alongside all the half-baked, hashed-up, unbelievable scandal they tried to drag out of Buckingham Palace for French week-end consumption.

The papers were full of the story. Franks and Cellini had done their work well. "*Better me than you, sir,*" was plastered all over the front pages, set as a streamer in most cases, chosen as if by a common decision, with all the history of General Murphy and Master-Sergeant Sligo underneath. There was even a strong emotional hint, in one paper which had got the old story of Murphy's life-saving in the lorry crash in Virginia, that Sligo had stepped deliberately into the path of the bullet. General Murphy was having a unanimously good press for the first time since his arrival in Paris. *Figaro* was quoting the impressive loyalty of the Veterans of the Bligues and the *New York Times* was demanding proudly that back home they should name an American Legion Post after the two of them.

The uproar in the Place de la Concorde had been almost pushed off the front pages. No one seemed concerned with whatever its organizers had been trying to prove. It had changed direction from the moment that the echoes of the shot at the Arc de Triomphe had eddied down the Champs Elysées, like the ripples when a stone is thrown into a pond; and all the men who'd been doing the shouting and offering all the insults had suddenly found they were on the receiving end of what abuse was being bandied about.

It was as though the crowd, sickened by all the unpleasantness that had been showered on General Murphy ever since his arrival, were suddenly on his side, and the little bawling groups had been forced to retreat and indulge in sporadic outbreaks among the funfairs and rifle ranges in the working-class districts of La Chapelle, Villette and Belleville. Banners and placards had been broken and torn down and still lay in fragments among the scattered chairs and torn leaflets and broken glass under the trees opposite the American Embassy, while the Santé Prison was fuller than it normally was.

This mad act, commented *Le Monde* with the staid conservatism of responsible France as it laid the blame squarely on the political groups of the extreme Left, *can only bind our transatlantic alliances tighter.*

If he'd done nothing else, Hardy thought, young Boderin had got sympathy at last for Murphy. It was strange that the very opposite of what he'd hoped for had happened. Instead of swinging the country behind the extremists who wanted the Americans out, he had done just the opposite and lined her up firmly behind Murphy.

If nothing else, France could appreciate courage, and Murphy's courage at the Arc, when he had stood up erect and unafraid under the firing while everyone else had been diving for shelter, had impressed the newspapermen. Ney's bravery still drew more admiration despite his final duplicity, than the icy skill of Davout, and Murphy's lack of fear had been noticed even by his enemies of the press, and their admiration showed in every line they'd written. For the first time, it seemed that Murphy had got them solidly and completely on his side.

By his courage and dignity, Le Monde went on, General Murphy acted in the finest of military traditions, and there can be no shame that French troops should be commanded by him. What was good enough for the men of the Bligues should be good enough for the rest of the nation.

Hardy stared at the papers a little longer. There'd been a murder in the Bois de Boulogne and the grisly details were all there. Josephine Baker was announcing yet another comeback, and there'd been another demonstration in Marseilles about sending conscripts to North Africa. But these were trivial compared with what had happened at the Arc. He threw the sheets aside irritably, suddenly tired, and lit a cigarette. Then he finished his beer and headed for the Métro station in the Place St Michel. Pushing his way through the cheerless corridors to the trains, he sat swaying in a corner until he reached Père Lachaise.

The night breeze was cool against his face as he came to the surface, for the stuffiness of the afternoon had changed to a light rain that moistened the roof tops and set the pavements gleaming. The faces of the tall old buildings in the Avenue Gambetta rose shutter on shutter on shutter to the weeping sky.

The road was in process of being repaired and was uneven and broken, but the traffic was still roaring by at fantastic speeds, heedless of the red lights and the need for brakes, swinging out round a slow-moving bus that joggled past with people hanging off the open platform at the back with the disinterested indifference of a crowd watching the bears at the zoo. As he tossed away his cigarette, an elderly drunk, propping up the lid of a litter bin with his head while he searched the contents, let the iron sheet fall with a clang and pounced on the cigarette triumphantly.

He turned into the Rue du Douleur and climbed the stairs to the Boderin apartment. He could hear a baby crying somewhere and the flat voice of a television announcer. The room beyond the door of the Boderin apartment was silent and he heard the bell peal distantly. It was Cellini who came to the door.

"Hello, Sam," he said, and he, too, seemed tired. "We seem to have done a lot of good for Murphy between us. Seen the papers?"

Hardy nodded and attempted to push past, but Cellini stood his ground, holding the door half-shut.

"It's no good, Sam," he pointed out. "She said you weren't to be allowed in here."

Hardy's face hardened.

"Why not?" he demanded.

"She won't say."

"What's wrong? Is she communing with the Boderin gods— in that private and privileged Valhalla they keep in French heavens for stiff-necked military men?"

"Sam"—Cellini's fact twisted with unhappiness in front of Hardy's hurt—"that's not fair!"

"No. I suppose not." Hardy shrugged, controlling himself. "Go on, Jimmy, you might as well tell me the truth. I've seen it coming for some time. She's decided to throw in her lot with the rest of them, hasn't she? Or is it with *you*?"

"God knows, not me, Sam," Cellini said sincerely. "Not yet, anyway."

"Doesn't she want to know what happened?"

"She knows. They came to see her. She's even been to identify the body. They sent a car. She's a bit knocked up."

"So am I. Let me in, Jimmy."

Cellini shook his head. "I can't, Sam. She won't let you in. She's got something against you suddenly but she won't say what."

"Ask her, Jimmy."

"All right, I'll ask her." Cellini looked apologetic. "But you'll have to let me shut the door."

Hardy stepped back. "Go ahead," he said. "I won't break it down."

Cellini closed the door apologetically and Hardy stood back and lit a cigarette. He could hear voices inside, then after a while, the door opened again. This time it was old Sergeant Blot. He'd already got a black ribbon across his lapel.

"Mademoiselle says you must not come in, monsieur."

Hardy shrugged and half-turned away. "Why won't she see me, Blot?" he asked. "Do you know?"

"I think it's because you told the police, monsieur, where to find Monsieur Robert when she'd begged you not to."

"*I* told the police?" Hardy stared. "But that was—Blot, does Monsieur Cellini know this?"

"I don't think so, monsieur. She won't talk to him either. But she told me."

"I see. I wonder——" Hardy stopped abruptly and gazed at Blot. "I'm sorry about your son, Sergeant," he said simply.

Blot nodded. "Naturally, monsieur. Thank you. They were two foolish boys with wrong ideas."

"I reckon so. Good night, Sergeant."

Blot nodded and Hardy walked out into the street again.

Almost without thinking, he drifted towards the Métro station, his mind stupefied with disappointment. This is like the end of a French film, he thought wildly. It's all down-beat. It's even more down-beat than the French like it.

He came out of the Métro at St Denis and, turning his back on the great brown stone gate, picked his way through the old canyons of decaying buildings. The news kiosks were still open and bright with the colour of magazines, apéritif signs and the affiches of theatres.

He was beginning to feel better now. Perhaps it was the finality of his dismissal. He knew there could be no hope of going back to Nicole now. She'd rejected him in favour of her family. Perhaps there'd never been much hope of anything else, really, because she'd never quite been able to put them behind her. They'd constantly crowded forward, demanding her loyalty, even when she'd had no wish to give it.

The pain began to subside a little and the bright neons around him, reflected on the wet paving stones like splashes of blood,

332

made him feel light-headed and cheerful as the crowding vitality of the city drove his misery away. Thank God for people, he thought. There was more sanity among them than most of them deserved.

He stopped on the corner for a second, catching the whiff of a Gauloise as a man in blue overalls passed him, gesturing wildly at his wife, and the scent of new-baked bread coming from a cellar grating, and the deep red smell of wine, the taste and flavour of France.

Thank God for Paris, he thought. Every corner of the place was a famous picture. The streets glowed just as Utrillo showed them, and the misty water shimmered just as Corot had seen it, and the ancient chestnuts, which even Hitler's minions had not had the courage to destroy, cast the same sunspotted shadows that had delighted Rénoir.

This was his city, this vast plain of stone and iron and glass. He could feast his eyes without effort for the rest of his life on its steeples, its domes and cupolas, on its centuries of life and architecture, on the grey colourings of zinc and slate and glass that could turn into gold and pearl and carmine and jade in a second as the sun went down beyond the Bois de Boulogne and the Meudon hills. He could stare at the Tour Eiffel, built of russet Paris lace; and at the Opéra where Orsini had thrown his bombs at Napoleon III and which he'd managed to visit only once in all his years there; at the lovely lost Place des Vosges, and the flattened roof of the Madeleine and the tasteless iron of St Augustin; at the Butte de Montmartre with the icing-sugar snow-castle of Sacré Coeur, and the children, like brides in communion white, on the steps that led down towards the Boulevard Rochechouart; at the severe simplicity of St. Germain-des-Prés and the uneven towers of St Sulpice; at David's St Eustache where Molière was baptized and Colbert was buried; at the Seine bridges which shone like snow when the moon came out; at St Germain l'Auxerrois which had sent out the signal for the Massacre of St Bartholomew; at Notre Dame and the slender perfection of the spire of the Sainte Chapelle; at the Panthéon, where they'd erected barricades in 1848 and the Place de la Concorde where they'd erected a guillotine and where the last King of France had parted from Paris; at the Gare de Lyon which led to the Riviera which he'd never visited; even at the ugly ironwork that carried the Métro over the Seine at Bir Hakeim. The names sounded like tocsins in his head, ringing like a call to arms.

Beautiful and ugly, honest and dishonest, lewd and chaste. There was something of everything, and so little of it was hidden. He felt he wore it like a jewel in his lapel. This was France, the land that all men loved because the sun shone sweetly on it as it did on no other place on God's earth.

He could hear across the old buildings the roar of the traffic in the Boulevard Bonne Nouvelle and somewhere in the bar the clamour of a juke box. There'd been a fight in the Méphisto and a man leaned against the wall outside, bouncing his head on the stone in his rage, the blood on his face bright in the street lights. The police had arrived and the crowd had gathered around a black van and were jeering at the culprits inside.

Hardy found himself stopping to watch them, standing in the dark where a pair of lovers held each other in a close embrace, indifferent to the racket around them. Then, as he moved on through the dimly-lit streets a couple of girls, their eyes fantastically made up, their lips so pale they looked faintly like corpses, their hair up in that curious Edwardian style they favoured, clattered past on high heels brushing him with their sleeves, filling his nostrils with their perfume.

He turned in at a door without thinking and began to climb the stairs. From somewhere up above he could hear the nostalgic whine of a piano accordion played as they knew how to play them only in France, coming down to him like an ancient plea, the thin wail of a baby, and the aimless banging of a shutter caught by the breeze. All the sounds and smells of the city seemed to be crowding in on him just then and he knew he could never leave it, whatever happened. In spite of the debts that were always picking at him. In spite of the disaster that was always brushing his sleeve. He'd scraped through before and he knew he would again.

It seemed odd, he thought, as he lifted one heavy foot after the other up the stairs, that Nicole had thought it was he who had told Schneider, when all the time it was Cellini. Probably she'd never find out now.

334

She'd wanted to leave Paris. Well, now she would. He supposed she'd marry Cellini eventually. She seemed to be heading that way. He supposed she'd drop everything that was Parisian about her and become a good American wife, taking the Boderins with her probably, a little ancient history to grace her future. On the other hand, however, perhaps she wouldn't. Cellini was tougher and more resilient than he appeared—like his country, able to take the knocks and the insults and, in spite of bewilderment at the lack of gratitude, coming back for more. It was as he'd said: They weren't such fools over there as Europeans sometimes thought, and she'd probably be absorbed into his vast, efficient, neon-lit world without even noticing, living in a dormitory town and sending Jimmy off to the city each day, while she brought up the kids in good American fashion, spraying the house with hygienic sprays, buying hygienic foods from hygienic self-service supermarkets, thrusting behind her all the grubby carelessness of this great roaring glowing city which had all the strength and weakness of her race.

She'd never wanted Hardy, he knew now. Their love-making had been too brief, too passionate, too insubstantial, with an illusive vagrant quality that would probably escape them now for the rest of their lives. They'd just happened to be two derelicts together at the same time, and she'd had the sense to realize that one failure couldn't help another and had turned finally to Cellini. Downbeat. That was what it was like. Like the music that was coming up the stairs from the juke box.

He came to a stop, suddenly aware of where he was. He looked back at the well of the staircase and saw the cards drawing-pinned to the doors. *Alphonse Daudi, Plombier*—*Theodore de Ring, Insurance de la Cité*—*Odette Bronsky*. The whole shabby lot. Every one of them a character from a novel by Hugo or Zola. They hadn't changed much in the days he'd been away. Even the roar of the traffic came spiralling up the stairs just as it always had, surging over the vast sea of roofs like a tide of sound.

He smiled suddenly and lit a cigarette. Beyond the door, he could hear Ernestine singing in a soft sad undertone, and he knocked happily.

There was an immediate silence, then he heard the quick click of high heels across the floor. As the door opened, the girl inside stared at him. She'd obviously been preparing for bed, because she'd been brushing her hair which fell over her white shoulders in a dark cascade. This is where I came in, he thought.

Her face stared back at him in sullen accusation while he did not speak, then unwillingly it softened and she stepped back to allow him to enter.

"Hello, Ernestine," he said cheerfully as he stepped through the door. "I'm back."

336